X
16

LISA BLACK

spent the happiest five years of her life in a morgue.
Strange, perhaps, but true. In her job as a forensic
scientist at the Cuyahoga County Coroner's Office,
she analyzed gunshot residue on hands and
clothing, hairs, fibers, paint, glass, DNA, blood and
many other forms of trace evidence, as well as crime
scenes. Now she works as a latent print examiner
for the police department in Cape Coral, Florida,
working mostly with fingerprints and crime scenes.
She has had over 741 hours of instruction in forensic
topics and has testified in over fifty trials.

LISA BLACK

THE
PRICE
OF
INNOCENCE

W★RLDWIDE®

TORONTO • NEW YORK • LONDON
AMSTERDAM • PARIS • SYDNEY • HAMBURG
STOCKHOLM • ATHENS • TOKYO • MILAN
MADRID • WARSAW • BUDAPEST • AUCKLAND

For Stanley Joe,
who probably would have gotten a kick out of this.

Recycling programs
for this product may
not exist in your area.

ISBN-13: 978-0-373-18979-3

The Price of Innocence

Copyright © 2013 by Lisa Black

A Worldwide Library Suspense/September 2015

First published by Severn House Publishers Ltd.

www.Harlequin.com

Printed in U.S.A.

THE
PRICE
OF
INNOCENCE

ONE

IN THE TEN minutes before the building blew up, Theresa MacLean packed her camera in its padded bag, peeled off her latex gloves and noted 'App S-GSW' on her crime scene check list. Apparent suicide, gunshot wound. She included the *apparent* purely to keep a defense attorney from saying she had overstepped her bounds, since only a pathologist could determine the cause and manner of death, while in reality her notation meant there would be no further investigation. She would go back to the lab and download her photographs and write a short report and go on to the next case. The homicide detective standing over her would go back to his desk and write a short report and go on to the next case. The ambulance crew, or body snatchers, would come and take the man's mortal remains to the Medical Examiner's Office for the standard autopsy, and go on to the next case. The man's family—well, she had no idea what the man's family would do. That most likely depended on the man.

'You don't see anything weird?' the detective asked.

'Single wound to the temple,' she said in answer, her forty-year-old knees creaking as she stood up. 'Stellate tearing, which indicates a contact shot. I felt inside the wound, no surprises there. No defensive wounds, no items disturbed as if there were a struggle, no signs of forced entry. The guy lost his job and his wife in rapid succession and was about to be evicted from this, his trendy loft overlooking the Cuyahoga.' The sour national economy had nothing on the sour local economy. Worry pervaded the city and sometimes fermented into despair. 'No, nothing gives me pause.'

'Nice gun.' The cop, Frank Patrick, nodded at the chrome-plated Smith & Wesson. This was something cops always noticed and this cop in particular. He spent his paycheck on cars and dates and yet had been trying to establish a gun collection since Theresa gave him a cap gun on his eleventh birthday. Which probably started him on the whole cop thing as his mother, her aunt, liked to point out to her with that baleful stare that only older female relatives can perfect. 'Ready to go, then?' They left the fashionable but now sparsely decorated apartment, its air already growing fusty and close. Frank locked the door behind them. He would now retrieve the patrol officer who had gone out for a smoke and instruct him to wait for the body snatchers.

Theresa crossed the wide hallway and pushed the bell for the elevator, noting how the rose walls and white ceiling made the most of the light coming through a wide window to the east. The Bingham apartments were tidy, expensive, and quiet. 'Who reported the shot?' she asked.

'He did. Called the emergency number and told them to come find his body.' Frank adjusted his overcoat, too warm in the sunlit hallway. He wore the standard detective uniform of trimmed mustache in sandy blond, dark slacks, white shirt and a loosened tie that had seen better decades. He lived on long hours and fast food, which made her worry, but managed to stay relatively slender, which made her envious. 'No one here reported a shot. Most people in this city can't afford rent like this anymore; those who can are probably at work right now to pay for it. The walls are thick enough to soundproof the sound from anyone who *is* home. The place is built like a bomb shelter. Literally,' he added, nodding at the small plaque on the wall next to the elevator bank, which said the building had been classified as a fallout shelter.

'Don't be silly. Who'd bomb Cleveland?' The elevator arrived. A young couple got off, as beautiful and trendy as their surroundings, the man in a silk sweater and the woman in strappy sandals worn too soon in the spring for real comfort. They looked too young even to know what a fallout shelter was. Hip to hip, arms around each other, oblivious to the rest of the world, and not even the very functional and unromantic briefcases they both carted could spoil the image of a fresh and perfect love. Theresa stared at the floor, carefully stepping over the elevator's threshold. If there were one subject she could permanently forbid her mind to ponder, it would be fresh, perfect love. Or old, broken-in love. Or even a strong case of lust.

'What else you got going on?' Frank asked, and pushed the *L button*.

Shake it off. 'I have to run the gunshot residue samples, put together some sort of lecture for my college alumni group, and I'm still sorting out fingerprints from that weekend homicide. Leo will start nagging every half-hour on the half-hour if I don't get that report on his desk. How about you?'

'I have to interview eight of the weekend homicide's closest friends and relations. All of whom will lie to me.' They emerged on to the ground floor, brightly decorated with white walls and retro furnishings. Trendy didn't always mean good in Theresa's opinion.

'That's a bit cynical, cuz.'

'Friends don't get too up front about dead friends' coke trade, especially when they're an employee.'

'Better living through chemistry,' she quoted. They crossed the lobby behind a man in a white shirt and tie, who held the door for them as they exited. From the landing Frank could scan the parking lot for the patrol officer and Theresa appreciated the sight of Cleveland in spring, the sky a cobalt blue, the breeze from the lake hinting at dead fish and summer. The weather could change to something dark and dangerous at any moment, of course, but that had to be accepted as a fact of life. It was apparently a beautiful day. The victim in his pricey high-rise had apparently committed suicide, another victim of the economic downturn. She and her cousin apparently had little else to discuss other than their jobs. She was apparently lonely.

She had learned from her years in forensics that true mysteries weren't as common as one might expect. What seemed apparent was, more likely than not, true.

A rumble sounded behind them, not like one man's gunshot muffled by the walls but a hundred such gunshots muffled by an entire building. At least that was how she thought of it later. In reflex her body began to turn toward Frank, to seek his input, when the world around her exploded into a blinding flash of noise and power.

TWO

SHE DID NOT lose consciousness, only felt the bewildering rush of uncontrolled movement as air and brick threw her into an abyss of sound that ended, painfully, in a tumble across the parking lot. Then her body lay, curled in the fetal position, on a paved surface covered with a vicious sandpaper of sharp grit. She tried to suck back the breath that had been knocked out of every last alveolus, and choked on dust and an overpowering smell.

Frank!

She rocked to her hands and knees, feeling tiny bites as thousands of shards of destroyed stone and brick and wood bit into her skin, breathing in only smoke and dust. Watering eyes opened on destruction as seen through a heavy fog and all noise had been dampened. She tried to call her cousin's name but produced only a rasping hack.

Mouth closed, try to produce some saliva, try again: *'Frank!'* Theresa heard a moaning sound, and for one terrible second thought it came from herself. Then she heard it again. She pivoted, tried to get her bearings as the air began to clear. She stood on what had been the sidewalk in front of the Bingham building, the eastern border of the property, now littered with detritus. Almost the entire building lay as a heap of rubble, and she had no way to guess how many human bodies lay crushed beneath it. A few moments before it had been a hive of beautifully renovated lofts; now, sharp stones pushed up into a still-swirling mist of plaster dust that persisted even in the Lake Erie breeze. A boot edged over the precipice of what was left of the fourth floor in the north-west corner of the building, the only part of the structure still standing. She hoped the boot would be empty.

West Ninth Street held some debris but seemed passable. Other Warehouse District dwellers crowded their windows to look down; some of the glass in nearby buildings had been broken by the shock or by flying rubble. Sirens wailed in the distance, coming rapidly closer and making it even more difficult for her shocked eardrums to listen.

'Frank!' Theresa focused her hearing, trying to eliminate the sirens and pick up that low moan again—one of the advantages of years spent in a school band. There.

Theresa scanned the ground somewhere to the left of her, which quickly turned from scattered chunks of building over black asphalt to an inclining and rocky terrain. The acrid smell became stronger as her feet disturbed the stones anew. 'Frank!' Flashes of color were everywhere, shards of appliances or furniture or clothing, but nothing moved, nothing appeared to be bloody flesh. She stopped and listened, a nearly impossible task with every fire rescue truck in the city now bearing down on her.

'Uuuh!' Not a hallucination or a trick of the air. Theresa scrambled into the pile of leftover building to her south-west, peering into the darkness between the bits. Then she heard, not a moan, but the soft *chink* of stone against stone.

There, about ten feet to her right. And then the moan came again. She crossed to the area and began to dig without full awareness of the motion, only of the stones under her unprotected hands and how some had smears of blood on them. Under the first few inches she found a brown leather shoe. When it moved, Theresa knew she was standing on his shin, and jumped to the side. More rocks and glass revealed torn denim jeans and a green sweater. This was not Frank.

She nearly stopped, because, of course, she needed to find *Frank*, but her body continued to work while her mind calculated how quickly she could abandon this stranger without overwhelming guilt. Heedless of the pain in her fingers, her hands scattered rubble aside until she got to the bloodied right forearm with the delicate wrist of a woman. Bone protruded from the black skin in two places. Theresa proceeded more carefully, still calling for her cousin as she dug.

The fire trucks arrived, sirens continuing to blare. Couldn't they turn them *off* now that they were here?

The woman's left arm had been pinned by a slab of concrete that ran under the rubble so that Theresa could not guess how far it went. She abandoned that arm as well and moved around to where the girl's head must be, trying to pick up and remove each shard rather than brush them, trying to function with both gentleness and all possible speed. Where was *Frank*?

Black hair sprang into view, twisted into knobs, the face too covered in blood to reveal much about age or appearance. The woman shifted her head slightly but did not make much effort to move. Was she conscious? What other bones had been broken? Had her spine snapped? What if— Someone reached her side, and began to pull the stones away as well.

The woman's eyes opened, and immediately narrowed in pain. She looked at Theresa but made no sound.

'Cuz, you OK?' asked the form next to her.

'Frank!' He was dirty, dusty and had streaks of blood

everywhere—probably much like herself, she realized—but he was alive, mobile and speaking.

'We'd better—'

'Hey!' Theresa glanced up at three firefighters, now crowding around them. 'Help,' she said.

'Get out of the way,' one told her in a firm but kind voice, and then firmly but kindly picked her up by the shoulders and moved her several feet to the side, so that almost before she absorbed what had happened the three men had finished excavating the woman as two more ran up with a backboard. Unneeded, she and Frank headed for the street, instinctively moving *away*. She held his hand for the first time since kindergarten.

Ten minutes later, Frank's extremely competent partner Angela Sanchez found them sitting on the curb across the street in front of the Waterstreet Grill. Frank stared at the smoking lot. Theresa had managed to hang on to the car keys she had stuffed into the front pocket of her pants; a mini Swiss Army knife, a present from her daughter, served as a keychain. She flexed her fingers over it, relaxed, flexed again.

Some of the olive color returned to Angela's face as she said, 'There you are. I was wondering.'

'I know you covet my desk,' Frank said, 'but this is not the way to get it.'

'It's your blotter I really want. Those vinyl corners just thrill me.' Her voice shook as she said it, though, and she settled on to the curb as if her legs were unsteady as well. She sat on the other side of Theresa. She did not hug her partner or even shake his hand. They were a man and a woman working together, both single and reasonably attractive. Distance, Theresa had long ago surmised, had to be maintained. At least in public. In private, they'd been sleeping together for six months.

'The powers that be are conferring. What about MacAfee?' Angela asked, referring to the patrol officer assigned to the scene with them.

Frank jerked his thumb over his shoulder at the restaurant.

'Lucky stiff came over here for a cup of coffee and a pack of matches, missed the whole thing.'

'Good for him.' She sighed in relief.

'He didn't want to come back out, though,' Frank went on.

'Kind of startled him a little, building collapsing his second week on the job. I sent him up the street to help with traffic.'

'I don't understand,' Theresa interrupted. 'The building fell down.'

'Yes, it did.'

'It *exploded*,' she said.

'Yes,' he agreed.

'Some kind of gas leak?'

'That would be my guess,' he said. 'Problem is, you smell any gas?'

'Not all gas has a smell. They have to add it to propane.' Some kind of odor wafted around, and she tried to place it—chemical-like, but not gas, gasoline or any sort of accelerant, not like a base compound or a medicine...more like a cleaner.

'That's true.'

'I lost my camera,' Theresa said. 'Leo will make me pay for it.'

'Don't let him,' Frank said.

'You two sure you're OK?' Angela asked.

'Peachy,' Frank said.

They sat for a while longer as the fire department roped off the block and refused to let any non-EMS personnel in. No one could know yet how many pounds of asbestos, lead paint or stored biohazards might lurk underneath unstable piles of rock.

As most humans would, Theresa sorted through self-ish considerations first: it seemed unlikely that she would know any of the victims. Her daughter was safely en-sconced at a college halfway across the state; her mother was home, probably doing laundry, and she had just left her favorite and even not-so-favorite co-workers at the Medical Examiner's Office trace evidence lab. Frank was here beside her, making it possible for her to react to the situation as impartially as she could.

To the north sat a garment warehouse, with at least ten broken windows on the second and third floors. Be-hind her, to the east, the blast had ruined the appetites of the lunchtime diners, who abandoned their tables to watch the EMS personnel scour the site for anyone left alive. So far, Angela told them, there had been five: two from the parking lot and three from the south-west cor-ner of the building, including a large and naked man who had been in the bathtub at the time. The porcelain shell offered just enough protection to save him as the apartment upstairs joined his.

With most of the west side of the Bingham gone The-resa could see the tops of the bars and warehouses in the Flats, if not the Cuyahoga running along its crooked course. The Lambert mansion-slash-factory which oc-cupied the rest of the block to the south did not seem to have suffered any damage beyond a few broken windows and gashes in the stone exterior. Its employees had been evacuated as a precaution and now blocked the intersec-tion, slender young men and women with glasses and T-shirts advertising video games. Most had their cell

phones out, videotaping the EMTs search of the rubble.
Cleveland's very own 9/11.

Theresa knew something about the Bingham. It had
been built in 1915 for Bingham Hardware, designed by
a well-known architectural firm whose handiwork could
be found in many other landmarks. More recently it
had been turned into lofts for beautiful tenants and had
done well, despite the fact that not really much had been
trendy about Cleveland since the turn of the previous
century. Well-intentioned developers kept trying to graft
some sort of style on to the city: building stadiums, closing off East Fourth to showcase local gourmet restau-
rants, adding a subway platform in Playhouse Square.
These efforts convinced no one, but Clevelanders loved
them no less for their contrivance.

But the lower levels of the building had not been
made fashionable, only left as the owners had found
them: functional, large and empty. Other businesses in
the city could rent this space for storage and the Medical Examiner's Office, crammed into three sixty-year-
old floors in University Circle, had done so. Decades of
files, X-rays, tissue slides and homicide victims' clothing had been stored in a room on Lower Level 2. And
that was how Theresa had become familiar with the
Bingham building, with the loading dock paved with
wooden bricks and the sublevel freight elevator so old
that it could be run only by building personnel.

So yes, the relevant items from every homicide in
the history of the Medical Examiner's Office had been
buried, at best, or had disintegrated at worst. It made
her want to cry. Her boss, Leo, would probably have
to be hospitalized. Equanimity had never been part of
his nature.

She asked of no one in particular, 'Do we have any idea how many people were inside?'

'Not according to the fire department. We can only hope that most of the tenants were at work, at ten-ten on a Wednesday.' It had to be some kind of accident, had to have some kind of, if not natural, than at least non-malicious origin. No one would kill that many people to collect an insurance policy, or to eliminate one particular enemy. She didn't even consider any political motivations. No one else in the country paid any attention to Cleveland; why would a terrorist?

Angela said, 'Here they come.' They got to their feet and moved away from the curb, Frank actually straightening his plaster dust-covered jacket. A phalanx of cops, suits and uniforms came toward them, or rather toward the center of the block. The briefing had obviously concluded and a plan had been formed. *Good*, Theresa thought. Cleveland saw its share of troubles, crime, unemployment and political unrest, but large-scale disasters—earthquakes, hurricanes, plane crashes—usually passed the city by. No way could she and DNA analyst Don Delgado handle a scene of this magnitude all by themselves. Even by combining with the Cleveland Police forensic unit— Too busy looking at the approaching army to watch where she was going, she stumbled over a brick and went down, keeping her knees safe but putting another gash in her left hand with a piece of glass. She surveyed the damage to her palm, not sure how much blood belonged to her and how much to the woman they had uncovered. Either way, the sticky red substance had collected dust, grit, two straws of dead grass and a cloudy crystal of rock. She pulled it off with her other hand and was about to throw it away when its smell stopped her, the same acrid scent she had been noticing for the past fifteen minutes.

'You OK?' Frank asked.

'Yeah.' She brought it to her nose, sniffed. Perhaps it had been used as a building material, some sort of insulation. She gave up and dropped the faintly purplish stone into the pocket of her jacket, wiping the blood on her pants. They were ruined anyway.

The arriving officers had fanned out a bit, surveying the scene, and paid no attention to Theresa or her cousin. Frank walked up to a man Theresa recognized as the Chief of Police, and asked, 'Where do we start?'

'We don't. The Fee—the FBI will be handling it, mostly just to hold it until Homeland Security can take over. The Region II Strike Team will be here any minute.' He nodded at a man and a woman in matching suits, both middle-aged and suitably grave. Actually, the woman looked grave. The man wore a pissed-off scowl, as if someone had blown up the city's bomb shelter just to make him look ineffectual.

'They'll ruin their shoes,' Frank said.

'Oh, thank God,' Theresa said.

The man glared at Frank. The woman smiled at Theresa. 'That's not the reaction we usually get,' she said.

Theresa didn't bother to introduce herself, since her windbreaker identified her as M.E. staff. 'I've been lucky enough to have a lack of experience in explosions. One thing, though, which my boss will want you aware of—we had our off-site storage on the second sublevel. It's buried, somewhere in there.'

'Ours, too,' the woman told her.

THREE

Tuesday

By the next morning both Theresa and the city had regained their composure. The cause of the blast remained unknown. The number of confirmed dead so far totaled a remarkably low seven, all building personnel except for one, who had apparently been visiting his storage area. The woman Theresa had found ran the snack bar in the lobby; the man pulled from the car had been about to move in that day; the man in the bathtub had been home sick from work. The pretty young couple had survived. The six dead employees included one maintenance man, three cleaners, one rental agent and the freight elevator operator/loading dock manager. The suicide didn't count, of course.

The building manager—who had held the door for Theresa and Frank when he left for a doctor's appointment, only to have the blast throw him across the street—reported that the man who had been visiting his storage area in the lower levels worked for an electronics importer and appeared to be of Middle Eastern descent. No one worried too much about that. If a malcontent wanted to hit something in Cleveland there were much more likely targets—political ones such as City Hall, all-American ones like the baseball or football stadiums or glitzy ones like Tower City. Most people still anticipated a rational explanation, rational but scary—if a stray gas

leak or an underground sinkhole had taken down the
Bingham, no structure could feel safe. Tall buildings in
the surrounding area had been all but abandoned, employees calling in sick to work and tenants deciding to
spend a few days with relatives in the suburbs.

Theresa had used Neosporin as body lotion to treat
the myriad of cuts, scratches and abrasions that covered
every inch of her body. The bruises were on their own.

The victims would be transported to the M.E.'s office for autopsy after the federal agencies did an initial
exam. There could be more, would almost certainly be
more, as excavations continued. Homeland Security arrived with an army and someone had had the sense to
inform them that Cleveland in the spring did not go more
than a day or two without rain, so they worked at breakneck speed to transport all the rubble to the Convention
Center where it could be searched through at leisure.
Still, they had not reached ground level, much less the
sublevels. Theresa's boss, Leo, had spent his time since
the blast articulating a mental list of every untried homicide in his twenty-five-year career and his concern
that all those killers would now walk free because the
evidence had been compromised. As much as Theresa
didn't care for dramatics, she knew he had a valid point.

'And just the historical significance,' Leo would per-
sist. 'The Sam Sheppard stuff was in there!'

'At least that case is over.'

'Don't be too sure. Conspiracy theories never die.'
With relief she went out on a call at about eleven o'clock
and met a patrol officer at the scene of a possible overdose which did not involve either conspiracies or explosions. The victim's house perched at the edge of Lake
Erie near Bratenahl, at the end of a long, wooded driveway off Lake Shore Boulevard. The view alone made

life worth living, the three-story mansion with the four-car garage merely icing on the cake. 'Why would a guy who lived like this want to overdose?'

'Wife left him,' the stocky cop told her. 'Which is why I never married.' Theresa dropped her *Support the Troops* water bottle into the console and pulled her basic crime scene kit from the trunk. Every movement brought to life a scratch, cut or bruise left over from the day before.

'I find it very disappointing that money can't buy happiness.'

'I'd sure like to give it a try, though.' He led her into the house, past the stainless steel appliances and Persian rug. The man of the house had sat in a brown leather armchair and flicked on the TV before taking a handful of prescription Xanax and washing it down with a Manhattan. Half of the drink remained in the glass with the cherry.

'He's fifty-five, two grown kids, owns all the Circuit Warehouse stores in northern Ohio. The soon-to-be ex-wife called us, said he hadn't answered the phone since yesterday morning and missed a meeting with their attorneys at nine. Door was unlocked when I got here. A detective should be out in a while, but I wouldn't hold my breath. They're all jockeying around trying to get in on the Bingham investigation. Did you see that place?' The cop stood about six-four with a few too many pounds attached to it, but plenty of muscle as well. He had curly brown hair and the requisite mustache and she guessed his age at a few years past hers.

'Yeah, I saw it.' She turned on the digital Nikon and took a picture of her clipboard with its form detailing the date, time, location and her name.

'Big, smoking hole in the ground.' She suppressed a shudder.

'Yep.'

'I've been a cop for twenty-three years, never saw anything like that. What could take out a whole building? I mean, that thing was *solid*.' She snapped a picture encompassing the man, the chair, the end table with the drink and pill bottle. 'No idea. Explosives are not my area.'

'They think it's that Arab guy. They have his name, I forget what it is exactly. I haven't seen his picture yet.'

'I don't think they think it's him.' Theresa felt compelled to interject some reason. 'There were other people there. And he wasn't Arab.'

'Why would they blow up the place they worked in?'

'Why would he blow it up if he was in it at the time?'

'He's probably nuts,' the cop said, looking away in a hurry as she caught him studying her rear end. 'All terrorists are nuts. I think they were trying to take out the Lambert place, get rid of all the technology that might keep us safe from them. Didn't work, not with how tough the Bingham is—was—and their stuff wasn't powerful enough. Stupid ragheads.'

'It looked pretty powerful to me. Didn't scratch the Lambert place, though, except for a few windows.' And there were so many better targets for politically motivated murderers—like the State Capitol in Columbus, where Rachael now attended OSU. Bad enough to fret constantly about school shootings, now this...how far did the campus sit from the Statehouse?

Rachael had called last night. She had no idea how close Theresa had been to the blast—Frank and Theresa would keep that their little secret, especially from

Frank's mother—but was now worried because her mother worked in Cleveland.

There would always be a reason to agonize about loved ones, and a reason for them to worry that you're worried—unfair, the pressure we put on others. No wonder so many cops were divorced.

A further thought occurred to the one in front of her. 'But you know what else? The FBI stored stuff there. They say it was just old training manuals and stuff, but you know they're lying. I bet it was the mob. The FBI probably had all the witness relocation information there and the mob stole it and then blew the place so they wouldn't be able to tell it was stolen.' He rocked as he spoke, as if impatient, but his gaze bespoke only enthusiasm for his theories—or her figure, she couldn't tell.

Theresa finished photographing and took a closer look at the victim's face. No foaming appeared in the nose or mouth, characteristic but not always present in a drug overdose. 'Seems like a lot of work to find somebody.'

'Not just one somebody. A whole list of somebodies, everyone who's ratted them out since the beginning of time. That might be worth taking out a whole building for.'

'It's as good as any other theory, I guess. I'm still holding out for a gas leak.' He smirked as if at her naivety, running one hand through his short hair. Two deep but obviously old scars ran up his forearm, leaving furrows in the hair. 'Do you need me for anything in here? I was going to canvass the neighbors, find out if anyone's seen him since yesterday morning. Though how they'd see anything at this house, two hundred yards up a wooded driveway—'

'Money might not buy happiness, but it sure buys

privacy. No, I'm OK in here. Just don't leave for good without telling me first.' He promised not to and she picked up the pill bottle as the cop's footsteps trailed off through the kitchen. The prescription had been written for sixty pills, a thirty-day supply, filled three weeks ago. Twelve remained. If he'd been taking them as prescribed that left only six unaccounted for. What Theresa didn't know about pharmacology could fill several books, but she didn't think six ought to kill him. Unless he hadn't taken them as prescribed, and swallowed all forty-eight right together. But she didn't see any other signs of over-dosing. Perhaps the man had simply had a heart attack.

She heard a sharp sound, not quite a bang but more like a sudden snap of air, and then another one, louder and more like a bang. Maybe a car had backfired, though she didn't think cars backfired any more, and certainly not the cars in this neighborhood. Perhaps someone had dropped something, something heavy.

The man's jaw muscles were rigid in rigor, and the reddish lividity in the lower extremities had fixed it-self in place. Early yesterday, she thought, and began to sketch the room on her crime scene form, the victim represented by a round head with sticks for limbs.

Could it have been a car door slamming, that noise she had heard? No, it had sounded too concise, too sharp. Perhaps a neighbor liked to shoot targets. Probably not legal, but maybe the wealth in this area let residents do whatever they wanted.

Without any conscious decision she found herself setting down her clipboard and retracing her steps back through the house. The door from the kitchen opened on to the driveway, with her county station wagon parked neatly on the concrete, directly behind the officer's marked patrol car. No humans or animals were in sight, and only the new spring leaves moved in the breeze off the lake, their surfaces a bright Kelly green against the weathered wood of the trees. No voices, not even a bird.

Theresa moved off the small porch, the soles of her black athletic shoes scratching loudly against the driveway, feeling every step in her aching muscles. The shade from the towering pines and oaks dropped the temperature in the yard several degrees and the chill reminded her that summer had not yet arrived.

She kept going until she rounded the front of the patrol car. Then she saw him.

The officer lay on the ground, face up, not moving. A pool of blood spread out from under his head.

She ran to him, took in the shredded forehead and the globs of brain leaking on to the concrete, flowing along with the blood, even before she noticed the open, lifeless eyes and the growing stain in the middle of his shirt. Then she did the only sensible thing under the circumstances—she pulled her phone from her belt and called Cleveland's police dispatch.

'Police Department. Can you hold?'

'No. This is Theresa MacLean from the M.E.'s office. Your officer is down, he's been shot, he's signal 7. Send help to forty-seven Sunrise Drive, it's off Lake Shore.' There, that sounded pretty calm. Coherent, even.

'Forty-seven?'

'Yeah.'

'Which officer?' She had no idea. He had just been another uniform, generic and interchangeable. By twisting her neck she read 'Davis' off the silver bar above his badge.

'He's shot?' the dispatcher asked, after shouting to someone else to send units to their location.

'Twice. He's dead.'

'Can you render aid?'

'He's dead,' Theresa repeated, knowing as she said it that the dispatcher would not accept that from anyone except professional EMS, especially not when it was a cop, so she didn't bother pointing out that Davis' brains were now coating the driveway. She also didn't confess that she'd never felt more reluctance to touch a dead body in her life, probably because up until now she'd never been chatting with one just a few minutes before he became one.

'Can you get him on his back? We're going to need to try CPR.'

'Sure,' Theresa said. 'OK.' At least he was already on his back. She couldn't help but fret about moving the body before photographing it; the policy had become that ingrained.

The dispatcher had a question first. 'Are you in a safe location?'

'What?'

'Is the shooter still there? Who shot him?' Theresa did a hasty three-sixty, scanning the area for movement, a flash of color, a madman with a smoking gun aimed at her, but the trees were alone and the only sound came from a now-relaxed chickadee. The lake breeze ruffled her hair.

'I don't know,' she said into the phone.

FOUR

LEO, HER BOSS, showed remarkable compassion when she returned to the office, which meant he gave her a cup of coffee before starting in with the questions. 'You didn't see *anyone*?'

'Peaceful as a cemetery, and just as tidy.' She took another sip to lubricate the lump in her throat. It had begun to rain again and the dampness settled into her bones, only aggravating the leftover aches and pains from the explosion.

A frown had long since become permanently etched into the skin over her boss's bushy eyebrows, and he had clothed his skinny frame with ill-fitting pants and a long-sleeved shirt in unfashionable plaid. With a tie. 'And no casings, no tire tracks?'

'No casings, concrete clean and dry.'

'Any reporters there?'

'Channel 15 showed up just as we drove away. Everyone else is still at the Bingham, I'm sure.'

'Did the officer fire?'

'He hadn't even unsnapped the holster strap.' The twenty-three-year veteran had not been concerned. The assailant had either caught Officer Davis completely by surprise—difficult to do in the middle of a driveway with yards of visibility all the way round—or had appeared utterly unthreatening.

'What did you collect at the scene?' Only Leo would leave unconsidered that perhaps she might not have felt up to working the scene. They spent every day hip-deep in dead bodies and had no reason to be freaked out by one. But she knew about and prepared for the dead people she encountered in her job. Stumbling on a body without expecting to, especially one she had met, spoken with...*that* turned out to be another category of experience altogether.

Of course, she *had* worked the scene.

'Only what I found right around the body—a hair that looks like mine, a cigarette butt that's probably been there since last summer, a piece of foam or lint or something, and a few pieces of dirty plastic. I processed his car, got some prints. I swabbed a sample of the blood from the driveway, even though it's obviously his. Officers searched the rest of the driveway and the lawn and into the trees, but didn't find anything worth collecting. I had no indication that he, the cop, had walked any distance—no shoe prints, no crushed grass in the yard or path through the trees.'

'Weird,' Leo summed.

She leaned one elbow on her desk. Blue-covered lab reports swam up against a photo of Rachael's high school graduation and a framed cross-stitch reading *Non illegitimi carborundum est*. (Don't let the bastards grind you down.) 'That's one word for it.'

'What if he came from the house?'

'Huh?'

'The killer. Maybe that's why you didn't hear a car.' She thought she'd finished freaking over the incident, but the idea of some malevolent being moving silently through the house she'd been in prompted a few last shudders.

Leo indulged the theory for a moment. 'The family has a lunatic son they keep hidden in the basement, and the father can't take it anymore. He swallows all his pills, distressing the son, who sees a stranger in the driveway and decides to defend the household.'

'And overlooks me, though I'm actually inside.' Theresa swallowed hard, and felt stupid for doing so. 'Besides, they cleared the house.'

'Yeah, it was just a thought. Probably some scumbag this cop put away, who just got out.' Leo dismissed it, moved on. 'I drove by to get a look at the Bingham, but it's still a pile of rock. It will take the Feds another day or two before they get close to uncovering what's left of our stuff.' At least Leo had abandoned the idea of having her and Don camp out as a twenty-four-hour guard for the evidence stored in the lower levels of the building. Technically, the chain of custody had been broken for every bit of it, since the location could no longer be considered secure—as if an intrepid criminal could get underneath the crushing layers, first to find and then to tamper with the evidence relevant to his or her case. But Leo wasn't exaggerating their concern. In any older case that came to trial the defense attorney would waste no time in pointing out, accurately, that a building had fallen on the clothing, slides and items of evidence stored there, and if that could not be defined as contamination, what could?

The thought made her heart sink, and she thought she saw a tear glisten in Leo's eyes. The loss was personal to him, she knew. Unmarried, childless, and without any hint of a family, a hobby or a social life, the M.E.'s lab defined his existence. Just because this consuming devotion failed to translate into some kind of a work ethic did not lessen its sincerity.

Then he shrugged and suggested she carry on. 'Any minute now the samples from the Bingham building bodies are going to be coming up here, so clear your desk.'

'How's Christine doing with strangers in her autopsy room?'

Leo chuckled, always vocal in his belief that the assertive doctor was too smart for her own good. 'Not happy at all. But apparently one of them is both unmarried and good-looking, so she decided to cooperate. Work. Now.' Theresa swallowed the last of her coffee; it had not warmed her. She put on her windbreaker, noted the tears and blood, and took it off again. In the process she discovered the rock she'd put in its pocket the previous day, and walked across the hall to the Toxicology department, heading for the cluttered desk in the rear.

If Oliver, rotund and ponytailed, had heard of her recent misadventure he gave no sign of it. The boundaries of his fortress had been composed using tanks of compressed gas, a cluttered desk and the mass spectrometer, and visitors were not welcome. So Theresa stood respectfully at its entrance and waited for acknowledgement from the pasty white behemoth.

Oliver ignored her, typing the narcotic levels of victims' bodily fluids into a report.

She held out her scratched and torn fingers with her version of the Trojan horse. 'I found this at the building site yesterday.'

'You mean the exploded building? The one that's now lying on the ground, the one that pulverized all our archives? That building?' Oliver spoke without turning from his desk.

'Yes, the Bingham. I noticed this weird smell—'

'A building that old is probably composed of little else but weird smells.'

'—almost like a cleaner, or disinfectant or something. Then I stumbled—literally—on to this little stone and it seems to smell the same way. I wondered if you could tell me what it is,' she finished, abject humility being the only way to Oliver's center.

He sighed with great forbearance and put down his pen. His chair squeaked as it swiveled. 'Terrific. If you're not bringing me something that stains, it's something that stinks.' He leaned forward and examined her hand, gave it a tentative sniff, then suddenly jumped back nearly on to his desk, crushing the keyboard under his massive buttocks and scattering his swivel chair. *'Shit!'* Then she saw something in Oliver she would never have expected to see.

Fear.

Her hand, still holding out the crystal, began to tremble.

'Don't move,' Oliver ordered as soon as he caught his breath.

'And don't sweat.' He rummaged through a drawer before coming up with a small metal tray, which he cleaned with an alcohol wipe. All the while she stood frozen in place like Lot's wife. Don't *sweat*?

'Now listen to me very carefully, Theresa. I am going to set this tray on my counter, like this. I want you to pick up that crystal with the fingers of your free hand and set it on this tray. Do not drop it even a fraction of an inch. Do not shove it into the metal. Don't squeeze it hard. Just place it there as gently as you possibly can.'

'Or?'

'You don't want to know about *or* right now.' She then violated the sweating ban. She used the fingers of her left hand to pluck the small stone from the palm of her right, and took two cautious steps to the workbench. Then she placed the stone on the tray, as carefully as instructed.

Oliver heaved a sigh of relief as she stepped away. She sighed as well, without even knowing why, and demanded, 'What *is* that?'

The toxicologist ignored her, picked up the phone and dialed a number. He told whoever answered: 'I need your bomb squad.'

'Oliver! What is that?'

He covered the phone with his fingers. 'That, my dear, is either nitrogen or ammonium triiodide. It probably blew up your building.'

'But—'

'Explodes when it decomposes, as when it's shaken, crushed or comes into contact with water. Where exactly did you find it, and what on earth possessed you to touch it? Did you sleep through your chemistry classes?'

'But I've been carrying it around in my coat pocket since yesterday!'

'I'm still on hold, do you believe it?' he complained with a tinge of hysteria in his voice. 'I'm glad this is merely a deadly explosive and not a real emergency. You've been walking around with this in your *pocket*?' He made her feel as if she'd been strolling down dark alleys, trailing hundred-dollar bills.

'Yes.'

'Then be glad you continually disappoint the male sex by not wearing tighter clothing, or you would probably have blown off one or both of your legs. Hello, I have to report an explosive. Who am I speaking to? Sir, do you have at least a working knowledge of chemical compounds?'

'Oliver—' She had to wait until he finished explaining the situation to the bomb experts at the police department. To her horror they agreed completely with his assessment, so that then she had to wait further, until the building had been evacuated and all her co-workers were standing outside under a gray sky. Most fretted about the work they had had to abandon, while some, especially the smokers, greeted the interruption as an unplanned break and used it as such.

The Medical Examiner, Elliot Stone, did not find it a lark. He stalked up to Theresa in a swirl of expensive, weatherproofed khaki. 'Do I have you to thank for this?' Theresa, still trying *not* to picture losing a leg, stammered.

'No—'

'Yes,' Oliver said.

'It was evidence,' she added.

Leo intervened. 'It's not our fault your tubby toxicologist overreacts at every opportunity.'

'You ask those guys in the full body armor if I overreacted!' Oliver shouted.

The M.E. moved away to do just that.

Leo went on, nearly nose to nose with Oliver and clearly unimpressed with both the toxicologist's assessment of the situation and the extra two hundred pounds the man had on him. 'Just so I have this straight—you called out the marines over a little rock that she's been carrying around in the pocket of her windbreaker?'

'It's nitrogen triiodide. I don't expect you to understand what that means.'

'It's made by soaking iodine crystals in pure ammonia and filtering until they'll explode at the slightest amount of heat, pressure or shock. It's a high school prank, something for nerds to cook up in second period. You honestly think they took the Bingham building out with nitrogen triiodide? No one could have enough of the stuff in one place without—'

'Without blowing themselves off the map,' Oliver finished.

'Which is exactly what they did.'

'They couldn't have accumulated enough to take out a building,' Leo repeated.

'Maybe it was only the detonator, used to set off another explosive,' Theresa thought aloud, though both men ignored her, as usual. Dark shapes appeared in the third-floor windows, the bomb squad invading Oliver's assigned territory. They moved promptly until they reached his counter, then stopped, obviously regarding the silver tray and its burden. Had Oliver been wrong?

Oliver said: 'It must have impurities. That's why it didn't blow up little missy, here. They used household ammonia instead of reagent grade.'

'Then how could it be powerful enough to destroy the Bingham?' The heavily armored men on the third floor still hadn't moved, or were moving very slowly. She took this to mean that Oliver had not been wrong.

He said, 'Not having been to terrorism school, I haven't learned all their tricks, one of which is obviously stabilizing nitrogen triiodide.'

'There's about a million more convenient explosives to use,' Leo insisted.

'More convenient, perhaps, but not easier to make. It's got two ingredients, iodine and ammonia.' Oliver's voice dropped, and he began to look thoughtful.

The bomb squad guys moved away from the window—very, very slowly, prompting Theresa to picture herself losing *both* legs.

'But if it's so stabilized, then why did it explode downtown?' Leo had begun to look thoughtful as well. 'It depends on how it's stabilized. It might just take more to detonate it, but once it does—'

'Boom,' Theresa finished.

They watched the armored men come out of the building, towing a small but apparently very heavy square box. They parked it on the loading dock where their vehicle could back up and use a built-in forklift to take the box into its interior. Slowly. The M.E. office personnel scattered, giving the whole operation a wide berth.

'It can't be done.' Leo decided, refuting the theory with all the fervency of a man whistling in a graveyard. Bad enough to lose the Bingham building, but a threat to his lab, his fiefdom, could not be imagined without abject horror. 'There's nothing to the stuff but iodine and ammonia.'

'Nothing else could bond to it,' Oliver admitted, 'without changing the compound—'

'And then it wouldn't be explosive.'

'Right.'

'Couldn't be done.'

Theresa said, 'Do we care? *Something* blew up the Bingham building. Whether it was this or something else, what difference does it make, unless it can tell us who did it, why and what they're planning to do next?' Oliver and Leo glanced at her, then back at the armored vehicle, now closing its doors. Slowly.

'It only has two ingredients,' Oliver said for the third time.

'Which can be more or less easily obtained,' Leo added. 'From any chemical supply company, even a school lab—'

'It's not like plutonium or something. Then, they only need to be mixed, and passed through any all-purpose filter paper. You wind up with an explosive that can be carted around or used without any special equipment. Other than a death wish, I mean.'

'Just one problem,' Leo said. 'It's not possible.' Oliver ignored him. 'Nor will it show up on a metal detector.'

Theresa said, 'But wouldn't airport "sniffers" pick up the nitrogen?' Sniffers looked for residues from explosive compounds on people and luggage, and most such residues were nitrogen based.

'Nitrogen *compounds*. Nitrogen triiodide decomposes into nitrogen gas, which is already present in the air.' Leo apparently thought, considered and rejected. 'It's impossible. It might be a similar compound, I don't know, probably detonated with an electrical charge.' All three fell silent as the bomb squad vehicle left the parking lot and the bomb squad. An errant beam of sunshine lit the area and warmed the bomb squad members until they pulled off helmets and gloves and guards. The sudden brightness didn't cheer anyone, however, and the M.E. staff waited in a somber silence to see what would happen next.

The bomb squad commander said something to the M.E., and Theresa pressed forward to listen in.

'So it is an explosive?' Stone asked.

'Oh yeah. If your chemist decided to start his analysis by chipping off a piece, well, it might not take out the wall but it would have broken a window or two, and put a hole in your counter. And killed him.' Theresa shuddered, long and hard. Behind her, Leo harrumphed.

'Having the compressed gas tanks right next to it might not have turned out so cool either.'

'It's nitrogen triiodide?' she asked.

He had black skin and caramel eyes and seemed rather young for a commander. 'We'll test it to make sure, but it looks and smells like it. I haven't seen it for about ten years, not since some kid at West Tech made a mess of his chemistry lab. You see similar compounds in meth labs, but crystals like that are, well, rare.'

'Is it the same stuff as what blew up the Bingham building?'

'Ye—' he began to say, and then stopped himself with a wry frown. 'I don't know. There's no official report out yet. You'll have to ask Homeland freakin' Security.'

'But you've heard rumors?' she guessed.

Again, the frown. 'There's always rumors.'

'Were they really after the Lambert place?' Oliver asked, letting his supercilious persona slip for one unguarded moment to admit there was something he didn't know. 'The Channel 15 anchor seems to think they were.'

'Well, I'm sure he'd know,' the commander said, with wry and admirable restraint. Then focused on Theresa. 'That's the only amount brought back from the site, isn't it? There isn't any more on the premises?'

'No,' she assured him, wondering if there could be crumbs in the pocket of her windbreaker. But if it had broken, it would have detonated, right? And probably cut her body in half.

The M.E. thanked the commander. 'This is why we need a new building,' he added to no one in particular, no doubt writing the press release in his head as he spoke. 'No more off-site storage. Every piece of paper, evidence and samples need to be under our roof at all times.' The commander nodded politely and left. The M.E. wasted no time in ordering his staff back to work, but Leo stayed at her elbow. 'You told him the truth, right? There's nothing else you're carting around?'

'No. Thanks for sticking up for me to the M.E.'

Her boss laughed, as if at her naivety. 'Every once in a while I have to make him toe the line. No one can berate my people like that.'

'Except you.'

He didn't hesitate. 'Exactly.'

FIVE

Wednesday

THE FUNERAL TOOK place in a sporadic rain, more like a heavy mist that provided a suitably grave atmosphere but also flattened some of her reddish curls and made others stick out in the wrong direction. It gave her yet another reason to hide underneath an umbrella, had she thought to bring one along with her inexplicable sense of guilt.

A large crowd trampled the wet grass despite the short notice. The local Jewish community had vast experience in making sure the funeral took place within a day, according to their custom. They had quickly put together a proper ceremony for Marty Davis even though he had never, so far as anyone knew, attended temple. Nor did his fellow officers hesitate to brush off their dress blues in order to support one of their own.

The men and women in uniform had all been decent to her, regarding her with more curiosity than censure, but still she felt culpable. She should have run, not walked, out of the house as soon as she heard the bang. She might have seen the guy, or guys. Why hadn't she heard a car, why hadn't she heard it pull in, or pull out? Had anyone been behind them when she followed Officer Davis' vehicle to the scene? Could anyone else have been in the house, around the back of it? Why hadn't she run down the driveway after seeing the cop was dead, even before calling Dispatch? Why hadn't she been more observant?

None of the cops at the funeral asked her those questions. That did not stop her from asking herself.

Internal Affairs *had* asked, of course, immediately after the incident, whipped her into one of those bleak little rooms with the built-in cameras, the rooms they used to question criminals, but they had only wanted to dot every i and cross every t. Each man—and she didn't remember any of their names hours later, she couldn't tell Frank when he was finally permitted to see her— had been kind, even in their frustration at her lack of knowledge. It frustrated her, too, embarrassed her to have to answer continually, 'I don't know. I didn't see, I didn't hear, I don't know.' One day later Marty Davis' death remained a complete mystery. He had no spouse or angry girlfriend, wasn't cheating with someone else's wife, did not have any unexplained sums of money. It seemed an unlikely neighborhood for a cop-hating thug to pull a drive-by. Marty had arrested a lot of people in his twenty-odd years as an officer and received his share of threats from same, but none so far had panned out into a serious suspect.

The Brooklyn Heights Cemetery thronged with blue uniforms, as well as civilian attire in respectfully dark colors. Theresa's eye caught one person who didn't fit in: hovering at the edge of the crowd stood a thin man whose clothes were dark but also worn and sloppy. He scratched at the fringe of a beard with the agitation of a drug addict and spoke to no one, indeed avoided the eyes of the men in uniform surrounding him. Theresa would have taken him for a cemetery employee or chauffeur, someone who did not wish to be there, were it not for the look of abject misery he aimed toward the open grave.

'Officer Davis had a lot of friends,' Theresa said to her cousin.

'I'll bet most of these people never met him,' Frank said. He had gotten away from the Bingham with fewer scratches on his face than she did, but had one rather deep cut near his left ear.

'But he was shot in the line of duty. It's a cop thing.'

'Well, of course—'

'It's also a photo op.' He gazed without expression at several men in the most resplendent uniforms present.

'Are you getting anywhere on the investigation?'

'No. You been OK? No nightmares, anything like that?'

She shook her head. 'Why would I be traumatized? It was over before I knew enough to feel afraid, and whoever did it obviously had no interest in me.' Her car had been parked right behind Davis'. The shooter needed only to come inside the unlocked house to find her, alone and unarmed. But he hadn't. He had come to kill Marty Davis only.

Leaving the body for her to explain, the day after she'd nearly been blown to bits. Theresa allowed herself a moment of self-pity. Suddenly she had been surrounded by bodies. So much death.

Then she remembered that she worked in a morgue and spent every day surrounded by bodies, and that absurdity forced out a strangled chuckle. To cover it she asked if Frank had located any family.

'None. Only a mother, now deceased, who bought these cemetery plots. She must have figured her boy for the eternal bachelor type. No siblings, no kids, no exes, not even a current girlfriend. He left all his belongings to some woman who's still in the area but hasn't contacted us yet. Of course he filled out the beneficiary form shortly after he began working for the department so she may have completely forgotten about him by now.'

'That's pretty sad.'

'I'll find out this afternoon when I go talk to her. Let's hope the bigwigs are brief, or we're all going to be soaked to the skin before this is over. I should go stand with the rest of the unit. You want to—'

'I'll stay here.' She still felt awkward, out of place.

'Probably a good idea. There's press here, you know they'll be on you like flies on honey if they recognize you.'

'I've got it. Say it's an open investigation and nothing else, not even the tiniest detail.'

'There's so little to go on as it is.'

Thanks to me, she almost said aloud, but instead just summoned up a smile as he squeezed her elbow, then threaded his way between two women in their thirties standing in front of Theresa. They were not in uniform. One sniffled, raising a damp tissue to her nose.

The melancholy settled on Theresa's shoulders once more. People weren't supposed to die on her watch. They were supposed to *be* dead already, before they got to her watch.

The mist abruptly stopped dripping on to her scalp, and a glance upward told her why. A tall blond man had stepped up beside her; by holding his black umbrella slightly off center he gave her some protection and still kept himself dry. She glanced up with a quick, grateful smile, which he returned. Then he returned his attention to the people closest to the grave, who were obviously preparing to speak.

The girl in the trench coat sniffled again. This earned her, instead of sympathy, a derisive glance from her companion. 'Come on. You didn't even know him.'

'I did too. I must have dispatched him to twenty calls a week, for the past four years.'

'He was just a voice on the radio.'

'They're all voices on the radio, but that doesn't mean I don't get to know them. I can tell when they're excited or they're bored or they're having a bad day. Can't you?'

'Yeah. And he was always having a bad day.'

Trench Coat sniffled again. 'That's not true. He would never get snippy with me, no matter how busy things got. You're just mad because he broke Devin's nose. That was three years ago.'

'Well, why did he have to brawl with his own friends? Why couldn't he be like any other self-respecting cop and beat up suspects when he needs to unwind?' She chuckled at her own joke. At least Theresa hoped it was a joke.

'He was too professional,' Trench Coat insisted, but weakly.

'Hah. He did a traffic stop on Sunday for a busted brake light, and after I ran the plate he let the guy go. You know why?'

'Shhh.'

The chaplain had cleared his throat and begun, 'Martin Davis spent more than half his life with the police department—'

The second woman lowered her voice, but went on. 'Because it was freakin' Bruce Lambert, that's why! The only guy in the city who can *afford* the fine, and little Marty gets stars in his eyes and lets him skate.'

'Shhh,' the woman in the long coat said again, and they quieted. Theresa listened as an officer described as Marty's best friend gave a long and rambling history of the man, from his youth as a budding criminal to his post-college-dropout epiphany when he realized that he could help send other people to jail or go there himself and resolved to turn his life around. His friends saw Marty as honest, humble and extremely hard-working, a thoroughly professional officer—this earned a snort from one of the women standing in front of Theresa, obviously still miffed about that broken nose—and a great loss to the police force, especially needed at this time when Cleveland found itself under attack. Listening between the lines, Theresa heard that the dead man had not been the brightest candle in the menorah, but he had been hearty and loyal.

The thin agitated man had backed up into a copse of trees, completely outside the circle of cops, wiping his eyes with the cuff of his jacket.

Next the bagpipes played—'Danny Boy', of course, which some sadist had long ago dictated must be played at all police funerals—and Theresa wiped her own eyes. Tears threatened all the more when, once again, her mind returned to two facts: that she, who hadn't even bothered to learn his name, had been the last friendly face Marty Davis had seen on this planet, and that if she had done one single thing differently that morning he might still be alive. She had no idea what that one thing might have been, but still it had to be, it stood to reason—if she had taken more or less time to get to the scene, if she had gone out to her car for equipment—And round and round.

When she began to sniffle like Trench Coat, the man beside her seemed to draw closer but without actually moving, and she glanced at him again. Broad without being heavy, he had blue eyes and a smile like a shy boy's. Quite tall, but the way he curved his back as if to apologize for it made her think he was not a cop. As the last of the bagpipes' notes faded into the air, she asked in a whisper, 'Were you a friend of Marty's?'

He hesitated before answering. 'He was nice to me during my wife's case.' As he had no wife with him, this seemed a daunting line of inquiry. Had the wife been assaulted? Forcibly committed? Killed? It had to be something serious to warrant coming to the funeral of the officer involved. It sounded as if Marty Davis had always worked patrol so how involved in any one case would he have become? Perhaps they lived in the same neighborhood, and it had been some ongoing thing. Or perhaps this guy was one of those weirdos who liked to go to funerals.

He seemed to flush just a bit, and she realized she was staring. Then they both faced straight ahead as the chaplain made a few closing remarks.

But he didn't seem weird, and at least the umbrella had salvaged what was left of her hairstyle. A little make-up covered most of the bruises and scratches on her face, but she still probably looked as if she'd recently been caught in the path of a Peterbilt.

The gathered officers all turned on their radios to go through the ghostly 'last call' procedure. An unseen dispatcher hailed Marty by his radio number three times, the numbers echoing unanswered, and the woman in the trench coat began to sob. Theresa felt like joining her. Her tissue no longer did any good at all and she fished a napkin out of another pocket, folding it in half to hide the cheery Wendy's logo.

The man touched Theresa's elbow, as if to support her, but then he leaned down to her ear and said, 'There's a reporter heading for you. Do you want to talk to her?'

'No.' She had not helped this investigation at all so far, and leaking details to the perfectly made-up young woman coming her way might harm it. Besides, she had nothing to add to what the press already knew.

'Come this way.' The ceremony over, the mourners all began to move at once. Some continued to sniffle while others struck up conversations in normal, even boisterous, tones. As Frank had suggested, few people were there from personal grief, many more simply to show the respect due a fellow officer. She stayed underneath the man's umbrella and they strolled behind a few trees and the group of high-ranking uniforms. When she glanced back, the young woman with the notepad had diverted to the fire chief.

'How did you know she was a reporter?' Theresa asked her protector.

'After a while you learn to spot them.' Like how a criminal recognizes a cop, no matter how they're dressed, she thought, but really didn't want to pry into what had happened to his wife or how he had become so cognizant of the media. Of course, she *did* want to know. 'How did you know she wanted to talk to me?'

'Her line of sight got really focused. Besides, I recognized you from the papers, so I'm sure she did too. You're the one who—who was with him, weren't you?' His face, already solemn, grew even more so with the question.

'Yes.' He opened his mouth, shut it again, watched the uneven ground passing beneath their feet—like her, he wanted to ask but didn't want to ask.

Unlike her, he did. 'Was it quick?'

'Yes,' she said. 'Very quick.'

He did the looking down, frowning process again and this time added a nod. 'Good. Well, I have to go.' They had reached the first line of vehicles.

'Thanks for sharing your umbrella.' He offered to let

her keep it and she refused. Then he looked over at the grave one more time—not that he could see it through the crowd—as if reluctant to walk away. Turned to go.

'What's your name?' she asked, surprising herself.

'David.' He shook her hand. 'David Madison.' She reciprocated, then let him slip his fingers out of hers and weave between the rows of parked cars. He did not look back, nor did he speak to anyone else. Drops of water once again penetrated her hair to dampen her scalp.

The reporter remained lost in the crowd. The bagpipers were hustling to get their instruments out of the wet weather and the woman in the trench coat had found a uniformed man to put an arm around her.

Frank popped up on her left. 'What were you talking to him for?'

'Huh? What?'

'That guy with the umbrella. Who is he? I know I know him from somewhere.'

'David Madison?'

'Yeah, that's it! He's the husband.'

'Whose husband?'

'Deirdre Madison, the teacher. Don't you remember that case?'

'No, what happened to her?' Please don't let it be too tragic, she thought. That man doesn't deserve tragic.

Frank glowed with the kind of regretful excitement any human feels for really good gossip. 'She's in jail. She had an affair with a student.'

'And she went to *jail*?'

'The kid was thirteen. Fifteen when they were caught, thirteen when it started.' Theresa stared at him.

'Sick, right? And they had two boys of their own, right around the same age. That's how she got involved with the kid—besides having him in her class, he played on the same soccer team as her son. Can you believe that? I wish we'd had teachers like that when I was in school. Oh, stop scowling at me. Every guy thinks the same thing.'

'You wouldn't if it was your son.' This conundrum stumped her cousin, and he pondered it for so long she punched his arm. *Men*.

'Anyway,' he sidestepped, 'it'd be bad enough to have your wife dump you for another man, but a little *kid...*' She turned away, searching until she saw David Madison reach a worn sedan. He closed the umbrella and got in. Did he glance back at her just before tucking himself into the car's interior?

'...what goes through the head of a guy like that?' Frank asked.

SIX

'THE BINGHAM WAS blown up by *what*?'

'Vlads,' Angela told him. Angela was relatively new to homicide and as carefully neutral as a woman, and one with some color, needed to be. At times he worried that this neutrality spilled over into their personal lives, that there were still worlds about her of which Frank knew nothing. On the other hand, he saw no reason to rush things. They'd both seen too many of their colleagues' relationships crash and burn.

'I nearly got disintegrated by a bunch of vampires?'

'No, Georgians. As in Georgia in Europe, not the place with magnolia trees and the Falcons. They say the current president there stole the election from a Vladimir Minksky.'

'So go blow up freakin' Russia or something,' Frank protested. 'Why us?'

'The Vlads say that the current president got much of his funding from expats in Cleveland. And there *are* a lot of them. Seven per cent of our foreign born population is from Ukraine and Yugoslavia alone, with other eastern European sites close behind.'

'What did they expect to accomplish? As if anyone in DC or freakin' Russia or Georgia or wherever would care if Cleveland got blown off the map.' Frank hit the brake for a red light at East Sixty-Fifth, maybe a bit too hard.

'You OK?' Angela asked.

'Why does everyone keep asking me that?'

'Because you *did* nearly get disintegrated and buried beneath four floors of rubble, and then your cousin winds up at the scene of a cop killing?'

'Thanks for reminding me,' he grumbled, wondering, not for the first time, if Angela and Theresa ever talked about him behind his back. Theresa was blood and Angela was his partner, but they were women, and women felt anything they did could be justified.

'My money's on the building owner. No one can afford trendy downtown lofts any more. Most of the units were vacant—just as well, kept the body count low—and he had to be running into the red.'

'Skirting it,' Angela agreed, 'according to tax returns. But not bankrupt yet.'

'Smarter to quit while you're ahead.' Frank steered past the sagging roofs and cars parked on lawns of East Eightieth. Accumulating seniority in the detective unit had its privileges; the Crown Vic had rolled off the assembly line a month before and still had that pristine smell. Angela had made Frank promise not to smoke in it if she would refrain from leaving empty coffee cups under the seat. So far, they'd stuck to the deal.

In any case, he had *not* been freaked out by the explosion, or taken it personally. The cop killing, however, was a different story. The powers that be and a particularly vindictive Fate had decided to drop the investigation for the killing upon the shoulders of Frank and his partner. He needed to be freaked, he needed to be obsessed, and most of all he needed to come up with a viable suspect. Do it fast and make it stick. Failure would be felt in his record, in the squad room, in the locker room, in the eyes on him everywhere he went. Failure, to put it mildly, was not an option.

They'd probably even take the car back. He and Angela would be driving a rusted Pinto from now until
retirement.

'Did you know him?' his partner asked.

'Marty Davis? No.'

'I talked to the guys on his shift,' she said. 'I even
looked up a few from shifts past, but they all sounded
pretty consistent. A stand-up guy, not on the take, not
the most powerful round in the ammo belt but reliable.
He lived to write tickets.'

'So who did he tick off badly enough to come gunning for him?'

'They all had a list of suspects. A few came up more
than once, a crazy ex-girlfriend—'

'Doesn't every cop have a crazy ex-girlfriend?' He
braked, enjoying the quiet rotors.

'I don't.'

'Crazy boyfriend, then.'

'Nope. Annoying, certainly. But the girlfriend has
since moved to LA to pursue her dream of working
at Disneyland, so she's out. Then there's an alderman
named Bevilaqua with fifteen outstanding parking tickets. He and Davis had been having a pissing contest
going back two years over the man's habit of parking
in the fire lane when late for a meeting. Apparently he
doesn't handle his temper any more efficiently than his
schedule and threatened to, quote, string Marty up by
his thumbs, unquote.'

'If he wants to intimidate a cop he needs to use a
threat coined in the last century. I mean the last last
century.'

'True, but he repeated this one on a number of occa-
sions. The third choice is the most likely. Marty arrested
him three times for domestic violence. The last time he

served four years and has a permanent restraining order to keep him away from both his wife *and* children.'

'Threats?'

'Lots of them, but only to other inmates, who relayed the info to the correctional officers, who passed it on to Marty when the guy, Terry Beltran, got out early for good behavior last month.'

'Has he approached Davis?'

'Marty didn't say anything to his friends, and they say he wouldn't have been shy about something like that. The guy's probation officer said he's been making his meetings, not with good grace, but showing up, and has neither mentioned Marty nor asked about him.'

'And that's it? The guy's a cop for twenty years and only has three enemies?'

Angela shrugged. 'You know what patrol's like. The scumbags talk big when you're putting the cuffs on, but once they're in the system you get crowded to the bottom of their payback list.'

'Problem is you never know which scumbag is going to be particularly good at holding a grudge.'

'And smart enough to keep it to himself,' Angela added. 'One of our instructors in the academy said we were signing up to walk around with a bull's-eye painted on our backs for the rest of our lives. I never forgot it. You ever had someone come back on you?'

'Not yet. But tomorrow *is* another day.' Frank pulled over to the curb, stopping in front of a tiny house near Superior. He heaved a sigh and unfolded his aching body from the car, hoping to find it—the car—in the same condition when they returned. The two-story home appeared ready to fall down, or at least think about it. An apple tree, the only concession to landscaping on the entire street, looked as old as the house. Apples littered the ground; frozen all winter, they had waited for these spring months to resume decomposition. Angela preceded him up two sagging wood steps to a screen door with no screening left in it. She reached through and knocked on the inner door.

'Yeah, yeah,' came a woman's voice. 'Just leave it.'

'Can't. We're the police. We need to talk to Lily Simpson.'

'Why?'

'We need to do a notification. She isn't in any trouble. Are you her?'

The voice continued from inside the house, to the left, and didn't seem to be moving. 'Yeah, but I'm really busy right now.'

'Sorry, but we have to interrupt.'

'Oh, for the love—' the woman shouted. 'Just come in, OK?'

'You want us to come in?' Frank asked. The department lawyers had said to clarify these matters.

'As in open the door your damn self! My hands are full.' Frank shrugged, pulled open the empty screen door and turned the knob of the inner door. Then they entered and saw what Lily Simpson had her hands full with.

Through a cluttered front room with an antique fireplace, the lady of the house stood at her kitchen table, bathing a small dog in a large plastic tub. The dog, a brown thing with long hair and perky ears, stared with pleading eyes from a coating of soapsuds.

Lily Simpson had hair the color and consistency of straw and not nearly enough pounds on her slight frame. Her driver's license reported her age as forty-five, but as Frank came closer he saw how the lines on her face belonged to someone twenty years older. Her eyes were bloodshot, with jumpy pupils, but no alcohol bottles in sight. Crack, he figured, or something similar. Her clothes, a T-shirt with rust stains and a pair of sweatpants held in place by a drawstring, had large wet spots.

'What do you want?'

'You're Lily Simpson?'

'Yes. What do you want? They didn't do anything.' Her hands must have relaxed ever so slightly, and the dog took full advantage, putting two paws on the edge of the tub and pushing. This accomplished nothing save for adding another layer of water to the already soaked tabletop. Lily got a firmer grip and continued sudsing.

'Who didn't?'

'The kids. Or me. None of us did anything.'

Frank decided to bypass the getting-to-know-you stage. 'Are you acquainted with a Martin Davis?'

'Marty?' This got her full and un-irritated attention. She stared at them until the dog made a leap for it, leaving itself stranded over the edge of the tub, half out, half in. Lily dragged it back into the water without moving her gaze from Frank's face. 'What about him?'

'We're sorry to tell you that Martin Davis was killed in the line of duty on Monday.'

She froze, but briefly, then went back to the task at hand. 'I'm not surprised. I always said that job would kill him. Why he wanted to be a cop—no offense.'

'None taken.' Frank waited for her to ask another question, but she kept her head down, concentrating on the dog, until he realized she was crying. 'What was your relationship with Officer Davis?'

With a twitch of her neck she dried one cheek on her shoulder before answering. 'We were friends.'

'Just friends?'

Now she looked up with freshly red eyes, before hauling the dripping dog over to the kitchen sink and drop-

ping him on top of two spoons, a plate and a cereal bowl
with corn flakes adhering to the rim. A cockroach scattered, but didn't make it up the side of the basin before
Lily turned on the tap. She adjusted the water to a comfortable temperature, and began the rinse cycle. Only
then did she answer: 'Off and on. I mean we were always friends, and off and on we were more. I've known
Marty, geez, seems like all my life. Since high school,
but we got together in college.'

'You went to the same college?' Frank tried to keep
his voice as neutral as possible. Neither the victim nor
this woman struck him as brainy.

He didn't keep neutral enough and a defensive tone
crept into her voice. 'Yeah, we went to Cleveland State.
I was going to major in elementary education, believe
it or not. That was before I knew what kids were like.'
She turned off the water and Frank noted the relief in
the dog's eyes. Its tail even gave a half-hearted wag as
Lily pulled a frayed terry-cloth towel from the edge of
the table. Half if it had already been soaked from the
washtub overflow.

'What did Marty study?' Angela asked. She had a
habit of that, popping up with these off the wall questions. Frank would have preferred to do the notification
and get out before one of the cockroaches decided to
hitch a ride on his shoe.

'Beer. Women. Video games, anything to have an
excuse to get away from his parents without having to
get a job. One of his room-mates had a Nintendo, and
that's what Marty studied more than anything else.'
Lily wrapped the dog and transferred him back to the
kitchen table, absently pushing aside two water glasses
and a magazine to make room. 'Isn't that funny, I don't
remember what Marty was supposed to be majoring in.

Chemistry, maybe? Or math? I guess it doesn't matter, he never graduated. Neither did I. I got pregnant with my first, and that was that.'

'Marty's?'

'What? Oh. No, Shawna wasn't Marty's, we were broken up by then, sort of. Her father joined the Army to get out of child support and died in the Gulf War, good riddance. I couldn't even get any of the death benefit because I couldn't prove she was his.'

'Paternity test?' Angela suggested.

'Those cost money, don't they?' The dog's mood seemed to improve under the vigorous toweling, though Lily didn't seem to be paying much attention to her own actions. Her countenance appeared to be a million miles away, or perhaps twenty-odd years. 'It don't matter. I can't see me as a teacher, anyway, wearing little sweaters and cutting things out of construction paper.' Something in her voice made Frank think she could see it, and sometimes did.

Lily dried the inside of the dog's ears with the towel, gently, then got out a brush. The dog never took its eyes off Frank, as if hoping he might have a treat with which to reward him for all this suffering. Frank decided to get the conversation back on track.

'We're here to tell you that Marty named you as beneficiary in his will.'

A look of panic leapt to her face. 'I can't pay for a funeral.'

'The police department has already taken care of the funeral. It was this morning.'

'Oh my God, I didn't even get to go to the funeral? Why didn't you guys tell me sooner?' She lowered the dog to the floor.

'You didn't see it in the papers? On TV?' A boy of

twelve or thirteen threw open the back door, took one look at the two cops, and began to back out again.

Frank said, 'Come in. No one's in any trouble.'

The kid maintained his position by the door, just in case. 'Who're you?'

'They're cops, Brandy. Nothing to do with you.'

'It's *Brandon*. Did Shawna get knifed in the shower room?'

His mother shrugged without energy. 'His sister's doing two years for grand theft. No, Brandon, it isn't about Shawna.'

'Too bad.' The boy appeared visibly disappointed. He also appeared to need a good deal of the care his mother had just lavished on the dog. Pasty skin carried a layer of grime and a cut festered on his left hand. He hadn't been starving, though.

'Go to your room.'

'Why?'

'Grown-ups are talking. Beat it, *Brandy*.' The kid shuffled off, with heavy steps and a few backward glares which tried for intimidating and came off as pouty. The dog, now the cleanest thing in the room, obviously lacked the intelligence to escape while it could and instead began to investigate Frank's shoes. Meanwhile Frank explained that they hadn't found the will until that morning, a preprinted form on which Marty Davis had filled out the blanks longhand. He had kept it stuffed into a pile on his dining room table, along with a collection of *Playboy*'s, a picture of his swearing-in, a tattered copy of the police union rules and notebooks going back to high school.

'Actually you were the contingent beneficiary after his mother, but she died several years ago. He listed her as emergency contact and we couldn't find an address book. He didn't have a lot of close friends, and none of them mentioned you.' She sat in one of the mismatched chairs, heavily, leaning one arm on the still-sodden table.

'Not surprised at that either. I'm from the first half of Marty's life.'

'When was the last time you saw Da—Marty?' Lily pulled a half-empty bottle of beer from behind the wash-tub and took a mouthful to think with. Frank wondered how close it had been to the overflowing tub, and tried to catch the expression on his face before it puckered up at the thought of drinking dog bath water. Not that it mattered. Lily's gaze focused only on the past.

Finally she said, 'A year ago, maybe more? After Christmas, but we still had snow on the ground. He dropped off a friend somewhere around here after a cop party—someone's retirement, or bachelor party or some-thing—and saw my house. He'd do that once in a while, come by for old times' sake—well, more for a beer and a lay, I guess. But those *were* our old times, and I guess he'd get sentimental now and then. I do, too. Did.'

'Did he ever mention a Terry Beltran?' These were probably stupid questions, since she hadn't even spoken to the victim in over a year. But they were standard ques-tions and if he didn't ask them then for sure at some point in the future he'd be asked *why* he didn't ask them, and Frank despised being asked why he *hadn't* done some-thing because there was never any way to answer with-out looking either lazy or stupid. So he asked.

She looked at him again, coming back to the pres-ent, and drank another swallow of Pabst. 'No. I don't think so.'

'Did he ever mention being afraid of someone, or perhaps worried about them? Maybe someone threat-ened to get back at him over something?' He must have imagined the faint, sharp, startled look that shocked her eyes into full attention, so quickly did it evanesce only to be replaced by a frown. 'What do you mean? Wasn't he shot in a hold-up or by an escaping prisoner or something? Car accident? You know—regular cop work?'

'Had he ever been threatened?'

'No. I mean, not that he ever mentioned to me. Marty wasn't afraid of anyone or anything. I always thought—no offense, I loved him—he just didn't have the brains to be.' She shrugged. 'If he was, he probably wouldn't admit it to me. I'm just the bimbo, remember. If a guy talked trash to him and he laughed it off, *that* he would tell me, but any real problem, no. Why? Who killed him?'

'We're not sure yet. That's why we're exploring all possible avenues of investigation. Are you sure you can't think of any past incident that might help us?' He waited for that startled look, that flash in her eyes that meant a name had popped into her head, but she showed nothing but confusion which gathered and massed into agitation. Best to get out before she demanded every detail down to the bullet's caliber. Frank held out a card. 'This is the number of our legal department. They can advise you how to claim the estate. I have to warn you there isn't much,' he added as a wild hope came into her eyes. 'He rented his apartment and cracked up his car last month. He had a small amount in the bank—about four thousand dollars—but we haven't found any other assets.' She took the card. 'Marty wasn't much of a saver. I'm sure he signed his paycheck over to the bartender every week.'

'Our condolences on your loss,' Frank added. His condolences weren't much, but then it didn't look like her grief, other than those first few tears, amounted to much either. At least she'd come out of it with a few extra bucks to keep her dog in shampoo, and maybe spare some for the kid.

Angela, true to form, popped up with another question. 'What do you do for a living, Lily?'

'I work for Downtown Courier. I deliver stuff.' She gave a smile, which seemed to be meant only for herself. 'Been doing that most of my life. Why?'

'That sounds like a good job.' Frank knew his partner's habit of working up to her questions, and left her to it.

'I don't like to sit still,' Lily said.

'What did you mean when you said you were from the first half of Marty's life?'

Lily scooped the dog from Frank's feet, regardless of its wet fur. 'From the bad half. The young and crazy half. The half when crack and meth were part of our study habits, before he saw the light and decided to become a cop.' She didn't exactly say 'cop' the way most people said 'child molester', but it came close.

'What made him see this light?' Angela asked.

'At the end of sophomore year—' the woman began, then stopped, reassessed, and clearly changed her course. 'Sophomore year, Marty got tired of both drugs and studying. They didn't work well together. When we were high we thought we were studying our brains out, expected to ace every test, you know how it is when you're cranked up—' Frank, who didn't, nodded.

'—and we'd bomb. Then we'd get all concerned and stop the drugs and really try to learn the stuff, but it was so damn *hard*, and harder still without a pop here and there to cheer you up. It wore Marty down. It wore me down. Marty decided to trash it all, including me, to work on the side of the friggin' angels. By the time summer came he had enrolled with you guys and I was pregnant.'

'That was it?' Angela pressed. 'No one particular incident that made Marty turn to police work?'

'He said he figured he could put other people in jail or go himself, and he preferred it to be them.' His wording still made her laugh. '*Preferred*. He'd get flowery once in a while.'

'Thanks for your time,' Frank said, and turned to go.

'Hey.'

'Yes?'

'I get all his stuff?'

'You're apparently his beneficiary, yes. Once it goes through probate.'

'Did he have a TV?'

'I don't know,' Frank lied.

Angela, too soft-hearted, said, 'Yes. A big screen, probably fifty-two inches.'

'Plasma?'

'No.'

'Oh. That's still cool, though.' She scratched the dog's ears.

'Thanks.' They left her standing in her damp kitchen and moved carefully down the wooden steps. 'Nice to brighten someone's day,' Frank muttered.

'It's not like they were that close,' Angela pointed out. 'She was going to say something else, about why Marty became a cop, and then didn't.'

'I noticed. But I don't really care what happened to him twenty-five years ago. I'm more interested in what happened to him two days ago.' At least, he noticed, their new car appeared unmolested, and he used the remote to unlock the doors. As they pulled away from the curb, a *thump* at the rear made him jump. Braking, he and Angela craned their necks round to see a browned, rotting apple splattered on to the trunk, its mushy guts glistening against the deeply black paint.

And from his sagging roof, his ample butt depressing the shingles underneath him, Lily's son Brandon grinned until the afternoon sun reflected off his teeth.

SEVEN

Thursday

THE DEATH TOLL from the explosion had been arrested at seven and the various sets of initialed agencies working the scene seemed fairly certain that all the victims had been found.

Theresa had not had the time nor the inclination to revisit the area but would have to, and soon. They needed a plan to excavate their stuff. She wondered if any other crime lab in the country had ever had a similar situation. What did the New Orleans PD do after Katrina? She should make some phone calls…

She'd spent all morning drafting a written plan of attack to excavate, move and store their stuff. Leo had requested the SOP and she had nearly finished expanding 'dig the stuff out, pack it into boxes, truck them back here and put the boxes into the garage' to three pages in true civil service tradition. Once she had completed it, Leo glanced over it, told her that the average fourth-grader could have produced a more comprehensive plan, demanded that she start over with a more clear focus on her professional responsibilities. So she changed five or six words and altered the font from Arial to Times New Roman. Leo grumbled while shuffling out of earshot, then went to the second floor and presented it to M.E. Stone as his own work. After fifteen years, Theresa knew the process.

Hence freed to get back to work, she hovered absently around portly Dr Banachek's autopsy table. He detailed this particular victim's injuries on a preprinted diagram as Theresa examined the body for any trace evidence left after the clothing had been removed. The dead person, a female in her forties wearing hospital scrubs, had worked in the building's fitness center. Beams from the collapsing upper floors had crushed part of her skull and compressed her chest into her backbone. She had not been burned, however. The fitness center had been located at the back of the building to the west, and the blast apparently originated between the center and the front, possibly in one of the lower levels. No other information had been released. The Feds were playing their cards close to the chest. They had only now released these bodies for the county to autopsy.

She pulled a white sliver from a gash on the woman's arm.

'What's that?' Christine Johnson asked. Her lab coat a snow white against the black skin, the pathologist stood at the next table over a body that only loosely resembled a man. Christine was young, fit and gorgeous, but Theresa tried not to hold that against her.

'Looks like ceramic tile to me,' Theresa said. 'I wish I knew what the rest of the building looked like before the blast. I never went anywhere in it besides sublevel two. And the suicide's apartment.'

'You sure he didn't set a fuse but then wanted a more certain death for himself?'

'No apparent connection.' Christine leaned closer to the burned and shredded man than Theresa would have been comfortable with. 'We're lucky the place didn't have more people in it.'

'The tenants are all yuppies, I guess, out at work.

Another thing that makes me think the explosion itself was accidental, that someone had stored stuff there that shouldn't have been stored there. Why purposely blow up a mostly empty building with no political or financial significance?'

'Yeah.' Dr Banachek, ungloved, used a plastic stick to prod the jagged edge of the dead woman's broken mandible. 'I see a whole lot of crushing injuries here and not much else. No burns or signs that she got too close to explosives, no signs that she was tortured into cooperating with terrorists. She doesn't even smell as nasty as some of the other ones. I'd say she was a good distance from the explosion. Just not good enough to survive.'

'Hmm.' Theresa used disposable tweezers to pluck a bundle of white fibers from the woman's ankle into a small Manila envelope. Then she sealed it up, smiled at Dr Banachek, took her collected samples into the amphitheater to store on a lab tray, changed gloves and returned to the autopsy room to start on the next victim.

'He ain't looking so good,' she pointed out to Christine.

'Nothing a little aloe and lanolin won't fix,' the doctor said absently. 'Maybe. This is Nairit Kadam, born in Pittsburgh, family from India. Fairly or unfairly, he is the closest the Feds have to a suspect, simply because he is the only victim who didn't live or work in the building and he was obviously closest to the explosion. Of course, if you were going to blow someplace up, you'd think you'd take great pains to be the *farthest* person from the explosion. Oh, and the Middle Eastern name isn't helping his case any.' The cleaning agent odor filled her nose. Theresa stared at the blackened husk, trying to sort the charcoal-colored protrusions into parts of a body she could recognize. 'The blast took off his hands and feet.'

'Maybe. Or they were crumbled to dust by falling concrete.'

'Why was he there?'

'For the same reason you go there, to store stuff. That's how they know who he is—or at least how they're making a guess at who he is; we'll have to wait for DNA results because I don't think dental is going to be completely accurate,' Christine said, squinting at the decimated skull. 'A little bird told me that Nairit here had signed in to visit his storage unit just before the blast, and we only know that because the building manager had been chatting up the receptionist when Nairit came in.'

'The same building manager who then left for a doctor's appointment?'

The doctor nodded. 'Which saved his life.'

'So what did Nairit store in his storage facility?'

'According to the lease, files and miscellaneous paperwork from a data entry company called Blount Enterprises.'

'Doesn't sound too explosive.' Theresa used a fresh pair of disposable plastic tweezers to pull a melted glob from the man's rib. He might have been wearing a polyester shirt, or he might have been standing near plastic when the explosion occurred. Or it fell on him from one of the eight upper floors.

'Except that Blount Enterprises doesn't exist.' Theresa nearly lost the glob before dropping it into an envelope. She had been so hoping for a rational, accidental, non-malicious explanation. Life didn't often strike her speechless but right now she could come up with nothing more than, 'Doesn't exist?'

'That's all I know.'

'So he has a fake company, but not a fake name?'

'Apparently.'

'Who is this little bird?' Christine smiled, without bothering to lift her eyes from her work, only made a scribble on the anatomy diagram to represent a fracture of the man's right ulna. Hadn't Leo said one of the Feds observing the autopsy had been single and handsome? Christine had only to look at the average man and he would chatter away simply to have an excuse to stay in her presence. If she smiled, he might cough up anything, from his own bank account numbers to gossip straight from the corridors of power.

'Can you tell if that occurred before or after death?' Theresa nodded at the right arm.

'Like maybe terrorists tortured him and then left him to die with his own explosives? Man, I wish I could say you've been watching too much TV.'

'I have,' Theresa said grimly. 'The non-fiction type.' They both leaned over the broken bone until their heads bumped.

After a few moments, Christine said: 'I can't be positive, but I don't think so. I don't see any change in what's left of the tissue around the break or any healing at the end of the bone. Most likely it's a post-mortem crushing injury.' Theresa retrieved another envelope and collected a piece of paper-thin fabric from the stump of the left leg. It remained entirely possible that someone meant to blow up the Bingham building and not themselves, using a detonator with a timer. She herself could have placed a nuclear reactor in the sublevel storage chamber without notice, as long as she brought it in piece by piece in cardboard boxes. Nairit could be an unlucky soul who went to drop off some data entry sheets exactly when the storage unit across the hall went kablooey. Maybe his company could not be located because they had moved, or had a name change.

Or Nairit had been manufacturing or storing extremely explosive devices, and accidentally—not even the most desperate terrorist would consider the Bingham worth a suicide attack—set them off. Explosive devices utilizing nitrogen triiodide. But why? What had he hoped to do with it?

And if he had achieved his goal, how many bodies would they have on their hands right now?

Christine straightened, rubbed her lower back with one hand.

'So what's on your mind?'

'Huh?'

'You seem distracted. What's bugging you?' Theresa glanced back at the dead fitness center worker, as Dr Banachek made the Y incision down her chest. 'Other than a building collapsing on a bunch of people as they went about their daily business?'

'Yes.'

'Not to mention on top of nearly every piece of Medical Examiner's Office evidence accumulated during the last century?'

'Yes.'

'And almost on top of me and Frank?'

'Your face is looking better, by the way. But yeah, aside from that.' Theresa paused to find a whitish crystal on the exposed patella, but it crumbled to dust—and without exploding—when she tried to remove it. Plaster. 'Well, I did have a police officer shot to death while at a scene. That hasn't been too easy to shrug off.'

'Uh-huh.' Theresa never knew how doctors did this, how they could look at the tone of your skin and gauge your weight and figure out what you didn't even know that you didn't want to tell them. They must spend a whole semester of med school on it. She tried again.

'I met a man.'

'Hah!' Christine exclaimed, so loudly that Theresa jumped away from the steel table and nearly stabbed herself with the tweezers.

'Sorry, I'll stifle myself. What man? What is he like? Where did you meet him?'

'Down, girl, down. I didn't mean it like that. I meant—' Theresa discovered she didn't know exactly what she meant, so instead she started from the beginning, and told Christine about David Madison. Then she added what Frank had told her about David Madison's wife.

'Eww. Weird.' The doctor wiggled a sharp object from behind the dead man's shin bone.

'Finding a sliver of concrete wedged between his tibia and fibula?'

'Having an affair with a thirteen-year-old. The concrete is clean, it probably got in there during excavation. It's one thing to have your wife leave you for another guy, but a kid? What does that say about you? Is he some kind of hulking brute that made her think of herself as helpless, so that she started to see this kid as a peer?'

'He struck me as a big teddy bear. Of course, I only talked to him for about three minutes. How do you sleep with someone who's the same age as your own child?'

'Men do it all the time,' Christine pointed out. 'Though we hope they're at least over forty and their daughters are grown. So you have to ask yourself, how much sympathy does this guy warrant? How many women have had to face the fact that their husband is sleeping with a student, or the office intern, or the babysitter? No one ponders what that does to *their* self-esteem.'

'Maybe his self-esteem is OK. He probably just wonders what to tell his boys. The older they get, the more questions they're going to have, if they haven't asked them already. He must cringe every time he sees a news camera.'

Christine hadn't left the topic of cheating men. 'It's not surprising men are attracted to younger women. Biology and society trains them for that. But when they cross the line from "younger" to "child", then—'

'They've crossed the line from scumbag to pedophile.'

'Exactly. And there's such a double standard for boys and girls, of course. Some people actually claim that early sexual activity isn't as damaging to boys because they can't get pregnant. Granted, it's not going to disrupt their life like having a baby at twelve would, but their minds aren't just going to brush it off because their bellies don't grow.' Christine warmed to her subject as she took a rubber hose and washed off a spot on the dead man's wrist. 'All I know is, kids have a right to be kids and grow at the same rate as their peers, and if that was my boy I'd show up at that woman's house with a two-by-four and not a jury in the world would convict me.'

Theresa opined, 'I say reverse the genders. If you would put a man in jail for molesting a thirteen-year-old girl, and of course we would, then you have to do the same for this woman. I just feel sorry for the ones she left in her wake. What do you have there?'

'He's got a deformity on the outer edge of his ulna.' She pointed at the bone that ran on the outside of the arm, from the left hand to the elbow. It had an indentation, like a rough crater, just above the wrist.

'An old break?'

'No, not a break, not a calcium deposit…it almost looks like a burn.'

Theresa raised her eyebrows. 'Burn? The man's entire body is *crispy*.'

'Don't get cute with me, missy. I mean an old burn. The bone healed around it.'

'Oh.' Theresa leaned in closer. The campfire smell of the body competed with the scent of iodine and ammonia until she had to back up again, or sneeze.

'Maybe not a burn,' Christine muttered aloud. 'But I don't know what else could cause this, a cut would have…too bad I don't have any flesh to see…we'll have to get his medical records, ask his next of kin if he had an injury to his arm. OK, I'm going to hose the rest. Are you done?'

'Yeah. I've pulled off every piece of trace evidence I could find. Do we *have* a next of kin for him?'

'The Feds are supposed to find out. The parents are deceased, they told me that, but they're searching for siblings, spouse, etc.'

'No.' A woman in a suit, the same woman Theresa had met at the scene, entered with her dour partner. 'Sorry we're late. They had a water main break on Euclid and we had to go around. I see you've started on our suspect.'

'Victim,' Theresa said. 'No, you aren't searching, or no, he has no next of kin?'

'No,' her partner answered. A man of few words. Though his face softened when he gazed at Christine, the Dudley-do-Right chin slacking just a millimeter. Christine's source, no doubt.

'None that we can find,' the woman expounded. Nothing softened the lines that the intervening days had etched into her face; the agents had probably been working around the clock.

'Parents died in Pittsburgh years ago, no siblings, never married.'

'How does an Indian guy wind up part of a Georgian splinter group?'

'The Vlads might have taken responsibility, but they don't make a lot of sense. They're a small group, no real activity on the board and we can't confirm their numbers. They've created some riots in Georgia but no bombings, and have never done anything more violent in the US than write letters to the editor.' The female agent said all this. When he could tear his gaze from Christine, the male agent merely looked around him as if he personally found everything in the room as repulsive as the flayed-open bodies.

'So you think they're just claiming the credit for someone else's work?'

The woman shrugged. 'It's a theory. It also means whoever *did* stockpile the explosives is not about to step up and claim ownership.'

'Sounds like they didn't really mean to blow up the building. Makes me feel a little better,' Theresa admitted.

'I don't see why,' the woman sighed. 'They were hoarding it for some purpose. If they didn't intend to use it on the Bingham—'

'Then their target is still out there.' The woman nodded, and evaded a few more questions. Theresa couldn't blame her. No one at the M.E.'s office had an official security clearance and several of them were incurable gossips.

Besides, Theresa told herself, this isn't my case. Even the samples she had removed from the body would be turned over to the Feds, to be analyzed and identified by their laboratories.

Of course, no one said she couldn't take a good look at them before she sealed them up. 'I'll just get out of your way, then.' She took her envelopes and left. She didn't ask if Nairit Kadam, when alive, had a deformity to his left wrist, or what he had done for a living, or how long he'd been in Cleveland. Christine, she knew, would question the agents without cease for every moment they were present. If one wanted to hang around that particular doctor's autopsies, one had to pay the price.

Maybe the dead man knew nothing more about terrorists than what he saw on TV. But maybe he did. Maybe more destruction would explode in the city, today, tomorrow or the next day.

Keep working, she told herself. Just keep working.

EIGHT

LILY SIMPSON MUST not have waited for the dog to dry before presenting herself to receive the booty of her inheritance, because she appeared in front of Frank the next morning as he stepped off the elevator.

'Oh, hi,' she said. 'I was just coming to find you.'

'Yeah?' He juggled a Styrofoam cup of coffee without a lid and a lengthy list of felons to re-interview regarding the depth of their dislike for Marty Davis. Angela had gone to get the car and he needed to get out to the Ontario Street sidewalk before she had to double-park and create a traffic hazard. RTA bus drivers cut no slack for official cars.

'I went to that lawyer like you said, and he said yeah I'm the beneficiary, but I can't go get Marty's stuff yet. It has to go to the probate court first or something like that.'

'Well, that's for lawyers to determine. It's really got nothing to do with me.' He sipped the coffee and tried to sidestep, but she moved more quickly and planted herself in front of him, bouncing her weight from toe to toe. She had put on jeans for her trip out of doors, with a thin sweatshirt and a zippered hoodie.

'But it belongs to me now, so why do I have to wait for it? I've got a daughter in jail who needs a lawyer *now*. Marty would want me to have it,' she added with solemn piety. 'Can't you hurry them up? You were his friend.'

'I never met him.'

'But you came to my house—'

'I'm investigating his death. I was not part of his life. I'm sorry, Miss Simpson, but I have to go.' He stepped around her and made for the revolving glass doors.

She stayed on his heels, even gaining ground during the trip.

'So you need to talk to me, if you're investigating. I know more about Marty than anyone.'

'You hadn't seen him for over a year.'

'I know what matters.' She plunged through the glass doors ahead of him. Angela waited on the other side of the row of marked and unmarked police vehicles at the curb, causing a minor backup. He circled through the doors and prepared to run the gauntlet of Lily Simpson, hoping to do so without spilling coffee on his semigood pants.

'I'm just saying,' she said as soon as he broke out of the pocket of glass, 'that maybe whoever killed him came from way back, too, like me.'

'Because of an old grudge? You got someone in mind?'

'No,' she admitted, drawing out the *o*.

He studied her eyes, blue and jumpy. 'Are you on something?'

'No.' This time with more firmness but less conviction.

Frank would have bet his paycheck that Lily had seen a windfall coming and celebrated, the only way she knew how—not with champagne but with another kind of crystal. He could haul her back inside, do a DRE exam by making her follow his pen with her gaze to check her pupils, and then arrest her if she failed. But Lily would be out smoking more of it before nightfall and he needed the time to investigate a murder. 'I really can't help you with his estate, Lily. As far as I know, those things take time and there's nothing anyone can do about it. He only died on Monday,' he added, wishing he could use the impolitic but blunt phrase *his body's barely cold*. He dumped the coffee cup—nothing without a lid could enter the pristine Crown Vic—and dove into the sanctuary of the passenger seat.

'Horns are blaring,' his partner informed him.

'They'll get over it.' Somewhere in the middle of this statement the rear door opened and Lily Simpson jumped into the back seat, just as the vehicle began to move.

'Um—' Angela said.

'Ma'am.' Frank still knew how to say the word with that voice of absolute authority, perfected during his patrol days, and he used it now. 'Ma'am. You can't *do* that.'

'We don't usually have people jumping *into* a cop car,' Angela remarked. 'They try to get out, yes, but not in.'

Lily seemed quite at ease there, her face slightly screened by the metal mesh divider. She hugged herself with both arms and said, 'I need a ride. My car died again, and I figure you guys are probably going to Marty's place anyway, right? I need to talk to his landlord.'

Frank said, 'Lily, I can't help you with the legal process, and we are not a taxi service. You're going to get out at the next light.'

'I can't get out. This is a cop car, right? Handles don't work in the back seat?'

'You would know,' Frank said.

'What?' Perhaps he could annoy her out of the vehicle.

'I ran your stats. They're pretty impressive for the beneficiary of a cop. Four warnings and eight arrests in the past fifteen years, five for drug possession and three for soliciting.' This only made Lily settle deeper into the upholstery and stare out the window with a sullen cast to her face.

Frank spoke to his partner instead. 'Convicted of three of these eight offenses, serving a total of two years in two different sentences.'

Angela said, 'That's our justice system. Eight arrests and she serves two years.'

'And now she gets herself revved up and hops in a cop car. Maybe the judge will be stricter this time.'

Lily couldn't maintain the pout, and leaned closer to protest: 'The drug stuff was misdemeanors.'

'Not the last one,' Frank said. 'You were carting around a little too much for personal use.'

'I wasn't selling it.'

'No,' he agreed. 'You can't get together enough money to make your own business. You were delivering it for someone who could.'

'I got kids to feed.'

'Doesn't everyone?' Frank said, though he didn't.

'Spare me the attitude. Half my customers were cops.'

'Really.' Frank made sure to speak in a tone of complete disbelief, but he wondered. Marty could have been one of those customers…though all his friends and co-workers had seemed positive that his only drug of choice came in a glass bottle with a twist-off cap.

'You think you knew Marty? You think you know all about your little fallen angel, but you don't. *I* knew him.'

'I keep telling you, I never met Marty. You got something to tell me about Marty, then tell it, because we're not your chauffeurs. Pull up to the federal building, Ang. We'll dump her on their laps.' Lily leaned forward, twining her fingers through the mesh divider. 'You think I'm some drug dealer? Who do you think I learned it from?'

'If I assure you that I don't think you're a drug dealer, only a dealer's crack whore mule, will you get out of my car?'

The insult didn't seem to register. 'Who do you think I learned it from? Marty, that's who.' She flopped back against the upholstery, face flushed, secure in her fait accompli.

'Pull over,' Frank said when Angela kept driving.

'We *are* investigating his death,' his partner pointed out, playing the good cop with a subtlety worthy of Hollywood. 'Marty dealt drugs?'

'Yeah,' Lily confirmed, nodding for emphasis. *'Yes.'*

'When? Back in college?' Frank guessed.

'Yeah.'

'What did he sell? Pot? Crack?'

'Meth,' she said. 'And we didn't just sell it. We made it.' Frank tried to picture Lily peering into a glass flask over a Bunsen burner. The mesh barrier diffused the look of her face just enough to suggest the college student she had once been, but only just. 'You cooked meth.' The disbelief in his tone apparently stung her.

'Yes. No—I mean, I didn't cook it. Neither did Marty.'

'Make up your mind, Lily, are you going to tell us or not? The statute of limitations on a few crystals of meth ran out long ago.'

'How about murder? What's the time limit on that?' The word hung there for a moment while Frank considered how much more of his day he wanted to spend on Lily's history, which, he suspected, gave the term *revisionist* a new dimension.

'Is meth what you smoked before walking into the Justice Center, which, by the way, is full of the people who are supposed to arrest people like you?'

'Why are you harassing me?'

'Lily, your pupils are dancing around like dust motes in a breeze. Besides, you jumped into *my* car, remember?'

She scowled for a moment, but the drugs wouldn't let her stop talking. 'We didn't do the actual cooking. That was two other guys. You had to be, like, a chemist to do that. It was complicated. It stunk, too.'

'Yeah, yeah.' Frank had spent a short stint in Vice and knew the rudiments of meth labs. The process usually began with cold relief tablets and from there took a variety of routes, which all used solvents like acetone, methanol, benzene or ether. These flammable compounds would be heated, cooled, filtered and heated again, making for an extremely combustible atmosphere. And they *did* stink. Frank loathed meth labs.

'But we were sort of a team. We all had a job. How do you think we could afford to be there at all, Mummy and Daddy? I don't think so. Mine helped me a little but Marty had been on his own since he was, like, twelve.'

'And what was your role in this operation?'

Lily rubbed her lips, pulling them out of shape, obviously wondering if she should shut up now. 'I made deliveries.'

'You were a mule. So not much has changed?' He expected her to snap at that but she didn't have an answer, merely bounced on the upholstery so that her foot slipped and she kicked the back of his seat. Apparently not much *had* changed. 'What was Marty's job?'

'We were kids, you know? So we'd sell to our friends and let them owe us the money. Only if they didn't pay, well, we couldn't let that go on.'

They drove past the *Plain Dealer* building. 'So Marty enforced your business relationship?'

'Yeah. He never hurt anyone, really. Not bad. He'd

threaten them and they'd pay up. He had more muscle than fat, then.'

'Where did you do all this cooking?' Angela asked.

'I told you, I didn't do it.'

'Where?'

'In the—place we rented.'

'And who else worked for this little company of yours?'

Lily rubbed her arms, though even her threadbare sweatshirt should have kept her warm enough inside the car. 'You don't need to know that.'

Frank gave his partner an exasperated look as they crossed East Ninth. 'Fine. But at least tell me this: how is a sideline from Marty's college days going to help us figure out who killed him this past Monday?'

'The sins of the past,' Lily intoned.

'What's that, the title of a book you read? You got any other information about Marty, maybe something more current? Because I have a hard time believing someone would kill him over a twenty-year-old drug deal. How about that murder you mentioned?'

Now Lily clamped her arms around her and pushed herself into the seat back as if trying to disappear. 'Never mind about that.'

'You brought it up.'

'Yeah, I shouldn't have. Let me out.'

'We're cops, Lily. If you mention a murder, we're obligated to investigate same.'

'It's nothing, forget it. I made it up.'

'Make up your mind. It's nothing, or you made it up?'

'I was just trying to get a ride.'

'And now you don't want one?'

'No!' She set on the door handle with both hands,

pushing and pulling, shading from hyperactive into manic. 'Let me out.'

Frank couldn't resist the urge to screw with her. 'If you have knowledge of a crime, we're obligated to hang on to you.'

'Forget it, OK? There was no murder! I made it up. Now let me out.' Without discussion Angela pulled to the curb, in front of the silver dome of the Cleveland State planetarium. Frank got out, still feeling each abrasion on his legs and arms, and opened the back door.

'And here we are back at the scene of your college days, Lily. Maybe you can raise the ghosts of your old customers and ask them if they killed Marty.'

She burst from the car nearly as fast as a champagne cork but without the happy *pop*. 'Asshole,' she told him, before stomping down the sidewalk, moving east, retracing their route. She did not look back.

He shut the rear door and slipped back into the passenger seat, feeling suddenly weary. 'At least it got her out of the car,' he said to Angela.

She shifted into drive. 'Finally.'

NINE

THERESA SETTLED DOWN with the samples she had removed from Nairit Kadam—actually the slivers of samples she had retained before turning the larger remaining amounts over to the nicely dressed federal agents—after setting up the scanning electron microscope to analyze the week's gunshot residue cases and completing the fiber comparison in a rape case. She had also written up the clothing descriptions for all the explosion victims, such as they were, since the clothing of those people closer to the epicenter, like Nairit, had either burned or melted off. This limited her descriptive abilities.

Now she opened an envelope she had labeled with a Sharpie, noting Nairit Kadam's case number and 'left shin', 'shin' sounding more pleasant than 'stump'. She tried to keep her notes PC and somewhat gentle, for fear of finding herself on the witness stand trying to explain the use of the phrase 'cat-puke yellow' to describe a piece of evidence. Attorneys leapt on any sign of humanness as a sign of incompetence.

Under the stereomicroscope, which functioned as a large, high-powered magnifying glass, she examined the paper-thin piece of fabric. Its fibers were unusually thin as well, and coated in black tar from the explosion. Even this tiny scrap brought a faint whiff of iodine to her nose. She pulled off a few fibers and washed them, first in soapy water and then in xylene, almost losing them entirely when the liquid made them hard to see.

Then she let the xylene evaporate. She did all this while breathing shallowly, lest an errant breath shoot her fibers into the wild blue yonder to be lost forever along the lab's worn linoleum.

Finally they were ready to analyze. Now the real fun began, as she tried to hold down one end of the fiber with tweezers and roll up and down the length of it, from the loose end, with a small metal roller. The fiber stuck to the roller at will, then let go of it again, so that even once nicely flattened it would get bunched up under the roller and wind up a wadded-up mess. Then she had to transfer it to a round, clear disk of potassium bromide about one centimeter in diameter and repeat the rolling motion, trying to get the fiber flat against the 'window' without scratching the soft salt disk with the metal roller—or, heaven forbid, breaking it. They cost well over a hundred dollars apiece and Leo would have a mild conniption if she ordered another one before the end of the quarter. So she worked with the fiber until it gave up and lay flat, and carefully picked up the window and dropped it into its slot on the infrared spectrometer's stage. All the while breathing very, very lightly. Only when she told the computer what to do and it sent a beam of light through the fiber did she take a deep breath, but still held it until the spectra appeared on the monitor.

Fibers could be a painfully annoying analysis, but they were not her *least* favorite task—they still had more variety and color than hairs.

The fiber's spectra turned out to be quite ordinary, a type of polyethylene.

'What's up?' Don hitched himself up on her workbench, his long legs dangling over her cabinets.

'Don't move, and don't breathe too much.'

'That's why I love coming to visit you. I always get such a friendly welcome.'

'You're breathing.'

'Duly noted.' Determining someone's DNA markers from bodily samples involved periods of waiting, during which Don would inevitably seek her out. He had made this even more of a habit in the past few days. Unlike Leo, Don *did* care about her emotional health.

Unfortunately she did not have such a free period at the same time. 'These are samples from the explosion suspect. Possible suspect.'

'I thought the Feds took the samples.'

'They did.'

'You naughty girl. So what is it?'

'Nothing exciting, just olefin.'

'And that is?'

'It makes excellent carpet—really stain resistant. I don't think it's used in clothing too often.'

'So it's carpet. Place blows up, the fiber sticks to him.'

'Who carpets a storage room, especially in white carpet? And it's awfully thin.'

'Maybe he wasn't in the storage room at the time. Maybe he didn't have anything to do with this explosion at all and we're all rushing to the profile a little too fast.' Don, half black and half Hispanic, knew all about profiling.

'Could be.'

'Or he set the charges and thought he'd get out of the building a lot faster than he did. Or the carpeting fell on him from another floor in the midst of the fireball. I don't know about you, but I think I'm glad the Feds have this one.'

'Yes,' she said, 'and no.'

EXCAVATIONS CONTINUED AT the Bingham building. In the next twenty-four hours they expected to reach sublevel two. Once that occurred Theresa would put in hours non-stop until all the M.E. office's warehoused evidence could be accounted for. The Feds expected this to be to-morrow, so Theresa figured to spend one more evening at leisure and then get a good night's sleep before she gave up both for an indefinite period. Her exciting eve-ning plans consisted of a meeting of the alumni board of her Alma Mater, Cleveland State. Normally she would have claimed emotional trauma to get out of it, but to-night's meeting would be held at the Lambert edifice and feature a tour, not to mention wine and appetizers, which made it the most appealing invitation she'd had all month. Her social life, she told herself while parking the car in the sprawling lot, left something to be desired.

But it couldn't be helped. She had joined the alumni's Futures Committee while in a funk of Empty Nest com-bined with a touch of Dead Fiancé, when her mother kept nagging her to get out of the house and even the dog had taken to gazing at her reproachfully. The Futures Com-mittee had been formed to investigate ways to make the university more energy efficient. Simply trying to heat and cool the sprawling complex of buildings in any sort of logical, centralized way presented a challenge. Class-rooms could not always be matched to the expected class size, so that rooms were under- or over-utilized. The ris-ing costs of natural gas had not helped. But questions of efficiency always appealed to Theresa's orderly soul, and at least it got her out of the house.

She had also, feeling generous, invited Leo to accom-pany her, since he had also graduated from Cleveland State at some point before she did. But he had turned her down, to her guilty relief (he was not good company inside the workplace, and she had no reason to think he would be any more pleasant outside of it), having 'stuff to do'. What that might be, she couldn't guess. If Leo had any more of a social life than she did, he hid all evidence of it with magnificent efficacy.

The ruined horizon of the Bingham building sat just north of Lambert's parking lot. It seemed that the large pile of rubble where the building sat had been moved, piece by piece, to a large pile of rubble in what used to be the parking lot. Progress of a sort. She wondered if it had gotten the Feds any closer to their bomber. Then she gave up thinking about it, stepping up to Entrance Number Two as expressly instructed via memo by Ginny Wilson, Futures Committee Vice Chairperson.

Bruce Lambert's mansion/workshop/factory loomed above the banks of the Cuyahoga, spanning an entire city block, and still seemed small for the amount of money it generated. One leaping advancement in technology after another had emerged, from mini-MP3 players to jet engines that used half the fuel of their predecessors, putting Bruce Lambert at or near the top of the Forbes 500 list in every year of the past ten. Theresa had toured his factory once; Rachael's class had taken a field trip there, a rite of passage for every Ohio student as much as the art museum or the Schoenbrunn Indian village.

Theresa remembered the factory, vaguely, as big, brightly lit and noisy, more of a think-tank than a factory since Lambert mostly produced designs for products rather than the products themselves. Prototypes were built, tinkered with, built again. Supposedly he recruited local talent to keep up Cleveland's growing emergence in the high-tech field. Whatever—most Americans were simply glad he hadn't moved his offices to China and most Clevelanders were thrilled he hadn't taken himself to Silicon Valley or San Francisco or even Atlanta. He could be considered Cleveland's answer to Bill Gates.

Entrance Number Two led to a gleaming white hallway and a friendly security guard, who pointed her to the conference room, decorated in deep cherry panels and burgundy carpet and smelling of clean plastic. A SMART board covered one wall, opposite a podium filled with enough electronic equipment to stage a community theater. On one side of the room stood three huge and ungainly *things*; they put Theresa in mind of a small crane crossed with a mammogram machine and then fused with a copier. She half expected them to come to life and transform into killer robots, but suspected they had merely been stored in the room and forgotten, sitting at odd angles and collecting dust. Boxes sat in another corner. A conference room is often to an office what a guest room is to a home, a convenient place to stash unwanted items.

At least twenty other alumni were already present and were, under the direction of Ginny Wilson, lining up the metal frame chairs in rows of ten with exactly six inches between each set of legs. Having left her water bottle in her car, Theresa made a beeline for the box of wine and the plastic glasses. It had been a long couple of days.

She couldn't stay unnoticed for long. Ginny eyed her outfit—in the dinky bathroom at the M.E.'s office Theresa had changed into a standard pair of black pants and a too-snug scoop neck top she'd grabbed by accident—but merely asked if she would stack the yearbooks on the table in a nice way. Once you've finished your drink, dear.

Theresa dutifully opened the cardboard flaps and began to stack yearbooks. They were a gift to the host for his 'museum', a collection of informational displays that also served as the front lobby for the mansion/factory/workshop. Bruce Lambert himself would probably be hard-pressed to come up with a theory as to why he would want thirty years of college yearbooks, but they were large, weighty and, most importantly, since they had merely been accumulating dust in a storage room, free. Plus they would serve to remind people that the very impressive Bruce Lambert had attended CSU before he'd strayed off to that snooty MIT.

Talk swirled around her, speculations upon and hysteria about the explosion next door. A few of her fellow alumni, finished with the chairs, asked Theresa what she knew. She told them: 'Only what you've already read in the papers.' They didn't need to hear how it had nearly killed her. They could figure that out from the bruises on her face and hands.

The Futures Committee Vice Chairperson returned to re-stack Theresa's artistically stacked yearbooks. Ginny Wilson didn't give a crap about when or how or why the Bingham building had blown up, too busy hyperventilating that the alumni association would be getting a tour of the factory not from some flunkey but, unexpectedly, from the top dog himself. Theresa dutifully stood by when the man walked into the room, in case Ginny fainted.

Bruce Lambert dressed the part of the hyper-intelligent nerd with so much flair it almost seemed put on. He lacked only a pocket protector and some tape on his glasses. But the slightly wrinkled plaid shirt gleamed with a pricey sheen, and the neatly cuffed trousers had to have been hand-tailored from the finest wool. He had fair skin and unruly chestnut-colored curls and no wedding ring (preferring to date an eclectic mix of women, from a Nobel Prize winner to a supermodel to a barmaid from his high school class). If a building blowing up only inches from his life's work bothered him, he did not show it, speaking to the forty or so people in front of him without the slightest sign of discomfort. During the tour he would show them how cars powered by electrical energy were now the logical choice, and gasoline-powered engines an expensive, inefficient custom of the past.

Theresa watched from beside one of the huge mutant robots. She could learn about electric cars or she could maintain access to the wine box and the baby carrots. Her choice seemed clear. It had been a *really* long couple of days.

'Hello.' She turned, and found herself staring straight into the collarbone of David Madison.

TEN

Theresa promptly choked on the orange vegetable.

He patted her back. 'You OK?'

'Um, yeah. Hi. Nice to see you again.'

'Under slightly more pleasant circumstances,' he pointed out, keeping his voice low.

'You went to Cleveland State?' she asked, stupidly, since his name tag sticker spelled out 'Class of 1988'.

'I'm the accountant for the alumni association.' Like Lambert, he dressed the part, in a white shirt, dress pants and a conservative but loosened tie. Unlike Lambert, none of his clothes had the sheen of money.

'Is that what you do for a living? Accounting?'

He nodded. 'It's exactly as exciting as it sounds.'

She tried to think of a follow-up question that showed she knew something about accounting. 'Do you have your own practice?' *Doh*, not good. Sounded snobby.

'No, I work for a company downtown. Gardner Supply. Hey, I think we're going on the move.' The assembled group stood up, en masse, and followed the pied piper out into the hallway.

'I'm going to stay in the back. I have to cut out early,' Madison said. 'But I don't want to hold you up if you want to hear this.' She shook her head, as content as he to stay on the fringes, just as they had at the funeral. Had it become a habit with him, avoiding the crowd, staying under the radar? It wouldn't be surprising behavior for the survivor of what must have been a media circus.

Or maybe he had preferred to camp by the wine box too, who knew? 'I thought your name sounded familiar.' Her voice bounced off the gleaming hallway floor, and she modified the volume. The couple in front of them glanced back at her. At least Ginny would be all the way at the front, on the heels of her idol. 'I probably saw it in the alumni newsletters.' He opened his mouth, seemed to think better of it, and then nodded. Perhaps he'd been about to say, 'Or the newspapers.' Their first stop turned out to be a lab at least six times the size of Theresa's, stocked with sinks, burners, fume hoods and what appeared to be welding torches. The clean plastic smell of the conference room gave over to the scent of solvents and metal.

'Two things have always kept electric vehicles from becoming a viable consumer alternative to the gas engine.' Lambert proved to be an excellent tour guide, his voice reaching each corner of the room. He paced a bit as he talked, absently picking up a clamp and then dropping it on the next bench. 'Range and speed. They can't go too far and they can't go too fast—well, they can, but then the price climbs so high that the average consumer can't afford it. If you're talking about a car that can't exceed thirty-five or forty miles per hour, then what you have is basically a golf cart with a nice exterior. That's annoying enough, but range is what really fills consumers with fear. No matter how far the vehicle can travel on a charge, fifty, one hundred or two hundred miles, if you get to the end of it and there's no handy recharging station there, then you are as dead by the side of the road as if you tried to go from LA to Vegas on fumes.' Theresa worked a piece of carrot out of her teeth and wondered about weight. Not her weight but the car's, because if electric cars were anything like those electric wheelchairs, those things were as dense as a block of lead and impossible to move once the engine quit—'Well, limits are a personal affront to me. My brother Carl and I always found it difficult to observe limits—just ask my parents! I believe human beings are limited only by themselves, so it may be just as well that I didn't become a physician like my mother wanted. People refer to me as an inventor. If they want me to pick up the check, they'll refer to me as a genius inventor, but I'll tell you the truth—I have never invented a thing in my life.

'What I do is take something that someone *else* invented, look at its end point, and say, why did you stop there? Completely electric cars come with too many limits. I took another look at the situation. What are we really trying to do? Electric cars might be better for the environment but they're still not great for it since that electricity has to come from somewhere. What we need is gasoline without the side effects.' The group began to move again. The climate control, Theresa had to admit, seemed flawless. Not freeze-dried, but not too warm even with the crowd of people. Good for Theresa as she tried to remember how to make polite conversation with someone who did not work in law enforcement. She kept her voice low though she couldn't even see Lambert from their position at the back of the line. Happily, Madison helped out, asking for her connection to the association and what the Futures Committee had been up to lately. The group shuffled past Lambert's office, furnished with a massive cherry desk; its owner joked that he never sat there, merely kept the room set up to convince his mother he had a real job. On the wall behind it spread a window which overlooked Cleveland from the east bank of the river to Tower City. A large print of the Vitruvian man hung on the wall. At least Theresa assumed it to be a print; with Lambert's money she couldn't be sure.

'I believe I've found that substitute in the much more convenient form of dry crystals,' the man was saying.

'What is it you do again?' Madison asked. 'The papers said you weren't a cop.' Theresa said she worked as a forensic scientist and then explained how her job in no way resembled the glamorous activities seen on popular TV shows.

'I don't have that problem,' David said. 'Hollywood has yet to glamorize accountants.'

'Give them time. So, how do you really feel about electric cars?' Ambient light bounced off every surface in the white hallways and intensified the blue in his eyes.

'When they have a recharging station on every corner, then I'll consider it.'

'If the price of gas gets high enough, I'll consider anything,' she said. The woman in front of them turned around again, this time with an actual frown, which only made Theresa drop back a few more feet. As the alumni strolled through the ergonomics section, she and Madison compared notes about their time spent at Cleveland State and how steadily college tuitions had risen across the country. She whined about the fees she had to pay for Rachael and he said he had two to go yet. Gazing at an automobile seat in some early stage of construction or assault—it was difficult to tell which—Madison complained, 'My older boy is fourteen and has already picked his place: the esteemed University of Hawaii.'

'Hawaii?'

'He doesn't believe in thinking small, and regards shoveling snow as equivalent to waterboarding.' Bruce Lambert guided the quivering Ginny into the prototype car seat, calling the inch-thick foam covering something that sounded like 'eva'. It didn't look too cushy to Theresa but Lambert sounded convincing as he made eye contact with every person in the crowd. He even caught Theresa's gaze at one point, the warm color of his brown eyes evident from across the room. It silenced her until he finished and the tour group moved on.

'Has he picked a major too?' she asked David Madison.

'Bovine science. Since they have all those ranches in Hawaii. That way he'll have a job there as well, and need never return to the forty-eight contiguous. He did graciously agree to call me on my birthday.'

'Don't despair. Rachael insisted on the Sorbonne until she got a D on her first French test. What about your other son?'

'I get a break with him. He won't need a degree to go directly on to the NASCAR circuit.'

'Good to know.' They paused as those ahead stopped to watch two men molding plastic headlights and taillights into the shapes they desired. The plastic pieces were held by clamps as the men applied heated pliers equipped with their own fan.

Madison faced her over the gleaming linoleum, all smiles having left the smooth skin over his cheeks. 'Theresa...my boys have been through a lot.' *Why is he telling me this? Because he's interested in me and, in the interests of honesty, wants to get the baggage out right up front? To explain why he can't be interested because he's too traumatized ever to trust again? To show how he doesn't have time to be interested because his boys are a full-time concern? Because whenever he does talk about it, women start falling over themselves with sym-*

pathy? Because he'd rather talk about *anything* other than electric cars?

She kept her voice low, but the noise from the fan helped cover their conversation anyway. 'My cousin told me about your wife.'

'So you know. My life has been a little—unusual.'

'I can imagine. No, actually I can't. Rachael's father cheated on me, but at least it wasn't with—'

A child. He gave that same sad, gentle smile she'd seen at the funeral. She resisted the urge to put her hand on his arm as they wound past the overpowering smell of melted plastic. 'It's the boys I worry about. It was bad enough at the time, but the older they get, the more those hormones start pushing, the more questions they have. I considered moving but I knew I'd need help with the boys, and I have a mother and two siblings here.'

They followed the other alumni back into the hall-way, pausing outside a set of windows as the plastic smell receded. The windows turned out to be an observation spot, looking down on a two-story-high room about thirty by fifty feet, as brilliantly lit as an operating room even without the skylight windows in the opposite wall. A suspended track bisected the length, and Theresa saw the shell of an automobile dangling from its pulley. In the center of the room, mobile robots surrounded another frame, also resembling a small vehicle, with all its parts scattered about it on the floor like an unmade jigsaw puzzle: wheels, seats, axle, engine.

Rimmed with workbenches, cabinets, the walls and floors of the fishbowl-like room were white but everything else stood out in color: books, models, drawing boards with sketches, phones, even a leftover bowl of popcorn. One desk held both a collection of fluorescent Post-it notes and a four-foot-long pipe cutter that looked too heavy to lift, much less use. Abandoned Tyvek jump-suits had been thrown over chairs and desks like shed skins. It reminded her of an amusement park tour ride. It only needed a caption: 'Genius at work'.

They watched the slightly hypnotic process as a crane on a suspended track ushered the shell across the room to be lowered on to a waiting chassis, tended by the wait-ing robots. Lambert explained that the process could be reversed as well; anything that didn't work would be dis-assembled down to the problem, or down to its bolts if necessary. A man in the audience asked if he'd be open-ing any future assembly plants in Cleveland. Lambert's reply was lost to her as Madison leaned down to speak quietly in her ear, 'Look, the reason I'm dumping all this on you is… I wanted to explain…'

'Why you hide from the crowd?'

'Yeah, well. I don't hide, exactly, more like avoid. But I also wanted to be straight about it, in case we… run into each other again.'

'I'd love to run into you again.' She choked, coughed, and added, 'Wait—did I say that out loud?' He laughed.

'Really, this isn't like me.' It would be impossible to describe just how *unlike* her it was. She hadn't chased a man since she'd been, well, a student at CSU, and then made the mistake of catching him. She'd been interested in her late fiancé from the moment they met, but hadn't let on for months. How did this particular man get past her defenses, and in such record time?

This was dangerous.

She stared at the robots.

'I'd like that,' Madison said. 'Right now, though, I have to go pick up Jake. His judo class will be over in ten minutes. The lobby's right here, so I'm going to take this opportunity to slip out.'

'Oh. Well, OK, then. It was nice talking to you.' Inane! She made herself look at him, and hoped her cheeks were not flushing.

'Yeah, I have such pleasant conversation.' He put a hand on her upper arm, nearly encircling it with his fingers, making her ever so glad she *had* worn the too-tight shirt. 'Thanks for listening.' She bit her tongue to keep from saying 'Anytime', and settled for smiling, curving up her warm cheeks. He skulked away down the catwalk without looking back. She made herself gaze at the workroom and stare at the nearly completed electric car without seeing it.

Then she took in a deeply contented sigh. Ridiculous.

Bruce Lambert caught her gaze again and she blushed anew, a sure confession that she hadn't heard a word he'd said about robotic assembly.

The crowd moved on. She followed.

You do not like that man. This is a silly flash of infatuation because you're bored and lonely and you drank wine on an empty stomach. And he's probably only trying to prove that he can still be found attractive by women who don't prefer little boys.

The group wound up back in the conference room. Some collapsed into chairs, as if that had been the longest walk they'd taken in months. Theresa headed for the wine box, ignoring the baby carrots entirely this time. Bruce Lambert moved on to the subject of fuel cells and how they lasted ten times longer than batteries but still ran out too soon and were too difficult to replenish. She wondered if he had agreed to speak to the board to help the school reduce its carbon footprint or to drum up new investors.

Her eye fell on the yearbooks. Ginny had stacked them in groups of five, sitting alternately on their sides and on their ends, with the tail stacks fanned slightly. The Vice Chairman would slap Theresa's fingers if she disturbed them.

She'd have to be careful. To disguise her errand, even from herself, she first located her own year and photograph, noting with a sigh how firm her skin had been. Then she moved four years back and found David Madison's. He hadn't changed his hairstyle much; the flecks of gray made it look lighter these twenty-three years later. Schoolgirl behavior, gathering information on her secret crush and squirreling it away. Next she'd be leaving notes in his locker.

Bruce Lambert wrapped up the discussion of thermoset composites and took some questions. Yes, he expected the car to be on sale within the next year, possibly the next six months. Yes, he had helped create the full-body scanning station for schools and no, he didn't feel they were an invasion of privacy. No, he had not proposed to his current girlfriend, that was a rumor. No, his brother Carl had not gone to CSU until his sophomore year; like the Kennedys, his father had planned for his eldest child to bring in riches and scraped and saved to send Carl to Columbia, from which he was promptly expelled for a schoolboy prank that remained a more closely guarded secret than Bruce's new fuel crystals, ha ha. Yes, the new cars would be available in an array of colors, including lemon yellow and something called electric poppy.

She turned another page, and once again David Madison's face jumped out at her. In a candid shot under the heading 'Campus Life', his younger incarnation hoisted a brew in the tradition of all college students since the beginning of time. He grinned for the camera with a bit more mischief than he had for the head shot. The caption

read, 'The chemistry club confers in the Rathskeller.'
Chemistry? He majored in accounting. No doubt the
yearbook writers meant it as some sort of joke, since
the phrase had not been capitalized. Or perhaps he'd
been there as a guest?

At the front of the room, Cleveland's resident genius
explained how his version of the internal combustion
engine was fueled by sand-like crystals. Theresa realized that everyone else had taken a seat, and sat down
at the end of the last row so that her complete inattention would not be so obvious. She flipped to the index of
the yearbook. The Chemistry Club had a nicely framed
group picture, which did not include David Madison
or anyone else from the Rathskeller photo. The caption
had referred only to the chemical compounds of hops
and barley.

The young man next to David seemed familiar. Perhaps she'd shared a class with him; if he had been an
underclassman in the photo, he might still have been
there when she attended. He had a round face and a little
too much curly brown hair to be flattering. She stared
at the photo, willing the memory to come back to her,
but it resisted until she gave up and examined the other
students at the bar. One slender boy in the back stood
with his shoulders hunched in, as if cowering, though
he smiled, and his body language made her think of that
squirrelly guy at Marty Davis' funeral.

She went back to the young man holding a bottle of
Pabst and leaning on David Madison. Maybe if she took
off twenty years and added some pounds—that was it.
She hadn't met him in a class but at the crime scene
where he'd been shot to death.

Marty Davis.

She paged briskly through the rest of the yearbook.

David said he attended the funeral because Marty had been kind to him during the brouhaha with his wife. Well, why not because they had been classmates first? She had wondered at the time why a patrol officer would have had steady contact with him after the case had been assigned to detectives—surely Marty would have done what he could to walk his old friend through the myriad of events that made up an investigation, arrest and prosecution. But why not say, 'I'm an old friend,' and leave it at that, instead of bringing up the errant wife?

Maybe the investigation loomed so large in David's life that he'd forgotten how he first got to be friends with Marty. Maybe some perverse impulse made him bring up his wife with any woman he felt attracted to—is he *attracted* to me?—the same way people pick at scabs.

She could imagine what Rachael would say. 'You work in a morgue and met this guy at a funeral? *Mom!*'

'I *am* in there,' Bruce Lambert said, materializing next to her. He poured himself a plastic glass of very cheap wine. 'Somewhere. I wasn't exactly Mr Popularity.'

After the initial shock, Theresa found her voice. 'Me either. I mean—' From some place nearby she heard a long, warning rumble. Then the floor began to quake.

ELEVEN

THERE WAS NO FORCE, no propulsion pushing her away. Just a deep-seated *sound*, at once too loud to have a rational explanation and too muffled to be identifiable. The room shook, glass shattered somewhere, and Bruce Lambert pushed her to the floor, partially under the table that held the wine and baby carrots. Suddenly her cheek pressed into the linoleum and his body partially covered hers while a wave of vibration passed through them, almost imperceptibly separate from the noise that followed.

Then it receded, and Bruce Lambert got to his feet, pulling her along. The air filled with dust that rolled toward them like a living thing. 'Are you all right?' She could only nod, stupidly. There must have been some sort of accident. One of Bruce Lambert's many experiments hadn't turned out so well.

Then a man somewhere to her left said, 'Was that an explosion?'

'They really are trying to blow this place up!' Thirty-odd college graduates scrambled for the doorway, Ginny Wilson leading the way.

Out in the hallway, a door three to the west leaked smoke and showed the erratic lighting of flames within. She followed Bruce Lambert toward that ominous glow.

Then she smelled it.

The wispy smoke carried odors of melted plastic and charred upholstery, but also a faint aroma of disinfectant. The same acrid smell from the Bingham building, and the crystal that she'd carried in her pocket. Nitrogen triiodide.

She pulled out her phone.

'You almost got blown up for the second time this week?' Frank demanded.

'It sounds bad when you say it like that.' She had been all right until now, calling the lab, retrieving her camera to take photos of the charred storage closet outside the fishbowl workroom, helping the EMT move a badly burned technician and forbidding him to move the engineer he pronounced dead, trapped beneath one of the overturned robots—they were much larger up close— all the while trying not to ponder why the area she had been in only ten minutes beforehand had turned into a smoking hole.

But now the tremor in her cousin's voice made her realize that neither one of them had even begun to deal with the close call they'd had at the Bingham building. She had grown accustomed to the physical threats of the job, and mostly of Frank's job, by not thinking about it— after all, there was little she could do to control it. But clearly that would not be sufficient, not for this round.

She tried not to cough. The air still stunk of iodine. 'I'm all right. Not even a scratch.'

Her cousin said, 'It's you. Someone's trying to kill you.'

'No, someone's trying to kill America's first truly popular electric car.' She glanced over at Cleveland's resident genius. Lambert stood over the dead engineer. Neck bent, he had one hand on his belt and the other covered his face, a still life of regret and grief. His brother Carl, a taller and handsomer version of Lambert, had draped one arm around his shoulders. The rest of the staff crowded in and out, gaping, exclaiming, some crying. All other movement had ceased. The huge robotic arms hung limp as if they, too, wept.

'You think so?' Frank asked.

Theresa explained what she had learned on the tour, the few things she had picked up when not distracted by David Madison. 'This is where they design robots that assemble parts and suchlike. Bruce says the explosion obviously came from a supply closet off this main workroom.'

'So now you're on a first name basis with the richest man in the country?'

'No, I heard him say that to the firemen. What I mean is, who knows how long the bomb could have been in there?'

'And it just happens to go off when you are up the hall.'

'Exactly—up the hall, not in the room.' Outside, the sun emerged from behind one of Cleveland's many clouds and surged through the skylights above them. Its beam picked up the swirling motes she'd been breathing in and turned the car parts, smoke and people into a masterpiece of surrealism. She did not mention David Madison's early exit. The man had been with her every minute and could not have snuck a bomb into the supply closet during the tour. From what she knew of nitrogen triiodide it would take a chunk the size of a concrete block to cause this much damage, and he could hardly have been carting that around in the pocket of his suit coat.

Of course, he could have planted it *before* the tour. But still, size of a concrete block, strolling around a strange facility...

'The security here seems adequate. Locked doors,

security guards. We all had to sign in, get a pass, had a monitor with us during the tour, not to mention the said richest man. I've seen cameras. Plus every member of the staff seems to be best buds with every other member. Shipping a box here would be much easier than trying to get in yourself.'

'Unless you already work there,' Frank said.

'But if you could get into this building, why blow up the Bingham next door? That sounds like someone who *doesn't* work here.'

'How long has that tour been scheduled?'

'At least three weeks.'

'What about Lambert? Any damage?'

'Not hurt.' Because he'd been lying on top of me underneath a table, she thought but didn't say. 'One of his engineers wasn't as lucky.' She and Lambert had worked to uncover the man's head and one shoulder. One of the assembly robots had fallen over, crushing him before he could die of smoke inhalation or extreme heat. Blood seeped from his scalp, the puddle now thickened with ash and debris.

'So the bomb was planted by someone with access who screwed up the timing and miscalculated Lambert's movements—'

'Or by someone who mailed it here in a box of supplies and didn't care about access or timing, who targeted the facility and not the people in it. The bomb squad will have to figure that out.'

'I have to go to a death call,' Frank told her. 'Try not to get killed in the meantime.' Snappy comments such as 'No guarantees' or 'I'll take that under advisement' stuck in her throat, and in the end she simply assented and then hung up, still without mentioning David Madison.

She snapped another photo of the dead engineer.

'Do you have to do that?' Bruce Lambert asked. He stood with a smudge on one cheek and a slump to his shoulders. He had lost his glasses at some point, exposing large brown eyes. His brother had disappeared. Two firemen combed the room for residual fires but stopped every foot or so to exclaim over some unusual gadget.

'Yes,' she said. 'I'm afraid I do.'

He squinted at her camera as if a bit perplexed. 'You *were* on the tour, weren't you? We were just underneath a table together, right?'

'I'm a fellow alumnus, yes.' She introduced herself, stating her position with the M.E.'s office.

'Did we have any classes together?' She shook her head.

'I'd have remembered you. *He* would have.' He gestured at the dead man on the floor. 'Aaron never overlooked a pretty girl. He said science didn't reward the unobservant and neither did cupidity.'

'You've known him since college?'

'I've known him since grade school.' The man collapsed into a singed task chair, unable to take his gaze from his dead friend.

'He was brilliant, generous, and sometimes a supercilious pain in the ass. He'd get ideas so fast that the rest of us couldn't keep up, then he'd want us to finish developing them so he could go on to something else.'

'I thought that was you,' Theresa said, having read several articles to that effect.

'It *is* me. It's also Aaron and every other guy here. We thrive on the pace but that doesn't stop us from driving each other crazy with it. My brother kept telling him to get married, that maybe that would channel some of that intensity and give the rest of us a few moments' peace. For the first time I'm glad he didn't.'

'The man who was hurt—did you know him personally, too?' Lambert finally looked at her instead of the dead man. 'Leroy, yes. Met him at MIT. He's one of those guys that got rich counting cards in Vegas. I convinced him to use his powers for good.' This brought the touch of a smile to his face, which Theresa returned.

'He loved to catch wild animals. They'd just migrate to him, squirrels, crows, raccoons, like he was some sort of St Francis. Then he'd leave them in my room. The skunk was the worst. I had a wild rabbit as a room-mate for half a semester. I couldn't get it out from under my bed so finally I just left it food and water and it would come out at night to drop little bunny bombs all over the carpet. Him, I'm glad he got married. His wife put a stop to that sort of thing.' Theresa leaned over, scooped up a twisted piece of clear material.

'What were they working on in here? The lights?'

'Headlights and taillights, yeah, and all the other molded plastic to be used in the design. The radio cover plate, the inside door handles. Gearshift. Battery cover, power steering tank. The entire body is a plasticized metal alloy.'

'Do you think whoever planted the bomb is trying to sabotage your car?'

Anger flashed across his face, hardening his features. 'Could be. It could also be half a dozen other things we're working on here, but the car is definitely the biggest project and the most far-reaching. It will change the face of the American landscape. It will also shift its power structure. This country has always been run by the most profitable corporations, insurance, banking and oil, and this will take one-third of that block out of the equation. It will also make me a tanker full of thousand-dollar bills, which I had hoped to use to ransom some groups of people from poverty, both here and internationally.' This did not sound like a speech, using the moment to stump an agenda. He spoke absently, as if sorting through possibilities in his mind.

She worried the chunk of plastic between her fingers. 'What about you personally? Any threats—enemies?'

His look changed to one of pity at her naivety. 'I have a lot of money. A *lot*. Everyone hating me comes with the private jet and the villa in Barbados.' Three people appeared at the far end of the room, moving cautiously over the rubble. The two FBI agents from the Bingham followed Lambert's brother. Johnny-on-the-spot, as always.

'I'm sorry,' Theresa told Bruce, 'for your loss, and because the FBI will now ask you all the same questions that I just had the audacity to ask you, and many more besides. But they'll find out who did this. We'll find out who did this.'

He climbed out of the task chair, stretching to an unexpectedly tall height, and regarded her. 'But I love women with audacity.' She had just begun to smile when Carl Lambert reached them and began speaking. 'These two are from the FBI. I don't know what they're doing here, and I don't think you need to talk to them.'

'Aaron's dead,' Bruce reminded his brother.

'That doesn't make it a federal case.'

'What are *you* doing here?' the male agent asked Theresa. 'How did you get here so fast?'

'I was taking a tour.'

'She's OK,' Carl Lambert insisted. His face was structured like his brother's—elongated with a shock of brown hair on top—but his eyes were a cool blue.

'*You* have no jurisdiction here. It's an industrial accident on private property.'

'It's not an accident,' Bruce gently pointed out to his sibling, nodding at the damage the bomb had wrought for emphasis.

The female agent put in, without rancor: 'We have the investigation at the Bingham building. This is obviously related, so this becomes our investigation as well.'

'It's not obvious to me!'

'It's the same explosive.' Theresa also did not want to enter this argument, but saw no choice. 'And it's a relatively unusual one.'

'How could you know that?' Carl demanded.

'By its smell.' He gaped at her, snorted, threw his hands up, turned in a short circle and then said to his brother: 'All right. I just don't like anyone federal poking their noses in our business, you know.'

'I know,' his brother assured him. This seemed to be a conversation they'd had many times already.

Carl thought another moment, then added, 'It always winds up with them raising our liability cap.'

'I know. But they have a job to do.'

Carl added to the agents: 'And you don't remove anything from this facility without my written approval!'

The female agent said, 'We're not here to pirate your secret designs, Mr Lambert.'

'All the same. I play golf with your boss, you know.'

'We're aware of that, yes,' the woman said, in a voice soft enough to lull a baby to sleep. Her partner rolled his eyes, but only after Lambert the elder had turned away.

Just then Theresa's phone rang, and she moved to the relatively unscathed hallway to answer it.

It was Frank. 'I need you,' he said.

TWELVE

THERESA FOUND THE house with the sagging apple tree in the yard within fifteen minutes, responding to the concern in her cousin's voice. She located Frank upon entering the house; he stood gazing at a TV set with a decently sized screen and a fraction of the dust found on the rest of the furniture. Nothing appeared on the TV and she saw no dead bodies. 'It helps if you turn it on.' His eyes but not his mind turned toward her. A small, well-groomed dog also looked up from its perch on the threadbare sofa.

'Frank? What's going on?' He didn't usually get so lost in thought—that had always been her bailiwick, and his the job of teasing her out of it.

'You all right?' he asked.

'Fine. I told you, I heard the rumble, that was it. Didn't even get knocked down.' Not by the explosion, anyway.

'This is Marty Davis' TV set,' he told her.

She waited, but that seemed to be the sum total of his explanation. 'How do you know that?'

'Because our victim is Marty Davis' beneficiary,' he said, with some irritation, as if she had not been paying attention. He wore the scowl that made weaker beings confess on the spot and his hair stood up as if he'd run a hand or two through it. 'He left her all his worldly possessions, of which this TV represents the crown jewel.'

'Where is the victim?'

'Upstairs, in the bathtub.'

'Drowned?'

'Only in her own blood. She slit her wrists. And then let her son find her when he finally decided to mosey home from school—this had to be the day he actually *went* to school, which I gather is not a regular occurrence. Great plan, huh? Let your kid find you?'

'Frank,' Theresa asked carefully, 'how long have you known this woman?'

That he did not seem to find this question strange only proved his agitation. 'Since yesterday.'

Angela Sanchez came in the front door at that moment. 'You all right?'

Theresa said, 'Fine.'

'And our resident genius?'

'Shook up. One of his staff dead, one critical. He seemed pretty upset.'

'You spoke to him?' the cop asked, staring, and Theresa realized that even the normally unflappable Angela was a bit star-struck.

'Isn't he, like, the richest man in the world?'

'Not *the* richest, I don't think. But in the top five.' Again, the slightly unfocused stare, but then Angela shook it off and spoke to her partner. 'The landlord let her take the stuff. Lily had a copy of the will proving that she was the beneficiary.'

'So he just let her waltz off with whatever she wanted?'

'He had no intention of waiting for the probate process to clean out the apartment. Says he needs to rent it, and likewise had no intention of storing all Marty's stuff for the duration. He wanted to get rid of it and she wanted to take it.'

'Terrific.' Frank did not seem able to tear his gaze from the TV set.

'Marty Davis had lived there for almost ten years, and the landlord knew Marty didn't have any close friends or relatives likely to protest.' Angela looked around. 'Where's the kid?' Theresa turned up her hands to confess ignorance.

Frank said, 'A Victim Advocate took him to a neighbor's. What about a car? If she got excited over a TV set, she must have wet herself to inherit Marty's car.'

Angela shook her head. 'A lease. The landlord called the company to come and get that before Marty's body had cooled.'

'Efficient guy.'

'He needed the parking space. He says Lily was distinctly unhappy when he told her that, but the mood didn't last long.'

'Not this afternoon, it wouldn't have. She was flying when we saw her.'

'So how did she go from high to slitting her wrists in one afternoon?' Angela asked.

They fell silent. Theresa tried to sort out this information into a timeline, and fill in the missing parts. 'So this victim—Lily?—went to Marty's apartment to collect her inheritance?'

'Three times,' Angela clarified. 'He says she broke in yesterday; it must have been immediately after we talked to her. I guess she had to check out her windfall. He came back from dinner to find the M.E.'s seal on the door broken, says he didn't think much of it and figured one of the other tenants helped themselves to stuff that Marty wouldn't need any more. He didn't report it. He figured they only waited that long out of respect for Marty, whom everyone seemed to like despite his occupation. His tenants, he tells me, are not of the highest quality.'

'So that was Lily?' Frank asked.

'He doesn't know. But she showed up bright and early the next morning, demanding to collect her inheritance. He wouldn't let her take anything, but he did let her go in and check it out while he dealt with a leaky pipe. Next thing he knows, she's running off with what looked like a red cardboard box that had been on the dining room table and something shiny, a watch, or jewelry or something.'

'And didn't report that either, did he?'

'Too busy with the leaky pipe. I'm guessing Lily then came downtown to get a copy of the will from the legal department—don't ask me how, she probably stole that too—'

'They might have given it to her.' He didn't exactly growl, but it came close.

'True,' Angela said, more cautiously. 'It's only one page long and hers is the only name in it—aside from his mother, who's dead. After she left our car she somehow got back to the apartment and showed him the will. That was enough for the landlord, who by then wanted to be rid of both Marty's stuff *and* Lily both.'

'How did she get that TV back here?'

'No idea. The landlord didn't see anyone else with her or know what kind of vehicle, if any, she had.'

'So Lily either got a ride or carried a fifty-two-inch, what, three miles?' Angela said, 'The TV's bigger than she is. Though she seemed to have a lot of extra energy. The landlord described her as "super-hyper" on the second visit.'

Frank nodded, finally turning from the TV set. 'So she helped herself to Marty's watch, probably pawned it, then used the money to stop and smoke some meth before bouncing down to the Justice Center and running into us. Then she used the rest of the money to get a ride and cart Marty's TV set home.'

'And some other stuff,' Angela said. 'There's a box on the kitchen table with some more jewelry, an iPod, a ton of CDs and a Nintendo model from four years ago with games to match.'

'No way she walked, then,' Frank said.

Angela said, 'She worked for a courier. She could have called a co-worker, someone in the area who could pick her up and drop her off in between deliveries. A job perk the boss doesn't need to know about.'

'Send a guy to her job.'

'Already did.'

'This all happened earlier today?' Theresa asked, still playing catch-up.

'Yeah. So how does she go from bouncing off the walls with excitement over her new TV set to slitting her wrists? That—' he faced Theresa with eyes full of anger— 'is what's bothering me.' She could see that. 'Show me the body.' Frank turned without speaking. She followed him through a kitchen cluttered with dirty dishes, unopened mail and loose food. Boxes of cereal stood open; one had fallen over and trailed Fruit Loops across the cracked laminate counter. Three cockroaches feasted there, too gorged to move as she walked by. A single navel orange, the only apparent concession to good health in the room, sat forlorn and forgotten behind the empty dish drainer. Theresa felt immense gratitude for her more hygienic upbringing.

Mail had been stacked on the table until the weight of it had pulled the top envelopes over. A number of them had warnings in red, dire predictions about the consequences of late payments, and seemed to have been soaked with water at some point. The cardboard box with the dead cop's belongings sat as Angela had described. Next to it sat a small, empty box with bright red designs which had once held a cell phone.

The dog had been no neater with his food dish, or perhaps someone had accidentally kicked the bowl as they went by, because kibbles crunched under her feet. Not a single drawer or cabinet door was completely closed, but one stuck at least halfway out. This seemed to be the standard kitchen 'junk drawer', full of twist ties, assorted tools, take-out menus and a can opener.

She snapped a few pictures as they walked. A filthy home didn't just represent a not terribly attractive lifestyle. It caused a serious problem in the investigation of the crime. At any scene investigators searched for items that didn't belong, that stood out, that seemed to have been recently deposited. How could she find a stranger's hairs or fibers on carpeting that hadn't been swept in a decade, or determine if an intruder had knocked over a pile of items when everything in the house normally lived on the floor? Did the ex-boyfriend rip all the clothing out of the woman's closet or did she simply find hangers too much trouble? There was a reason why investigators on TV always went to wealthy homes. How hard could it be to find a wayward casing in the rug when the maid had just vacuumed that morning?

The steps to the second floor creaked and Theresa stepped carefully to avoid tripping on the many loose strings—the floral tapestry runner reminded her of her grandmother's house, as did the dark wood of the steps. Generations of footsteps had worn a groove into each one.

The upstairs held three tiny bedrooms and one bath,

the conditions of all four on a par with the kitchen. The bathroom came first, at the top of the stairs. From the landing Theresa could see the too-white hand extend out over the edge of the porcelain tub and the puddle of blood on the floor. But she did a quick walk-through in the bedrooms first; once in the bathroom she would remain there for quite some time, so she might as well get a rounder picture of the victim before that. One bedroom must belong to the kid Frank had mentioned. It contained the electronic accouterments of a teenage boy's life and smelled like team spirit.

'What's his name?' she asked Frank, who leaned in the doorway. Over his shoulder, Angela watched Theresa.

'Brandon.' Some memory made him chuckle, a dry, mirthless rattle. This case bothered him, but she didn't want to ask him about it with his partner standing there. No matter how close he and Angela might be, Theresa doubted they were to the point where Frank would be comfortable discussing a weakness. And letting your cases get to you was, in his view, a definite weakness.

A mattress on the floor and a stained comforter, shoved to one side, made up the bedding. A battered dresser with clothes overflowing from its drawers would have looked ransacked, but a healthy coating of dust on the edges made it clear that the compartments had been in that position for some time. Two notebooks sat neatly aligned at the foot of the mattress. Had young Brandon walked past the bathroom with his mother's body to come into his room and drop off his school work?

'Was the bathroom door closed when he came home?'

'I'm not sure,' Frank said.

Angela said, 'From the way he described it, the door was not completely closed, but he said something about knocking on it before going in.' Partially closed, so he probably had gone to his bedroom first. A boy would hardly want to walk in on his mother in the bathroom. But if he found the house unlocked he would assume she was home and eventually get curious about her location. Or simply need to use the toilet. 'What about the house? Locked?'

'Open.' The next bedroom belonged to a female, one who wore tiny, shimmery tops and thong underwear. She also hadn't been there in a long time; every item and surface had a half inch of dust on it. Frank explained about the daughter in jail.

Lily Simpson's bedroom appeared similar to her son's but with a slightly more feminine aspect. She seemed to be the same clothing size as her daughter but not as interested in dressing to appeal, owning mostly T-shirts and thin sweatpants, jeans and athletic shoes (called, in Cleveland, 'tennis shoes', despite the fact that few of its citizens had played the game since the mid-1970s). She had three books in the room, a dictionary, a paperback romance and the Bible, and one magazine (*Cosmo*). Two scratched CDs, Milli Vanilli and Tom Petty. Lily at least had a bed, with a wooden frame of indeterminate age and a set of unmade, threadbare sheets under a velour blanket with an assortment of dried stains. Theresa took a picture, and then gingerly pulled the top sheet back. None of the stains there seemed fresh.

A lamp stood on the nightstand between the bed and a badly painted wall. Next to it sat a box of tissues, a wadded-up bundle of bills, and three quarters. Theresa counted the money by its edges, without substantially moving the stack. Twelve dollars.

Also on the nightstand sat a wooden tray with an assortment of drug paraphernalia. Two butts left from marijuana cigarettes, a roach clip to hold same, a crack pipe made of pretty blue glass with cooked-on black residue in its bowl, a few of the inch-square baggies used to hold cocaine or heroin. No syringes, though, so the baggies must have held crack, or at least some drug that did not need to be injected.

'I guess she never really got away from it,' Angela said.

'Drugs?' Theresa asked.

'She made it sound like a thing of the past. Maybe that's why she felt a need to smear Marty Davis' name a little. He got off the stuff. She didn't.' Frank moved away from the door.

THIRTEEN

THERESA FOUND HIM in the bathroom, a space barely large enough to hold the tub, a toilet and a single sink. The cabinet beneath it had only one door but held a healthy supply of toilet paper. Old-fashioned, undersized squares of white tile covered the floor, making the pool of blood seem even brighter by contrast. Plasma had begun to separate from the red blood cells, creating an outer halo of clear yellow liquid. Her clothes sat in a pile on the floor next to the toilet.

Lily Simpson lay in the tub, naked and white. Her knees were bent, her feet flat against the outer wall with her shoulders wedged into the far corner on one side of the faucet. Her head rested against the tiled wall so that she could stare at the cracked plaster ceiling with open eyes. Her dirty blond hair was dry and she wore no make-up. Many suicides put water in the tub, thinking that will somehow help them to bleed faster or simply make them more comfortable, but Lily had not bothered with that.

The box cutter she had used on her wrists lay in the bottom of the tub under her right shin. Her left arm stretched over the floor to create that dramatic pool but Theresa suspected that most of the draining had been accomplished through her right wrist, which lay on the bottom of the tub with a direct line of red between it and the drain. Her life had escaped neatly and efficiently.

Theresa began to photograph. When done with that,

she sketched. Occasionally she asked a question. The landlord said she left Marty's place about four o'clock. No one yet knew how she had traveled from there to home.

Frank said, 'Most of the neighbors didn't pay any attention to her and didn't know her friends. One woman across the street would hang out here occasionally; she knew some people who came by but only by their first names, of course. Never noticed their cars. Never knew Lily to mention suicide, either, but said she kept up with the drugs. Low-key, but constant.' Theresa checked the medicine cabinet—aspirin, and a well-used safety razor. An empty pill bottle for a three-year-old oxycodone prescription. 'She didn't keep them in here where the kids could get them.'

Frank snorted. 'Sure. She hid them in an open box next to her bed. That would really keep Junior from helping himself.'

Theresa checked the drawers. 'No razors.'

'That's why she used the box cutter.'

'Who has straight razors in the bathroom these days anyway? No one uses them to shave anymore,' she chatted, just to keep the conversation going, to stave off that awful silence emanating from the dead victim and maybe get her cousin to open up about why the suicide of a drug addict had rattled him, now that his partner had gone back downstairs. 'Scraping wallpaper, that's about the only time I've used a razor blade in the past twenty years. They're more likely to be found in the garage or the tool box.'

'Mmm.'

'She probably pulled it—the box cutter—out of that open drawer downstairs, walked up here, took off her clothes and cut her wrists. Didn't even take the time to

write her kids a note.' Frank leaned casually against
the door jamb, with nothing casual in the way he stared
at the frozen hand stretched out over the tile, the palm
turned up in supplication or abandonment or in one last
contented sigh. 'But why? She's bouncing around all
morning, harassing everyone she can find to get what
she wants, and then offs herself? Why? She thought
Marty would have a million dollars stashed in his mattress? She found out what cable costs? Why?'

'Suicide isn't always logical.'

'It's never logical.'

'Some people consider it a viable alternative.' They
had had this argument many times, so she skipped right
to her concluding remarks: 'If you don't understand it,
you won't understand it, so don't try. In this case, if she
had taken a healthy amount of meth earlier today, she
might have crashed. Methamphetamine dumps a ton
of the body's neurotransmitters into the nervous system at once. It's like getting socked with a boatload of
adrenalin.'

'You don't have to lecture me in basic drug chemistry. I did my stint in Vice.'

She persisted. 'The person becomes nervous and hyperactive. The problem is, this depletes the body of its
supply of neurotransmitters, so once the high starts to
fade the person doesn't go back to normal. They go way
below normal, to a sluggish depression. The same chemistry that caused the surge of energy causes a surge of
fatigue.'

'But not that fast.'

'No.' Theresa frowned. 'She should still have been in
the high stage, at least until tonight, maybe for another
two or three days. It all depends on how much she took
and its purity.'

'Plus she's been taking meth all her life, and suddenly she gets suicidal? There's no history of suicide attempts.'

'That we know of,' she clarified. 'Maybe she never took that much before, so this crash was worse than anything in her experience.'

'She wasn't *that* high. Just enough to be noticeable. You think I would have let her keep walking around if she'd been completely insensible?'

'Of course not. But meth—that's why it's so insidious. It's different from other drugs. Like cocaine, it lurks between the brain's neurons, blocking the re-uptake of dopamines. But only meth actually goes inside the cells to push the dopamines out. These neurotransmitters eventually wear out, making it impossible for a chronic user ever to feel truly good again. Nothing would stimulate Lily like it once did, not a good meal, the love of her family, sex, nothing gets the blood flowing except meth, and that only in larger and larger quantities. So maybe she didn't take too much, she just didn't take enough, and finally realized that even *with* meth life really didn't hold anything worth struggling for.' Frank stared at the floor.

'Look—I don't know if that's why she did it. But I can tell you this: I don't see any signs of foul play here. There's no sign of a struggle, nothing knocked over. The clothes are in a single pile. There's no bruises on her arms—' here she reached one gloved hand to the back of the woman's skull—'no signs of trauma, no one hit her over the head, no petechiae in the eyes or lips to indicate smothering. There's no sign of forced entry downstairs, right?'

'The kid said he found the back door unlocked. That's why he assumed Lily was home. She could have let someone in.'

'Unlikely, since amphetamines make the user paranoid as well as hyper.'

'So if she let someone in, it would be someone she
knew,' Frank said, following the thought.

'Or she simply forgot to lock it when she came home.
There's also no sign of overdose, no foaming in the
mouth or nose.'

'What if she started to OD, at least became uncon-
scious? Then someone could have put her here and sliced
her wrists without creating bruises or signs of a struggle.' Theresa checked the dead, open eyes and then the
pile of clothing. 'Actually an overdose would explain
taking off her clothing, since it raises the body temperature until the person sweats profusely. But there's no
dampness on her clothes to indicate it, and her pupils are
not dilated. That implies that the stimulation had worn
off, setting her up for the depression stage. Everything
here, cuz, is consistent with this woman coming home,
walking up those steps and killing herself.' Frank said
nothing, but he had that stubborn frown he'd employed
since his grade school days.

'What's bothering you about this victim, in particular?'

'I told you. She comes into a sudden windfall, excited
as hell, and an hour or two later, she's dead.'

'Again, that could be the result of the crash. When
the amphetamines pass, the dopamine neuron activity
is suppressed for a while, so she might have been physically unable to feel any pleasure over her good fortune.
It ceased to be a factor in her thinking.'

'Maybe.'

'What else is bothering you?'

'No note.'

'Most suicides don't leave notes. And who knows if

suicide was even her goal. Meth users—especially long-time users—can experience a host of visual and auditory hallucinations. Meth users all over the country report hearing and seeing black helicopters over their homes. Another saw the heads of his former customers sitting in a tree outside his house, monitoring his movements to report back to the police. Another very carefully combined every chemical in his lab together and then set it on fire to destroy evidence. He caught on fire himself, but didn't think that was a problem until he woke up in intensive care without most of his fingers. In other words, there's no way to guess what she was thinking. It's quite possible she thought her blood had turned to poison and she needed to remove it to save herself.'

He sighed, rubbed his neck. 'I know. But a cop and his beneficiary both wind up dead in the same week? That's adding up to way too many coincidences for me.'

She gave up on subtlety. It never worked on men anyway. 'I know you hate coincidences. But you seem to be personally upset over the death of a woman you only met yesterday.' It occurred to her that she had only met David Madison the day before yesterday, and already felt quite personal about him. She couldn't define it any more clearly than that, just…personal.

'Maybe because I called her a dealer's crack whore mule last time I saw her?' Frank suggested.

'Oh.' Theresa looked at the dead woman, then back to her cousin. 'Well. You've said harsh things to people before. Sometimes it's the only way to get them to talk.'

'Yeah. Sure.'

'Between her kids, her drug habit and the logistics of trying to get a big-screen back to her house, I'm sure she had more on her mind than a passing insult from a cop.'

'Yeah.' He shook it off, literally and apparently figuratively. 'So it's clearly a self-inflicted, as far as you can see.'

'Yes.'

'Me, too,' he said. 'I doubt her children did her in to get their hands on Marty's vast estate.'

Theresa added, 'Maybe it's not coincidence, the deaths coming so close together. Maybe thinking about Marty and their college days only made her feel worse, magnified the gap between her teenage dreams and the reality of her life. Crashing from the meth gave her the last little push she needed to fall over the edge.'

'Maybe.' There was a pause.

'But just to be sure—' Theresa began.

'But I have to look under every rock. A cop is dead, and I don't want to have to explain to other cops how I missed the solution by blowing off a possible connection. Sorry, what were you saying?'

'I think I'll fingerprint the edge of the tub before I start manipulating the body. Just in case.'

Frank gave the first hint of a smile she'd seen in days. 'Thanks, cuz.'

'That's my job.' Theresa disliked fingerprinting, a messy and tedious task. The fine black powder got everywhere and she could never train herself to keep her face well away from the surface as she applied it, so that the tiny particles would settle on her skin until some itch or jostle smeared them into a black streak. No one would ever tell her so, and she'd discover the marks only by accident the next time she entered a ladies' room. She'd also be sneezing black powder for the next few days. Didn't coal miners get black lung from carbon dust?

But of all surfaces to fingerprint, white porcelain is the best. Smooth and glossy and intrinsically cool, it holds prints beautifully and its whiteness only makes the blackened ridges easier to see. The edge of the tub gave up several palms and fingertips, most with a distinctive whorl in the hypothenar area at the outer edge of the palm. Theresa glanced at Lily's upturned palm. It had the same whorl.

Frank had disappeared and she heard him rustling in the bedroom.

Encouraged by this success, Theresa quickly covered the tiled wall of the tub with powder, working quickly but trying not to let too much fall on to the body. She found mostly water spots but retrieved a few prints, of lesser quality than the ones on the edge. Lily must have cleaned the tub once in a while, but not the backsplash.

Theresa pulled off the blackened gloves and got a fresh pair, and wrestled the body to its side just enough to view the back. Lividity had turned the skin a dusky rose color where the blood pooled, the pressure points—such as the bottom of the buttocks, on which the weight of the body had been resting—a stark white. This, too, appeared consistent with Lily dying in exactly the position in which she'd been found.

Theresa placed a brown paper lunch bag over each of the victim's hands and secured them with tape. She would scrape the fingernails at the lab, not something she'd normally do in such a clear-cut suicide case, but having already gone the extra mile with the fingerprint powder she might as well go another one. The box cutter went gently into a small cardboard box. Theresa would probably fingerprint that too, though the surface had too much grime and too many ridges and convolutions to hold anything good. A thin line of blood traced along the cutting edge of the blade, which didn't look too sharp. Lily Simpson must really have wanted to die.

After that, Theresa could see nothing else to do. She

went back into the bedroom and collected the box with
the drug use odds and ends, in case the tox screen came
back with a bizarre result and the pathologist wanted
to compare the residues found in the house. She tilted
it toward the light before dropping it into a paper bag.
The box and its contents all had a layer of dust on them
at least an eighth of an inch thick. But Lily had apparently taken a large dose only that morning.

She found Frank downstairs, going through the mail
on the table. 'You thought she bought her meth with
whatever she stole from Marty's apartment this morning, probably this cell phone? Took, I mean, since the
items legally belonged to her anyway?'

He chuckled. 'That's OK, you can say she stole it.'
Theresa checked the garbage can, which sat next to the
back door and had been filled to the top with beer cans,
paper towels and chicken bones. No drug paraphernalia.
Theresa went back upstairs, kicking herself for forgetting such an obvious move, and checked the pockets of
the jeans Lily had been wearing. She did so gingerly,
in case Lily had moved from smoking her drugs to taking injectables. But nothing pricked Theresa's fingers,
and she did find a baggie and a tiny glass pipe in the
back pocket. It didn't have the pretty blue filigree running through the center, but it also didn't have quite so
much blackened residue, either. Theresa dropped it into
a Manila envelope.

She checked the hooded sweatshirt and found twenty-
six dollars and seventy-five cents in the right pocket.
The left pocket held a pawn slip, an item that had so
much more cachet in the pages of old detective novels,
when it was only a small ticket with a number on it and
no other information. Running down a pawn ticket had
been like a treasure hunt, with no idea what item you

might uncover. Today's pawn slips were a detailed form on a full-sized piece of paper, containing everything you could want to know from a complete description of the item to the name and address of both the pawn shop and the person selling the item, as well as their thumbprint. Since stolen property often wound up in pawn shops, having the burglar leave their print behind had become an extremely helpful addendum to the legal process.

Lily had pawned a gold Armitron watch, a silver chain necklace and a silver chain bracelet that morning at 11:53 a.m., at a branch of Goldie's Pawn on East Seventy-Fifth. No cell phone. The shop had given her thirty dollars for all three items.

Theresa could feel her brows coming together. She didn't know what a rock of crystal meth cost, but she bet it was more than $3.25.

After photographing the items, she put the slip and the money into separate envelopes and took them downstairs. Frank had moved on to the open drawer and now paged through a worn address book. Theresa told him what she had found. 'I need someone to witness the money for me, and I don't want it to be you.'

He didn't look up from the address book. 'You don't trust me?'

'You're my cousin. I don't want internal affairs saying that because of our personal relationship we conspired to rob Lily Simpson's children of her twenty-six dollars and seventy-five cents. Dot every i.'

'And cross every t,' he muttered. 'So if Lily didn't buy drugs this morning with the money from the pawn shop, how did she buy them?'

'Maybe she already had money. She has a job.'

'Then why go directly to the pawn shop?'

'Maybe she thought she'd need more. She was still working out how to get that big-screen home.'

Angela walked in from the living room, snapping her phone shut. 'I've got that, believe it or not. I sent patrol to Lily's workplace and one of her friends 'fessed up right away, a woman named Monique. Lily called her at lunchtime. Monique had three deliveries in this area and in between the second two she picked up Lily and her TV set at Marty's apartment building. She even helped Lily wrestle the TV from her trunk to inside the house and on to the stand. She insists the whole trip didn't take her longer than ten or fifteen minutes or more than a few miles out of her way, so the boss didn't get too upset about it—at least not in front of our officer.'

'So we've solved that mystery,' Theresa said.

'Lily didn't work today?' Frank asked.

'Wasn't scheduled to,' Angela said. 'And the son, Brandon, is asking when he can come home.'

'What home?' Frank tossed the address book on the table. 'There's a whole fifteen people listed here; only seven have addresses, and none of them are named Simpson. Unless some kindly grandma comes out of the woodwork, it looks like foster care. His mother's dead and his sister's in jail. That kid's chances in life were slim to begin with and just plummeted to none.' Theresa and Angela said nothing, unable to offer any hopeful words. They'd both seen it too many times. Children learned what they were taught, and those that grew up surrounded by crime and drug activity spent their lives in crime and drug activity, scraping by from day to day, watching beautiful lifestyles on television without the slightest idea of how to get one, or maybe they'd even been denied a chance to do that. Theresa's sister, a school nurse, had a term for these kids. *Doomed*.

Someone rapped at the back door, startling them all.

FOURTEEN

HIS VOICE CALLED OUT, 'Lily!' a split second before he pulled the frame open and walked in.

They definitely startled him more than he startled them, and Theresa could swear the only reason he didn't bolt like a rabbit was because his short, undernourished body couldn't outrun an arthritic Chihuahua. That, and he needed an answer to his now-obvious question: 'Where's Lily?' The other three people in the kitchen stared. The man wore stained denim pants held up with a leather belt and a T-shirt advertising a band Theresa had never heard of. A scruffy growth of light brown beard disguised some of his old acne scars. His hands fluttered without cease, on his hips, shoved into pockets, scratching his head. She recognized him instantly. The squirrelly guy from Marty Davis' funeral. The one who had given both cops and reporters a wide berth.

'Where's Lily?' he repeated, putting more insistence into his quavering voice.

Frank asked who he might be and he gave his name as Ken Bilecki, friend of Lily's. He had taken his customary approach through the back yard, so he had missed the cop stationed at the front door. Frank hadn't posted one at the back, not for an apparent suicide.

When told that Lily had died, the man reacted. Violently. He burst into tears, moaned 'No, no, no, no,' and sank to his knees, then rocked himself and sobbed. The dog came up and licked his fingers, but he didn't seem to notice. Theresa noticed her feet backing slowly away, away from someone else's grief. Times like these were why she chose to work with dead bodies and not live ones, why she opted for the lab instead of becoming a cop.

Frank and Angela waited for the storm to subside without much expression. They had, no doubt, noticed the man's eyes, the disproportionate fear of strangers and the scabs on his arms. Chronic methamphetamine users grew paranoid and often scratched at their skin, feeling as if bugs were running underneath the epidermis.

'Sit down,' Frank said when he could be heard over the sobbing, and pulled out a chair. The dog wandered into the next room. The man wiped his face with both grimy hands, and then used both again to crawl into the seat. Only then did he look up.

'Who killed her?' he asked.

Frank told him no one had, she killed herself. This set off a fresh burst of cries and again Theresa thanked her lucky stars that she had never become a cop. She couldn't take exposure to this kind of raw emotion on a regular basis. That the drama had been no doubt intensified by drug use did not make it any less heartfelt.

Again Frank waited, but this time the man spoke first.

'No way.' He shook his head with a fierce power. 'Lily would never have done that. She had her life together. She had a job and kids.'

'She took meth,' Frank stated.

'Well, yeah,' Bilecki agreed without hesitation. 'But just a little.'

'A little.'

'Seriously. She had it under control. Not,' he added

in what might have been a moment of rare insight, 'like me.'

'You take more than a little?'

The man turned his face away, his gaze glancing off everything except Frank. 'Where'd the dog go?'

'Never mind the dog. How do you know Lily?'

'I've known Lily for years.'

'How?'

'What do you mean, how? We're friends. We were friends.' Forcing himself to use the past tense produced another round of sniffles. Theresa plucked a nearly empty box of tissues from the counter and held it out to him. He looked at it as if wondering what it could be, glanced at her as if wondering when she had arrived, and took a tissue. He didn't use it on his nose, however, merely turned it over in his hands.

'From college, right?' Theresa asked.

He gave her a surprised, direct look. 'Yeah. How'd you know that?'

'I saw your picture in the yearbook.' It *was* him in the Rathskeller photo. She tried, physically tried, to keep from asking the next question. 'Do you know David Madison?'

He could not have been capable of faking such a blank look. 'Huh?' Angela looked fairly confused herself. Only Frank narrowed his eyes at Theresa until she felt herself blush.

But he turned back to the man and continued with this line of thought. 'You were friends with Marty too, right?' Bilecki's eyes welled up with water and his lips trembled, and Theresa felt so bad she continued to hold out the box of tissues.

'Yeah, Marty. Lily and Marty both dead now? Tell

me that's just a coincidence.' Theresa stopped blushing. She and Frank exchanged a look.

'Why would you think someone killed Lily?' Frank asked.

'Don't know.'

'You immediately assumed someone killed her. You must have a particular person in mind.'

'No. It's just something I said. It don't mean anything.' Drugs lowered one's inhibitions, but also one's defenses. A five-year-old could have lied better than this man. He stared at the others as they spoke, until a question came along that he didn't want to answer. Then not just his gaze but his entire head turned to the floor.

Problem was, the drugs also made him a bit paranoid while giving him a quite rational reason to avoid any entanglement with the police. All this added up to an unproductive interview.

'Did you sell Lily the meth she took this morning?'

'She scored some? Today?'

'Yes. Did you sell it to her?'

'I didn't know she wanted any. She swore she had finished with it for good after the last time.'

'What happened the last time?'

'She went to jail. No, that was the second-last time. The last time she went to pick up Brandon at school and those bitches called Children's Services on her.'

'They noticed she was high?'

'Yeah,' he told them, indignant. 'And she was only a little bit. But she still swore off it after that.'

'So what are you doing here?'

'Huh?'

'If you and Lily didn't have a drug habit in common any more, why are you hanging around?'

'I told you. We're friends.'

'Just friends.'

'I got friends,' he insisted, as if Frank had implied he didn't.

'Since college. You and Lily and Marty.'

'Yeah.' The tears threatened again but he pulled them back, apparently determined to present his memories with a touch of dignity. 'We went to Cleveland State and flopped in this pit on Payne. It was all we could afford.'

'Did you graduate?'

'Hah! No, I flunked out the third quarter. Lily and Marty made it a little longer. I quit after—'

'After what?'

'After I flunked.'

'And you stayed in touch all these years.'

'Yeah. I got friends,' he repeated, defensive again, and then abruptly chuckled with a low, rattling laugh. 'Not that Marty wouldn't arrest me if he found stuff on me. Marty took that cop shit seriously. But he would loan me a few bucks, too, if I was clean.'

'And Lily?'

'She didn't have a lot of bucks, but she'd make me something to eat once in a while.'

'Where do you live, Mr Bilecki?'

'Um. Around.' Homeless, and mooching off the same friends for twenty-five years. Not much of a life. Theresa wondered what he had studied in college. Frank asked when Bilecki had last seen Lily—two weeks prior— and Marty—two months prior—and if he knew who might have a grudge against Marty or any other reason to kill him. Bilecki said no, and that he figured it had to be some scumbag that Marty had put away, while obviously not including himself near that category.

Then Frank came full circle back to the beginning. 'Why did you think someone had murdered Lily?'

'Nothing. I wasn't thinking. I can't think like this, in times like this.' He repeated this theme for a few more sentences before running down into silence, wrapping both arms around himself and rocking slightly, his gaze darting to every item in the room except the faces of the other three people present.

The other three people waited. Obviously Mr Bilecki had something he wanted to say, and simply had to make up his mind whether to say it.

Unfortunately, the small dog chose that moment to re-enter the kitchen, and Bilecki made the most of the distraction. He scooped the squirming animal into his lap, petting and cooing in a nauseating, baby-like patter.

Frank gave up the waiting game. 'Mr Bilecki. Why did you think Lily had been murdered?'

'Isn't this a great dog? Lily loved this dog.'

'Mr Bilecki.'

'What's going to happen to him? Is he going to have to go to the pound? I'd take him, but obviously I can't afford it. I can't even afford myself. Poor puppy.' Theresa tossed the box of tissues on the counter. It apparently hadn't occurred to him to save some of that sympathy for the woman's son.

Angela stepped in, gently removed the dog from the man's lap, and took it into the living room.

Left with Frank's question, Bilecki dissembled further. 'I didn't mean anything by it, I mean…it's a rough world, you know, and sometimes Lily met bad types…' It took a few more minutes of this before he stopped trying to look innocent and said, 'It just seems weird that Marty and Lily both died in the same week. Doesn't it?'

'It does. Maybe Lily killed Marty, and the remorse made her suicidal,' Frank suggested, though Theresa could tell he didn't mean it.

'No way! She would never have killed Marty. Lily couldn't kill anybody.'

'Then who did? Let's suppose, for a moment, that Lily didn't kill herself and someone murdered her. Why? Who would hold a grudge against both Lily *and* Marty?' Bilecki looked at him then, with a sudden, keen concern, so that Theresa believed that not only did he think such a person existed, he knew exactly who it might be. Frank saw it too.

'Mr Bilecki?'

'I don't know,' he said, exhaling breath so foul that Theresa could catch the scent from five feet away. 'I don't think that's possible. They didn't have much to do with each other anymore, not for years and years. I don't know why Lily would—do this. At least she had this place, somewhere to stay.' He stood up as he spoke, and placed one foot behind the other, slowly, moving toward the back door. 'Lily never did anything wrong. Neither did Marty. We were just kids.'

'No one's saying they did. But someone murdered Marty. They might not have had a very *good* reason, but there must have been something. So if you have any suggestions, we'd love to hear them.'

'No. Nothing. I have to go now. Sorry about Lily— will there be a funeral?'

'I don't know. Can you tell us who were her closest friends, or relatives? Besides her children?'

He paused to think about that, but shook his head. 'I didn't really hang with Lily that much. I didn't meet friends, and I don't think she ever had no family.'

'What about Marty?'

'I didn't hang with Marty. His friends were all cops.' So he'd stop by for a handout, but stayed in the shadows, Theresa thought; again, a lousy way to live.

'I've got to go now.' He made a dash for the door, opened it, and then stopped. 'I can go now, right?'

'Sure,' Frank said.

The door slammed. It had grown dark outside, and Kenneth Bilecki disappeared into the gloom.

'I can't hold him,' Frank said as Theresa raised one eyebrow at him. 'This isn't a homicide, and I doubt—'

'Hey.' Bilecki stuck his head into the kitchen again, hanging on the knob as if he might swing on the door. 'Is there going to be a funeral?'

'You asked that already, remember? I don't know yet.'

'Oh, yeah.'

'Here—take my card. If you remember any details about Marty and Lily that you think we might need to know, you'll call me, right?'

'Yeah. I mean, no, there aren't any. Nothing.' He backed into the night as if it had plucked him from behind and swallowed him whole, leaving the door to shift gently in the open space. Coldness pressed into the kitchen.

'Junkie,' Frank muttered.

'He's kind of—skitterish,' Theresa said, in the understatement of the year.

'They're all like that, meth heads. Why did you ask him about David Madison?' She explained where she had been earlier in the evening, just before where she'd been had exploded.

His eyes narrowed again. 'Uh-huh. And why were you talking to David Madison?' She became suddenly interested in the lump of melted plastic from the Lambert place explosion, which she had just rediscovered in her pocket. 'Why not?'

'Tess.'

'Have you ever been to an alumni board meeting?

They don't exactly rival the latest James Bond movie for entertainment value.'

'*Tess.*'

'What? Geez, I'm not thirteen any more. You have no authority to comment on my choice in, um, whom I'm interested in.' He literally clapped one hand to his forehead, as if she had announced a decision to become a nun or get a nose ring.

'*Interested?* Are you out of your mind? The man's a walking disaster! He drove the last woman in his life into the arms of a thirteen-year-old! How's that for a rec-ommendation?' She would have gotten angry, but her cousin had judged every male she'd ever dated equally harshly so that now she couldn't help but laugh. And at least it got his mind off Lily Simpson.

'That's just mean. You can't blame her pathology on him. My ex-husband's probably tucking a dollar bill into the G-string of some girl our daughter's age as we speak. Is that my fault?' He hesitated so long that she punched his arm for the second time in as many days.

'Ow! No, I'm still trying to word my objections to this Madison guy. You turn down dates from every single guy in my unit because you don't want to deal with drama and baggage, and the next thing I know you're cozying up to someone who's nothing *but* drama and baggage. Why? Because he held an umbrella for you?'

'It's the quiet things that speak the loudest.'

'You get that off a fortune cookie?' Angela re-entered the kitchen in time for the tail end of this conversation.

'You shouldn't torment him, you know,' she told The-resa. 'He'll go back to the station, run his name for war-rants and get his DL history.'

Theresa dared her cousin: 'Go ahead. I'll bet he doesn't even have a parking ticket.'

Frank rubbed one eye. 'Fine, just expect to see your picture on the screen behind the anchors on Channel 15, that's all. And don't come crying to me when you do. What d'ya got, Angela?'

His partner grinned at Theresa before checking the small notepad in her hand. 'Kenneth Bilecki, on a one-man quest to rid the world of methamphetamines, one pipeful at a time. Arrested fifteen times, ten for possession, two for sale of, two for passing false scrip and one for loitering. Convicted only on eight of the possession charges and one of the false scrip. Never married—big surprise there. He has parents but they no longer wish to be contacted by law enforcement in regard to their son.'

Frank said, 'Convictions on nine out of fifteen—I don't know if that means he had a good lawyer or a lousy one. At any rate he's spent his life staying under the radar, and hardly likely to have graduated from minor drug charges to cop killer.' They decided to wrap it up. Theresa replaced the lens cap on her camera and zipped the case, patted the dog on the head and collected the various items of evidence she'd bagged up, all the while wondering why Ken Bilecki had referred to himself and his two friends as 'just kids'. Perhaps that was the last time they were all together. Perhaps their college days seemed like yesterday to the man. Perhaps they were the only ones in his life on which he cared to dwell.

Looking around at Lily Simpson's present, she could see why. Her phone rang, and showed Leo's number.

'I hope you've got a pair of waders,' he said.

'I hate it when you begin conversations that way. It's never a good sign.'

'Homeland Security has excavated down to the first lower level. They've given us the green light to go in.'

'In?'

'It's time to bring our boxes and slides and bloody clothing and other little babies of evidentiary value home. Don will meet you there.'

'It's nine o'clock at night.'

'And the county will pay you overtime, isn't that exciting?'

Not as exciting as a decent night's sleep. 'Where will you be?'

'At the office, setting up the inventory and storage. Did you think I'd be home in bed while my troops labor in misery?' Why not? That had always been his technique in the past. Theresa quite regretted having only carrot sticks for dinner.

'And dress warm,' he added. Leo tended to speak as if he held all the wisdom of the ages, despite having only four or five years on her. 'You know, layers, and all that.'

'Right,' she said. 'Layers.'

FIFTEEN

AT NIGHT, THE remains of the Bingham building resembled footage of London during the Blitz. Ringed by blinding halogen lights, the irregular piles of brick and debris seemed like an alien landscape of bright hills and deep shadows. The warmth of a spring day had disappeared with the sun and Theresa had, indeed, gone home, laid on another coat of antibiotic ointment, and changed into layers. After a lifetime spent in Cleveland she had accumulated enough cold weather wear to travel the Arctic in comfort.

'Are you wearing long johns?' Don asked, noting the cuff of the thermal pants peeking out from the bottom of her jeans.

'You betcha. Aren't you?'

'There's only one way for you to find out.'

'I would never take such liberties. Your virtue is safe with me.'

'That's disappointing.' He pulled on a pair of heavy leather gloves and asked, 'Where do we start?'

'Good question.' Homeland Security staff—or FBI, or Army or whoever they were—had used yellow caution tape to rope off a series of walkways. Most of the rubble had been removed to what had been the parking lot and divided into two sections, one for simple debris and another, much smaller, for stuff they wanted to take a closer look at. She and Don had been told upon arrival that they would not be allowed in either area. Not that they cared much. They had more than enough to do.

HS staff also informed them that Bruce Lambert had graciously opened the lobby of his adjacent factory for workers who needed a bathroom, a rest or some warm air. The lobby had also been stocked with coffee, sandwiches, water and donuts.

'Dunkin's or Krispy Kreme?' Theresa queried the slender Homeland Security agent.

'Presti's.'

'Bless the man.'

Don snorted. 'PR—the richest man in the country being nice to the little guy.'

'Good for him,' Theresa defended. 'Us little guys need a lot of nice.' A temporary metal staircase led to the first sublevel and their huge storage room. Originally, a section of the room had been closed off by a chain-link fence and a padlock, to which only the trace evidence section had the key, and stored boxes of evidence and row after row of victims' clothing. Now the fence had been mangled and most of the clothing racks flattened, though some of the cardboard boxes had survived—they'd been stacked against the wall, which remained in parts. The rest of the storage unit had been filled with file cabinets of old case files, X-rays and histology slides (slides made from sections of tissue for the pathologists to use in making a diagnosis). Along with Theresa and Don, one histologist, one toxicologist, two off-duty deskmen and poor little Dr Banachek had been recruited to work at the site.

All of them plucked their items from the collapsed stones and carted them to the road where the county had rented a U-Haul box truck for this express purpose. This work could not be outsourced. These items were not bricks or books or furniture. They were evidence, and had to remain in the custody of the M.E.'s office at all times. It was mindless manual labor instead of intelligent forensic work, the stuff that 'other duties as assigned' covered in the job description, the tasks that came along more often than TV would suggest, but Theresa had long since become accustomed to them. She only wished she'd thought to bring a radio. Every job went more smoothly with tunes.

She and Don assembled the supply of new cardboard boxes to fill with the clothing from victims past. For approximately forty years the bloody shirts and pants and underwear had been stored on hangers, covered with thin dry-cleaner's bags and hung on wheeled racks, like closeouts from the old May Company's bargain basement. Nowadays all items were sealed in breathable paper bags after thorough drying, better for forensic testing though not necessarily easier to handle, and certainly no more impervious to tons of rubble suddenly falling through the roof. Theresa pulled a piece of crushed fence to the side to reach the first rack. They both wore heavy leather gloves to protect their hands from broken glass and stone.

'Usually these smell kind of musty, with that dried-blood smell,' she commented to Don. 'But now I don't even notice it over the iodine fumes.'

He folded the clothing into a fresh box. 'At least it helped the dogs sniff out any remaining unexploded crystals. Wouldn't want you filling your pockets again.' She shuddered at the thought.

Don changed the subject, sort of. 'Correct me if I'm wrong, but aren't iodine fumes carcinogenic?'

'Yep. That's why we don't often do iodine fuming for fingerprints any more except in a fume hood or a very well-ventilated area. It works great, but it just might kill you.'

'I'm surprised OSHA doesn't object to our being here.'

'We're government employees.' She mashed the sets of clothing into the bottom of the box in order to fit as many items in as possible. It would all have to be sorted out later; the objective now was to move as much as they could as fast as they could. 'OSHA doesn't apply to us.'

'You're kidding.'

'I am not. Government employees are exempt. Always have been. We're covered by the Ohio Department of Health, which—' she panted a bit while hefting another thick set of bloodied clothing into the box— 'subscribes to all OSHA guidelines, except they don't do surprise inspections.'

'So they instruct all government offices to take care of us, but never actually check to see if they do.'

'We're civil service. It's another word for expendable.' She pushed on the stack of clothing inside its cardboard walls with all her weight, but it would not budge. It had taken all it would take. Don held the flaps closed while she taped them with red tamper-proof evidence tape, then added her initials over this seal with a Sharpie pen. Then they motioned to the two deskmen, who now had the unenviable task of maneuvering the very full box up the temporary staircase and out to the moving truck. When the truck filled, either she or Don would have to ride back to the M.E.'s office with it. The garage had been emptied of vehicles and all available basement space had been pressed into service as temporary storage.

'Not that I'm complaining,' she went on. 'Because you can have all the rules and guidelines you want, but when it comes down to something like this, one fact always wins out.'

'You gotta do what you gotta do,' Don supplied.

'Exactly.'

They worked in silence for a while. Then Don said, 'Not much of an explosive. It's bad enough it has to destroy something, but make it smelly and possibly mutagenic too?'

'It's an extremely odd choice for an explosive. Oliver says it would have taken between one thousand and two thousand *pounds* of nitrogen triiodide to take down this building. That's like a cubic yard. That's like over five hundred gallons. That's, like, a *lot*. They must have stockpiled it here, just like we stockpiled our old X-rays.'

'Or they made it here. I wonder if the Feds found any equipment in the wreckage.'

'If they did, they're not going to tell us.' Theresa picked up a small metal box designed to store glass slides, listening to the disheartening tinkle of the broken shards inside. 'It might not have been that much, if there had been other explosives in the room, or potentially combustible compounds throughout the building, like metal shavings or pervasive organic materials. Sugar dust took out that company in Georgia a few years ago. The shock wave from the NI3 would have set off anything else. Though I can't see a combustible dust problem in a residential building, and apparently the explosion generated from one point, that gaping black hole next to us.'

'So we're back to a big ol' pile of NI3.'

'Which Leo insists is the most impractical explosive ever; he says no one could have brought that much of it together without blowing themselves to tiny bits long ago. On top of that it tends to decompose, quickly, even if treated well and sealed up. The iodine would begin to subliminate and produce smelly, staining purple gas.' He helped her place the slide box into one of the fresh large boxes. 'Do they still think it's this Kadam guy? For any reason other than being of Middle Eastern descent?'

'They have a few more reasons than that. Christine gave me a few more details. His employer supposedly rented the space here but his work address comes back to a vacant lot. Kadam's own personal history fell off the charts three years ago. No address, no income tax return, no credit cards.'

'How did Christine find that out?'

'I didn't ask.' She helped him seal up the box and maneuver it up the steps.

'This should finish off the truck,' Don said. 'If I don't return, I'm on my way to the office. Want anything?'

'A cot and a sleeping bag would be nice.'

'How about coffee?'

'That, too.' If she had thought it would be lonely in the near-center of downtown in the middle of the night, she now learned the error of it. Cars came and went, with the Doppler principle affecting the sound as they moved up the street. At least once every half-hour a police car from the nearby police headquarters or a lone ambulance fired up the siren. Theresa wondered how the tenants who had lived in the Bingham's trendy lofts ever got any sleep. The blast site, ringed with blinding light, teemed with not only the M.E. staff, but Homeland Security and FBI agents. Other people's conversations formed a background hum like a radio played in the next office, only loud enough to catch a theme here or there but not the whole song.

Theresa peeked over at the FBI's storage area, well on the other side of the building. 'It looks like a bunch of old paperwork,' she told Don when he returned. 'Nothing interesting, like our stuff.'

'Should we loan them a few boxes of bloody clothes?'

'It would be the neighborly thing to do.' Having passed her fortieth birthday the previous year, Theresa cared for few things less than pulling an all-nighter. But once resigned to the idea that she would not see her bed that night, it wasn't that bad. Don made regular trips to the Lambert lobby for coffee, as much for the warmth as for the caffeine. The constant activity, though she would no doubt feel each muscle tomorrow, kept the time moving. And she had too much pride to falter in front of either the much younger Don or the much older Dr Banachek.

She kept an eye on the portly pathologist. Occasionally he would ask Don for help in wrestling a mangled drawer from its file cabinet but then would become lost in its contents, reliving past cases through X-rays of the victim's broken bones or gunshot wound. One of the histologists would have to prod him gently back into action.

Around three a.m. Theresa sealed up the last container of clothing. 'Time for a break before we start on the rest. I need a ladies' room and some more coffee. Want a donut?'

Don shook his head. 'I've had enough sugar for one night.'

'Silly boy. There's no such thing as too much sugar.' She took her water bottle to refill and climbed the metal steps, then followed the yellow tape path out to the sidewalk and turned to the south.

This would be her second visit to the Lambert mansion/workshop/factory in less than twenty-four hours. Strange. Now the lights were subdued and the noise near church level. What appeared to be a giant plastic frame had been erected over the damaged Entrance Number Two.

The lobby doors of frosted glass swung open with a mere whisper, ushering her in to a silent cavern. The room served as both museum and lobby, with marble floors and a vaulted ceiling. Glass cases ringed the area and huge diagrams and photographs hung on the walls. A long table with coffee urns, boxes of donuts and even a fruit plate waited for her on the left, but she turned away, in no hurry to rush back to work. Besides, she needed to find a bathroom first.

The story of Bruce Lambert began there to the right, with a blown-up photo of his humble beginnings in a weathered house on Fulton Road. Smiling parents, a maintenance man and a jewelry design assistant, flanked three boys dressed for Halloween. One, a scrawny thing with big ears, wore a magician's outfit. According to the display text they suspected their son's potential when he won his third grade science fair. And every science fair he entered after that, the placard added.

The glass cases did not follow the same chronological order, however, and the one nearest her held a blown-up model of a microchip that Lambert had developed when he—and Theresa—had been in their early thirties. The chip had earned Lambert his first million.

The next wall display jumped ahead to the college years, when Lambert took his undergraduate degree from Cleveland State and headed to MIT, which, the wording implied, only financial considerations had kept him from attending in the first place. Theresa hoped none of the alumni association staff noticed this placard, or Lambert might receive a sternly worded letter about loyalty and the lack thereof. He would have to put Ginny's yearbook collection on display as a peace offering.

No mention of sending brother Carl on his short trip to Columbia, or who the youngest boy might be.

Next, a collage devoted to the rich man's humanitarian efforts—providing Katrina victims with hyper-efficient generators and experimenting with a new kind of smart building by constructing an orphanage in Abkhazia, on the coast of the Black Sea. A footnote told how Carl fell in love with the country and its children and especially a teacher at the orphanage. They married and adopted two of the boys.

The next few cases and displays explained each area in which Lambert had become interested in turn, always leaving behind a trail of better, faster, cheaper products for the American people to use. The most powerful processor, the cordless phone with the highest range, the cleanest diesel fuel. The latter led him to the gasoline crisis and the internal combustion engine.

She leaned her elbows on a glass display case and read the printing around small models of six-cylinder engines; the leaning eased some pressure in her lower back. Electric cars were too inconvenient and unlikely to be accepted by Americans in any real sense, the writing proclaimed. The internal combustion engine had functioned well for a hundred years. All that was needed was to find something besides compressed gas vapor to provide the small, controlled explosion that pushed away the piston. After many experiments, Lambert believed he had found the answer in nitrogen crystals.

Did nitrogen come in crystals? And why did Theresa seem to find herself surrounded by nitrogen all of a sudden?

No joke intended. It *did* comprise nearly eighty per cent of the atmosphere. Humans sucked in much more nitrogen with each breath than any other element.

Could it be explosive? Not normally. She might know more if she had listened to Lambert's tour instead of chatting up David Madison. Her weary brain needed a connection between all these events, the Bingham explosion, Marty Davis' assassination, the Lambert factory explosion, Lily and her meth habit… Theresa formed the only link, and a completely random one. She rapped her knuckles on the display in frustration.

A voice startled her. 'Please don't tap on the glass.' In the dim corner near the entrance to the rest of the building, behind a small podium, sat a black man in a nice suit, with the body type of a Buddha statue and the immobility to match.

'S-sorry.'

'That's all right.' She approached him, gingerly, as if he were a new species of amphibian which might leap at any moment. His eyes were invisible behind tinted glasses. She couldn't even tell if they were open.

'What kind of crystals?'

'I beg your pardon, ma'am?'

'The new engine. The display says it uses nitrogen crystals, but pure nitrogen doesn't come in crystals and they aren't flammable at any rate.' He—or at least his glasses—regarded her for a while, no doubt wondering if she always sounded this incoherent in the wee hours.

'I'm Mr Lambert's chief of security. Not usually here at night but then these aren't usual circumstances. So though I may be just a teensy bit slow from being up past my bedtime, can I help you?'

'Um…it has to be some kind of compound, but what else is in the compound? If it's going to fire a piston, there must be…' After another long minute, her Buddha took a deep breath and said, 'Seeing that this is the answer to the gas crisis and a way to free America from dependence on the oil of those hostile to us, and that the first Lambert Industries IPO is scheduled to be offered next week, I suppose Mr Lambert didn't care to post his formula in a glass box in a public lobby.'

'Mmm, yes, well.' There didn't seem much to say to that.

'How does it work, then? I mean, gas is a liquid and a vapor. How do you convert an internal combustion engine to working on—'

'Sand,' the security chief said.

'Sand?'

'It's like sand. That's how tiny the crystals are. They're in a plastic ring. You ever have a cap gun when you were a kid?'

'No. But I got one for a Halloween costume once.'

'Yeah? What did you go as?'

At this, the first spark of interest in the man's voice, she didn't have the heart to tell him she couldn't remember. 'A cowgirl.'

'Ah.' He paused, clearly trying to picture her in that outfit, and she squirmed. 'Well, you know how caps for revolver type cap guns come in a preformed, plastic ring? Same thing here. Only instead of caps, the sections on the ring feed the sand into the cylinders one grain at a time.' The wide face beamed, as proud as if he had invented it himself. 'It fires like a gun, so there's no spark plug to gum up. The engine oil dissolves any residue, so there's little maintenance.' Theresa sorted out the idea in her head. 'What happens when the ring runs out of sand?'

'You take that ring out and put in another. They're only a foot in diameter and weigh less than a pound, so it's not like it's hard. A warning light will tell you when you're low, just like a gas tank, so you don't wind up dibbser.' At her frown, he added, 'DBSR—dead by the side of the road.'

'Oh.'

'Mr Lambert says dibbser is what Americans fear most of all, and no alternative engine will ever catch on unless we can assure them that will never, ever happen.'

'That makes a lot of sense. So where do you buy these rings—oh, duh. Here.'

'At first. It's not a complicated design, and any chemist could break down the formula for the crystals, so Mr Lambert knows there will be knock-offs available almost immediately. If he can just keep the patent on the engine, he'll be happy.'

'What about the EPA?'

'They love it. No harmful fumes. No lead, no benzene. Nothing to leak out of underground tanks or spill on the freeway. Well, the sand could spill, but it can be swept or vacuumed. Much better for human beings all around. You can store extra rings in your garage or your trunk. No more making a weekly stop at the gas station.' There had to be some drawback—there always was—but without knowing more Theresa could not guess what it might be and had no doubt that Lambert had found or would find a way around it. Trying to out-think Bruce Lambert was like trying to out-golf Tiger Woods or out-sing Barbra Streisand.

'Very interesting,' she told him. 'Have you been working with Mr Lambert a long time, to learn all this?'

'Only a couple of years, since I got out of the service. But I've been a friend of his older brother since they lived in the hood.'

'Cool,' she said, and meant it.

'A lot of the guys here are from when we were kids. Mr Lambert doesn't forget his friends.'

'I can respect that.' The conversation lagged, and she asked for directions to the ladies' room.

'Right down here, ma'am,' he pointed to a hallway behind him, 'past the workrooms.'

'Really.' It didn't make much sense to have the restrooms not in the public area, seemed to be a flaw in the security system.

'It's OK, ma'am.' Buddha still smiled. 'All entrances to the factory are closed. You can't get lost.'

'That's a relief.' She set off once again, feeling that it could not be good to wander into Bruce Lambert's workspace. She might find herself pulverized by a robotic sentry with a ray gun. Or another bomb. She made a beeline for the ladies' room, then found her way back along the corridor.

She could still smell the faint odor of iodine, unless it was just her imagination. Either it or the healing scratches made her skin itch.

She looked through the window as she walked, seeing the room she had toured through only hours earlier. It still had a large hole in the wall, but most of the blackened, destroyed items had been removed and an effort made to clean the walls and floor. It wouldn't surprise her to see it back in operation by tomorrow—things could get fixed quickly with all the money in the world—but the room on the left had not been badly damaged. She studied it, once again mesmerized by the chaos of invention. A lightly cushioned, molded seat had been brought in and sat on the floor next to the still ash-covered chassis. The engine block—which appeared to her to be a standard, six-piston engine block—sat on a table covered with tools. The entire car frame dangled, caught in the four prongs of a huge crane claw. No doubt this piece of the puzzle would be lowered on to the chassis at some point, but for now the car frame looked like a toy forgotten by a gargantuan child who had been called to dinner.

Bruce Lambert had come a long way from his mother's garage, but Theresa wondered if he truly found the slick, modern fishbowl more comfortable. 'I couldn't work like that,' she said aloud.

'Yeah, I know,' snorted a voice to her left. 'I don't know what I was thinking when I designed it.'

SIXTEEN

THERESA STARED IN surprise at her third encounter that day with Bruce Lambert, über-genius. She would have been both startled and self-conscious had she not been so completely exhausted.

He had cleaned off the blood and plaster dust and changed into a plain T-shirt, a well-worn pair of jeans and a weary smile. 'I wanted my place to be transparent, I guess. I've always loved clear stuff, glass, those telephones in the clear acrylic so you can see the mechanism, Wonder Woman's invisible jet. But it came out more like—' He glanced around at the windows, the room, the hallway suspended across the center of it, mouth working as if searching for the right word. 'Like—'

'Disney World?'

He half turned, looked directly at her. 'Exactly. I wanted the process to be visible, so people could distinguish it from magic. Invention doesn't require magic. It doesn't even require genius. All you need is time and persistence.'

'Don't you worry about people stealing your ideas, if they can stand here and watch you work?'

'Nah. The lobby is only open to the public three times per week, and even then it's mostly school groups. Industrial spies don't usually collaborate with fourth-graders. At least I hope not. Electronic transmissions are monitored, and there's no cell service past the lobby. The entire building is one giant Faraday cage.' At her look, he said, 'A Faraday cage is—'

'A container that shields all electronic signals, yes. We use the bags for seized cell phones so no one can delete information by remote. But I received a call standing in your workroom.'

'That was because someone had just blown a big hole in the wall, so the bag had a leak. Check it now.' She did. No bars.

He went on, 'If someone wants to steal my plans, they get a job here. That's happened four times in the past two years.'

'Could one of them have left that bomb in your supply closet?'

'No.' She didn't ask how he could be sure of that, knew that he would have his ways. Bruce Lambert presented himself to the world as a curious little boy, the geek that made good. But there was nothing geek-like about the tightly coiled body under that T-shirt and no one built such a financial powerhouse without both shrewdness and cunning. If the bomb had been an inside job, it had been left by a new threat, and obviously Lambert would be much better placed to figure that out that she could hope to be. Perhaps he would let the Feds help him, perhaps not. People at his level made up their own procedures for justice and resolution. The rich *are* different.

That said, at the moment he just looked tired. 'You should get some rest.'

He chuckled and slumped against the window. 'I've been out at Leroy's house. Two kids and one more on the way. I have no idea what they're going to do if he dies. Leroy had to grow up without a father, said that's the one thing he would never do to his own. And in the end he may not get a choice about it.' There was nothing she could say to that, nothing anyone could say.

Then he added, 'I never asked what you thought of the tour.'

'I think I should buy some stock in Lambert Industries.'

He chuckled again. 'You'll get your chance next week. The IPO comes up first thing Monday morning.'

'I heard.' This would be a significant change for him. People who knew business and industry only wondered why he had waited so long. 'Going public', or offering stock in the company for public sale, meant the owner could shed the liability while increasing personal profits—provided the stock remained popular, and this stock would. Bruce Lambert, surmised the business section of the *Plain Dealer*, would move from being the fourth richest man in the country to the richest man in the world by Monday's closing bell.

No wonder he couldn't sleep.

'So how does your sand crystal engine work?' she asked.

His grin widened. 'You would know if you hadn't been chatting up that guy instead of listening.'

'Sorry.'

'That's all right.'

'The crystals are nitrogen triiodide?' He looked surprised, then intrigued, then amused in rapid succession.

'Interesting idea, but impractical. Too unstable.'

'So what are they?'

'Remember what I said about science not rewarding the unobservant?' She raised her eyebrows, waiting.

'It doesn't reward the inattentive, either. And now I have to go, but it was a pleasure talking with you.'

'You too,' she said, and watched him walk away,

wondering how to categorize his brush-off: clever or petulant? She decided on petulant, though couldn't really begrudge him a bit of rancor for a woman who would find David Madison more fascinating than a gas-free internal combustion engine which might revolutionize the globe, alter foreign policy and make Cleveland the center of the country once again.

But then, he hadn't met David Madison.

She carted three cups of coffee back to the wreck of the Bingham, puzzling over both her sudden attraction to the unusually situated David Madison and the equally sudden significance of nitrogen to her life. Was the nitrogen triiodide that destroyed the Bingham building a bad batch from Lambert's prototype? But why store it next door? Why store it at all? Lambert disassembled his failures, didn't waste space on them. Had Kadam somehow stolen the compounds from Lambert? Perhaps he'd been one of those four former employees. But how, and why store them next door? None of it made sense.

She sighed, making her careful way down the metal staircase. If an answer existed, her brain was too fried to find it.

'Everything come out OK?' Don asked, raising his voice over the noise of the generator.

'Why do men think that's so freakin' funny?'

'Because it is. OK, clothes are done. That leaves us all this boxed-up stuff piled against the wall. What is it?' Don asked. He had not had the pleasure of removing items to storage quite as often as Theresa and her overdeveloped sense of order had.

'Just that. Stuff. Quite a variety of stuff. Take this, for instance.' She hefted a rectangular cardboard box, still in fairly good shape as it had been tucked up against the outer wall. 'Remember our window washer who fell thirty-eight floors?'

'Distinctly.'

'Well, after OSHA had finished inspecting the harness, I called them to see if I could get an OK to destroy it. The guy there said they had completed their work with it, but there might be other interested parties, so to err on the side of caution I asked him to send me a list. His letter included seven, from the victim's family to the harness manufacturer down to his union. I said forget it, put the thing in a box and sealed it up.'

'Your campaign against clutter had hit a wall.'

'You could say that.' She tucked the box with the harness into one of the new boxes and followed it with other items, including an unwrapped axe with a faded yellow tag and a bicycle wheel, the only residue of a mob boss who went missing in the early seventies during his daily ride.

Dr Banachek abandoned his X-rays for a while and came by to chat. He rested himself on a folding chair which someone had left in the storage room long before and had survived the explosion with only minor mangling. It listed slightly when he settled on it, but did not fall over. 'Remind me again why we had to do this in the middle of the night.'

'I would if I could,' Don grumbled. 'Law enforcement agencies seem to be addicted to the wee hours.'

'Aw, man,' Theresa exclaimed in disappointment, holding up a shattered glass case which held a human skull, its surface chalky white with areas of brown. 'It broke.'

'Is that real?' Dr Banachek asked.

'It's a real skull but not the result of homicide. A supposed satanic cult bought it or stole it from a medical school or some such thing.' She removed the gaping shards of glass from the frame, setting them on top of the crushed fencing.

'Don't cut yourself,' Don said. 'I suppose we should have stored it in something sturdier.'

'Well, we couldn't have known the ceiling was going to fall in. Besides, it's not evidence of any crime. Leo hung on to it for sentimental reasons.'

'Only a forensic lab would hang on to a skull for sentimental reasons,' Dr Banachek said.

Theresa picked up yet another box, this one from a crime scene on Payne Avenue, and pivoted to place it with the others.

Wait.

Where had she heard the name of that street lately? Not that such a mention would be unusual—Payne Avenue stretched through a mile and a half of downtown Cleveland.

Ken Bilecki. He said he, Lily and Marty had lived in a 'pit on Payne' when attending the university. The label said 2401, which would have been only a block from the school. She checked the date—spring, 1985. If they had been in the class of '88…

The label also noted 'explosion'.

'What's that?' Don asked, no doubt wondering why she had become as still as Lot's wife.

'It's from an explosion on Payne Avenue over twenty years ago. I didn't know Cleveland was such a volatile city.'

'Aside from the East Ohio Gas disaster, I didn't either.' He moved past her to brush gravel off another container, prodding gently. 'I *would* like to be out of here before breakfast.'

'Sorry. It's just that this guy Frank questioned about

the suicide last night mentioned living on Payne when he went to Cleveland State, and—' Dr Banachek stirred, producing creaks from the deformed chair.

'Oh. The chemistry students.'

Theresa stared. 'You know this case?' Don sighed.

The portly doctor sighed too. 'I couldn't forget it— the first time I saw a body burned beyond recognition. Unfortunately, not the last. Only a week later they brought in a family of four from a house fire, an old Berea duplex, the upper floor fell on to the lower. The couple in the upstairs—'

'But what about the students?'

He blinked, eyes big behind round lenses. 'Oh yes. It was my first explosion case…actual explosions are rare, as opposed to fires…they'd been living in a building converted to student housing and a room on the ground floor blew up, burned the rest of the place pretty bad. His own fault, too.'

'He started the fire?'

'The police thought he'd been cooking methamphetamine—making his own chemistry. And it killed him. He had no hands or feet by the time he came to us.'

'Ouch.'

'That was the early days of the meth epidemic. Bad stuff. Could easily be curtailed, you know. Pharmaceutical companies could make cold medicine with an optical isomer of pseudoephedrine that could not be made into meth.'

'What's stopping them?' Don asked from behind a pile of boxes.

'Their lobbyists. They get paid a lot of money to water down any bill that might inconvenience their bosses.' He patted Theresa's box. 'But I could be mixing it up with another case, you know. They all blend together after a while.'

'Yeah, I know.' Don had filled the rest of the container, finishing with just enough space to fit the box she held. He went to take it out of her hands but she pulled it away. 'Not this. I want to take a look at it later and that garage is going to be a Rubik's cube by the end of the day.' She set the box aside with her tote bag full of snacks and an extra pair of work gloves. Then she dutifully helped Don and the deskman maneuver the filled box to the truck. When she returned, Dr Banachek once again stood at the severely damaged file cabinets, removing X-rays to new file boxes.

The trace evidence department enclosure had only one slide cabinet and approximately twenty cardboard boxes of various shapes remained. Don hefted one up, heavy for its size. 'This is dense.'

'It's a solid block of index cards. That's how we used to sign evidence in and out, before the printed voucher forms.'

'Sounds cumbersome.' Don had been weaned on a keyboard and hated writing anything longhand.

'A little bit. But we never lost anything and you can pull out a card thirty years later and see what was submitted, what analyses were performed, the results and who picked it up. Nothing got lost in cyberspace.'

'Only in real space. So what is so fascinating about a twenty-year-old meth lab?'

Theresa explained how Marty Davis had lived on Payne Avenue during college with Lily Simpson and Ken Bilecki, and that Lily said Marty had been part of a meth cooking operation. 'Cooking and selling, I mean.'

'So you think this cop could have been killed in revenge for the death of a student in his meth lab twenty-odd years ago?'

She carted another box of index cards, thinking. 'I guess it *is* a silly idea when you put it like that. It's bubbling in my mind because the few facts I know about Marty Davis keep coinciding. But those facts are such a small fraction of his life. There must be worlds more to it than what I know.'

'Sure.' Don picked up the red sealing tape.

'All the same, it can't hurt to look up the case.'

'No, it can't. Is there any more coffee?'

'Come on, kid! I've got eleven years on you and I'm still going.' He laughed, and they moved the box to the truck, gingerly scooting past two FBI agents in the narrow walkway. Theresa recognized the female agent she had run into three times in as many days.

The truck had filled again, and Don climbed into the passenger seat to escort their booty back to the office. Theresa stood in the chill of West Ninth Street and wondered at the rules they followed. Did anyone care enough about these ancient cases to steal into the rubble of a ruined building to find the evidence relevant to them? Why? If the evidence could incriminate them, it would have done so long ago. Plus they'd have to search through the piles of items to find the one they wanted, assuming they could interpret the archaic numbering system. It would require a determined and intrepid criminal, a cut well above the hapless, thoughtless murderers and violent types she usually dealt with.

Perhaps it *would* make more sense just to dynamite the whole lot. Her thoughts moved to the cardboard box now tucked underneath her purse.

Ridiculous. The twenty-year-old fire had been quite forgotten. At least she assumed so—she would have to ask Frank. The investigation could have been reopened without either of them knowing. She opened her Nextel, saw the time and date and decided her question could wait until a more reasonable hour. He would not appreciate her input at four thirty a.m., no matter how ingrained the habit had become of telling each other every fact, insight or wild guess at the moment it occurred. She would not call a non-blood-relative homicide detective as continually. She never knew if being related to Frank made their working together more effective, or less. They communicated more freely because of the relationship, which should be a good thing. But perhaps they focused on each other's well being more than the case at hand. What had Lambert said about inattention going unrewarded?

'Excuse me.' Theresa looked up to see the two FBI agents, struggling with a bulky plastic container to load on their own moving truck. Instead of trying to go around them, Theresa simply backed up along the caution-taped walkway and made use of the serendipitous meeting.

'How's the investigation going? Do you guys know why this happened yet?'

'No,' the woman panted. The man, a different agent than the man who had been with her before, ignored Theresa entirely.

'Can I help you with that?'

'No, we got it.' Rules to be followed. Non-authorized personnel prohibited. Theresa continued, walking precariously backwards along the path.

'The explosion seems to have started in one place, right? That's obvious from the gaping hole in the center of the building. It's not like he put charges at strategic points, wanting to take the whole building down.'

'Did a pretty good job of it anyway,' the woman said. She didn't seem to be any happier with the wee hours than Don.

'We used this place for storage.' Theresa reached the sidewalk and nearly fell over it, but recovered and accompanied the agents to their truck. 'I guess you guys did too.' They didn't bother to answer, needing all their breath to heft their box into the waiting arms of two agents in the moving truck. Must be nice to have so much manpower at your disposal. At least they hadn't worn suits and ties, just sweatshirts, jeans and jackets with *FBI* emblazoned on the back.

When it had been settled to their satisfaction, Theresa walked with them back into the site, dogging the two like an unwanted kid brother. 'Is Kadam still your main suspect?'

'Yes,' the woman said.

'Ask Homeland Security,' the man with her said.

'Even though there's absolutely no strategic significance to this building,' the woman sighed. The man glared at her. The lateness of the hour had lowered her defenses.

'I don't know what you had stored here,' Theresa said, 'but have you considered the possibility that the purpose of the explosion might have been to destroy your records?' The man made a sound, a cross between *pfft* and *pah*.

The woman took a swig from a bottle of water which dangled from her belt. 'I doubt it. How would he know a particular file was here and not in our offices, and these were all old, mostly closed. Why go after them now?'

'I had the same thought. But—'

'Besides, if he targeted a storage unit and didn't simply blow himself up by accident, it would have been

yours.' Theresa stopped, and looked down into the evacuated hole. Standing at street level she could see what
the woman meant. The FBI's section had been in the
south-east corner, the M.E.'s unit in the north-west corner. And the worst, most blackened, most gaping part of
sublevel one had been right across the hall.

SEVENTEEN

Friday

BREAKFAST HAD COME and gone by the time they finally finished, and driving back to the office in rush hour traffic made Theresa think perhaps working during the night had not been such a bane. It would have taken their little truck four times as long to make each trip back and forth during working hours. But then, she was running on the fumes of adrenalin and feeling a bit punchy. At least that was Don's explanation.

'Why *not* us?' she explored aloud, gazing at the many empty storefronts on Euclid Avenue. The decline of the once-revolutionary industrial city was not just a punch line or the exaggerations of fund-seeking politicians. The city hurt, and its citizens felt helpless to do anything about it. 'Why bomb a mostly empty building of trendy apartments? There are only two logical targets existing in that building, us and the FBI. And the epicenter of that particular quake occurred much closer to us than to them.'

'Take out a whole building in order to conceal some moldy old evidence that everyone, including us, had forgotten about?' Don uttered a mild curse as they failed to make the light at Fifty-Fifth.

'Maybe they're stupid. Or maybe they're super-cautious.'

'I think the Feds are leaning toward the first theory.'

'Why?'

'Christine said her source said they found more wires and suchlike than would have been needed for one explosion.'

Theresa pondered that. 'So it wasn't a criminal trying to destroy our evidence or a terrorist who came in and set a charge to take down the Bingham. A terrorist stored all his charges there in order to take down other buildings.'

'Makes sense. Everyone else rented storage there, why not a terrorist? He'd hardly want to keep the stuff in his apartment.'

'He could spend hours there, working on bombs. The rooms are so huge, with such thick walls. No one to notice noises or smells. People coming and going all the time with no one really paying attention, or assuming that box he's carrying contains nothing more than files. Until something went wrong.'

'Really wrong.' Theresa settled back into her seat, the box from the Payne Avenue explosion at her feet. Many arsonists and bomb-makers died, accidentally, by their own hands. More walked around with scars and burns to remind them of their errors. 'I sure hope that's it.'

'Your feelings would be hurt if a criminal tried to take out our store of evidence in order to help his own case?'

'Well, then it would be *personal*. And you didn't tell me that Christine had said that! After we've just spent twelve—no, fourteen hours together, and you've been holding out on me.'

He glanced at her, sideways. 'How many cups of coffee have you had?'

'I lost count. But if it really was an accident…'

'Yes?' He pulled into the Medical Examiner's Office parking lot, coasting to a stop in front of the garage.

'…what does it have to do with Marty Davis?' Don killed the engine.

'Nothing! You happened to go to both scenes. That's all the connection there is. There is no more.'

'Maybe you're right,' she said, with a complete lack of conviction.

'No more caffeine today, Tess, seriously. Tell Leo you're done and you're going home.'

'And forfeit all the overtime I just racked up by sleeping all day?'

'Yes. *I* am.'

She wrenched the door handle until it opened. 'You don't have a kid in college.' Leo had made the county public works department install a barrier—it appeared to be a wooden barn door held in place with metal brackets—to section off one bay of the three-car garage for the trace evidence department, in order to preserve its integrity and maintain the chain of custody…as if the fifty-year-old overhead door would pose a serious obstacle to anyone who wanted to get in, as if they could find what they wanted once they got in, and as if anyone even cared to. The true threat might not even be a criminal who didn't want to see a particular piece of evidence in court, but a rabid fan of the forensic TV shows who wanted a 'real' souvenir.

At any rate, the volume of material which had seemed manageable when spread—or smashed—throughout the Bingham building's storage space turned into a floor-to-ceiling, wall-bulging mass in their assigned one-third of the garage. 'Good thing we're done,' Theresa said. 'She canna' take much muhr, Captain.'

'I'm not sure we can even fit this truckload,' Don

said, eyeing the precariously stacked, near-critical mass of boxes. 'If someone blows *this* place up too, I'm getting into another line of work.'

'And give up this glamour? What could be better than the smell of decades-old bloody clothing in the morning?'

'I mean it, Tess. No more caffeine. I have to take a leak, so I am leaving you to guard our fortress against any marauders, with your life if necessary.' Theresa collected her tote bag and her water bottle and her box from the passenger seat floor and dropped them on the truck's bumper.

'Fear not. I am armed with the Urn of Eternal Life and the Last Season's Fashion Tote Bag of Death. The lost treasure of the Bingham is safe with me.' He turned to go into the building.

'Unless any orcs show up,' she called after him. 'Then all bets are off!' She saw his head shake, and then she was left in the parking lot with a crammed garage space and a crammed moving truck, wondering how to fit one into the other. Might as well get started. She picked up the box from Payne Avenue to scoot it to the end of the bumper, out of her way.

The sun now peeked through the gathering storm clouds to warm her. Her clothes were caked with dirt and dust. She had sweated and chilled and sweated again until she couldn't stand the smell of herself, or at least what she could smell over the iodine odors clinging to the inside of her nose. Her mouth tasted like the concentrated ashes at the bottom of a coffee pot that's been on the burner for five or six hours. Her make-up had long since sunk into and clogged up her pores, revealing the latest shade of her bruises. Her skin had the shininess of an oil slick and she didn't want to think about what her hair looked like.

'Good morning.' Of course she turned to see David Madison.

He wore work clothes, pleated trousers of a weighty material and a white shirt with a tie, underneath a light-weight trench coat. It made him look even taller. He carried a briefcase, and seemed to study her as unob-trusively as he could manage. 'Sorry if I startled you. I had a meeting at the hospital next door and I knew the M.E.'s was here and I thought I'd go to the front desk and ask the receptionist if you were in, but then I saw you here…are you all right?'

'Um—yeah.'

He watched her face, picking his words. 'You look…'

'Like death warmed over? I know. We were at the ex-plosion site all night. What are you doing here?'

'Meeting. Butterfly Babies and Children's—' he gestured at the sweeping hospital system situated one door over from the M.E.'s office—had a few problems in their account, numbers not quite adding up. Some-times a quick meeting unties the knots a lot faster than phone calls. Otherwise it just snowballs—you must be really tired.'

'No, actually. Around three or four in the morning a second wind kicks in and you start running on adren-alin.' She wished he would turn his back for one sec-ond so she could at least blot her face. Maybe she could point out the clock tower on the medical school—'Can I get you anything? Coffee?' She laughed, the sound too long and too tinged with hysteria, and his face shaded from sympathy to worry. He set the briefcase down and used both hands on her elbows to guide her to the mov-ing truck's wide bumper.

'Maybe you should sit down. I hope you're going to go home now, get some rest. Do you want me to take that for you?' And he took the box holding all the evidence that remained of the Payne Avenue explosion, twenty-five years previously. It reminded her of her unanswered questions.

David Madison barely gave it a glance as he set it on the truck's bumper, next to her left hip.

'No,' she said.

'I'm sorry?'

'No, I'm not going home.' She explained how overtime used in the same week it accrued would not be counted at time and a half, so that she'd lose the extra half per hour, and that with another coffee and maybe a Diet Coke she'd make it through the day just fine. Her body coped better if she stayed on the daytime/nighttime schedule and somehow fooled it into forgetting that it had lost an entire night.

'Does that work?'

'Not really. Did you get the hospital's accounts all straightened out?'

'Yes. Our account, anyway, Gardner's.'

'And what does Gardner's supply?'

'Chemicals.'

She felt her face freeze before the word even registered and, even then, didn't know why. 'What kind of chemicals?'

'All kinds. Mostly stuff for factories and other manufacturing processes, solvents and caustics, but some diagnostic reagents for hospitals and other labs. Places like yours, I guess.'

'Oh. That's kind of strange, that we're in similar lines of work.'

He crouched on the asphalt, so that he could look

up into her face rather than vice versa. 'No, I crunch numbers. It doesn't matter if Gardner sells chemicals or bowling balls or clothes. They're only numbers to me. What you do sounds a lot more interesting.' A deskman came out for a smoke. He watched them with undisguised curiosity, a hallmark of the Medical Examiner's Office, where nosiness was considered an occupational qualification. She smiled at him—to do anything else meant rumors of clandestine parking-lot meetings would make the rounds by lunchtime.

'So what was the problem at Rainbow?'

'Alcohol.'

'I'd love some.'

'I don't blame you. They had an extremely high amount of reagent alcohol on their bills and protested. It turned out to be a typo on the purchasing secretary's form. That will prove to be my excitement for the day.'

'This is mine.' She stood up. 'Just a lot of heavy lifting.'

'Can I help you?'

She eyed the boxes in the truck. 'We need to get it stored before the rain, but they're dirty. They were covered with dust before the building collapsed. Now they're covered with regular dust and concrete dust and plaster dust and nitrogen triiodide, and in some cases water from the fire hoses hit it and turned it all into a coating of dust mud.'

'Wow,' he said. 'I'll hold them away from my good tie, then.' He pulled the smaller boxes off the truck, one by one, and walked them the ten feet to the garage, where Theresa scaled the mountain face to stack them as close to the ceiling as possible.

No space could go unused.

'Heaven help us if we need something for court before they find us a new storage area, or a miracle occurs and we move to our new building. And we will—need them, that is. Nothing in a county bureaucracy moves at a breakneck pace. Six months from now these boxes will still be here.'

'I can't criticize,' Madison said, gingerly plucking a particularly grimy box of index cards from the moving truck. 'I still have unpacked boxes in my garage from after—after my wife went to jail and we moved to another house. Only a few streets away from our old one, but I thought a new place would help the boys start over.'

She hefted the box up, leaving a fresh streak of dirt on her sleeve. 'Did it?'

He shrugged. 'I don't know. Maybe. If you ask me, nothing helped. They've stopped talking to me about it, of course, because I'm from the Stone Age and there's no point in communicating with a fossil. But I see it. Every time there's a love scene on TV or a sexy ad in a magazine or their friends are whispering the kinds of things that teenage boys talk about. I see the wheels turning. It's not getting better. It's getting worse.' He leaned on the stack, two hands on the dusty boxes, while she searched about for a gap in the monolith for her latest brick and listened mightily. The words poured out as if he couldn't stop them. Perhaps he had not had anyone he could talk to about it for a long time, if ever. Perhaps he wanted advice from another parent and figured, given her line of work, not much would shock.

'It's the older one, especially. Jake. He was the same age as this kid, they were in the same grade. That's how Deirdre justified having this kid around all the time, she told me Jake liked having someone to play video games with instead of his little brother. But Jake never liked him. I—' his expression showed just how much disgust he felt for his own naivety—'didn't think a thing of it. She was always taking some misfit under her wing, the kids who struggled, the ones who didn't speak English well. I just didn't think about it. I didn't question.'

'Who would?' Theresa said.

Madison retrieved another box. 'So first Jake has to face the fact that his mother had sex with a child the same age as him. That has to raise all sorts of questions in his mind—if one boy, why not another? If she looked at one thirteen-year-old boy that way, then—' He paused, obviously forcing himself to put these unthinkable thoughts into words. Theresa's skin crawled. She didn't want to hear any more, but this man needed to talk. So she waited, quietly sliding another box into place. 'Then had she ever looked at him like that? Her own son? I don't believe that for an instant,' he added hastily, 'but even if I tried to convince him, would he believe it? Can I even know that for sure? On top of that, he's beginning to realize how young thirteen really is. With every day that passes, it becomes more unbelievable.

'Second, it will occur to him, if it hasn't already, that his mother used him as an excuse to have this affair right under our roof. Third, she's been in jail for three years and she's up for parole. She's going to want to see the boys. She might even want *custody*.'

'Have the boys ever visited—'

He passed her a milk crate of old weapons, wrapped in brown paper. 'I took them there a few times, at the beginning, because they just missed her so much. But it would throw the boys into a tailspin for days. They began to resent her, resent all that pain, and she finally told me not to bring them anymore. She sends cards on holidays, is all.'

'That's so sad.' The words were inadequate, but she didn't have any others. Theresa deposited the crate atop the mountain and made her way back down, sat on the lowest level of the stack and, her legs dangling, gave him her full attention.

'On top of that, this kid is still walking around the neighborhood. Nothing happened to him, of course. He's a victim.' A touch of bitterness leaked out into his words and he reeled it back in. 'At least I got Jake into another school. It's not as good academically but I had to do it— they would have been in the same *class*. Bad enough that all his friends know and boys never get tired of talking about sex. It finally began to taper off, but a parole hearing is sure to make the news and that will start it up all over again. If she actually gets out, cameras will follow her every move to see if she gets back together with— him.' Never his name, only 'that kid'. To depersonalize the situation? Or to remind himself that the boy was exactly that, a child, a victim of the situation.

Just not the only one.

The hell with showing some restraint around someone she barely knew. She reached out and grasped his hands with both of hers. The smile he flashed melted her with its gratitude.

Then he coughed and changed the subject, freeing his fingers to gesture at the garage. 'So did you find out why all this is necessary, why the Bingham blew up?'

'That's not my job. My job was to tote that barge and lift that bale.' The cardboard flaps beneath her sunk a millimeter. 'And I'd better get off this particular bale.' He helped her off her perch before it could collapse, lifting her by the waist without any apparent effort. Then he promptly backed off so she could return to the truck bumper and take a seat on something she couldn't outweigh. Maybe he realized that she was a professional at work and needed to behave as such. Maybe she smelled worse than she thought.

'And you were at it all night, no less, toting those bales. I hope they pay you enough.'

'Ha. It is to laugh.'

'I, um—' he suddenly found a piece of lint on his knee that required attention, then traced the label on the box with the tip of his finger—'wanted to see if you wanted to get dinner, tonight…with me, I mean…but I'm sure you're too tired to now. Maybe another time.'

She put her hand on the box to steady it on the bumper. 'Tonight would be great.'

'Really? But I'm sure you're exhausted. Tomorrow night—well, tomorrow night Anthony has a basketball game, but the next evening—'

'No, tonight would be terrific.' His mouth turned up, either at her answer or her enthusiasm.

'You're sure?'

'Absolutely. Another Diet Coke or two and I'll be great. Maybe three.'

'All right. I don't live too far from you, I'm in Parma. How about seven? Is that too late?' She said it would be fine and gave him her address, which he did not write down. She watched him walk toward the parking garage at Rainbow Hospital, and wondered if the rush of blood she felt came because of the proximity of an attractive man, thoughts of what the evening might be like, or relief that he had to have seen the Payne Avenue address on the box of evidence and had not reacted to it in any way.

'Tessie's got herself a man,' the deskman said as she climbed the steps to poke her head in the rear door to see what had become of Don. 'You never smile at me like that.'

'You lie. I smile at you every day.'

'*You* lie,' he grinned. 'Never like that.'

EIGHTEEN

THERE ARE NO secrets in a government bureaucracy and certainly not around doctors. 'What are you smirking about?' Christine demanded before Theresa even reached the elevator. 'You look like a really tired cat who caught the canary. Or the cat who caught another cat. What's up?'

'I'm punchy. Pulling an all-nighter at my age produces a state of euphoria as my body, denied sleep and food, turns on itself to find a new source of energy.'

'Smart aleck. I have something interesting on your cop.'

'Marty Davis?' Theresa started up the steps, and Christine followed. The elevator took too long.

'We have another dead cop around here? Step into my office. Want some coffee?' Theresa giggled like a hyena until Christine rescinded the offer. The young doctor's office had once been a supply closet and still resembled one, except for the shelf of heavy books and the scattering of knives, disabled guns and less common fare like brass knuckles and a ninja throwing star.

'Do you want my chair?'

Theresa knew she must look really bad. Usually she had to perch on a surplus ammo can. She leaned against the wall and insisted, 'No, I'm fine.'

'The tox report on Marty Davis,' Christine began.

'He had crystal meth in him?'

'What? No, no drugs at all. A touch of alcohol, probably left over from the night before—unsurprising given the condition of his liver. No, we found poison.' Theresa stared. Perhaps 'punchy' described her condition after all.

'I had Oliver run everything we could—because the brain cells had some funny damage that couldn't have come from the gunshot, because the victim was a cop, and because I like giving Oliver orders—and the GC/Mass Spec found ricin.'

'Ricin? Someone poisoned this cop with ricin and then shot him?' Theresa found the ammo can and sank down to its uncomfortable top. 'I don't get this. This guy was nobody—I mean, nobody like the rest of us are nobody. He went to work and drank beer with his friends and that was about it. He didn't carry a stainless steel briefcase handcuffed to his wrist or vacation in Biarritz. Some ex-con with a bad temper shooting him, that I can see. Poisoned like a Russian spy, that I can't.'

'I hear you. But the GC/Mass Spec doesn't lie. Neither does Oliver. He may be a pain in the ass, but he's a truthful one.' Theresa stared at the cabinets under Christine's desk, without seeing the yellowed cartoons taped to them or even the funny magnet signs. She stared so long that the doctor stretched out a foot and kicked her shin, gently. 'Don't you want to hear the rest?'

'There's more? You're going to tell me someone smothered him, too, or maybe garroted the body when we weren't looking?'

'Calm yourself. Being the astute and thorough physician that I am, I then asked myself, how did this guy get ricin in his system? It didn't kill him, after all, the gunshot did. Perhaps he'd chewed a castor bean or otherwise ingested it earlier, and it had made him sick but he'd recovered by the time you saw him. But his stomach contents were negative. So were the lungs. His brain cells, however, were swimming in the stuff.' Theresa waited, her own gray cells too tired to keep up. Christine sighed, and went on without her: 'The bullets used were 380 Glaser safety rounds, also called anti-personnel, the kind of handgun bullets that act like a shotgun. Instead of a solid slug of lead, they have a hollow copper jacket filled with tiny lead shot, held inside by a plastic plug. When the bullet hits the person, the impact breaks off the plastic plug and the tiny shot is free to keep moving through the body, shredding the organs and tissues in its way.'

'What's safe about that?' Theresa asked, though she knew the answer. A bullet that mushroomed and disintegrated inside the target took the target down, whereas a solid lead bullet might pass completely through the person threatening you and leave them able to continue threatening you. The bullet might also continue on to hit other people, bystanders for whom it had not been intended.

Christine knew she knew that, and didn't bother to answer. 'We had pulled out most of the shot and the shell fragments, of course—'

'Ballistics?'

'Maybe. There's a few shreds of the slug base, if we're lucky they have some usable toolmarks. Point is, I had Oliver test the pieces. Tiny lead shot hadn't been the only thing contained behind the little plastic plug. The shot had been coated with ricin before being released inside this officer's skull.'

'So someone didn't just want him dead. They wanted him dead, gone and buried before I could even step out of the house.' Theresa rubbed her forehead, feeling the knots in her temples. 'Who needed this cop dead

so badly? Who the hell *was* Marty Davis?' Theresa
scrubbed her face and changed into a clean shirt she
kept around for such emergencies. Unfortunately after
a month or two in her desk drawer it had absorbed the
odors of the lab and now smelled like a combination of
xylene and nitric acid. She tucked the Payne Avenue box
under her desk and washed down a granola bar with a
fresh cup of coffee. Then she reported the night's events
to Leo, who appeared entirely too bright-eyed to have
remained at the garage all night to supervise the unpack-
ing and storage. It came as no surprise to learn that he
had given the keys to Don and then gone home for a cozy
dinner and eight hours of beauty sleep. She would have
glared at him had she had sufficient energy left to do so.

He absorbed the information about Marty Davis' ricin
bullet with the same uncomprehending disbelief that she
had. Then he told her that the pathologists were cutting
Lily Simpson as they spoke and Theresa must write up
her report posthaste so they could ship the body off to
the potter's field. 'You have to get with the receptionist. Some guy keeps calling the switchboard wanting
to know what will happen to the body, when the death
certificate will be available and did she really kill herself or did she have help? He's driving her so nuts that
she's transferring the calls to me, and that is *not* going
to continue.'

'Ken Bilecki, I'm sure.' Just like Lily's pestering of
Frank.

'These meth addicts are so impatient.'

'Hyper,' Leo said. 'They're like that in the up phase.
That's the beauty of meth. They can work double, triple
shifts without ever having to eat, drink, sleep or go to
the bathroom. And won't even slur their words.' Theresa
nodded, knees drawn up to her chest, fingers pressing

her eyes gently to keep from rubbing them and creating wrinkles.

'The beauty and the curse. That's how meth has hung around long enough to get a stranglehold on this country, especially in the heartland where people pride themselves on being hard workers. It's a drug for people who *want* to work, without the social stigma of laziness like heroin or even pot. Heck, it used to be legally prescribed in the United States for everything from weight loss to post-natal depression until the 1970s.'

'You could use some right now,' Leo observed.

She shuddered, only partly for effect. 'No, thanks. Like all drugs, it only feels good for a while. Once it's depleted your neurotransmitters, nothing feels good any more except more meth. Then the neglect your body has suffered begins to show up, in dehydration, sleep deprivation and paranoia.'

'Then before you know it you'll be telling me that black helicopters are buzzing the lab. I had a cousin who saw them, insisted they were going to Napalm his house. His house wound up strafed, all right, but by irate customers. He'd gotten so fond of his own product that he was using everything he cooked, and selling rock candy for a hundred buck a bag. That bought him about twenty minutes before they came back and shot him to death.'

'Wow.' This marked about the third time in fifteen years that Leo had ever mentioned a friend or relative. 'Were you close?'

'We grew up together. Don't forget to give me your comp time request for last night's work by the end of the day.' He shuffled off to his office.

Theresa, trying without success to picture Leo as a boy, made a prompt exit with the box from the explosion on Payne Avenue tucked under her arm. She had earned herself a break. Ken Bilecki and the receptionist could wait.

File cabinets ringed the records room on the second floor, leaving space only for the door. Usually Theresa could chat with Norma and then request any file she liked, for she got on well with her. Sarah, however, never approached friendly by so much as a mile, and liked to pretend that she had the right to refuse access—to non-doctors only, of course. Doctors, even doctors for dead people, were second only to gods. Theresa crossed her fingers that Sarah would be occupied.

However, the same crisis which had kept her up all night now interrupted the secretaries' day, for the files from the Bingham building had to be resettled, and Norma had her hands full directing the traffic. She and a deskman hauled a file box to the very top of a precarious pile of such boxes. As all three people at that end of the room watched the stack sway, Theresa ducked into the archive room, found the Manila folder bearing the correct case number, and got back out while the getting was good.

One flight down took her to the ground floor. In the autopsy suite, a diener sewed up Lily Simpson's torso with heavy black thread and a practiced hand. 'Find anything interesting?' Theresa asked him.

'Aside from her bein' dead?'

'I should hope so, seeing as you've taken all her organs out. Who did her?'

'The Block,' the man sighed, and tilted his head toward the back of the room without missing a stitch. He referred to a recently hired transplant from a tiny former-USSR country, but the nickname didn't refer to the eastern bloc. It alluded to the doctor's build, as close to a monolith of granite as a human could get and still breathe. Theresa found him sectioning the liver, explained about the victim's connection to Marty Davis, and asked that Lily Simpson's bloodwork be given the full treatment, every assay that the Toxicology department had at their disposal.

'Leo in hurry for results,' he protested.

'Leo's always in a hurry.' She told him about the ricin, and he found that fascinating enough to push threats of Leo's ire from his mind. He also told her that the inside of Lily Simpson's body looked like—he muttered a few foreign words which he then translated to mean ten miles of bad road, but neither that nor any other detail of it seemed surprising. Her stomach had been empty, lungs clear of foaming, no indication of overdose.

Theresa thanked him and moved to the amphitheater. The old teaching room gave her the closest thing to privacy and peace that she could find in the cramped building. Even better, it had not yet been pressed into service as a storage area and the examination table gave her room to spread out. She opened the box.

NINETEEN

PHIL BANACHEK, HIS handwriting a bit firmer then, had kept the autopsy report brief. Firemen had removed victim Joseph Darryl McClurg from 2401 Payne Avenue, a former hotel which had been converted to student housing. The victim's body had been near the center of the building and 'at or near the point of origin'. Both hands and both feet were missing, not terrifically unusual in bad fire cases. The collections of small bones which make up the extremities could easily be consumed in a very hot fire, or simply fall away to be lost in the surrounding debris. The body had been identified via dental records as Joseph McClurg. Cause of death, smoke inhalation, as his lungs had been full of the stuff. He had definitely been alive when the fire began. There were no apparent pre-mortem injuries to the bones, she noted, and took this to mean that no one had hit the boy over the head or slashed his body—at least not deeply enough to strike the skeleton—and left him there in the fire to cover it up.

Two parents were listed as next of kin, Robert and Rosemary McClurg. No address noted.

Phil left no other notes about the cause of the fire or the circumstances. The dead body had been his responsibility, and only the dead body. The rest of the file contained the death certificate, the body release form made out to a funeral home on the east side, and a newspaper clipping about the fire—only two paragraphs, which surprised Theresa. Residential building fires usually got a lot of press. No subpoenas or trial dates had been noted. No one had ever been prosecuted for the death.

According to the *Plain Dealer*, the hotel on Payne had been turned into twenty-four efficiency apartments, all occupied by CSU students who would be displaced from their living quarters indefinitely, perhaps for good, since the extensive damage to the ground floor threatened the integrity of the entire building. The state fire marshal now worked to find the point of origin as well as the cause of the fire, but the police had implied that a clandestine methamphetamine laboratory had been operating at the location. Students on the second floor reported hearing a loud bang several minutes before they smelled smoke. McClurg had been the only victim. Four other students had been treated for burns and smoke inhalation and released.

She would have to get Frank to look up the case. The cops would have interviewed all the students and the victim's parents, and confirmed the presence of a clandestine lab.

But first, she'd open the box.

The cardboard box from the 2401 Payne Avenue case held four sealed bags and one quart-sized paint can, with notations in black magic marker listing the case number, item number, and a description of the evidence inside. There were additional numbers and letters in a thinner blue marker, in an unfamiliar hand and giving unfamiliar details—obviously work had been done by some agency other than the M.E. Indeed, three yellowed sheets of paper also enclosed turned out to be the state fire marshal's report. She snatched them up.

But the report only listed the volatile compounds found on the evidence in the four bags. Referencing the fire marshal's numbers explained which results related to which items. Theresa pulled a fresh piece of brown butcher paper over the examination table and cut open the first bag. A collection of broken glass fell out, tinkling gently.

It had been clear glass at one time, and the larger pieces appeared to be curved. Meth cookers would have used rounded glass flasks, probably pilfered from the school's chemistry labs. She had spent plenty of time in such labs with such flasks. It seemed that every organic chemistry lab assignment required distillation, which added an hour to each procedure. She still resented the very word.

But some pieces seemed too thick to be delicate chem lab flasks; they were heavier, like Pyrex bakeware. Soot and smoke residue coated each piece, overlaid with water drops, except where the fire marshal's investigators had apparently swabbed off samples for analysis.

She returned to the report. Remnants of methanol, toluene, acetone and other organic compounds had been found. All these compounds were used in the process to synthesize methamphetamines and all were extremely volatile. This was why meth labs were so prone to explosion and fire, Theresa thought to herself, because at least half the ingredients used were flammable. Combine that with the locations in which the work occurred—old, run-down rooms that no one cared about and that were not likely to be visited by any responsible party, sometimes abandoned places rigged with temporary power, with careless wiring and inadvisable hook-ups. Ventilation would be kept to a minimum lest the noxious odors alert the neighbors, increasing the potential power of any explosion by containing it. Housekeeping would also be kept to a minimum, both by the typically less-than-organized nature of the participants and by the need to keep evidence from the prying eyes of neighbors and garbage men, so that large amounts of trash piled up to serve as kindling. Add in any booby traps that the cooks might include to protect their merchandise from thieves, to destroy, if necessary, anything the police could use as evidence, or simply because too much use of their own product had made them paranoid. By definition, every meth lab became a powder keg, needing only a spark to remove itself from the face of the earth.

Along with the usual solvents, however, the fire marshal had listed iodine. Iodine was not particularly flammable in itself, and she knew it could be used in one of the several routes to crystal meth. Why had she had run into iodine—and nitrogen—at every turn lately? A deep sniff of the broken glass didn't bring any of the Bingham building and its nitrogen triiodide odors to her nose—but then it had had twenty-five years to dissipate. She folded the paper to funnel the broken shards back into the bag, sealed it and went on to the next.

The second bag held another piece of apparatus—a metal clamp designed to encircle a rod, brace or glassware at each end, while able to pivot in the middle so that the items could be maintained at any given angle to each other. Standard chemistry lab fare; Theresa had a pile of them in the lab upstairs. Not the kind of thing one would normally find in a dorm room.

A clump of bluish material like melted plastic clung to one of the rounded brackets, and she considered pulling it off for further study. But she thought better of it. The plastic most likely belonged to some item of clothing or upholstery destroyed in the fire and identifying its compounds would not be of any help so many years later. Besides, she could not warrant consuming any of the meager evidence left out of mere curiosity.

And why *was* she so curious? Why was she doing this? Because she felt guilty about Marty and Frank felt guilty about Lily. And if David Madison had any skeletons in his closet she wanted to know about them.

And the curiosity might not be so mere. Lily had suggested that Marty's death related to his college days, and now Lily was dead.

The third bag measured only two inches across. Inverted over a clean piece of paper it coughed up a ring, a blackened, dented piece of metal barely recognizable as jewelry. Theresa switched on the magnifying lamp attached to the table. Her eyes, having passed their fortieth birthday, had begun to grow balky in tight quarters.

Designed as a plain band for the most part, about one-quarter of the circumference had an overlay of a vine-like decoration, broken at one end and tapering down to two wispy tails at the other. She rubbed at it with one gloved finger, offsetting some of the tar. The vines didn't meander but entwined each other in a uniform manner, with equal space on each side, up to a leaf at their top, which protruded slightly from the edge of the ring. It seemed somehow familiar.

She turned the ring on its side and recognized the design. The two vines weren't vines, they were snakes, surrounding a central rod with wings at the top—a caduceus, sometimes used as a symbol of the medical profession. Perhaps the unfortunate McClurg had been a pre-med student. Or the ring belonged to a doctor father.

The paint can apparently contained a piece of the victim's clothing—denim cloth, of course, what else did students wear? The can seemed to weigh almost nothing and she did not open it. It seemed unlikely that a scorched piece of denim would prompt any insights and she did not want to release the compounds that a sealed paint can could easily contain, even for a quarter of a century—just in case the idea came up to re-analyze the evidence.

She put the can back in the box and picked up the papers. The fire marshal's report stated the obvious: that the ring had been found with the victim's body, having probably been on one of his fingers before the bones were crushed by the collapsing upper floor, and that the clamp and the glassware would have been used in a chemical process such as methamphetamine production. The situation seemed clear to the report's author. Analysis indicated a healthy amount of toluene with smaller amounts of acetone on the denim. No wonder the kid died. He had been soaked in solvent when the place went up.

Given the extreme volatility—the report used those exact words, extreme volatility—of the environment, the fire expanded quickly. Too quickly for him to get out, she surmised, though the report did not go out on such a limb and left the reader to imagine the scene for themselves. Perhaps the glassware exploded, spraying him with solvent. Perhaps he'd been overcome with fumes before that point.

It did point out that there were no indications of a secondary point of origin, or the presence of any sort of booby trap. It had been an accident, pure and simple.

She read the report through again but still had only Lily's vague insinuation that Marty had anything to do with this fire or Joseph McClurg. Theirs had probably not been the only meth lab operating at that time. So why would McClurg's parents or siblings or ex-girlfriend blame Marty Davis for this death, or come to extract revenge twenty-five years later?

Unless it turned out Marty Davis had been one of those other students treated for burns at the scene, and someone had decided, albeit belatedly, that Marty bore responsibility along with the scars Theresa had seen on his arm.

Theresa picked up the ring again. Twenty-five years. Perhaps McClurg had fathered a child just before his death. He or she would now be at a perfect age for violence—young enough to feel reckless, old enough to have the brains to track down the target.

Theresa wet a cotton swab with some distilled water and scrubbed at the inside surface of the ring. Perhaps she'd get really lucky and there would be some sort of engraving…but the only marking told her that the ring had been made from sterling silver. She folded up one of the preformed boxes for the swab and sealed it up anyway, having already collected it. She'd give it to Oliver later, and invent an intriguing enough story to make him test it. Or maybe the truth would suffice.

Leo appeared at her elbow, having shimmied in on little cat feet designed to give no warning to loafing staff. 'What's that? Stuff from Bingham? You know you're supposed to turn over any rubble to the Feds. They take a dim view of people filching their evidence.'

'Relax. I had enough work there to keep me busy last night without trying to do their jobs for them.' She explained, very briefly, about Marty Davis, Ken and Lily, the building on Payne Avenue and the dead student.

Leo listened without expression, and certainly without enthusiasm. 'Let me get this straight. We had a building blow up last Monday and scatter our evidence to

the winds where any Tom, Dick or Harry could contaminate it—'

'That's an exaggeration. It remained under the protection of the proper authorities at all time. We just weren't
those authorities, that's all.'

'—and then we had a cop shot, and then we had a
few more suicides and a homicide just to round out the
week, and all the clothing and evidence and accouterments from those cases are sitting in the drying room
while you poke through a box from a twenty-five-year-
old accidental fire?'

'Just curious,' she told him.

His face began to flush to an ominous shade of puce.
Not the dangerous red yet, only the puce, but it meant
she had better pull up.

'OK, OK. I will take care of the clothing examina-
tions and then—'

'Not right now you won't. Your cousin's here. He says
he needs to get enough for a search warrant on some
guy named Terry Beltran and wants to borrow you for
an experiment. I can only hope it involves needles, and
maybe electric shock.'

She blinked at him. 'My brain has been up all night
and is distinctly unhappy about it, so I'm not tracking
very well. You said Frank—'

'His word, experiment. He's in the lobby. I'll take
your box, and I took the liberty of bringing this down
for you.' He held out her tote bag with two fingers on
the straps, as if the bag or the water bottle sticking out
of the top might somehow contaminate him, which,
given the places to which she dragged it, was not entirely impossible. 'And then, Theresa—get some rest.'
Good Lord. For a moment there actual empathy flickered across Leo's face.

Forget appearing tired, exhausted or even cadaver-like. Her looks had obviously deteriorated to a new, as yet unnamed category.

And she had a date tonight.

TWENTY

THE HOUSE IN Bratenahl where Marty Davis had died
appeared exactly the same as when Theresa had last
seen it, except for the two cars in the drive which hadn't
been there on her last visit. They belonged to the dead
owner's wife and son, the latter of whom did not appreciate their visit. 'We just buried my father, you know,'
he said, a pale, slender man in his thirties.

'Is this going to take long?'

'I don't mind,' his mother, the nearly-ex-wife of the
victim said.

'This is kind of interesting. What's going to happen?'
Theresa had been perfectly comfortable in the room with
the dead man, but not with these two people watching
her as if waiting for her to launch into a tap dance. She
tried to explain, though it sounded lame even to her. 'I
was inside when the officer was shot. They want to see
if I can hear a car pulling into the drive from this room,
and also what the gunshot sounds like with and without a silencer.'

'They're going to shoot a gun out there?' the son
asked, despite the fact that Frank had gone over this
with them twice already. An expensive education obviously didn't guarantee a sharp mind.

'Only blanks. It's just the sound we're looking for.
I'm sorry to take up your time.'

'That's all right.' The mother appeared more rounded,
in both appearance and effect, yet avoided so much as

glancing at the chair where her husband had died. She kept her back to it and watched out the window, informing them all as to what the officers were doing. This might affect the experiment—if Theresa's mind was alerted that a car had pulled into the drive, wouldn't she be more likely to hear it only because she knew it was there? What did they call it, that by observing a phenomenon you could not help but affect it? Was it the Rosenthal effect? Or Heisenberg?

Theresa kept her back to the window and purposely gazed at the chair, as if she and the dead man's ghost were partners in this endeavor. There were people who said they could talk to the dead—and if ever there was a line of work for which that would be an advantage, this would be it.

'Why didn't you guys do this when you were here the first time?' the son asked. 'I had to cut an appointment short for this.'

'You didn't have to be here,' his mother pointed out.

'I need to keep an eye on things.'

'Like the silver?' Theresa could answer the first question: because Frank had received a tip that Terry Beltran, the paroled felon who bore a grudge against Marty Davis, had lost his driver's license and been reduced to getting around via bicycle. The question of whether Theresa had or had not heard a vehicle drive into the yard suddenly took on more importance, and Frank wanted a definite answer. Theresa had argued that, either way, the results would not be conclusive—she could miss a plane buzzing the house if sufficiently involved in work—but he had wanted to try.

On top of that, Mr Beltran's recently paroled former cellmate had been a talented gunsmith who specialized in making silencers. His burgeoning business in the illegal and the untraceable was how he came to be Terry Beltran's cellmate at the Youngstown state pen in the first place.

Of course, she would not be mentioning a suspect by name to these two civilians, and so said nothing. They continued without her input anyway.

The mother said, 'You're wasting your time, trying to guard your trinkets from me. Your father and I were still married. It's all mine now anyway.'

'Not if he got specific in the will.'

'Your father wouldn't make out a grocery list. What on earth makes you think he could be bothered to write a will?'

'No one was talking last time I was here,' Theresa pointed out.

'It was quiet.' The faces of mother and son, eerily similar, made it clear that the police department and its dead cop did not figure highly on their list of priorities, but they fell into a cooperative and most likely short-lived silence. Through the stillness Theresa heard the unmistakable sound of an internal combustion engine making its way toward the house.

It sounded distinct and louder than she expected. On her first visit she had been busy with the dead man, her thoughts, as usual, spinning in their own orbits, but still it seemed to her that she would have heard a car if it had approached. It was hard to tell, to adjust for the everyday autopilot of all functioning humans. One could drive home from work and not remember anything on the route, have a conversation and completely forget it five minutes later. Could she have heard the car, and her mind filtered it out as background noise?

She didn't think so. Her mind would have listened, worried that a hysterical family member had appeared on the radar. To the best of her knowledge, then, the killer did not approach by car. At least that had been—'I hear that,' the mother said. 'You can't miss it. I'd always know when he came home.'

The son said, 'This place always had crappy insulation. The wind off the lake in the winter can kill you.' A gunshot cracked through the air, startling her, making the mother jump and the son gasp. Yes, she would have heard that, too.

So the killer had used a silencer, which worried her. Silencers were common on TV but not so much in real life. They could be made at home but only for a single use, and did not work at all the way TV portrayed. The bang made as a gun is fired results not so much from the bullet leaving the barrel, but from the fireball of burning gunpowder behind it. The gases from that fireball burst out of the end of the barrel with a loud noise. A silencer gives these gases a contained place to go, which contains some of the noise but not all. Gunshots by no means become truly silent, not a discreet *phut* but more like the slam of a car door. The gun also needed to be an automatic (the gaps in a revolver's chambers defeat the purpose of a muzzle silencer), and she had not found an ejected casing.

In addition the bullet, usually moving at supersonic speeds, creates its own little sonic boom. The safety slug could have been a low-powered round designed to travel at subsonic velocity. It had been used in relatively close quarters and designed to stay in the first target it struck, so a lot of power would not be necessary.

Damn, hadn't she found a few pieces of plastic at the scene? Home-made silencers often utilized a two-liter pop bottle, which flew apart with the first shot. The killer wouldn't have had time to remove the shards of one and tape on a second in the short interval between the two shots. The second one had been louder, but still muffled, which a shredded two-liter bottle shouldn't have been able to accomplish. And why hadn't she found more than a few pieces? No, this killer had moved beyond home-made fixes downloaded from the Internet. He had something more sophisticated.

Also, the killer might have shot Marty through an opened window, retaining the casing inside the vehicle. That would explain why she hadn't heard a car door slam.

'I'm missing an appointment for this,' the son groused again.

'How important could it be?' his mother asked. 'It's not like you have a real job.' Theresa bumped into Frank and Angela as she went out the kitchen door.

'Hold up, there, pard,' he said. 'You were supposed to stay put.'

'I got claustrophobic.'

'How can a seven-bedroom house be claustrophobic?'

'Believe me, it can.' She gave him the results of their experiment.

Frank seemed to mull this over. 'That supports the idea that this Terry Beltran came up on his bike to get his revenge.'

'You weren't crazy about that theory,' Theresa reminded him.

'I wasn't until this morning, when we talked to his parole officer again.'

Angela explained to Theresa, 'Terry Beltran began to look for his ex-wife and kids the minute his feet hit real pavement. Apparently he doesn't think restraining orders apply to him. At the end of last week he finally cornered a relative and found out that the ex, who apparently wised up during Terry's most recent incarceration, had got herself and the kids out of town. No forwarding. Her own mother doesn't know where she is. The relative took three broken teeth and a sprained wrist before he could convince Terry of it, but Terry finally accepted the fact that he had no way to find her. Then he burst into tears and rode off on his Huffy. So we're figuring, without the bloodhound work to keep him busy, he turned to revenge.'

'And he's got his ex-cellmate to touch for a silencer,' Frank added.

Theresa said, 'Where would he get the money? He just got out of jail.'

'I don't know, but they always do. Maybe his cellmate owes him a favor.'

'You can't put him away for assaulting the relative?'

'He's too understanding a guy to press charges. In other words he's got a stolen credit card business to protect and doesn't want our help.' He glanced at her, glanced again. 'What's bothering you?' She scowled at the driveway, the house, the driveway.

'Come on, cuz, spill.'

'If Beltran's on a bike, then he had the sense to pick up the casing before he left.'

'Maybe he did. Or it flew somewhere in the lawn and we didn't find it.'

'We used a metal detector.' Frank shrugged. Casings and bullets could wind up anywhere, including the shoe treads of EMS staff.

'Would Marty Davis have let Terry Beltran come right up to him without at least unsnapping his weapon?'

'Beltran's been in jail. People look different. We have no idea what he wore, a hoodie, a low cap, who knows? Marty might not have gotten a look at his face until it was too late, and who knows if he would even recognize him then? Beltran was just one more arrest. A guy on a bicycle never looks too threatening, especially in this neighborhood.'

'But why so quiet? Why use a silencer? We're isolated from the other houses, why even bother?'

Angela said, 'He couldn't know he'd be able to track Davis to such an isolated spot, and had planned for a more populated site. That Davis came here just made it better.'

'I didn't hear any raised voices. Wouldn't he want to tell Marty why he was about to kill him?'

'And give him time to go for his gun?' Theresa sighed, glared at the house again. Mother and son glared back from the kitchen window, no doubt wondering when the police department would stop cluttering up their driveway. 'What's creeping me out is that maybe he kept quiet because he saw the other car in the drive, and knew Marty was not alone. Maybe he watched us both arrive.' She couldn't shake the idea of the killer standing right where she stood, watching for any sign of activity inside the house, any hint that he had a witness he now needed to dispatch as quickly and dispassionately as he had dispatched Marty Davis.

'He knew you were here,' Frank agreed.

'So why didn't he kill me?'

TWENTY-ONE

FRANK AND ANGELA went to try to find out how Terry Beltran had been spending his time since his release, leaving Theresa to her own devices. Before they left, however, she asked to know what they had found out about Kenneth Bilecki, in addition to the basic rap sheet information Angela had looked up the evening before. Frank shrugged, but Angela, with the endless curiosity about the people she encountered in their investigations, had dug a little further. Bilecki subsisted on the kindness of strangers and by working at various unskilled jobs long enough to get laid off, stringing out the sparse unemployment checks. When asked for an address he often gave a street and number off Addison, which apparently belonged to a soft-hearted friend who let him flop there once in a while. His only other appearances on the official record occurred at a methadone clinic on Carnegie, which he would visit at least twice a month. This made no sense to Theresa, as doctors used methadone to treat dependency upon opiates, such as heroin or morphine, not a stimulant like amphetamines. Apparently, when Bilecki would crash down from the high of meth, the resulting discomfort and depression convinced him that he felt pain. Since pain was usually treated with opiates—most patients at any methadone clinic had become addicted to prescription painkillers like OxyContin—Bilecki assumed that methadone would help him feel better. He very rarely convinced the medical personnel of this, but he kept trying, especially in the winter when the waiting room gave him a warm place to sit and drink free coffee. Angela had an extra copy of the appointments, which Theresa took to give to Dr Banachek. Given that Bilecki and Lily Simpson were friends, perhaps she frequented the same clinic for the same reason. It might shed some light on her medical history.

At least that had been Theresa's first, and innocent, goal. But as the taillights of the detectives' shiny car wound up the drive, Theresa realized that Bilecki liked to make his visits to the clinic on Fridays. Sometimes a Thursday, but usually Friday, around three or four in the afternoon. Maybe this fit into the schedule of whatever else he did with his time, or he had some theory that doctors would be more liberal with the prescription pad when they were trying to get out of the office and start their weekends. Today was Friday, and—Theresa checked her watch—coming up on three p.m.

It couldn't hurt to swing by. It wasn't *so* far out of her way, really, and Leo would believe her tied up with Frank and his sound experiment. Bilecki might be talkative, looking for a little comfort after hearing of his friend Lily's death. If not, no harm done.

She drove away from the expensive home. Two faces in the window watched her depart.

Twenty minutes later, having wound through the plentiful downtown traffic—rush hour began at any time after noon on Fridays—she passed between the baseball park and the Erie Street Cemetery and turned right on Carnegie, named after steel baron Andrew Carnegie. Several industries had built Cleveland, but steel led the pack…especially in Theresa's mind. It had fed and clothed her for much of her life.

The methadone clinic existed on one of those one-way streets so that she had to make several turns before she could approach it from the right direction. The old stone building could have been anything before being pressed into service for the clinic—apartments, a store, offices. The front steps were still bracketed with granite banisters that ended in a swirl, but the people resting against them appeared anything but classic. Two women and a man waited and smoked, their clothes old and their faces worn. All three gave Theresa and her car only the barest of glances as she fed a few coins into the meter and went inside.

It could have been a waiting room in any low-rent hospital. One bathroom, one white-jacketed woman behind a Plexiglas window, and one closed door leading into the rest of the building. Patients would not be permitted to wander the halls. Chairs ringed the room and made a line down the center. Every human being present turned to look at Theresa as she hesitated in the doorway, wondering who she might be and if she had an appointment, and either way would she get in before they did? The only person who did not look up was the woman behind the Plexiglas.

Most of the—her mind didn't know what to call them: junkies? clients? patients?—lounged back against the walls and more than one appeared to be asleep. Others stared with unblinking eyes at the television, streaming twenty-four-hour news with the volume turned down so low it might as well not be on, leaving viewers with nothing to do but read the cryptic tickers at the bottom of the screen. One unlucky woman had to make do with the ring of chairs in the center of the room. Without a wall to rest her head against, she had doubled forward and laid her head on arms crossed over her crossed knees.

I would need pain medication after two minutes in that position, Theresa thought.

She forced herself past the sets of eyes, over the dingy linoleum, up to the window. The white-coated woman must have heard her approach and smiled a welcome. She had graying blond hair and not enough muscle or even fat on her bones, a white wimple on her head and a large wooden cross around her neck. A nun. Theresa wondered if she worked out of St Vincent Charity Hospital. 'Hello, dear,' the woman—Betty, according to her name tag—said. 'What can we do for you?'

'I was wondering if there's a Ken Bilecki here.'

'We have no one—oh, you mean a patient?'

'Yes.'

The nun's gaze flicked over Theresa, or at least as much as was visible through a waist-high window. 'I can't give out any patient information,' she said, but gently.

'I don't need any. I only wanted to ask him if he's seen a mutual friend.' This was sort of true. She wanted to ask him about mutual acquaintances, two dead and one a mere possibility, but sort of true didn't really count with a nun. But surely Sr Betty simply wanted to know that Theresa had not come to harass the patient, which she hadn't. Bilecki had no current trouble with the law to the best of her knowledge. Unless they got to talking and he confessed to participating in a meth lab that killed a student twenty-five years ago, but Theresa would cross that bridge when the black and yellow gate lifted. 'I know he usually comes here on Fridays at about this time, and I hoped to run into him here.' Again the gaze flickered. Theresa could confuse people. She did not have the wariness, the constant alertness, to be a cop, yet there existed a sense of authority. She had grown used to this puzzled look.

But it cleared and the woman told her, 'I still can't give out any patient information. However, if you care to take a seat, he might pass by.' Theresa took the hint, smiled her thanks and turned away, nearly bumping into a block of granite thinly disguised as a man. He wore a heavy flannel shirt under a leather vest and tattoos up both sides of his neck. Various metal studs and jewelry pierced parts of his head. Theresa froze, her body warring between fight and flight.

'Excuse me,' he said solemnly. 'Hi, Sister Betty.'

'Good afternoon, Ralph, dear. What can we do for you?'

'I got my three thirty.' Theresa scoped out the seats in the waiting room. No one had moved, so she headed for the chairs in the center.

She heard the nun say, 'I see your new tattoo has healed up nicely.'

The man's voice brightened. 'Yeah. It come out good.' Theresa sat catty-corner to the hunched-over woman, their backs to each other, and focused on the TV mounted on the wall. The pretty heads there continued to talk, with only a background photo now and then to give a hint as to the content. Theresa gazed and thought, not for the first time, what a handy talent lip-reading would be.

After a while, when she felt that her fellow waiters had grown bored with the new arrival and returned to sleeping, reading and staring at their shoes, she dared to examine them.

Across from her sat a woman whose clothing belonged to a twenty-year-old, but the drugs had sucked all the youth from her skin until she appeared nearly twice that. Theresa pegged her as a factory worker and mother of at least two school-age children, a younger one learning to write or draw who had left slashes of permanent marker in two different colors on her right hand, and an older child responsible for the letter on her lap. Theresa read the heading upside down—Cleveland Metropolitan School District—and its paragraphs appeared as ominous blocks even from across the aisle. The woman read it over and over, smoothing it out with battered fingertips, three of which were bandaged. Perhaps her job required working with machines which tended to catch fingers—or her addiction problems made her fingers too careless. Or she had an abusive husband who had designed creative ways to abuse. This was the trouble with clues: they could, almost always, mean more than one thing. That was the problem with forensics, with crime investigation, with life. Interpretations could shift at any moment. Everything depended.

The black man next to the woman read nothing, couldn't see the TV from his angle and did not care to make eye contact. The premature wrinkles and sagging skin made it impossible to guess his age. The top of his skull rested against the wall and he had scooted forward in his chair to form a forty-five-degree angle with his body, long legs extending well into the aisle. She could not reach any conclusions about him. Too clean to be homeless and yet thin enough to suggest hunger. His clothes had no identifying labels and she couldn't see his hands, tucked up under his armpits. He stared, unblinking, into the middle distance. The ramrod position did not look restful and Theresa watched his chest for a few minutes to see if he still breathed. He did.

Time passed. Two people went in and two came out. Theresa checked out the other waitees, forming more theories. After approximately fifteen minutes, Ken Bilecki appeared from the inner door.

The nurses must complete the checkout procedure inside the offices because no one stopped at the window on their way out, and Bilecki was no exception. He walked directly to the door, pausing only to wave and say goodbye to Sister Betty. Theresa caught up with him in the foyer.

TWENTY-TWO

AT FIRST HE became startled by someone saying his name, but as they spilled into the street he did not find her sufficiently threatening to bolt. He did not seem to recognize her at first but then his face smoothed out. 'Oh, yeah, you were at Lily's. You're not a cop, right?'

They always knew. 'No, I work for the M.E.'s office. I would really like to talk to you for a few minutes.' He didn't bolt at this, either. In fact, Ken Bilecki seemed distinctly relaxed. Either the doctors inside had given him something for temporary relief or he simply had the usual euphoria one felt upon escaping a doctor's office. She suspected the former.

He actually smiled when he asked, 'What about?'

'About you and Lily and Marty.'

His expression became appropriately downcast. 'I am really going to miss Lily, man. Marty, too, but Lily never stopped looking out for me. That's why I came here today, I was in so much pain…now I'm really thirsty, though… I could use something to drink. Just pop would be OK.' She took the hint and guided him to a Subway, where, in the off-peak hours, they would have quiet and space in which to talk. He ordered a meatball sub with all the trimmings and some side snacks, along with the largest Coke they had.

When settled down with his sugar and starches, he said, 'Someone killed Lily, didn't they?' Theresa bit back the 'no' before it passed her teeth.

'There is nothing to indicate that. What makes you think so?'

Bleary brown eyes gazed at her solemnly. 'Well, how come she winds up dead in the same week as Marty?'

'I don't know. Why don't we start from the beginning—did the three of you meet each other in college?'

'Yeah.' He spoke around the meatballs. 'Well, I met them. They'd known each other before that, high school, I think. I met Lily in a bar and we got to talking. We all needed a place to stay—actually all of us could have stayed with our parents, but we didn't want to—so we split the rent.'

'You got an apartment on Payne Avenue,' she prompted.

The chewing paused, ever so briefly, and then a hard swallow.

'Yeah.'

'Where there was a fire in 1985. That would have been your sophomore year.'

'Well, I didn't pass two of my classes, so credit-wise I was still a freshman.'

'Did you know the student who died in the fire? Joseph McClurg?' A few words of graffiti etched into the tabletop suddenly captured his attention, and he traced them with one index finger.

Then he took a sip of Coke. Then he traced the graffiti again.

They'd be there all afternoon at this rate, and she had a—gasp!—date. 'Ken, you know I'm not a cop. I'm not interested in getting you in any sort of trouble. I only want to find out if someone could have had a grudge against Marty Davis.'

'It was so long ago.'

'Yes, it was. But it's all I have to go on at the moment.'

And before I go on that date tonight, I'd like to know if David Madison had anything to do with a meth lab that blew up and killed someone.

'I really need to hear about it.' It took waiting through the rest of his sandwich, but finally Bilecki said, 'Yes. I knew about that Joe kid.'

'He was friends with you and Marty?'

'Not me. And not a friend, really. It was business.'

'The meth business?'

'Yep.' The pace hadn't picked up much. She tried another tack. 'What kind of process did you use? Reducing ephedrine, or the phenylacetone and methylamine route?'

Lips wrapped around his drink straw, he stared at her, the huge brown eyes clearing in what seemed to be delight. 'You know how to make meth?'

'I know the rudiments—'

'We did the red phosphorus and iodine.'

'You scraped the phosphorus from match heads?'

'No! Way too labor-intensive, right? Doc and Da-Vinci were both chemistry majors and teaching assistants. They got the chemicals by ordering them, same as they ordered the stuff for students to use in class. Reagent-grade chemicals! Pure. We made the most perfect crystals ever.'

'They stole them from the college chemistry lab?'

He grinned, giving her a too-close view of meth-ravaged teeth. Chronic use of the drug had exceedingly detrimental effects on enamel. 'No. They *bought* them from the supply companies.'

'But—didn't the teachers notice—'

'No, no, that was the beauty of it. DaVinci was a genius, man.' He pushed the Coke to one side and leaned over the table, breathing out enthusiasm and garlic. 'A friend of his, Bean, set up a bank account in a name that sounded like CSU, but wasn't. Then DaVinci started separate accounts with three supply companies. Da-Vinci—teaching assistant, remember—would receive the supplies for our stuff, pay them out of our bank account, and no one ever figured it out. The teachers were ordering and receiving exactly what they wanted. The supply companies were being paid in full. No crime committed.'

Theresa pictured this. 'So DaVinci had a separate business running out of the same space as the normal college lab, with nothing to alert any of the three parties involved—school, company or bank—that something was going on.'

Bilecki slapped the table. 'Exactly! We had the sweetest set-up ever.'

'What was DaVinci's first name?'

'Uh—I don't know. We all called him DaVinci. 'Cause he was, like, a Renaissance man.'

'What about Doc? What was his name?'

The sudden onset of amnesia continued. 'Don't know that either. We were a business, man. We weren't in each other's hip pockets or anything like that. I'm not sure I ever met Doc. I dealt mostly with DaVinci. Like the guy who died—I guess he was one of our cookers, but I never met him.'

'Joseph McClurg? He wasn't Doc?'

Bilecki reclaimed his Coke cup, and considered this. 'I don't know. Could'a been. Can I have a cookie?'

'What?'

'They got those cookies here.' He pointed to the counter. She gave him two dollars and he trotted off to get his sugar fix and a napkin. She wondered why he wouldn't confirm Doc's identity—the boy had been dead for twenty-five years and had been considered guilty of meth cooking for all that time, so it could hardly be out of respect for the kid's reputation.

He returned and wiggled into the booth, neglecting to hand over her change. She let that and Doc's identity go for the moment.

'So the ingredients came from the school. And you set up the lab in the apartment you rented on Payne?'

He shook his head, spewing a few crumbs. 'No! Meth's dangerous stuff and it stinks. On top of that it's kind of incriminating to have in your own space. Here's the situation.' He gestured at her with the chocolate chip-laden cookie. 'The building we lived in had been a hotel. The landlord could squeeze a penny until the copper turned his fingers green. He bought a hotplate for each room and rented them as efficiencies. I don't think he even vacuumed the carpets before hanging out a "vacancy" sign.' Theresa nodded to show her attention, though it did not seem necessary. Ken Bilecki had been dying to relive his past, in any way, shape or form.

'It had been a hotel, right? So on the ground floor it had a kitchen and restaurant that would cost too much to rip out and certainly too much to run. So he boarded it up, used it for storage. Now, do you know what the limiting reagent is, in the manufacture of methamphetamine?' It seemed funny to hear a homeless guy talk about a chemical reaction using proper terms, but she did not smile. Obviously Ken Bilecki qualified for a PhD when it came to cooking meth. He referred to the reagent that controlled the yield of the reaction, usually whichever reagent you had the smallest amount of, percentage-wise—in the same way that if you only had one cup of sugar you could only make one batch of cookies, even if you had several sacks of flour.

She ran through the process in her head. The ephedrine would be extracted from cold pills with methanol, then washed with acetone, then boiled with toluene. Sodium hydroxide would be added to change the pH, then condensed, then distilled, then crystallized with hydrochloric acid.

Methanol, acetone and toluene. No wonder the place went up like a Roman candle soaked in kerosene and placed on a pile of paraffin and straw.

Back to the limiting reagent. 'The iodine?' she guessed.

He shook his head, delighted to have stumped her. 'Heat.' She raised her eyebrows.

'Heat,' he insisted. 'You have to heat the oil bath for the reaction, and later the flasks for the distillation process, for hours. A stove in your average kitchen can give you about two kilowatts of power. This limits the size of the flask, or number of flasks, you can heat at any one time.'

'Oh. But—'

'But our kitchen wasn't average. It had been designed to feed a few hundred people. We could double the batch, triple, quadruple. We could cook enough in one session for two months of sales.'

'Didn't your fellow tenants complain of the smell?'

'Sometimes, yeah. We set up ventilation fans and the exhaust vents already went directly to the roof… I suppose to keep the kitchen smells from the rest of the building, back when it had been a hotel. I bet it had been a pretty nice hotel,' he added, momentarily distracted by the thought of a glorious heyday for his old home. 'Solid, you know? Anyway, I'm sure they smelled it, but they were kids, like us. No one would have ratted us out. No one did.'

'So you cooked a whole lot of meth.'

'Exactly! I'd find the customers, then me or Lily would make the deliveries. Usually in the hallways, student lounges, sometimes right in class.'

'And still, no one noticed?'

'Of course not. It was school, man. Kids trade stuff all the time, pens, calculators, notes.'

Theresa ran down the personnel in her head. 'Where did Marty come in?'

'Not that much, really. He'd go with Lily lots of times to make deliveries, make sure nothing bad happened to her. Customers tended to pay up a lot quicker with Marty standing there. Lily, they'd give her a sob story or invite her to a party, and she'd let them slide. She was soft-hearted, like me.'

'Then she and Marty would give the money back to DaVinci?'

'Yeah.'

'Any problems there?'

'Hell, no. The proceeds would all go back into the school account—well, the fake school account—to pay for the chemicals. And we'd go round again. I told you it was the sweetest set-up ever.'

'You didn't make a profit?'

A full-throated laugh floated up from his belly. 'Hell, yeah! The extra money would go into another account and Bean would pay our rent out of it. Then he split the profit equally among us. It kept me in shoes and babes and meth—DaVinci made me pay for mine, the cheap bastard—the whole time.' He sighed. 'It was perfect.'

'Until the fire.'

The laughter ended. 'Yeah. Until the fire.'

'Were you there when it started?'

'No, man. I wish I had been, maybe I could have done

something. I'd gone to a party, and when I came back, one-fourth of the building was wet ashes.'

'What went wrong?'

The happy memories went up in smoke. 'I don't know. I didn't know who that guy was who died and what he screwed up to make the place go up like that. DaVinci thought it had something to do with the sodium hydroxide. He was mad as hell, too. I never saw him that mad.' NaOH—otherwise known as lye, it could explode on contact with water, but that shouldn't have occurred during the meth process. Unless Joe McClurg had made a mistake.

'What did sodium hydroxide have to do with it?'

'You have to condense the pseudoephedrine crystals with the iodine and red phosphorus over a hot oil bath. Then you add sodium hydroxide to bring the pH up, but DaVinci seemed to think that the guy added ammonium hydroxide instead,' Bilecki explained morosely. 'I don't know, and I didn't really care. He kept muttering about NaOH and NH-four-OH and the oil bath, and I kept asking where we were going to cook meth now.'

'Where did you?'

His face crashed into wrinkles of pain. 'We didn't. DaVinci said he was tired of the whole mess and he couldn't do it without Doc anyway. Time to go our separate ways. I thought maybe he wanted to start again on a smaller scale, cut the rest of us out—because by then he thought I had gotten kind of…unreliable. But if he did, he did it somewhere else, because the whole campus went into a meth shortage without us. I flunked out and so did Marty and Lily. It just fell apart.' He sighed. The best time of his life had ended.

'Did the police suspect you?'

'Nope. I mean, they questioned all of us, everyone

who lived in the building, but no one 'fessed up and they couldn't tie us to it. Any of the tenants could have broken into the kitchen.'

'The other students staying there didn't tell them—'

'We were careful going in and out of the lab, we'd use this back service hallway from the restaurant. Everyone in the place knew *someone* was cooking meth, but I guess they didn't know who.'

'What about the money?'

'Cops never found the dummy accounts. Bean officially closed them, even wrote a letter to the suppliers that the school had discontinued the study program, so that no one would be calling the school looking for our fake department. Then he closed the bank accounts the next day. Even if the cops found them, they couldn't tie them to any of us. DaVinci thought of everything.'

Quite the criminal mastermind. 'Did you know Joe McClurg?'

'The dead kid? No.'

'Then what was he doing in your lab?'

'Cooking, I guess. I never knew who did all the cooking. DaVinci wouldn't let me near it.'

'Wasn't Joe who you call Doc?' she pressed again.

'Sure, could'a been. What difference would it make?' he asked, still mourning the loss of twenty-five years ago.

'Because maybe someone shot Marty in revenge for his death.' Bilecki snorted.

'Maybe it was DaVinci.'

'Hah!' The more Bilecki thought about it, the funnier it seemed, and he burst into giggles. 'DaVinci never cared about anyone else in his life. And besides, why would he blame Marty? Why would anyone blame

Marty? He only worked as a collector now and then, he had nothing to do with the lab or the actual cooking.'

'Then maybe someone who didn't know that, someone who knew Marty was part of the operation but not what part. Or who didn't care, held you all equally responsible.'

Bilecki paled a bit. 'Wow.'

'Did this Joseph McClurg have parents? Brothers or sisters?' Siblings often attended the same school and might know the same players. Though why it would take them twenty-five years to catch up to Marty Davis—whose name and address appeared in the phone book, she had checked—Theresa could not guess.

'I told you, I didn't know him.'

'What did it say in the newspaper? Reporters would have interviewed the family.'

'I don't read the paper.' He made it sound roughly equivalent to joining the rowing team or wearing a pink tutu. 'You think this person killed Lily too?'

She tried to keep him on topic. 'What did DaVinci say about Joe? You all must have rehashed the incident over and over in the next few weeks.'

'Not really. He said to scatter, stay away from each other so the cops and the teachers wouldn't notice us. We had to find other places to stay anyway. The apartments were condemned. The few times we were together, DaVinci kept talking about the sodium hydroxide and getting Bean to close all the accounts, and telling me that we couldn't cook more meth.' He sighed. Theresa hoped that, with the years fallen away, he could see how truly callous their actions had been. A boy their age, a friend or at least an acquaintance, had been killed working by their side and they had covered their tracks and denied even knowing him.

But then Bilecki said, 'It really was the sweetest set-up ever.' In the story she had told Frank, the fingerless addict learned to work a cigarette lighter with his palms in order to continue smoking meth. The single-mindedness of the addict.

'And no one ever came looking for McClurg's acquaintances, asking questions about what he'd been doing? I mean, after the original canvass regarding the fire.'

'Canvass?'

'When the cops questioned all the neighbors to see if anyone saw anything or knew anything. It's called a canvass.'

'Oh. No. No one ever asked us another thing.'

'What about other than cops? Other students? The victim's family?'

'No. No one knew we had anything to do with it. We got away clean.' At least he did not seem triumphant or even proud of that, simply stated it as fact. They had gotten away, and DaVinci, at least, had had the sense to quit while ahead.

A thought struck her. Instead of the shooter tracking Marty down to get revenge, perhaps Marty had done the tracking—but not for revenge. For blackmail. 'DaVinci, and Bean—were those their real names?'

He blinked, slurped his cola. 'I guess.'

'First names or last names?'

'Dunno.'

'Could be nicknames?'

'I guess.'

She stifled a sigh. 'What happened to them? Did you ever see them again?'

'Nah. Went out of state. Probably never came back.'

He seemed a little squirmy on this point, though he seemed squirmy in general.

'Are you sure? This could be really important, Ken.'

'Pretty sure.' *Slurp*.

Frank had once arrested a meth cooker who had been outside when the police arrived. Instead of going into his house, which contained an arsenal sufficient to hold the cops off for days, the man had stretched out, face down, in his yard's drainage ditch, convinced the officers would not be able to see him there. Most of Ken's life could well be a blur by this point. 'Could Marty have looked one or both of them up? Maybe demanded some money or he'd go public with the fact that they'd been partially responsible for Doc's death?'

'Marty? Blackmail someone? You got to be shittin' me, man. When Marty became a cop, he became a cop. Straight arrow. No drugs. No bribes. No shakin' down hookers.' Bilecki grew more adamant with every word. 'He didn't do *none* of that. I *knew* him, man.'

'You're probably right,' she soothed. 'Why would he wait twenty-five years, anyway? He could easily have found them before that, right?'

'Yeah, exactly. He was a cop, he could find anybody. Besides, he never tried to get anything from Lily or me, and he certainly knew where to find us.' She didn't point out how there would be no sense in blackmailing people who couldn't pay. But again, why wait twenty-five years, unless he had lost track of his fellow students? Or if they didn't have any money to take until now, or if he didn't particularly need any until now.

But she had no reason to think Marty had any sudden need for cash. To all appearances he had been perfectly content with his life.

What about the accountant? 'What was Bean's real name again?'

'It was *Bean*, man. But I hardly ever saw him. He stayed on one end of the production line and I stayed on the other.'

She swallowed, then enunciated each syllable as she asked: 'Was his name David Madison?'

'No.' But the question gave him pause. He drained the last of his Coke with a noisy gurgle, and frowned.

'Do you know David Madison?'

'No…yeah! I know who he is!' Her throat seemed to plummet to the bottom of her stomach, like a dumb waiter with a cut rope.

'He's married to the chick teacher who slept with the little boy!'

The rope began to repair itself. 'I thought you didn't read the papers.'

'I saw it on TV, a couple of years ago. They say she's still in touch with the kid. That's messed up, man. That's really messed up.'

'Yeah,' Theresa agreed.

'I mean, why couldn't they have teachers like that when I was in school?' Theresa rubbed her forehead.

TWENTY-THREE

SHE BOUGHT KEN BILECKI another sandwich, two cookies and a Coke for the road, and headed down the alley to Carnegie. The spring sun had fallen behind the buildings, plunging the streets into a night-like gloom. The nine-to-fivers had already fled to their respective 'burbs and she passed no one.

Even Carnegie's traffic had dropped far below daytime levels and she could cross it in safety, pondering what she had learned from Ken Bilecki. All in all, it didn't seem to be much, save for the intricate details of their illegal methamphetamine lab operation. A student had died back then but this seemed unlikely to have any connection to Marty Davis dying now. Maybe she should leave the cop's death to those who got paid for it, like her cousin, and get back to her own job of examining clothing and analyzing gunshot residue and figuring out just what they were going to do with that garage crammed with old evidence.

She paused, the heels of her shoes sounding abnormally loud against the concrete sidewalk.

Four men were hanging around her car; one had actually seated himself on the hood. Not that they had a lot of vehicles to choose from, as only hers remained on the street. They wore a common uniform of oversized pants, oversized athletic shoes, skintight T-shirts with warm-up jackets lettered with embroidered words so large she couldn't make sense of them. Shiny jewelry. A bulge at one's hip that had to be a gun. At least two cell phones each hanging at their waistbands. Expressions that bore no resemblance to the spaced-out, uncaring looks she'd seen in the methadone clinic waiting room—these faces seemed thoughtful, guarded and very, very aware.

She stopped, considering her options. She could call their bluff, get in her car and drive away, leaving the one on the hood to fall or jump to the pavement. There might be women with the right attitude to pull that off, but Theresa knew she was not one of them, and even if she were would not want to bet her safety on a risky play like 'attitude'. Nor did she fool herself into thinking that because she was in a public place before dark, nothing bad could happen to her.

She could retreat inside the methadone center, call for a patrol drive-by, but the clinic's closed, dark door made it clear that the staff had gone.

The men didn't move, didn't speak to each other. They merely watched her, and waited.

A car drove by. A man in a jacket and tie spoke on his cell phone, eyes on the road, not glancing at Theresa. She considered throwing herself in front of him, but figured he would simply run her over and continue on.

That left turning and running—unlikely to help if they truly pursued, since she had never been able to run very fast, and making her look quite foolish if they didn't. But she had looked foolish before and surely would again.

Or she could take out her cell phone now and dial 911. She hated to take up their time with escort service, but she had heard it a million times—*trust your instincts. If something feels wrong, it probably is.*

She didn't have time for this. Didn't these guys know she had a *date* tonight?

She had dialed the first digit when someone grabbed her.

A strong hand clenched her arm, and her mind mentally clenched a fist. *You idiot! How could you not think to look around you, that they might be a distraction while one came up behind*—'Good evening,' Sister Betty said. 'Did you and your friend have a nice chat?'

'Uh.'

'Is that your car, my dear?'

'Uh-huh.' The little nun looped one bony hand though Theresa's arm.

'Well, you'd better move it. I think the meter expired. It's after hours, but we don't want some traffic cop getting any ideas, do we?'

'Um—no.' Theresa allowed herself to be guided up the sidewalk, toward her own car and the waiting group, keys clutched in her trembling hand, wondering if the tiny knife attached to them would discourage or merely annoy the men. 'But, Sister—'

'Mario, get off this lady's car. I hope you didn't scratch the paint.' The man on the hood slid off with a sheepish grin. Sheepish or wolfish, Theresa couldn't decide.

'No, Sister Betty. No scratches.'

'Good boy. Good evening, DeJean, how is your mother?'

'She's a little better,' the biggest of them said. He stepped backwards, carefully, scraping his soles along the concrete, his feet checking for obstructions before taking the next step. His gaze never left the two women.

Theresa sucked in shallow breaths. Perhaps this was not smart, perhaps Sister Betty was relying on attitude as well and that might not be the best course…she tried to get the key in the lock without looking away from the men, failed, and chanced one split-second glance to do it. 'Can I drop you somewhere, Sister?'

'Oh, no, these boys are going to walk me home.' Door open, men on the other side of the car, sufficient time to get in and close it, but first she turned to the little nun.

'Are you sure? I could—'

'Oh, quite sure,' she trilled. 'They do it every night. Now you have a pleasant evening, dear, and bless you.'

'You too,' Theresa breathed, and got in, shutting the door but not locking it, as some sort of show of good faith and apology, boys, for assuming you were a bunch of gang-bangers. She turned the key but waited there until Sister Betty had crossed in front of her grill and climbed back on to the sidewalk, where she took De-Jean's arm and began to stroll up Carnegie Avenue. The other three fell into a tight grouping and all of them began to chat with no little animation.

Theresa said some extra prayers on the way home, including several for Sister Betty.

TWENTY-FOUR

SHE HAD NOT yet passed the Denison Road exit before her phone trilled.

'You wanted to know the toxicology reports on the Simpson woman?'

'Yes, Oliver. Thank you.'

'Whatever. Normally, of course, I would not be allowed to release this sensitive and confidential information, but our new doctor of the unpronounceable name left an imperious and illegible sticky note instructing me to do so.'

'Kotylyarevsky. He's from Moldavia. And if it's illegible, how did you know what it said?' No response, until she began to wonder if he'd hung up or if she'd truly stumped him, not a wise thing to do when she needed information.

But he went on with: 'Here are the results—the unfortunate Ms Simpson had taken a lot of meth.'

Theresa braked, momentarily stuck behind a box truck driving, of all things, at the speed limit. 'No surprise there.'

'A *lot* of meth.'

She found herself glancing at the cell phone in surprise. Oliver didn't usually emphasize, or repeat himself. 'Define a *lot*.'

'Enough to intoxicate five men of greater body weight than her.'

'But she didn't seem out of her mind. And she didn't overdose.'

'No,' Oliver agreed. 'She did not.'

'Are you saying that she took enough meth to over-dose?'

'I'm saying she took enough meth to die instantly.'

'Move, buddy!' she fumed at the driver of the box truck. To Oliver, she said: 'That doesn't make any sense.'

'No. It does not,' Oliver agreed again. 'Are you driving while you're on the phone?'

'Hey, you called me. My eyes have never left the road.'

'Refusing to check your mirrors once in a while is nothing to be proud of.'

'How do you explain that? The meth levels?'

'I can't. Not to you, or to anyone else who doesn't have at least a master's in organic chemistry.' Theresa looked over her shoulder, signaled and merged into the right lane with a quick jerk. Her bottle of lightly flavored water fell on to the passenger seat floor and she left it. After three Diet Cokes with Ken Bilecki, the last thing she felt was thirsty. Then she said, 'Try.'

'You know that methamphetamine stimulates the nervous system by releasing neurotransmitters, norepinephrine, dopamine, serotonin, etc.'

'Yes.'

'The amphetamine then metabolizes to four-hydroxy-methamphetamine. That's what I find in her bodily fluids, more or less. But there's another compound present, some form of amphetamine but with a few extra—OH bonds. So I checked the residues from that baggie and pipe you took out of her pocket. Same thing—extra compounds.'

'A designer drug?'

'A new one, if so. It's not MDA, it's not ecstasy, it's not one of the local variations.' She slowed through the notorious Linndale speed trap.

'New, and dangerous. It makes the user much higher?'

'Not exactly. Try to follow: the meth stimulates the neurotransmitters to release dopamine into the system. The person feels high. Normally, the cells have safety mechanisms that take up this excess dopamine, but meth blocks those reuptake transporters. The meth also blocks the synthesis and release of serotonin. Levels of the dopamine and other neurotransmitter levels become low as the ones dumped into the system pass away and fresh ones are not immediately available.'

'The downside,' Theresa said, meaning the crash and depression that most users experienced.

'It's a somewhat gradual process as the dumped neurotransmitters pass out of the system. But in this case, the extra compounds riding along with the metabolites bond with the OH and the NH group on the dopamine.' He said this as if it were important. 'OK.'

'Bond with it,' he emphasized, 'and don't let go.'

'So the meth isn't making them very euphoric?'

'Not if the neurotransmitters are bound up instead of doing their happy dance. The chemist could adjust this effect by mixing regular meth with the adulterated version. A small amount of the latter would not make much of a difference, but a large amount would change the entire experience.'

Theresa could not have drawn the exact chemical pathways on a piece of paper, but felt she was getting the picture. 'So the high wouldn't necessarily have been higher, but the low would have been lower.'

'Exactly. The user thinks their dose is a dud, and takes more to get to that up stage. Then instead of sliding into the down stage, they're plunged into it. Not, of course, that any of this is easily discovered—I'm definitely going to get into the *Journal of Forensic Sciences* with this one.' She could hear his voice smile at the thought of his name in print.

'So first it made Lily Simpson a little high, and then it threw her down a black hole.' She hit the brakes for the daily slowdown at the 71–480 split. 'Who would invent such a thing?'

'Someone who wants to rid the city of meth addicts?' Oliver suggested.

'Or one particular one.'

TWENTY-FIVE

THERESA'S BED BECKONED to her. *Come and lie with me, love*, it said. *You're tired. You need rest.* She could almost hear it speak, in deep Barry White undertones. *Just for a minute.*

She resisted, too occupied in clawing through her closet with increasingly desperate motions, trying to keep the damp towel from slipping off her damp body, wondering what the hell a forty-year-old woman wore on a first date. She couldn't even remember what a twenty-year-old had worn on her first dates.

It had been that long since she'd had a date that hadn't been simply going to dinner with a man she knew fairly well already. David Madison was a stranger, possibly a stranger with an unpleasant and criminal past. So, the red satin shirt? Or the white camisole?

Perhaps he had asked her out only to keep an eye on the investigation into Marty Davis' death? After all, why her? A man with David Madison's boyish handsomeness must encounter any number of women willing to help ease him through the pain of his ex-marriage. Theresa was old, with a weird job and a belly getting soft and laugh lines—oh, let's be honest, crow's feet—and a pimple forming on her left temple.

And why the hell was she wasting time on a date anyway, when a mad bomber, a cop killer and a fatally virulent methamphetamine stalked Cleveland?

Because the Feds wouldn't share their information

about the bomb site, Frank had the cop killer in his sights and there didn't seem to be much she could do about Lily's meth supplier. They'd already released the scene and Oliver would alert CPD Vice to the new version of the drug.

So she had time for a date. David Madison had asked when she had lank hair and no make-up and hadn't slept in twenty-six hours, so she couldn't look any worse, right?

Except that now it had increased to thirty-seven hours, and she couldn't deny the pimple. Maybe some Oxy 10— The doorbell rang. He couldn't be early, could he? She would *not* answer the door wrapped in a towel like some meet-cute in a rom-com. He'd have to wait. Unless it were the FedEx man, because she had ordered a few books. It couldn't be her mother, who would simply come in and shout a hello.

That left the FedEx guy or David Madison, and for either case she pulled on a pair of jeans and the white camisole. She didn't want David to think of her as some dweeb who couldn't even handle being ready for a date on time, and she didn't want to frighten off the FedEx guy before he could leave her order.

She opened the door just in time to remember that her hair remained damp and she hadn't covered up the pimple.

It wasn't the FedEx guy. David Madison had foregone the shirt and tie ensemble of the workday and softened into a plain beige tee under a blue button-down shirt of such quality it made Theresa wonder if his wife had chosen it for him, it suited his eyes so well.

'Hi,' he said. 'I see I have the right place.'

'Come in. I'm sorry I'm running a little late.' *Little?* She didn't even have socks on. She hadn't opened her mail or fed the cat or patted the dog, the small but very firm routines a single person develops. But she'd have to worry about that later.

'I'm not surprised, after the day you've had.'

She closed the door. 'Where are we going?'

He snickered as she guided him into the kitchen. 'I'm sorry, I got distracted thinking up smart-aleck answers like, do you mean metaphorically speaking or in a more literal sense? As in, will the human race overcome its baser instincts or did I have a restaurant in mind? But you're probably not in the mood for smart-aleck answers, are you?'

'That would depend on their level of wit,' she said, noticing with some dismay half a sink full of dirty dishes, and whirled around to keep him trapped in the hallway. 'I'll settle for the literal sense.'

'Don's Pomeroy House? According to Google, it's designed to leave a favorable impression on one's date.' There was that word again. 'And only ten minutes away. Perfect in all respects.'

'I'm sorry,' he said, with a gentle smile and no trace of smart aleck. 'You really are tired, aren't you?'

'Oh, I don't know. I think I'm getting a second wind. But I'll have to change into something better.'

'That's a pity—I mean, you look—you look great in that,' he stumbled, and changed the subject. 'Is this your daughter?' After Rachael left for her first year of college, Theresa took the liberty of erecting a mother's shrine: a series of similar frames along one wall. Left to right, they began with Rachael in infancy and progressed, two or three years at a time, to her high school graduation.

'What gave it away?' He peered at each one, then stepped back against the opposite wall to take in the whole array at once.

'This is nice. I should do this for my boys, even though they'd probably sue me for gross embarrassment. I don't have any artistic ability, anyway. Our house is like a locker room—a little disgusting, but we like it.'

'Good.'

'You miss your daughter a lot?'

'I do. But I'm better about it now.'

'Good.' In the closeness of the narrow hallway she could smell his aftershave, or cologne…whatever it was, she liked it. 'Before we go, there's one thing I'd like to get out of the way.'

'What?'

What, indeed? She hadn't intended to say this, but now she had to keep going. 'When you went to Cleveland State, did you know a Ken Bilecki?'

No one could fake such blankness. 'No.'

'You said you knew Marty because of your wife's case?'

A puzzled frown. 'Yes.' She explained about the year-book photo she'd just happened to see, leaving out the part about looking up his school picture like a lovesick tween. The story still made him look at her a bit oddly, but she couldn't blame him for that.

He nodded. 'Yeah. Marty and I had a class together. English, I think…and we'd hang in the bar with a group of regulars. I didn't see him again until my wife's arrest. He came with the detective—Deirdre taught in Cleveland, so it was their case—recognized me, and after everyone left he gave me the rundown on what would happen, the booking, the arraignment, and so on. He kept tabs on the case, would try to give me the heads-up when the detectives were going to question our friends and when the prosecutor would announce the charges, that sort of thing. He couldn't do much, being a road of-

ficer, but he did what he could. He was a good guy.' She
put her hand on his arm again, but this time she felt a bit
guilty about it, as if trying to soften the fact that she had
just questioned him about a cold case under the guise of
romance. But the fact that it wasn't a guise made it even
more important to know the extent of his involvement
with Marty Davis' past.

'Did you know a friend of Marty's they called Da-
Vinci?'

His eyes flickered, as if they had seen an incoming
blow. 'No.'

'Are you sure?'

'Yes. Why are you asking me about Marty?'

She removed her hand. 'Because he died at my feet.'

After a moment, he said, 'I'm sorry. I'm sure that
must have been terrible. But what does Marty's college
career have to do with some felon gunning him down
last week?'

'Maybe nothing. Maybe everything. What about Doc?
Do you remember a Doc?' He shook his head, and she
hated to see the warmth begin to fade from his face. If
she ruined this date, she'd regret it forever.

But then, if she never asked…

'There were a lot of kids called Doc in college. Usually the ones who sold drugs. But that has nothing to
do with Marty. He was a good guy…loyal to a fault.'

'Why do you say that?' she pressed.

'Look at what he did for me—just some guy he used
to have a beer with, and he went through a lot of effort
for me. It's the way he was.'

'When was the last time you saw Marty?'

His weight shifted from one side to the other. 'Maybe
once after the trial, about two years ago. I'm not sure.'

'Did you know a Lily Simpson?'

The warmth definitely fled and left behind a calculating look, as if he had two columns whose totals did not agree. 'Marty dated a girl named Lily, in college. Why?'

'When did you last see her?'

He snorted. 'If it's the same woman, probably twenty-five years ago. *Why?*'

'Because she's dead too.' The words hung over her dim hallway, dampening down the life around them to make room for the death. He would ask a question now, and she waited for it before moving on.

'How?'

'Overdose.'

'Oh.' That answer relieved him. Because she hadn't been murdered, like Marty? Because it made him unlikely to suffer the same fate?

'Did you have—'

'Is this an interrogation or a date?' he asked simply.

She looked at him, his handsome solidness, and felt that if she closed her eyes she'd be able to locate him in a room by feel alone, picking up the aura through an outstretched hand. 'I'd really like it to be a date.' The longing in her voice startled her, and seemed to surprise him.

Maybe we don't know how lonely we are until we stop being it.

He reached out, ran one thumb along her cheek. 'Then maybe there's something else we should get out of the way.' Slowly but steadily he used both hands to pull her closer. Then one went around her waist while the other cupped her cheek, both burning wherever they touched. His mouth came down to meet hers, pressing lightly, then a little more firmly, then, lips opening, harder still. It gave her plenty of time to resist if she wanted to, if she could.

She didn't, and couldn't.

After one panicked thought trying to recall if she had brushed her teeth, she stepped into it, their torsos now up against each other, a shock of heat that made her gasp. His fingers on her face slipped around to her neck, twining through her hair until her mouth opened and his tongue ran along the inside of her lower lip. The hand at her waist moved first up and then down, guiding her hips to his. She stepped in further, leaving him no room for retreat if he wanted to, if he could.

This isn't me, said one of the few coherent thoughts bouncing through her brain. *I don't do this. Not with someone she'd only just met, and knew so little about.*

But apparently she did, because her toes arched to get her face closer to his and her hands pulled out the bottom of his T-shirt so her fingers could touch the peach-fuzz feeling of skin and hair underneath. Clothes suddenly seemed an encumbrance, an artificial barrier between humans that had grown wearisome. She stroked upward from his stomach to his chest and it became his turn to gasp.

Then her fingers found a channel to follow, a streak through the soft hair where the skin stayed abnormally flat and smooth. Like a river. Or a burn.

She tilted her head back slightly, giving him only enough room to say, 'It's a scar. I got caught in a fire a long time ago.'

With her lips one-quarter inch from his and still tingling with hunger, she asked, 'On Payne Avenue?'

TWENTY-SIX

To FRANK'S DISMAY, the new-car smell had begun to fade. On top of that, Angela had introduced contraband.

'I thought we agreed.'

She sipped from the foam cup, the aroma of fresh-ground beans infiltrating the upholstery without pause. 'We're parked. This doesn't count.'

'How do you figure that?'

'It can't spill. The car isn't moving.'

'You've never spilled something when you weren't in a moving car?' She appeared to give this some thought, then more thought, then apparently gave up any attempt to answer because, of course, he was right.

'Well, why don't we get out and go serve our search warrant and then I won't be drinking coffee in the new car?'

'Nah. According to the group home coordinator, Beltran always comes back for dinner. The man does not miss a meal, ever.'

'Searching his room might go easier if he's *not* here.'

'Yeah, but guys get really ticked off when forced to watch you toss their stuff. Ticked-off guys say things they shouldn't say and without waiting for a lawyer. I want him here. If he doesn't show up for the chow line, we'll go ahead without him. It's only another ten minutes.'

'OK.' Angela often got antsy about working overtime. She didn't like her son to have too many unsupervised hours after school let out, worried about what that might lead to. They had both seen how the guys in handcuffs seemed to get younger every year. He covered her hand with his.

'There he is,' Angela said, gesturing with the cup.

'Don't—'

'It didn't spill.' He examined the carpet to be sure, but then turned his head to watch ex-convict Terry Beltran approach the Calgary halfway house on East Forty-Ninth. The man's history didn't quite match his description. He had no more than average musculature and weight.

He had only one tattoo and the sleeve of his shirt covered it. His short hair and trimmed goatee could look either sinister or mischievous, depending on the clothing he wore. Put him in a shirt and tie and he could be a banker with a maverick streak. Today he strode along in a very average pair of jeans and an oversized football jersey, not particularly intimidating until you added the knit cap and the irritated way he swung his arms. Then he became someone you would cross the street to avoid.

'Let's go,' Frank said. He and Angela exited their vehicle, Angela taking her cup with her, so at least he didn't have to worry about her setting it on the floor and then knocking it over upon re-entry. Behind them, two guys emerged from a marked unit to join in.

Beltran saw them, had seen them the moment Frank touched the door handle, and bolted—but not away. Instead, he turned and ran up the sagging wooden steps into the house.

'Damn,' Frank sighed.

Angela dropped her cup in the middle of East Forty-ninth and launched herself toward the house. She and Frank took the steps in unison, and he thought the combined pounding would rip off the entire porch. But the house had withstood plenty of pursuing cops over the years and barely quivered.

Frank could see Beltran's feet disappearing up the top of the stairs as he yanked open the screen door, which had swung shut behind their felon. A skinny, middle-aged black woman stood behind a heavy reception desk and gave them a look which would have stopped a bullet train, but momentum kept Frank going. He slowed only long enough to shout 'Police! Warrant!' before his foot hit the first step. Somewhere on the second floor, a door banged.

Beltran had gone to the right, right, as they came through the screen door? 'Did he go—' Frank asked Angela, or at least began to ask Angela. But when their feet, still in unison, hit the seventh or eighth step, the entire house exploded into a white heat of light and sound, and he felt himself falling backward, falling while knowing that eventually his head and the rest of his body would come into contact with something hard and it would not be pleasant, yet unable to stop his mental debate as to whether Beltran had turned to the right or the left.

TWENTY-SEVEN

THEY SAT AT her kitchen table, the polished oak slab having been the scene of many a confession over the years. Theresa had learned a lot while seated on one of the four striped cushions: that her husband had lost his job for sleeping with the boss's wife, that Rachael had developed a crush on Matt Devereau in her algebra class, and that there is no good way to tell a sixteen-year-old that her parents are splitting up.

Now she waited to learn whether or not the man she had fallen for had once been a party to drug dealing, fraud and manslaughter.

'So you were Bean,' she prompted after blowing the steam from her teacup. Brewing a cup had given her heart rate and other bodily indicators time to slow down from the too-brief make-out session in the hallway. She hadn't wanted to stop. Even now, she felt willing to ignore everything she had learned about crystal meth and explosions and dead students just to get his arms around her again. But she had to know the truth before going any further. She had an obligation to report a crime, though the statute of limitations on the drug charges would have run out by now, surely. And as long as the death had been accidental…maybe it had something to do with pride. She would not love a man who lied to her. Not again.

'Yeah, I was Bean,' he said, finally turning his gaze up from the table's surface. The fact didn't come as a surprise, but the way it made her feel as if her heart had slid five inches down her spine did. 'Look, I'll—I'll tell you everything, but you can't tell anyone else. Not your boss, not the police, especially not your cousin.'

'How did you know Frank Patrick is my cousin?'

'It said so in the article about Marty's death.'

'Oh.' The media did mention the fact every so often, either because they found it suspicious and indicative of some Vast Government Conspiracy against innocent civilians, or because they simply thought it was cute. 'I'm not trying to get you in trouble, David. I know it was twenty-five years ago.'

'It's not for me, it's for my kids. I have to protect them.' He leaned forward, blue eyes still shocking in the intensity of their color. 'My ex-wife comes up for parole next month. I would really like to keep her in jail—not to be vindictive, but it would solve the whole question of whether or not she's entitled to custody. But I have to assume she'll be released, at least until she violates her parole by contacting that kid again, and I know she will; she'll probably stop at the first pay phone outside the prison—'

'David.'

'Sorry. I mean, she's sure to get visitation rights and there's a good chance a judge will give her custody. Her parents will give her a place to live and her lawyer— she's got a good lawyer—will harp on details like Anthony flunking English and Jake getting suspended for three days for using a cell phone in class and that concussion he had last fall, even though I bought him a helmet for the skateboard but he won't wear it because it's not cool. I took it away after that until he promised to but I think sometimes when I'm not home—'

'David.' She put one hand on his wrist, risking the

disruption to her emotions that the physical contact brought on. 'No one's going to give custody to a parent who just got out of jail.'

'They might if the other parent produced and sold drugs that caused the death of a kid.' This harsh reality settled over them. Now she understood why he always seemed to walk with his shoulders pressed down—not to downplay his height but because he felt the weight of his children's future on them.

She put her hand over his, and again felt that rush of blood from the contact. Despite that, she would not promise to keep a secret from Frank. 'Your crime occurred twenty-five years ago. Hers was three.'

'In the eyes of a lot of people, hers wasn't much of a crime.'

She didn't know what to say to that, and fudged some more. 'I already know most of what occurred twenty-five years ago. But if anything is going to...*happen* between us, I need to hear it from you, David.' He hesitated so long she thought he might refuse, and had time to ponder what she should do if he did. Could she really blame him for placing his kids above some new squeeze? Did she care? Could she, in good conscience, bed him anyway? After all, who was the dead Joe McClurg to her?

But what if it *did* have something to do with why Marty Davis had bled out next to her car?

What if it didn't?

'Yeah,' David said again. 'I was Bean.' She didn't move, didn't breathe, for fear he would stop.

'As in bean counter,' he went on. 'DaVinci loved to hand out nicknames, like we were all Russian spies or something.' Or so that twenty-five years later, Ken Bilecki couldn't remember Madison's real name, only his assigned tag. DaVinci seemed to be a guy who thought ahead.

'I set up two accounts for us, one at Ameritrust and one at Ohio Savings. We used the business account to pay the chemical supply companies, and our profits went into the other one, the checking account, so DaVinci could pay the rent and the other expenses. We'd all have to buy cold pills, spreading ourselves over every suburb down to Akron so that none of us went into the same store twice in six months. He kept track.'

'I'll bet he did.' She sipped the hot liquid. Theresa drank coffee for caffeine, but tea for comfort. 'Where is DaVinci now?'

'No idea.' He looked her straight in the eyes when he said it, too. But then, he'd been looking her in the eyes since they'd met, when he told her he knew Marty Davis through his wife's case and had never heard of Doc.

'It sounds like he ran your lives for about a year, and you have no idea what his real name is?'

'He ran the business, not our lives. All I had to do was place the orders, write out the checks and buy Sudafed once in a while. I had nothing to do with cooking or selling the drugs. I'm not making an excuse, Theresa, I'm not saying I'm any less guilty than Marty or Lily. But DaVinci was good at keeping us separate, at assigning us only the tasks we needed to do. I never touched the meth, never took it, never sold it. I don't blame you if you don't believe that, but it's true.'

She did believe him, but only on that point. 'Didn't you all live together?'

'In the same building, not the same rooms. I had my own unit. Marty and Lily shared one, but otherwise we were separate. They were only converted hotel rooms, not big.'

'So you committed felony crimes with these people for, what, a year or two? And you never knew your boss's real name.'

'I never asked. I didn't ask about a lot of things. It seemed safer that way.' She would not have believed this, except that Ken Bilecki, who had been so in love with the entire operation, had not known David's name. She described him, and David quickly nodded.

'I think I know who you mean. Bug.'

Bug. What else? 'Because he picked at the imaginary insects he felt running underneath his skin? That's common in meth addicts.'

'No, because he'd bug you to death about every little thing, especially about our…business. Hyperactive. It's a wonder he stayed in school as long as he did—he only went to class to find more customers.'

'He was your salesman, Marty the enforcer, and Lily the mule.'

He looked at her with a pain in his face that could break her heart if she let it get close enough. 'Why do you want to know all this, Theresa?'

'I don't *want* to. But Marty is dead, and there may be a problem with Lily.'

This seemed to perplex him. 'I thought you said she overdosed.'

'Not exactly.' She summed up what Oliver had told her, in extremely general terms. She should not be sharing such information with someone outside the M.E.'s office, but she had to make him see that his situation might be more than merely embarrassing. It might be dangerous. If Lily had been murdered, she was the second from their little circle of six inside the past week. David Madison might know who had killed Marty Davis, and surely it would be better for him to reveal that information through her than to be hauled into police headquarters and questioned. She had to make him see that.

Though it wasn't her job to interrogate suspects, she had watched her cousin do it. She tried a more open-ended question. 'Tell me about the fire.' He sighed, coughed. She pushed the teacup toward him as he explained about the meth lab in the old hotel kitchen. His account matched Ken Bilecki's in every respect. However, David had entered it only twice—once to see the original set-up, and then when it caught on fire.

'We'd get in through the service entrance at the back of the building. If we walked through the old restaurant to get to it, it would be too easy to be noticed by other tenants if they happened to be in the lobby. This also made it easier to unload supplies from the back parking lot.'

'I thought you didn't work in the lab.'

He frowned at this show of mistrust. 'I didn't. But I helped set up the equipment the first time. It required a lot of stuff. Anyway, I never went near the kitchen again until—that night. I came back from class—Economics of the Public Sector—about seven thirty. I came in through the front door that everyone used, started to go to the elevator and heard this *boom*. Like, loud but muffled, you know? I had no idea what it was.' So many years later, he still shuddered at the thought.

'I could smell the meth, but that was not new. It had gotten into the ancient carpeting and wallpaper in the lobby until it always smelled of meth—at least I thought so, but it could have been my guilty conscience. All the tenants were college kids and either didn't know what it was, or did and knew better than to get involved.

'I stood there for a second or two, hoping it might

be a hot water heater or a gas line or somebody shooting at somebody, anything but the meth blowing up. I knew the chemicals were volatile, I saw all the warnings that came with the invoices. So I went back out again, down the alley to the back of the building. We used the service entrance. I had a key. DaVinci had changed the locks so we could use it.'

'Didn't the landlord—' She stopped. He hadn't noticed a meth lab in the kitchen; why would he notice a changed lock?

'He lived in Youngstown, I think, and never came around. As soon as I got inside, I could see the flames through the kitchen door and the smoke practically pushed me back out. I remember dropping my books and pulling my shirt up to hold over my mouth and nose. I just wanted to check the kitchen, I figured someone had to be there. Even without chemistry courses I didn't think stuff blew up by itself. My eyes watered from the smoke, but I could see him.'

Theresa took a breath. 'Joe McClurg?'

'I didn't know who it was. I mean—I couldn't tell. It was on fire. *He* was on fire.' And this very tall, very strong man shuddered again. She fought the urge to put her arms around him, lest she interrupt the flow of words. He seemed to have gotten past concern about his custody case or his job or anything else; she wondered if he had ever spoken of it to another living soul in the past twenty-five years.

'He was by the center island, where we'd set up most of the equipment over the ranges. I couldn't see any of it left except for some of those metal dowels that they'd attach the glassware to. I couldn't tell, really, because every surface had become nothing but flames. At first I thought the kid was running up the aisle, trying to get to

the door, but he was just flailing because then he stopped
and took a step backward. He—' Here he paused again,
and took a deep breath, pushing the words out even as
they trembled. 'He was completely on fire, like some
kind of…cartoon, or movie or something. I couldn't understand how he could still be on his feet, and just as I
thought that, he toppled over.

'I went in. I remember wondering how I was going to
grab his hands to pull him out, since they were burning.
I couldn't use my shirt, I needed it to breathe. So I held
the material to my face with my left hand and grabbed
his arm with my right, which was stupid, since I'm right-
handed.' Theresa turned his right hand, gently, until the
palm faced upward. Only a few patches of scarred skin
remained, and could have been taken for calluses. She
stroked them with one thumb.

'Even the *floor* burned, which I didn't understand,
linoleum burning. The chemicals must have sprayed
all over in the explosion, like an oil spill on the ocean.
The soles of my shoes got sticky—they were melting.
I grabbed the kid's arm and pulled.' His hand clenched
in reflex from the memory.

Theresa rubbed his fingers, trying to massage away
the pain. It didn't seem to work. 'You were brave.'

'No, I was stupid. I pulled him, but my hand felt like
someone had stabbed it a hundred times. I stumbled and
let go, and his arm fell back on me—that's how I got the
burn across my chest. I pushed it away and tried to grab
his wrist, where the shirt had burned off, but it still felt
like it was on fire to me. I was choking, and couldn't
see. The ceiling was on fire, the walls were on fire, the
whole world was on fire, and suddenly I thought the
upper floors would cave in and trap me there.' Theresa
waited. She knew what would come next.

'I left him.'

'David—'

'I got up and ran out. I left him there.'

'You couldn't have saved him.'

'You don't know that,' he said, his eyes angry and wet. 'I might have. I ran into Marty outside the door. He helped me put out my shirt. He asked if anyone else was inside and I said no.'

'He'd have died if you'd let him go in. As you would have.'

'I remembered to pick up my books on the way out, did I mention that? Even with my burned hands. Even with another person incinerating in the next room, I picked up my books from the rear hallway so that no one would know that I knew about that back entrance, so that no one would connect me with the meth lab.'

'It wasn't your fault.' He wouldn't look at her, and dug one fist into his eyes instead. This time she did not resist. In one quick, unthinking second she straddled his lap, wrapped both arms around his head and pulled his face into her neck. She felt wetness at her throat, and great heaving gasps of breath.

After a few moments these subsided, but she felt no hurry to release him, enjoying the warmth and the smell of the short, silky hair her fingers found their way into. Just as she began to tell herself to get up and finish the conversation, she felt his lips on her shoulder and that decimated any remaining resolve. Words were crowded out in an instant.

As she slid her tongue into his mouth and wrapped her feet around the lower rungs of the chair for leverage to pull her groin more tightly against his, it occurred to her that she hadn't asked him if Joe McClurg had been the one called Doc or if he, David, had only asked her out in order to keep tabs on the investigation, hoping that Marty Davis' past, and by extension his own, would not come up. But surely he could not be faking this, surely the way his hands crossed her back to bring her closer, pressing almost hard enough to bruise, could not be an act.

She wanted the answers to those questions, but not enough to stop what she was doing. Hell, she couldn't stop assaulting his mouth long enough to pull his shirt off even though desperate to feel his skin again—Two things happened.

The door to the garage opened and her mother walked in. Then the phone rang.

Theresa stared.

Her mother stared.

David gulped. His Adam's apple moved against her arm, still wrapped around his neck.

The phone rang again, and Theresa realized with a crushing disappointment that she had to do a few things right now besides kiss David Madison. She got to her awkward feet, greatly peeved.

'I'm so sorry,' her mother said, cheeks bright red under the gray hair. 'I didn't mean to—'

'Mom, this is—' David introduced himself. He did not stand up, indeed did not move, either because he didn't know what to do or to try to hide the evidence of his excitement. Theresa felt a rough, nasty sort of hope that it was the latter and snatched up the phone. 'Hello?'

'Is this Theresa MacLean?'

'Yeah, what do you want?' To her mother, she said, 'Come on in, Mom, it's all right. I know this must be—' Then the man on the phone identified himself as a sergeant with the Cleveland police department, and asked if Theresa would please sit down.

TWENTY-EIGHT

'I DON'T UNDERSTAND,' she said to the sergeant an hour later.

'Though I seem to be saying that a lot lately. I really have to come up with a better response to explosions than endlessly confessing that I can't figure out what the hell is going on.' The sergeant looked at her with an odd expression, and patted her arm.

She choked her emotions down—not easily, as they'd been on quite the roller-coaster ride for the past hour— and tried to sound more professional. 'How close were they to the bomb?'

'On an inside staircase, I guess. It took out most of the second floor.' She had never met this sergeant, a well-toned black guy with acne scars and gorgeous eyes. His name badge read *Altman*.

'The other tenants were lucky. Most of them were downstairs waiting for dinner. Two were at work, and the other two were far enough away to be hurt but not killed. One's in surgery now but expected to make it. Beltran's the only one who died. He must have been right on top of it.'

'So Frank and Angela were going to search his room, but when he saw them he ran inside?' Theresa asked.

'Yep. A few seconds later, boom.'

'Boom.' The sergeant leaned on the nurses' station desk, and nodded at a security guard who walked by. The emergency room seemed to be functioning at its usual level of controlled chaos. 'We figure he went for the explosives, either to hide them, or maybe to use them for some kind of stand-off. They detonated. Or he detonated them because he'd rather die than go back to the joint or because his wife left him, but I don't go for that, really. Types like him never take themselves out. It would make life too easy for the rest of us.'

'Why would Terry Beltran even have explosives?'

'Who knows? You can learn a lot in the joint. Maybe he came out with a new skill, only he wasn't too skilled at it yet.'

'Why would he shoot Marty Davis, then? Why not put a bomb in his car?'

'I don't know,' the sergeant admitted. 'All I know is that the halfway house staff said no one was staying in Terry Beltran's room except Terry Beltran, and that they don't inspect the rooms because it doesn't set the right tone for their felons' little self-esteems. I said they might still have both halves of their halfway house if they had worried a little less about self-esteem. Let me tell you about the self-esteem of your average criminal. It's pretty darn good. They all think no one matters but them and that they happen to be the baddest mother in the valley.'

'Can I see him?' Theresa asked. 'I need to see him.'

'Sure.' The sergeant pushed off the desk and led her down the hallway. 'But I have to warn you—'

'He looks bad?' Theresa tried to picture her cousin as a blackened, twisted fire victim, having burned as David Madison described the dead student—'His looks are fine,' the sergeant said as he pulled back a curtain.

'It's his mood that's bad.'

'Like that's news,' Frank said.

Her cousin had been stripped to the waist. Both arms

and the left side of his face had red patches where some shiny ointment had been applied, and there was a bandage over one wrist, but otherwise he appeared blissfully unhurt. The worry she hadn't acknowledged broke into a relief so sharp that tears came to her eyes.

'Don't you start bawling,' he warned. 'And don't call my mother.'

She perched next to him on the bed since her knees no longer wished to support her. 'Too late.'

'Damn! What did you tell her?'

'Same thing I told my mother. That you and Angela had a few scratches and that was it.' Theresa took a closer look at his injuries. A red patch on his neck seemed to have a straight edge, as if it had come from something rigid and very hot. An area next to his belly button formed a more amorphous splotch. 'Does it hurt a lot?'

'Not as much as losing our prime suspect under seriously questionable circumstances. Or what happened to my car. Did I tell you about the car? I worked so hard to keep that new-car smell, and what happens?'

'Does it involve flying debris?'

'A piece of the damn *house* fell on it! Big chunk of wall and part of a window. The hood is bent in now.' He pinched the bridge of his nose as if trying to blot out the memory.

'Sorry about your car. How is Angela?'

His jaw tightened until it looked like his teeth might break, but of course all he said was: 'Better or worse, depending on how you look at it. I landed on top of her.'

'Ouch.'

'Cracked one of her ribs. It softened my landing, yes, but it also meant that most of the burning debris landed on me and not her, so that makes us even. On top of that she owes me for waiting for Beltran.'

'What do you mean?' Frank accepted a pill from a comely nurse; under less trying circumstances he would have noticed the appreciative glance the woman in white cast toward his torso.

Instead, he merely growled, 'This had better be Oxy-Contin. Because, cousin, if we had gone in to search his room, it might have been us who stumbled on his little cache of blow-up stuff, and it would have been us it blew up. Obviously it had a hair trigger.' Theresa slid off the bed, stepped a foot closer and hugged her cousin, putting her face to his neck, just as she had so recently done with David Madison. Odd how the same gesture under different circumstances produced such different feelings.

'There, there, cuz.' Frank patted her back. 'I know you love me.'

'I do—love you, I mean—but that's not why I'm smelling your hair.' She backed up. 'Did you notice the odor?' He sniffed. 'I haven't noticed much of anything in the past hour and a half—oh.'

She nodded. 'Yeah. You smell like iodine. Terry Beltran had the same explosives in his room that brought down the Bingham building and the Lambert workroom.'

THERESA WENT TO check on Angela. The poor girl had to sit up very straight and breathe very carefully while the orthopedist spent more time gazing at the contents of her bra than applying the Velcro binding. Theresa did what she could to help by glaring at the doctor until he regained his focus and finished up.

Then she went back and waited with Frank until the hospital got around to discharging him. While driving to his apartment for a change of clothes, they bounced around possible connections between a violent parolee and a terrorist stockpile in the Bingham building. None seemed to make sense, though one fact remained—terrorists did a great deal of recruiting in prisons. A captive audience of the disconnected and disaffected provided fertile ground for their ideals. Frank planned to examine every prisoner or ex-prisoner with whom Beltran could have come into contact during his tenure there for some tie to Nairit Kadam. This would not be easy; it would require either cooperating with or duplicating the work of the FBI agents, and according to rumor they had not yet found *any* ties to Nairit Kadam. He seemed to have led an ordinary, law-abiding and utterly apolitical life until three years ago. Then, according to any and every fact recorded on the planet Earth, he ceased to exist.

So finding a link between him and Beltran would not be easy. Kadam had never been to jail, and even if they worked for the same organization they might not have known each other. 'That's how they try to work,' Frank had said as she drove. He fidgeted, searching for a comfortable way to lay his arm on his lap. 'So if one is caught, there's only a few others he can take down with him.'

'None of this would explain why he killed Marty Davis.'

'That could be what we first thought—revenge—and have nothing to do with his other activities.' Nor might a twenty-five-year-old meth lab explosion have any relation to Terry Beltran and terrorists. It most likely had no relation to anything, save her worry about falling in love with one of the involved parties.

Unless Terry Beltran had some connection to Joe Mc-Clurg, and had heard the account of the college group while in jail. Inmates had nothing to do all day but talk, after all. When had Ken Bilecki last been incarcerated?

But she could not picture Ken Bilecki involved with a political cause, unless it involved legalizing certain drugs. And Beltran didn't need to stumble on a motive to kill Marty Davis; he already had one. No, her brain had gone punchy with weariness, that was all.

Still, she said nothing to Frank about her talk with either Ken Bilecki or David Madison. She certainly didn't mention pinning the latter to a kitchen chair while Frank was getting blown on to East Forty-ninth Street. Or how much she wanted to do it again.

What a mess.

TWENTY-NINE

WHEN SHE RETURNED home for the second time that evening, she found an attention-starved dog, a hungry cat and David Madison's car still in her driveway. Moreover, David Madison was in it.

He got out as she parked. 'How's your cousin?'

'A little banged up, but fine. You didn't have to wait here…' She leaned against the warm fender of her car, weariness seeping through her bones. As much as she wanted a rematch with the man, tonight could not be the night. If she didn't get some sleep she'd collapse.

'I needed to—look, I'm sorry.' The cat meowed from the stoop, and the yellow retriever bounded between her and their guest, unsure which smelled more interesting.

'Geez, David, it's not your fault. My mother will be fine with it. Granted it wasn't the best way for you to make each other's acquaintance—'

'Not that. I mean, I am sorry for startling your mother,' he added with the hint of a grin that reassured her he wasn't *too* sorry. 'But I have to ask you for a favor, and I apologize in advance. I know you've had a hell of a day and you're exhausted.'

'You were the only good part of it,' she said. 'So go ahead.' The dog had made his choice and slapped his head against David Madison's thigh, to be petted as the man spoke.

'My neighbor called. Channel 15 is camped on my front lawn.'

'What? How could they have connected you to Marty Davis—'

'No, no. It's my wife. She is going to be released by tomorrow morning at the latest. They want to capture the happy family reunion. Newspapers, magazines and certainly the TV stations have been calling me for the past two days about it.' He looked more weary than she felt, which she would not have thought possible. 'I sent my boys to my sister's. At least it's the weekend, so we don't have to worry about school or work. I can't have them ambushed by a news crew during recess. They're just *kids*.' Theresa bent into her car to retrieve her purse from the seat and her water bottle from the floor. Then she said, 'Come inside.' It ought to be easier to control herself this time, too spent even to consider romance.

'Last time this happened,' David said, standing next to her coffee-maker, his body at an awkward tilt, 'a woman from some Hollywood show walked up to Tony as he waited for his school bus, and asked if his mother had ever tried to sleep with him. He was eight. He didn't even know what she *meant*.'

Theresa slumped into a chair. 'I'm sorry, honey.' The endearment slipped out without thought as she tried to picture reporters following Rachael to school. The idea made her want to beat someone.

David nodded. 'So the favor I'm asking is—can I stay here tonight?' Her mouth fell open, ever so slightly.

'I mean, on the couch. On the floor, I don't care, I just need a place to hide out. I've been through this once already—if I can avoid them for a few days, they'll get bored and go on to another story. I can't go to my sister's; her neighbors will see the car and then the media will find the boys. Maybe tomorrow she can get me some things from the house and meet me at a hotel, but

I just couldn't face the thought of it tonight. Desk clerks have called reporters on me before.' The dog turned to her with a second set of pleading eyes, making it clear whose side he took.

'OK,' she said. 'Sure. You can have Rachael's room.'

His shoulders slumped in relief. 'Thank you. Thank you. I know how this must look, and I promise I'm not usually such a basket case.'

'Neither am I.'

He laughed. 'I also promise this isn't a sneaky way into your bed. I know we—' he leaned over the table and touched only two of her fingers with his, producing a dangerously electric shock—'feel some attraction for each other, but I'm not going to exploit that.'

'Meaning you won't try a wee hour visit?'

He shook his head with a smile. Then he added, with equal amounts worry and hopefulness, 'Unless you want me to.'

'Desperately,' she admitted. 'But not tonight.'

A crushingly relieved smile. 'I agree completely.'

'David, can't you get a restraining order or something? Do you have a lawyer?'

'I can keep them off my own property and school ground, that's it. Everything else is a free for all. You didn't tell your cousin about me, did you?' he asked suddenly. 'About my connection to the meth lab?'

'No,' she said uncomfortably. 'But he wouldn't tell anyone anyway. The fire was an accident and the drug charges have expired.'

'It doesn't matter. Everything counts in a custody case.'

'He wouldn't expose you just for the fun of it. If it turned out to—' —*have something to do with Marty Davis' death*, she had been about to say, but David interrupted. 'Yes, he would. Nothing against your cousin, Theresa, but cops are not my friends. I'm a freak to them, the guy who couldn't hang on to his wife, who couldn't compete with a child. I'm a joke to everyone in this city. Except you.' Now he took her hand, and held it. 'My boys are at stake here. Help me.'

She nodded. After a moment she extricated her fingers, reluctantly. 'Rachael's room is the pink one—you can't miss it. The sheets are clean, and the hallway bathroom has towels and soap and shampoo. Help yourself to anything, and that includes whatever you can find in the refrigerator. It won't be much.' Then she went upstairs to her room and shut the door. And, after some thought and with much regret, locked it.

SHE DID WAKE UP, somewhere in the wee hours, but not because David Madison was rattling her doorknob. A slight sound wafted up from the kitchen below, the faintest creak of a floorboard. David had probably decided to forage. He must be hungry; they never did make it to Don's Pomeroy House.

What a strange situation. She had never had a romantic interest sleeping in her house other than her now exhusband (who surely could not say the same). She had not allowed Paul to stay over while Rachael still lived at home, and preferred to meet Chris at his place. She felt a sudden and completely unexpected nostalgia for her ex-husband Rick, for the time when every night would find them in their assigned places—husband, wife and daughter. Her life had not been especially happy, but at least it had been consistent. Now she had this new man shaking her up with his proximity to too many crimes for comfort.

Perhaps she had over-thought things. So many events

had occurred that week, perhaps she had jumbled them up. There were really two distinct crimes, or sets of crimes. First, the DaVinci meth lab ring from twenty-five years ago, involving Marty, Lily, Ken, David, the unknown DaVinci and Doc, presumably Joe McClurg. Then she had the explosion at the Bingham, involving Kadam and apparently Terry Beltran, if the odorous information Frank had given off meant anything. Terry Beltran could be connected to Marty. So two circles of events, which intersected only in the person of Marty Davis. A coincidence. Cleveland wasn't *that* big of a town.

Still, perhaps she should put any questions about Lily Simpson's death to rest before getting any more involved with David Madison.

She had time. Time to get to know him better... She dozed, dreaming of the process involved.

The peal of a telephone ripped her from it.

'Tess? It's Frank.' She collapsed back on the pillow. 'Hell. Don't you *ever* sleep?'

'Not this week,' he told her. 'Apparently.'

THIRTY

Saturday

Theresa threw on some clothes and brushed her teeth, tossing on a little mascara. That represented the maximum cosmetic preparation she felt willing to put into early-morning calls. The door to Rachael's room remained shut, and she did not see the need to disturb David. If he stuck to his plan, he'd be gone by the time she got came home from work. She left her cell phone number on the table in case he wanted to call, grabbed her water bottle from the refrigerator and edged her worn Ford out of the garage and around his car. Impressive considering she'd had about six hours of sleep in the past forty-eight.

She picked up Frank in nearby North Royalton, since Fleet Management had taken his car in order to pound out the dent in the hood. He wore a loose, long-sleeved T-shirt instead of his usual collar and tie and carried a small bottle of pills, shaking one into his palm. 'How's the arm?' she asked.

'It would be better if the hospital gave me real pain-killers. They're so worried about prescription drug abuse they just give you sugar pills these days. Angela got Vicodin. I got friggin' heavy-duty Tylenol because my burns were only a *little* blistered so the doc didn't feel they were *truly* second degree. Damn drug addicts have ruined it for everyone.'

'I'm glad she's all right,' Theresa said, knowing quite well what was really hurting him.

Of course Frank ignored this and tossed the pill into his mouth. Theresa offered him her bottle of flavored water— 'Fortified with vitamins and antioxidants and no additional calories, tastes like very weak Gatorade.'

'No thanks.'

She headed for the freeway. 'Where are we going?'

'West Sixth and St Clair. Right in the shadow of our beloved Terminal Tower.' He sighed, settled back in the passenger seat as she braked for a light at Bagley Road. 'Routine patrol checking the alleys found Ken Bilecki's body at twelve thirty this a.m. It took a half-hour to identify him because he didn't carry ID, but they traced a receipt from the methadone clinic to his name. Then it took another hour or two to notice the flag I'd put in the system after what you told me about Lily Simpson's tox results. You always drive through red lights?'

'It was yellow. I thought we'd make it.'

'Dangerous, cuz. They've already sent the body to your office, so I don't think there will be much to see in the alley. I thought we could take a look and then go to the morgue.'

'Medical Examiner's.'

'Yeah, OK. That one's definitely red.'

'Damn! Who'd think there would be all these cars on the road at four a.m.?'

'The workday starts early.'

'It's Saturday.'

'Maybe they're heading home from Friday night, then.'

'Don't these people have *jobs*?' She had to stop again just before the on-ramp, which infuriated her. 'Why did they move the body?'

'Because the responding officers hadn't looked under "notes" on the report screen. I don't think it's too bad—as I said, I doubt we'll find much in the alley. It looks like a standard OD.'

She took another sip and hit the gas. 'Which alley?'

'It's off West Sixth. They found him next to a dumpster behind a diner there. He still had the glass pipe in his hand.' Theresa sped up to get around a meandering SUV, picturing the scrawny little Ken Bilecki waiting to be taken away with the trash.

'That's so sad.'

'It is sad. It was also inevitable. He's been working up to it for twenty years.'

'That's so *sad*!'

'You're getting a little close to that truck. I wouldn't even have woken you up for this, but I have to know if his tox results are going to show something bizarre like Lily Simpson's. Even though,' he went on, apparently thinking out loud, 'all that means is that there's bad meth on the streets and they both got some. They probably bought it from the same dealer—why not, they kept in touch. It doesn't mean it had anything to do with Marty Davis.'

'But—'

'But what?' But another member of their circle is sleeping in Rachael's bed, Theresa thought, reminding herself at the last minute not to speak out loud. She knew she could trust Frank, though he had the same laughing attitude about the libidinous teacher as every other guy in the city. Men were so unreliable when it came to sexual things. Why did they have to be like that? But Frank would keep a secret if she asked him, wouldn't he? 'I don't know what to do.'

'Get in the right lane,' her cousin suggested. 'Around that Kia. How fast are you going?'

'Um, eighty.' It had gotten warm in the car, and she rolled down her window as they sped past the I-480 interchange. A jet came at them, heading for the Hopkins airport on her left. The rush of air seemed exciting, intoxicating.

'Slow down. There's not that big of a hurry.'

'We have to get there before they remove anything else from the crime scene.'

'I told them to freeze it. Seriously, Tess, slow down. You're starting to scare me, and that's not easy to do.' He put a hand on her shoulder, and she felt such intense comfort from it that her eyes welled up again. She could trust him, of course. But she had promised David. Better to say nothing for now. Besides, if Lily and Ken's deaths had nothing to do with their past, then David and his family troubles were irrelevant. 'So you think it could be some kind of killer meth? But Ken didn't kill himself—did he?'

'No, an apparent OD. I only want to make sure, or we might have meth addicts dropping like flies—look out!' A tractor-trailer materialized in front of them. Theresa screamed and jerked the wheel to her left, cutting off a small Volkswagen. Its driver tooted the horn in protest.

It took a moment to return her car to steady travel, as her heart pounded hard enough to make her ribs ache. Frank clutched the dashboard and she laughed at him. 'Do you *believe* how people behave on these roads?'

'What is the matter with you? You never drive like this!'

'But we're in a *hurry*.'

'Theresa MacLean, what the hell is the matter with you?'

'I mean, to be found by a *dumpster*. What a life.

Somebody must have cared about him once, encouraged him once. He went to college, or tried. Isn't that sad?'

'Pull over.'

'What?' This bizarre question roused her from melancholy over Ken Bilecki's death. *'What?'*

'Listen to me carefully. Take your foot off the gas. Move into the right lane—there's no one coming, go ahead. Now go on to the shoulder.'

'But we're not there yet.' Hell, they hadn't even passed the old Mead sign.

'On to the shoulder, now. Slow-ly. There's plenty of room here. Come on.' She protested past 117th Street, where the houses break off into deep woods, the landscape too undulating to build on. But he nagged, slowly and steadily, until she slid the car off the pavement and on to the rough shoulder and stamped on the brakes hard enough to make the car jerk. *'What?* Why are we stopping when we have to get to the crime scene?'

'Look at me, Tess. Stop, and turn, and look at me.' Her cousin had pulled out a tiny flashlight and now pointed it at her face, which she found *really* irritating.

'What?'

'I want you to follow my pen with your eyes.' The smooth and phoney way he spoke only added to her annoyance, as if he were talking to a child or a rabid dog. She knew what he was doing. This was called DRE or something like that, wasn't it? To test for—'That's it, just look at my pen. What did you do tonight, Tess?'

Kiss David Madison, she started to say, then bit it back.

'Nothing.' Cars zoomed by; each one that came close made the Ford quaver a bit.

'Before you came to pick me up, what were you doing?'

This she could answer with confidence. 'Sleeping.'

'Did you feel all right all evening?'

Depending upon the exact moment, better than all right. 'Yes.'

'You're not sick? You didn't take any medications?'

'No. *Will* you get that light out of my face?'

'You're sure there's nothing you want to tell me about?' Yes, she thought—David Madison. *What am I doing? How much baggage is too much baggage? How much does our past determine our future? Am I merely infatuated? Should I take a more objective look at him? How can I, when objective is the last thing I feel capable of being every time I'm with him?*

Receiving no answer, her cousin went on without her, 'Because right now, my dear cousin, you are higher than the Goodyear blimp. I'm getting out and you're going to slide into the passenger seat. I'm taking you to the hospital.'

THIRTY-ONE

THERESA'S SECOND VISIT to the Metro General emergency room in twelve hours proved even more unpleasant than the first, as this time it became her turn to be poked, stripped and made to give up her bodily fluids. All the while, her mind raced and her mouth tried to keep up.

'I have to take a little more blood,' the nurse said, her black skin glowing with youth and a touch of sunburn. After a long Cleveland winter, sunny spring days could prove impossible to resist.

Theresa protested with what she felt was reason. 'You've already taken three tubes, or four, I lost count. When you get up to a pint you have to stop, right? They only take a pint when you're donating blood. I like the curtains here, between the beds. I suppose blue is supposed to be soothing.'

'Yes,' the nurse agreed. She had apparently discovered, during the past trying hour, that agreeing with Theresa made the process smoother. At least then the chatter stayed at comfortable decibels. Silly, of course. Theresa had not been shouting, no matter what Frank said.

'I read a book on the great influenza epidemic of 1918—it took forever to get through but it was really interesting—and that's when they started putting curtains in between patients, not for privacy but to try to keep infection down. People would catch it from sick people coughing on them. They caught it from everywhere, really, so the curtains didn't do much in the long run. I'm glad we have them now, though.'

'Me too,' the nurse agreed. She had a deft touch; Theresa didn't even feel the needle sliding into her arm. Still, why couldn't they get everything they needed at once and stop putting holes in her skin? She had passed her fortieth birthday and her skin needed all the TLC it could get.

'How could this stuff have gotten into your system, Theresa?' Frank asked for the fourth time. Beside him stood the homicide division chief, a tall black lieutenant in jeans and a rumpled sweatshirt. Frank had called him in on Theresa's insistence. Frank could not be seen to have covered up or glossed over a relative's drug use. Her mind really was working quite well. 'Did you smoke anything last night?'

'I don't smoke! You know that. I gave that up before Rachael was born.'

'*Around* anyone who smoked?' the lieutenant intoned.

'No.'

'Injected anything?'

'Hardly. I couldn't prick myself to learn blood typing in a college lab; you think I could put a needle into myself?'

'We're just trying to help,' Frank told her, hulking uncomfortably by the curtain. The blue color had not soothed him. 'Calm down.'

'Francis,' she said through gritted teeth, 'I don't know how and I don't know why, but apparently I'm up to my eyeballs in stimulants. The one thing I *can't* do is calm down!'

'OK, OK.'

'And I can't figure out where it came from either. It's not like I have drugs sitting around my house.'

'She really doesn't,' Frank confirmed for the lieutenant, who nodded with less than complete conviction. 'Can methamphetamine be ingested?' he asked Theresa.

She thought. 'I don't know. Drugs really aren't my field. It's not the usual route…but then you can make brownies with pot and people who smuggle cocaine in their stomachs will OD if the bag breaks, so I suppose so. We have to ask Oliver. We have to talk to Oliver anyway—he has to test my blood.'

'They can do that here.'

'But the hospital lab might not know what it's looking for. Oliver has already seen the extra compounds that killed Lily Simpson. Get my Nextel, his number is in the contacts—it's clipped to my belt. I think they put the clothes in that bag there. There.'

'I've got it.'

'What did you ingest last night, then?' the lieutenant asked.

'And where did you get it?'

'Nothing, that's the point. I had some lunch about one, and that was it. I hadn't yet made dinner when they called to tell me Frank got blown up, and when I got home after that I went straight to bed.' She could feel some comfort in clearing David Madison—he had given her nothing and they had not had either food or drink together, except for a spot of tea, and she had made that herself.

'I did have a pop at Subway, when I talked to Ken Bilecki.' The men stared. She expected Frank to be put out by her questioning one of his witnesses, though Bilecki wasn't, really, he hadn't witnessed anything about Marty's murder, so she couldn't understand why the lieutenant looked—oh, yes. Ken had died tonight. No wonder they were interested.

'You interviewed our victim—' the lieutenant began.

'You talked to—when? Where?' Frank demanded. *'Why?'* This could get sticky. She could explain the twenty-five-year-old case without mentioning David Madison, but if Frank really began to look into it, he still might come up. 'That's kind of a long story. Is it cold in here, or is it just me? I felt so hot all this time but now I'm getting a cold flash. It raises your body temperature, you know. Meth.'

'Tess—'

'Is there another blanket?'

'Tell us about your meeting with Ken Bilecki,' the lieutenant said, in a tone which brooked no argument, stalling or confabulation. So she did. But only in general terms, leaving out any part about David Madison.

'Why the big interest in such an old case?' Frank asked her.

'Idle curiosity?' He gave her that narrowed-eye look that let her know he did not believe her, but did not know enough to call her on it.

'Because I found the box of evidence in the basement of the Bingham building, which also exploded, so I got to thinking…'

'Could Bilecki have put something in your drink?' the lieutenant asked.

'I don't see how. I bought them, and I never walked away or turned my back on the table.' She had gotten him that refill, but she'd been done with her cup by then, hadn't she?

'What did you order?'

'He drank Coke, I drank Diet.'

The lieutenant exchanged a glance with her cousin. 'Maybe the guy behind the counter is Bilecki's source, and he mixed the drinks up. We'll have to check out that Subway.'

'But would it have taken that long to take effect?' Frank asked.

'Don't know. Maybe ingesting instead of smoking takes longer. I'm going to go out and talk to the Vice guys. They might have some insights.'

After he left, Frank said to her, 'Did you have anything else to eat or drink last night? And would you cover your legs in front of other people, please?'

'Why?' she asked. 'What's wrong with them?' But she let him fold the bed sheet over her lap and ticked off her beverages—tea she had made herself, water from the tap, coffee at the lab, coffee at the site, and water from a water bottle she had refilled herself.

'And you felt perfectly fine when you went to bed last night.'

'Uh-huh.' Physically, yes. Emotionally she'd been a little perturbed.

'Is there any way someone could have tampered with your water bottle?' She had carried it all over the city today, at the site, at the lab, in her car. She had left it in her car while talking to Ken Bilecki. Ditto for her trip to the hospital to see Frank. Then she had added more water and left it in her refrigerator, while she let a man she barely know bunk in her daughter's room. 'Well—'

'Could someone have broken in? I've been telling you to replace those French doors for months now. A school kid could get those open.'

'No—yes! I did hear—or thought I heard—someone in my kitchen, shortly before you called. I brushed it off as house creaks, but maybe it wasn't.' And David's door had been closed when she came out of her room and she had not heard him come back up the stairs. The risers had too many noisy spots for anyone, particularly a man of his size, to get up them without announcing it to the whole house. Not even Rachael had mastered that, and not for lack of trying. She should call Rachael. She hoped the girl was studying, especially her calculus. And that the bomber hadn't moved on to the state capital, less than three miles from her daughter's dorm.

But wait. Wouldn't that would mean *two* unexpected visitors had been in her house during the same night? It stretched credibility. But she'd rather stretch than believe that the man she had gone more than a little crazy for had tried to poison her.

'Don't start crying again,' Frank said. 'I need you to focus.'

'But why would someone want to kill me over a twenty-five-year-old meth lab? I mean, that's *ridiculous*.'

'I agree. I think it's more likely someone would kill you over a three-day-old murder of a police officer. The whole city knows that you were there. Maybe the shooter worried that you saw him. We went after Terry Beltran, and the chief just told me they found some scribbled notes about that Georgian splinter group in the rubble of Beltran's room. They've got to be somehow connected to the Bingham explosion, which makes this bigger than even a cop killing. But he might think we showed up at Beltran's place because you saw him at Marty Davis' murder site. So to be safe this partner took out Beltran, and now he needs to get rid of you.'

Hardly a comfortable line of thought. 'But why not a bomb in my house? Why something more subtle like a meth overdose?'

'Because he doesn't want your death connected to Beltran's. And we don't even know if it *is* meth in your system. It could be something else entirely.'

Theresa hoped so. She did not want to have ingested the same stuff that had killed Lily Simpson and maybe Ken Bilecki. 'Call Oliver. Either he can tell the hospital lab what to look for, or you'll have to run a tube of my blood out to him.' He shook his head and flipped open the Nextel. 'It's five a.m. He's not going to appreciate this.'

'He'll be up. He doesn't have a life outside his job—isn't that *sad*?'

'Yeah, sad.' But correct. The man in question picked up, and Frank elucidated the situation as best he could, what with Theresa interrupting every two seconds to add some detail that Oliver might need to know. Every detail except David Madison. Every time she thought of him, her nerve endings shot off tiny flaming arrows.

But every time she thought of keeping a secret—possibly quite a relevant secret—from Frank, she started sweating again.

'Oliver says yes, it can be ingested,' Frank said to her, covering the phone, then listened some more. 'He says he has to have your blood sample, that the equipment in most hospital labs is not remotely able to reach his standards for precision or accuracy.'

'Ignore him on that. Oliver's a terrible snob,' Theresa said for the sake of the nurse, lest she take offense, but the nurse had apparently left the room at some point.

'He also said to tell you he analyzed the swab you took from a ring?' Ring, ring—the caduceus ring from the old meth lab case.

'Yes?'

'He says it has residue from nitrogen triiodide on it. What does that mean?' he asked into the phone. 'I know, but—well, you don't have to get so uppity with me, I just asked—fine, I'll get her blood out to you.'

He hung up. 'Man, that guy's a bastard. I don't know how you work with him. Tess—what's the matter?' The twenty-five-year-old meth lab explosion also involved nitrogen triiodide. This fact splashed into the pool of facts in Theresa's mind like a baseball smashing into an electric scoreboard, sending out a shower of brilliant, blinding sparks.

Her circles—Lily, Marty, David, Ken and the meth lab, and Marty, Terry Beltran and the Bingham destruction—now intersected at more than the one point of Marty Davis. They also intersected at a second point, the explosive used. What were the odds of that?

She didn't have two circles, she had one. One spanning twenty-five years.

Twenty-five years ago someone had learned—perhaps accidentally—about the destructive capabilities of nitrogen triiodide. They did not forget the lesson. Fast-forward to the present, as terrorism became a burgeoning industry. Someone brushed off their old chemistry notebooks and went back to work. Someone who was not Marty, Lily, Ken or the presumably dead Doc. That left DaVinci.

And Bean.

Theresa collapsed down on to the bed, pulling the tangled sheets and blankets up to her chin. The world needed to forget her, because someone this stupid could be of no possible use to it.

'I'll get this to Oliver,' Frank said, holding her red-taped tube of blood.

She managed a nod. They had to know if the same altered meth that Lily Simpson had smoked now coursed through Theresa's veins, ready to plunge her into the same black hole of despair. She already felt it coming but not because of the drug—she should feel this bad. She *deserved* to feel this bad.

How much worse would it get? Would the nurse come back? Would anyone keep an eye on her, keep sharp objects away? Could one hang oneself with the IV tubing? What about Rachael—'Frank!' Her hand shot toward him as he began to turn away.

'Don't leave me.' He stopped, looking down at her with a surprised expression. Then he took the out-stretched hand, curling her fingers into his palm with a gentle squeeze and an even gentler smile which terrified her since *gentle* had never been the adjective for him.

'I wasn't even going to think about it, cuz.'

THIRTY-TWO

NOISE CAME AND went around them, mostly came. The emergency room at Metro never stopped. 'Saturdays,' the nurse had said to Theresa, probably trying to distract her from the sewer-pipe-sized IV needle as it entered her vein.

'Weekday mornings we get the car accidents, people driving to work. Saturdays we get the home repair projects. Guys fall off ladders, kids swallow paint. A lady just came in, sliced her hand open with a carpet knife. Thirty-two stitches. I'll keep my apartment. Houses can kill you.' Theresa remained in the emergency room, napping in between sirens and blood draws. The hospital did not plan to admit her, assuming she'd be ready to leave once her bloodwork reached acceptable levels. Besides, should this embarrassing little incident ever come to the attention of a defense attorney against whose client Theresa was testifying, 'treated and released' would look much better than 'hospitalized'. Besides, Theresa thought, nothing would be gained by wasting the next twenty-four hours staring at white walls and daytime TV.

Not that she knew what else to do.

The IV dripped, dripped, dripped, supposedly washing out the meth and adding serotonin and other feel-good things to her bloodstream, but Theresa did not feel the effects. Besides, if drugs like Xanax and Valium worked in a way similar to meth, by stimulating the release of neurotransmitters which had already been released, weren't these additional drugs simply trying to draw water from a dry well? She should ask the nurse about that, but couldn't summon up the energy.

She pictured sodium hydroxide, seeing the atoms as neat, bulbous little things, the sodium connecting to the oxygen and then the hydrogen. Or ammonium hydroxide, the nitrogen surrounded by hydrogens, in an ionic bond with an oxygen-hydrogen pair. Then nitrogen triiodide, the simplest, just a nitrogen atom in a triangular arrangement with three iodines. In her mind she picked up these little structures, trying to fit them together like puzzle pieces.

Frank dozed next to her, a difficult thing to do in a metal folding chair, his head resting against a box of latex gloves mounted to the wall. No point asking him. He had made it through high school chemistry only with help from her, two years his junior. He knew no more about elements and compounds than, supposedly, David Madison.

Yet Madison worked for a chemical supply company. He had proven himself adept at creating shadow accounts to cover up the activities of a meth ring—how much harder could it be to cover the activities of a terrorist group? Theresa knew terrorism functioned on its funding just as an army once marched on its stomach. Who would be better suited to serve their purposes than an accountant? She didn't see why he'd be involved with Georgian independence, but then, the college meth business had been a moneymaking venture, so home-grown explosives could be the same—available for sale to the highest bidder.

Marty would have let David walk up to him without drawing his weapon. Lily and Ken would have bought meth from David. For all Theresa knew, David had never stopped selling it, had used the business to pay for private schools and lawyers. Perhaps he had a reason other than embarrassment to avoid the scrutiny of the media and the police.

But why use the meth? Why not merely strangle her in her own bed and leave? No one could place him there. Her mother had seen him, but earlier.

'Frank!'

He nearly slid from the chair. 'What?'

'Call my mother! She stopped over my house earlier and if he's tying up loose ends then he might worry that she saw him approaching my house and—'

'Relax.' Frank leaned his head against the wall and once again closed his eyes. 'I just talked to her a half-hour ago. You didn't think our late-night foray would go unnoticed? My mother and yours have already had an early-morning conference call and decided that these late nights are going to break down our respective immune systems. They watch too much Discovery Channel.' Then he seemed to nap once more.

Theresa sucked in a deep breath. The momentary panic had sharpened her mind, though, and she continued to apply reason to the situation. Or very slightly educated guesswork that might pass for reason, she couldn't be sure.

Why use such an uncertain method as meth intoxication? Even if she killed herself, people such as Frank and her co-workers would be much less likely to accept it. Theresa didn't have Lily Simpson's life and, psychology aside, he had to know every possible tox screen would be run. The adulterated meth compounds would be found.

Perhaps he'd hoped for a fatal car accident—she used

the water bottle for her commute. But a tox screen would still have been done.

Maybe her death was not strictly necessary. One way or another her condition would be noticed, and then any testimony offered would be discredited. Who would believe a morgue ghoul with proven drug usage when she started spouting theories of terrorism and its ties to an ancient meth lab?

Hell, the *truth* sounded unbelievable. She let a complete stranger stay in her house overnight and he then poisoned her bottle of water, having no idea if or when she would ever drink it, with some bizarre version of meth that managed to be odorless and tasteless.

Right. And on top of that, she had a crush on the guy, this man who only wanted to make sure she knew nothing useful about who shot Marty Davis. He had approached her at the funeral and she had not recognized him. Good. He came back again, perhaps to see if any new information had turned up, and found her holding the evidence that might tie him to the old meth lab. Not good. Now something had to be done.

Theresa had to be neutralized. So much for her taste in men.

'Frank,' she said, once more startling him from his position against the box of gloves. 'There's something I need to tell you.'

THIRTY-THREE

LEO FOUND HER at the infrared spectrometer when he returned from lunch, her hands still a little shaky, with eyes that felt as if the inside of her lids had been coated with sand. 'About time you got here. What are you working on?'

'The plastic I found in the driveway next to Davis' body.' People and their actions and their stories only continued to confuse her. Time to get back to the plain facts of physical evidence and she had too many of them still outstanding. 'I thought it came from a home-made silencer, like a plastic two-liter bottle. It's the right material—polyethylene—but it's thicker than pop bottles.' Leo surveyed her, carefully, eyes darting from her wayward hair to her scuffed Reeboks and settling on her face. The flushed face, bare of make-up, made him cringe, and the very un-Leo-like look of concern made *her* cringe. If Leo felt sorry for her instead of bawling her out for embarrassing the department, then that was it. Her career, looks and competence were in the toilet. She might as well shoot herself.

But all he said was, 'Any residues?' She sighed. 'Only the usual stuff from gunshots—barium and antimony from the primer, and copper from the jacket. A little bit of lead, probably left over from earlier firings since the lead shot from the round wouldn't be exposed until it hit its target.'

'What did he stuff the bottle with, then?'

'Good question,' she said. Usually home-made silencers were filled with rags to absorb the sound. She would have found tufts of cloth along with the few pieces of plastic. 'I don't know.'

'What's that?' He pointed to another glob of plastic, one that had softened and rounded into a rough oval.

'I picked that up at the Lambert factory explosion—don't even know why. Just something to do with my hands, I guess, while talking to the superbly rich guy.'

'You're running it? Why?'

'Why not? Because it's here, and I need more plastics for my database anyway.'

'You don't have enough to do that you've got to run unnecessary samples? Seriously?' he grumbled, then reached out a hand. 'Give it here.' She frowned.

But her wrinkled eyebrows were no match for his trademark scowl. 'The fine equipment in this lab is intended for the analysis of evidence, not random debris. Evidence. The stuff the attorneys want to hear about, that the juries need to see. That stuff.' She gave in... largely because she had already scraped off a sample for the FTIR window. He dropped the glob into his pocket, then gave her one last worried scowl before trundling off toward the coffee pot.

Speaking of which— 'Hey, what did you do with my box?'

'I'm not responding to that one, missy. You're not going to slap any kind of sexual harassment charge on me.'

'The box from the Bingham building that I had in the amphitheater yesterday. Where did you put it?'

He rolled his eyes. 'Back in the garage, of course.' She started to ask for more specifics, but didn't bother. No doubt Leo would have dropped it just inside the door.

She knew no room remained to go much farther and he had never been one for exploration. After he refilled, she went on: 'Did they call us to the Forty-Ninth Street scene?'

'No, that's the fire marshal and Homeland Security, and best of luck to them. They did bring us the body, complete with fire marshal department escort who insisted on telling me all about it with both a color and a play-by-play version. Firemen. They never have enough to do.'

'What did he say?' Her boss paused, hitched half of his bottom over the workbench edge and sipped from a steaming mug.

'He took the paint cans we collected from the victim. Only two—blue jeans and a melted plastic glob. I guess the guy had been wearing a nylon sports shirt. I don't get wearing football jerseys when you're not, at that moment, playing football.'

She eyed his plaid shirt. 'Anything else on the body?'

'A few pieces of bling, they're in Property. I asked if the guy was a terrorist and he said they were working with that theory, since the explosive seemed to be the same stuff from the Bingham building.'

'Nitrogen triiodide.'

'Yeah. Weird choice for a bomb, but easy to make. The point of origin seemed to have been against the interior wall, next to a dresser or in one of the drawers. He rigged it with a mercury switch, to go off when disturbed. I guess he didn't count on being the guy who disturbed it.'

'Why would you booby trap your own place?'

'Because a bomb is a little hard to explain when the maid or a pilfering neighbor stumbles on it? They don't lock the doors there. Honor system.'

'So he blows them up?'

'Does a guy like Beltran strike you as a guy deeply concerned for his fellow men? He shot a cop down in cold blood.'

Theresa lined up her shard of plastic on a microtome, slicing a thin sample from the piece. 'Then he panicked when the cops showed up at his door? Do you think he was going to try for some sort of stand-off? Threaten them with the bomb if they didn't let him go?'

'We'll never know now, will we? But they found a gun in his hand—a hand no longer attached, by the way. His body became almost completely disarticulated but by God he didn't let go of that gun. So the marshal's theory is that the victim went to that drawer to get the gun, forgot about the bomb or forgot he armed it or was in too much of a hurry to be careful. So he grabs the gun and boom.' And Frank came within about ten feet of going *boom* with him.

Theresa caught her breath, held it, let it out. 'What kind of gun?'

'Nine mil.' The same caliber that killed Davis. It might be able to be connected, if the shell fragments in Marty Davis' brain had any usable toolmarks. 'So he left an armed bomb in his dresser drawer? Where would a guy like Terry Beltran learn how to make a mercury switch?'

'Prison. You can learn anything there.' Leo shook his head. 'Or the Internet. Seems you can learn pretty much anything there, too. How is your cousin?'

'OK. He'll be all right,' Theresa said, pleased that he had asked. Her pleasure evanesced with Leo's next words.

'And he's going to keep any mention of you ingesting methamphetamine out of any report anywhere, right?'

'It wasn't my fault!'

Leo gave her a look both sad and stern. 'You want to explain that to a jury when you're asking them to accept the professionalism and expertise in your assertion that this fingerprint matches that one or that you found gunshot residue on the suspect's shirt? That you *accidentally* got higher than the combined attendees of Woodstock?'

Theresa began to feel nauseous. 'It wasn't accidental. It was a murder attempt.'

'Yeah. And Ross Perot dropped out of the presidential race because someone tried to blackmail his daughter. We have got to keep this out of print, Theresa. I cannot emphasize that enough. And you have to recuse yourself from this entire case.'

'Marty Davis' murder? Leo—'

'The Davis case, the Bingham explosion, everything. We have plenty of more standard homicides and suicides which are every bit as important. Work on them.' Again that look, equal parts *sorry* and *don't screw with me*. 'Whatever you have, give to me, your evidence, your reports, everything. No arguments, MacLean. You know this is how it has to be.' She did. Leo would do everything he could to protect her career, but he would do everything to the tenth power to protect the lab. Period.

She put the piece of plastic back into its envelope and handed it to him. She even gave him the piece from the Lambert explosion.

'Sorry, kid,' he said, and seemed to mean it. She went next door to see Oliver.

Most of the staff had left for lunch and it took much pounding on the door and shouting before the man would rouse himself from the workbench to let her in. The unexpected activity obviously left a bad taste in his mouth. 'Have you come for another assassination attempt? Carrying a little C-4 in your pockets, are you?'

'I need more chemistry.'

'I don't know about that.' He moved past a bench with Nalgene jars of bodily specimens and the gas chromatograph, back to his lair, and left her to follow if she wished. No flashes of empathy here, to her relief. Coming so soon after Leo that would add one more layer of surrealism to her day. 'You might be all right if you combed your hair, and got the proper amount of sleep. And stopped taking drugs.' A response to this seemed quite beyond her present abilities, and in her silence he relented enough to say, 'It shouldn't be all that bad. You didn't get the same stuff that killed Lily Simpson.'

'Yeah, Frank said that. So he dosed me with plain old meth?' Technically this violated Leo's edict, but surely she had a right to know what she had been poisoned with?

'I didn't say that, either.' Oliver took a large bite of what appeared to be an egg and sausage muffin, and not a feeble fast-food version, either. This muffin had at least a five-inch diameter. An oversized Styrofoam cup of coffee steamed next to it and she wondered when she had last eaten. Yesterday—lunch? Had she eaten lunch? 'He—do you know who this mysterious *he* is, by the way?'

'Um, no—not yet.' Naturally she held out a tiny, foolish hope that David Madison had *not* tried to kill her, but circumstances refused to throw this hope a bone. Frank had immediately sent the local police to her home, but David and his vehicle were both gone. His children were, as he had said, at his sister's and had not seen him since Friday after school. Frank issued a BOLO but so far neither the man nor his car had been sighted. 'We're working on it.'

Oliver's eyes, surrounded by puffs of flesh, peered out from behind round glasses. 'Uh-huh. Well, he used the same stuff he gave to Ken Bilecki. Plain meth, as you might say, none of the additional compounds that bind the neurotransmitters. Chemically, no different than any other meth that turns up in an unhealthy portion of the victims we see here.'

'Not *chemically* different.'

'No. The difference is in the purity. Most meth is not perfect to begin with and laced with unintended impurities, having been cooked by street thugs who barely made it out of grammar school. Then it is cut with some innocuous substance to add volume without additional expense—same way snack foods are often sold in boxes one-third larger than they need to be. It fools the consumer into thinking they're getting more. So most meth is also laced with intended impurities.'

Her brain did not feel like following Oliver's ping-ponging interests. 'And the stuff I got?'

'No impurities at all, intentional or otherwise. It's the most chaste, most potent methamphetamine I've ever seen.'

She tried to assimilate this. 'So he would not have had to add much to my flavored water. It wouldn't alter the taste. And if a chronic user like Ken took the same amount he usually did—'

'He'd be guaranteed to overdose.' Ken and Lily, both killed by bizarre forms of meth—forms tailored for each of them. The killer didn't only know chemistry, he knew his victims. He knew them well.

Of course this only added to the mounting evidence against David Madison. When this case ended she would lock herself in her bedroom and throw the key down to her mother lest she ever make the acquaintance of another man. And if she lost her job in the wake of this morning's incident, it would only make hibernation that much easier to accomplish.

OK, move on. 'Did you get anything from the samples I sent you from our Bingham victims?'

'In indirect violation of federal instructions regarding the evidence? Oh yes, my dear, I know about that. What do you mean by anything?' Oliver functioned as a particularly cranky form of Google. Make your search parameters too narrow, and you might miss some results.

'Anything interesting?'

'More residue of what you tried to kill me with, nitrogen triiodide.' Oliver chewed, swallowed, flicked his ponytail back over his wide shoulder and added, 'Found some phosphorus, too.' Theresa had been staring at the mass spectrometer to distract herself from the sausage and egg combination, which, of course, was not permitted in the lab, but rules did not apply to Oliver, especially when no one else was around. Now she switched her gaze back to the portly toxicologist.

'Phosphorus.'

'Chemical symbol P, number fifteen on the periodic table. A multivalent non-metal. Surely you've heard of it.'

'I have a theory,' she said. 'About why the meth lab blew up twenty-five years ago.'

He washed down his breakfast with approximately a pint of steaming coffee, taken all at once. 'Oh, excellent. A biologist with a theory based on chemistry. I do have to hear this.'

'Ken Bilecki told me DaVinci—'

'Who?'

'Long story. DaVinci mentioned ammonium hydroxide. They synthesized the meth using iodine and red phosphorus. One of the steps calls for the addition of sodium hydroxide, to bring up the Ph. If the dead student used ammonium hydroxide instead, maybe he wound up with a bunch of nitrogen triiodide crystals instead of meth in the bottom of his flask.'

Oliver considered this. 'Hmm. Might be an interesting experiment. Though I'll bet workers' comp wouldn't cover any maiming injuries, party-poopers that they are.'

'As long as the crystals are kept cold and wet, nothing bad happens and he doesn't know anything's wrong. However, the next step in the meth process calls for heating the flask.'

Oliver licked his fingers. 'Ka-blooey.'

'Just so. DaVinci figures this out. Maybe the red phosphorus coordinates with the NI3 molecule, maybe displaces the ammonia molecule. And the phosphorus stabilizes the NI3.'

Oliver stopped licking, his eyes focused on another plane where protons and electrons combined and recombined. 'But it still blew up. Rather forcefully, one might add.'

'I didn't say stabilized *completely*. It would still be a dangerous explosive, but a little easier to transport and store—or walk around with in a coat pocket without maiming oneself. It's how he amassed enough of it in the Bingham basement to take it down before he finally screwed something up and triggered the reaction.'

'So our chemist learned from his college days—'

She couldn't resist an Oliver-like digression: 'Which, after all, is the purpose of education.'

'—to become a terrorist, or at least a supplier, today.' It did not surprise her to hear him tie past and present cases to each other. She doubted anything could surprise her at this point.

Famous last words.

Her Nextel trilled, and she answered it. Leo, of course, who would rather call than walk thirty feet across the hall to get her.

'Come back here right away. We have a call on hold for you, and you're going to want to take it.'

'Why all the drama? Who is it?'

'I think,' Leo breathed into the phone, 'it's your new boyfriend. The one who tried to kill you.'

THIRTY-FOUR

SHE TOOK THE phone from the wide-eyed secretary.

'Theresa? I caught a bit on the news and it said some-one attacked you? Are you all right?'

She tried to speak, choked, tamped down her anger and tried again. 'Yes, someone did. We all think it was you.'

A pause—of shock, or to regroup? 'Me? How could it have been me? Didn't you see him?'

'Of course not, but—' The police had indeed tried to keep the name of their oft-testifying expert witness and mention of drug intoxication from turning up in the same statement. To the media they had characterized last night's event as an assault only. David was either inno-cent, or he was fishing. 'Where are you?'

'I've just been driving around, mostly. I don't know where *to* go—the media is still camped in my driveway. Are you sure you're all right?'

Then why hasn't someone picked you up on the BOLO? she had the sense not to ask. *And there are no TV vans, no spectators in your driveway because your wife is news but not big news, and I know that because Frank has two officers parked around the corner from your house.*

No, she'd have a better chance of convincing him to come in if she kept things cordial. 'Yes. Look—'

'Why would you think I attacked you?'

'Well…when I went back home, you were gone. That seemed kind of suspicious.'

'I heard you leave for work, so I got up. I'd already imposed on you enough and I didn't want your mother to see my car in the drive.' How thoughtful of him.

'I need to see you.'

'I'd like to see you, too,' he said, with the correct amount of wistfulness in his voice, just enough to make her hope, with an intensity that brought tears to her eyes, that they were wrong about him. 'I have to tell you something.'

'About Marty Davis?'

'Yes. I think I know who killed him.' Yeah, you, she thought, the hope choking on its own naivety.

'Really? Who?'

'I need to explain this in person. Can I meet you at your house?'

Not a chance, she thought. Someplace public, but with a little privacy. She thought fast. 'Are you downtown?'

'Huh? Yeah, I'm on the Shoreway.'

'Perfect. You know the Eastman Reading Garden at the public library?'

'Yeah. But—'

'Half an hour.' She hung up, clamping the receiver on to its body and holding it there. To Leo she said, 'If he calls back, tell him I left and you don't know my cell number. I can't give him an opportunity to change the meeting place.'

'You aren't going there alone, are you?' Her boss actually seemed concerned for her safety, and she smiled in response.

David had been lying to her from the first moment. About why he had attended Marty's funeral, about knowing Lily Simpson or Ken Bilecki, about why he needed to stay at her house yesterday.

'I may have been born at night,' she said to Leo, 'but it wasn't *last night*.'

THE EASTMAN READING Garden, decorated with adorable bronze figures by Tom Otterness, lay enveloped in dusky shadows as the main branch of the public library blotted out the sinking sun. Theresa perched on the edge of the small fountain, shivering in a thin sweater.

'She should have a coat on.' Frank, at the window, spoke to no one in particular. As if Theresa catching a cold wasn't the least of his concerns at present.

'He should be here any minute,' Angela said, with an uncomfortable breath. 'If he's going to show at all.'

Frank glanced sideways at the stiff way she held her damaged torso. '*You* shouldn't be here at all.'

'Of course I'm here. This is Theresa.' His cousin had picked a good spot, more or less. The garden was nestled in the seventy-five foot space between the original library building and the modern Stokes wing. The doors from the garden into the library were already locked for the evening so that Madison would not be able to escape into the library, still full of civilians. The iron gates at each end, opening on to the sidewalks of Superior and Rockwell, remained the only way in or out. The walls of this new wing were made of glass, so that Frank and ten other cops could watch every inch of the Eastman garden. Library staff stood at the ready to open the doors and let them spill out in an instant. They would not loan out the keys. Librarians could be quite firm on certain matters.

Five other cops were stationed along each of the two streets to the north and south, watching for Madison's arrival. This represented a lot of manpower for one stake-out, but Frank didn't fool himself that the men had been assigned out of concern for either Theresa or himself. No, Frank had told his boss he could—tentatively—link David Madison to the Bingham building explosion. That pulled a handful of strings. Theresa would be safe.

He kept telling himself that.

Unless Madison pulled out a gun as soon as he stepped inside the garden, or got close enough to use a knife. They could grab him the moment he appeared, as they had more than enough to hold him for question-ing…but Frank felt curious to know what he planned to say to her. Catching people in lies played well to a jury. It might put Theresa at risk, but they needed to know if Madison really *could* be connected to the Bingham explosion.

Why would Madison show up at all? Theresa had told him they suspected him of the murder attempt and then refused to let him come to her house. He either thought he could get away with her poisoning and planned to brazen it out with a posture of innocence, or he planned to finish the job.

But why? Theresa didn't have any evidence to con-nect him to the Marty Davis murder, and she had already told Frank about Madison's connection to the meth lab explosion. Madison might not know that for sure, but again, he would have to assume it at this point. So what exactly did he hope to gain by silencing Theresa?

Unless she knew something she didn't yet know she knew. Some connection she hadn't made, but would eventually.

Either that, or the cuckold really was innocent.

Two black teenagers ran through the garden, hand in

hand, weighed down by heavy backpacks. Theresa's gaze followed their path, head swinging from north to south.

Frank watched her shiver again. Madison should have been there fifteen minutes ago.

A screech of brakes came from Superior. Had one of those kids gotten hit by a car?

Frank saw Theresa stand, craning her neck to see what had occurred. At that moment, David Madison appeared at the north end, the side bordered by Rockwell. He wore dark clothes and an unzipped hoodie. He hung on the open gate until it swung shut behind him. His mouth opened.

Theresa turned immediately. Don't go near him, Frank thought.

Make him come to you.

She began walking toward Madison.

Theresa! What was she doing?

Frank did at least register the shapes of his two fellow detectives coming up behind Madison, outside the iron gates, but still found himself pounding on the glass exit doors. A slender librarian hastily unlocked the door, her keys flying as Frank burst through it. While he banged his shin on one of the iron tables, he saw his cops pulling the gate open as Madison lurched forward and grabbed Theresa.

His cousin sank to the ground.

Frank vaulted the next table set and arrived just as the two cops pulled Madison back by the shoulders and Theresa looked up at Frank, one upturned palm sticky with a red liquid.

She said, 'I think somebody shot him.'

THIRTY-FIVE

'WHAT ARE YOU doing back here?' Leo asked her, sounding sincerely irritated at the idea. 'I would have thought you'd had enough for one day.'

'I've had enough for one lifetime.' She settled back in the task chair and rubbed her eyes. 'But I've got a whole bunch of facts and I can't make them add up, so I came back to the evidence. I finally took a closer look at that tuft of foam I found next to Marty Davis' body. Why are you here?'

'Forgot my book.' Her boss hung his trench coat on the rack inside his office, then began to make coffee. Theresa shook her head. As much as he complained about the job, Leo never seemed able to tear himself away from it. He needed a life outside the lab.

But then, so did she.

Leo returned and leaned against the infrared spectrometer. 'The radio said they got him, or rather that he'd been taken to Metro with a gunshot wound. How'd it go? Did he try to kill you again?'

'Sorry to disappoint you.'

'Did your cousin shoot him?'

'Sorry to disappoint you again. Nobody shot him— exactly. It looked that way until they found his car on the next block, run into one of those concrete garbage can holders. His dashboard exploded, forcing enough debris and shrapnel into his chest to kill him.'

'But it didn't?' That seemed to surprise him. It surprised her, too.

'Not yet,' she sighed as the coffee finished perking and they both filled their respective mugs. 'He's still in surgery.'

'Nitrogen triiodide?'

'None. The mechanics are poring over it now. It could still be some really bizarre design flaw, but I doubt that.'

'Ya think? Maybe it's the wife. Did she teach physics?'

'Social Studies.' Leo snickered. Theresa didn't have the energy to glare, but she tried.

'And she was in jail until this morning. So now I'm back to square one. Or maybe circle one.'

'What do you mean?'

'I think David is innocent.'

Leo gazed at her with great skepticism. 'You know, the guy's wife left him for a thirteen-year-old. You think something like that comes out of the blue?'

'I think I didn't drive my husband into the arms of a twenty-two-year-old stripper. He did it himself, and with my gas card. If David wanted to poison my water bottle, he could have broken into my house and done so. Why stay there, letting me and any observant neighbor know it? Why not just strangle me in my bed and quickly leave, narrowing the time frame to nothing?'

'Because he doesn't have the guts to look his victim in the face while he's killing them?' The idea made her stomach roil, but she went on. 'The only motive he'd have to kill me is to keep me from telling anyone else about his part in the meth lab explosion twenty-five years ago. He couldn't be sure I hadn't already told Frank, when I went to the hospital to see him.'

'Did you?'

LISA BLACK   297

'No.'

'Maybe he's a better judge of people than you are.' She scowled.

'I'm serious. He's got you thinking with the wrong part of your anatomy. Forget him.' Leo finished off this advice with a slug of coffee, as if it that took care of it. As if it were that easy.

'Then who rigged his car?' she asked.

'An exploding dashboard has none of the subtlety of tailored meth.'

'Neither did shooting Marty Davis in the head.' Leo opened his mouth, apparently could not find an appropriate response, and shut it again.

'I keep coming back from the circle from twenty-five years ago, our meth cooking entrepreneurs. McClurg— or Doc—Lily, Marty and Ken are all dead. If David dies, that only leaves one living witness to the operation. DaVinci.' Leo blinked, frowned, the storm clouds gathering. Before he could remind her that he'd taken her off all these cases, she rushed on: 'He's the only one left outstanding. And since David's lying on an operating table as we speak, I'm willing to bet DaVinci's been responsible for this all along. I think that's what David came to tell me. He'd been hiding from his old schoolmate, not the media. But when I nearly died he realized that DaVinci would not stop until he'd obliterated every connection to the past. David couldn't run forever.'

Leo sighed heavily. 'And you know who this DaVinci guy is?'

She sighed, warming her hands on the coffee cup. 'That's where it gets really interesting.'

FRANK LEANED OVER and pressed the fast-forward button on the console. Through the glass in front of him he could see the room of dispatchers, six women and one man, each gazing at their own glowing terminal in the darkened room. The supervisor had set him up with the digital recordings of Marty Davis' radio transmissions from his last week on the job, but it proved to be a slow process.

'Why don't you go home already?' he said to his partner, seated next to him. 'Theresa is safe, Madison's in custody, nothing has blown up lately. You haven't had the easiest couple days, either. Go home and lie down. I'll be fine.'

'Have you ever had cracked ribs?' she asked mildly.

'No.'

'There *is* no comfortable way to lie down. There's no comfortable way to recline, sit or stand. At least here I have something to take my mind off it.'

'You could read a book.'

'I tried. Holding something up gets uncomfortable after a while, even something small.'

'Watch TV.'

'I don't have a TV.'

He stared at her, then shook his head. 'I knew there had to be something wrong with you, Angela Sanchez.'

'Tell me about it. Besides, you're not home nursing your burns. What are we listening for, anyway?'

'It's a hunch of Theresa's, something she overheard at the funeral. A dispatcher said Marty had pulled over our local boy wonder in front of the Bingham building but not written a ticket, an unusual turn of events. Apparently Davis really enjoyed writing tickets.' He paused while they listened to Marty Davis reporting his arrival at a disturbance call, then the fact that the situation had cooled in the meantime, and that the incident could be closed out.

Angela waited until the tape ended. 'So we still have another player out there—whoever tried to shred David Madison's chest.'

'I think Madison contacted DaVinci. Three of his old pals are dead, and he calls to say, don't kill me, bro; there's a sworn affidavit in a safety deposit box somewhere that will come to light if I die. Least that's what I would have done.'

His partner said, 'Or he called to say, I know it's you, pay up or I talk. He'd need money for the upcoming custody battle.'

'Except DaVinci is a guy who can concoct designer meth, silent cars and exploding dashboards. He'd have to be some major kind of stupid to mess with that. Maybe he figures that out, calls Theresa, plans to turn himself in. But DaVinci gets to him first.'

They listened through a lost child call, then Angela pondered aloud, 'Why after twenty-five years? If even a couple of meth addicts managed to keep the secret this long, why does DaVinci think he needs to take everyone out now?'

'Something changed. And it all started with the Bingham explosion. I think he knew his former partners would recognize his work, and then it wouldn't just be trying to hide their own youthful indiscretions any more. If large numbers of people started dying here and now, he might not be able to count on their silence. I think he's got another bomb set somewhere, and needed to keep us off his back until it goes off.'

Angela rocked in agitation, but the pain from her body apparently convinced her to stop. 'We could ask Madison when he wakes up.'

'The doctors aren't completely sure he's *going* to wake up.'

'Oh.' Frank moved the cursor to the next call on the screen. The speakers resting on top of the console spit out another recording. This one bore a label of Sunday the tenth, the day before the Bingham explosion, at 11:32 a.m. Marty Davis' voice told the dispatcher, with some relish, that he had pulled over a Porsche with a broken passenger side brake light. Two occupants. He read off the license plate number.

After only a short pause, the dispatcher came back on the line and had found the vehicle's owner of record, Bruce Lambert—hardly surprising as Davis was practically on the doorstep of his factory.

Frank and Angela heard Davis say, 'No kidding? I know him. Exiting the vehicle.' A longer pause, until Davis returned to the radio and said he had let the man off with a warning. He made no further comment, merely relayed the proper codes to indicate that the call had ended and he would now continue his patrol.

The screen's cursor flicked to the next recording.

'He said he knew him,' Frank pointed out.

'Bruce Lambert? *Everyone* knows him.'

'Yeah.' Frank drummed his fingers on the counter for a moment, then let them slow to a stop. 'We need to see the in-car video for this call.'

'It's Bruce Lambert,' Angela reminded him, as if he might have forgotten.

'Who else in this city could design killer meth and exploding dashboards? This stop occurred in front of a building that blew up the next day. The day after that someone came up to Marty Davis and shot him. We've got a boatload of unanswered questions and I'm ready to grasp at anything that might float.'

'Won't say another word,' his partner assured him.

THIRTY-SIX

LEO DID NOT receive Theresa's theory with nearly the same equanimity. 'Bruce *Lambert*?'

'I know it's a leap.'

'It's not a leap. It's jumping the Snake River Canyon!'

'The man fits a lot of facts. He attended Cleveland State at the same time as the others. Ken Bilicki said DaVinci left after their sophomore year, which Lambert did. He switched to MIT. He studied chemistry.'

'Bruce *Lambert*.'

'Bilicki kept referring to DaVinci as a genius, first, simply for recognizing the potential of an abandoned commercial-grade kitchen, then for making chemically perfect meth *and* running the business side of it as well. Lambert's more than proven himself in both fields. Assuming DaVinci is behind the Bingham explosion—'

'That's one big damn assumption, isn't it?'

'Not really. We have the same explosive, quite uncommon in large quantities, turning up at both sites. He may have learned how to stabilize the nitrogen triiodide, something no one's ever been able to do, from the meth lab explosion twenty-five years ago.' She didn't mention Oliver's input to this theory, as the two men did not care for each other and she would have a hard enough time selling this story to her boss. She had a hard time selling it to herself. 'Then he found a way to approach Marty Davis silently and, almost silently, shoot him twice. Then he tinkered with methamphetamines to turn them into poison. Then he got a bomb into Terry Beltran's apartment to make him a perfect and conveniently dead fall guy. He got into my house silently and left yet another perfectly designed form of meth to take care of me. The killer *is* a freakin' genius, and as far as I know there's only one in town.'

'Putting an unsubstantiated accusation in flattering terms will not help. He'll still sue us down to our toenails. But do go on. Why do you think someone other than the budding boyfriend poisoned your drink?'

'Because the budding boyfriend is on an operating table right now, fighting for his life.' The words hesitated in her throat, but for once did not stick. 'David had proven more difficult to approach than the others. David probably didn't make any connection to the Bingham explosion, but Marty's murder put his antennae up. David and Marty were liabilities to Lambert. With his IPO coming up, what would it do to his potential millions if America's heroic genius had been the head of a meth ring in college, one that ended with a boy burning to death? He couldn't afford that. Lily and Ken, chronic drug users, would be ignored even if they did talk, but Marty and David were professional men. Not perfect— Marty's career was not particularly distinguished and David has that embarrassing wife—but potentially convincing in the hands of some gung-ho prosecutor out to see his name in the papers. They had to be removed or at least neutralized. But David and Marty also had reasons to keep quiet—Marty had his job and David, his custody case. When I ran into him at the Lambert factory, he stayed tucked in the back and then left early. At the time I thought he wanted to be alone with me, but I think he wanted a way to show Lambert that he would not approach him, not call attention to him. That he could be trusted to keep the secret. But Lambert doesn't trust anyone.' Leo pulled on his lab coat. The lab air had chilled in the late evening hours. 'This freakin' genius, as you put it, seems to have left a lot to chance. What if your new squeeze drank your water instead of you?'

'That would have worked, too. Whether David is shown to be a killer or a drug user, Lambert still achieves his purpose. No one's going to listen to any tale he spins about Cleveland's resident Renaissance man and a meth ring from their college days. Neutralized.'

'This still sounds like a lot of hot air.'

'Not air. Chemistry. This entire case has revolved around chemistry, truly brilliant chemistry, carefully formed to serve the purposes of one particular individual. The meth had been altered for no productive reason such as stretching the product or making it more addictive, only to kill Lily Simpson. He changed it up again to kill Ken Bilecki, dispatching them both in ways that would seem consistent with the rest of their lives, ways that no one would question. *Because he knew them.*'

'Knew them twenty-five years ago, according to your theory. Lambert's got a better class of friends these days.'

'But he keeps in touch with his roots. That's why everyone likes him, because he's a former poor guy from the hood who surrounds himself with his childhood friends, giving them jobs, giving their families jobs. He has people who will protect him and who might possess the necessary roughness to do any task he assigns, including selling poisonous meth to his former partners.' A door slammed in the hallway outside as a lone toxicologist, the weekend's skeleton staff, left for the day. Oliver had gone home hours before and the secretaries and clerks on the second floor departed by noon on weekends. 'Seems like an uncertain method to kill someone.'

'If it didn't work, he could always try again. He experiments. Failures don't stop him. And any drug use incident discredits the target, at the very least.'

'OK, OK. It's a very nice theory. But here's the only real question: why? Why blow up the Bingham building? Why kill Marty Davis? *Why?*'

She sighed. 'Every indication says the Bingham explosion was accidental. He stockpiled an explosive he thought he had stabilized and something went wrong.'

'OK, stop there. Why would Bruce Lambert be stockpiling explosives to begin with? You're going to tell me he's working with terrorists?'

'He may have nothing to do with terrorists.'

'At last, a note of reason.'

'I think he uses it to power his car engines. He keeps referring to it as nitrogen "sand", but it sounds exactly like nitrogen triiodide. Small and highly explosive— great for powering a reaction, but the safety organizations in this country would never allow it. Americans aren't desperate enough to drive around with mini-bombs in their tanks. Rival car companies would exploit their fears. He needed to hide the formula until he could test his ability to stabilize large amounts of it. Of course he didn't want to take the chance of blowing his own building sky high—'

'So your genius suspect kept his pile of nitrogen triiodide next door?'

'Conveniently close yet plausibly deniable. I'm sure he had it calculated down to the last joule of energy liberated. The basement of the Bingham could function as a bomb shelter. He knew it wouldn't damage his own place other than to break a few windows, and that only made him look like a victim instead of a suspect.'

'You've taken meth before today, haven't you? Because it's eroded your synapses. The man has more money than God. I'm sure he could have found a more appropriate space to do all this in if he wanted. He could probably buy a small city.'

'He doesn't want to. He likes everything tucked up around him. Look at the man—he stays in the town he grew up in. He surrounds himself with people he grew up with. As DaVinci, he lived only a few floors up from a commercial-grade meth lab capable of taking out the entire hotel.' She leaned forward. 'He's a control freak.'

Leo shook his head as if to clear his ears of some annoying blockage. 'OK. Back to my first question. Why kill Marty Davis?'

'Because Marty Davis pulled him over on a traffic stop the day before the building exploded. Though he had a reputation never to give breaks, he let Lambert off with a warning. The dispatcher assumed he had been wowed by Lambert's star power. I think he did it because it was an old friend. Marty had great loyalty to his friends.'

'So Lambert returns the favor by killing him?'

'Lambert's life has been pretty busy the last couple of years. I bet he had forgotten all about his college days and dead Joe McClurg. But when he ran into Davis, he realized how vulnerable his little empire really was. When you're rich and famous, you attract enemies. Any chink in his armor, and they'd swarm in. It would not be that difficult to prove his involvement in the meth lab and McClurg's death, if anyone really tried. Who knows, maybe given this opening, Davis wanted to get together for a beer. Lambert wouldn't say no, not with his common-man persona, plus he was trying to get out of a ticket, but he had to realize that Davis was a liability. His life wasn't that great and he drank too much. Exactly the type of guy you *don't* want knowing a secret that could destroy you.'

'Interesting,' Leo said, but the wideness of his eyes belied the heavy sarcasm in his voice. 'But pure theory, meaning if you ever breathe a word of this outside this lab I will fire you in an instant. There is no way I'm bringing the wrath of the soon-to-be richest man in the world upon our staff, including yours truly.'

She helped herself to another cup of coffee. 'It's more than theory. Remember how the plastic used for a silencer seemed too thick for the usual pop-bottle job, and I didn't find any pieces of cloth? It's polymethyl methacrylate. It's what they make taillights out of. It's what I found in Lambert's workshop after the explosion.'

Leo's face darkened. 'I took that glob from you. I took you off this *case*.'

'Yeah—except I'd already taken a slice off…so I ran it anyway…' Her voice trailed a bit as a rolling shade of puce passed under the skin on Leo's face. 'The major functional groups match. My point is, Lambert has a station for molding his own car lights. I saw it in his workroom.'

'They make a lot of things out of PMMA, Theresa. It's Plexiglas.'

'Yes, but it's still interesting. If you give me my samples back, oh wonderful broad-minded boss, I can talk Oliver into letting me use the mass spec for further testing on the silencer plastic versus that lump I took from the factory explosion. It's probably different, but just in case…' This suggestion did nothing to soften Leo's expression, so she tried another tack. 'Speaking of Lambert's workshop, he also has stations for disassembling the prototype vehicles. He could have cruised up to Marty in a nearly silent car, shot him, gone home and had the car disassembled. It wouldn't matter if he had been seen by witnesses, driving up the street or the driveway. The car would no longer exist for them to identify.'

'Then if it can't be proven, it doesn't bear mentioning, does it?'

'Then there's this piece of foam I found in the driveway. I think it's ethylene-vinyl acetate, or so I gather from the infrared spectrum. EVA foam, it's called. It's often used for the molded seat cushioning in electric cars.'

'It's also used for cushioning kid's bike helmets and Crocs shoes. It's used for a million things.'

Sometimes Leo's devil's advocate role got a bit wearisome. 'But I'm betting this type will be unique. It seems to have a few too many methyl groups on it. If it matches what Lambert has in his workshop, we have him.'

'You'll never know what's in his workshop. That would require a search warrant, for which you have no sufficient probable cause. *That* much I'm sure of.'

'Not so fast. That's where the ring comes in.'

THIRTY-SEVEN

THE PATIENT DISPATCH supervisor sent Frank and Angela over to the equally patient Evidence supervisor, who kept watch, among other things, over all in-car videos. It took twenty minutes to locate the correct tape, but Frank, who remembered the prior system, didn't think twenty minutes was all that bad.

He and Angela watched Marty Davis move through the third-last morning of his life, passing out tickets, going into a ramshackle home to take a burglary report, watching a group of teenagers who might be up to no good. Finally he drove east on Lake Shore Boulevard and made his rambling way to West Ninth.

After listening to the Dispatch tape, it felt almost anticlimactic to see Lambert's Porsche through the windshield. Frank recognized Lambert as the driver, his unruly curls familiar to anyone who read the newspapers. His passenger did not turn, did not show any interest in the police officer or his car behind them, did not swivel his head toward Lambert. He even held his arm up across the passenger window, so that the side mirror reflected only a dark sleeve.

Marty called it in, received the response they had already heard, and got out of the car. He approached the Porsche and had a short but apparently amiable conversation with the driver. Frank could almost read his lips. 'Hey, Bruce! Long time no see! I haven't seen you since sophomore year. You've done great for yourself, or so

I read in the papers,' Frank guessed. The cop went on, smiling, laughing, doing most of the talking, sealing his own death warrant with every word.

The passenger never turned, not even when Marty ducked his head to get a better look at him.

The cop's amiable chatter lasted for two and a half minutes by Frank's watch. Then Davis paused to listen. Maybe Lambert made a comment about the time and someplace he needed to be. Marty Davis seemed to stifle a frown, grinned instead and clapped his old schoolmate's arm as he released the Porsche back to the open road. He grinned still as he returned to his own patrol car, glowing with the little rush that comes with running into an old friend. He disappeared from the camera's angle, but Frank knew what had happened. After climbing back into his seat, Marty Davis had picked up the radio and closed out the call without hesitation.

The driver's side brake light on the Porsche went out and the car began to move forward. Only then did the passenger turn to glance back at the cop, desperate to know that they were truly free. For one moment before he snapped his head to the front again, with the interior of the Porsche illuminated by a particularly sunny spring day, Frank saw his face.

Nairit Kadam.

'I CAN'T WAIT to hear this,' Leo said, with heavy sarcasm. He didn't budge from his task chair, letting the lab grow dark and still around them.

Theresa explained about the caduceus ring from the meth lab explosion. 'I assumed it belonged to the dead Joe McClurg, aka Doc, but it hadn't been found on the body, only in the rubble. I don't think it belonged to McClurg, at least not originally.'

'More guesswork.'

'Lambert's mother was a jewelry design assistant and she wanted him to be a doctor. How much you want to bet she made him that ring, an individual, unique piece of metal?'

'I'm not betting anything, because you can't prove it.'

'Not yet. But all we need is one ex-girlfriend who remembers it, or one old photo of him wearing it, and we will.'

'Don't give me this "we" stuff if you expect some teenage girl to recall a ring from half her lifetime ago.'

'A woman,' Theresa intoned, 'never forgets a piece of jewelry.'

'Maybe,' Leo said. He seemed to be absorbing her framework with a great and heavy concern, most likely imagining the firestorm of belligerence a man with Bruce Lambert's resources could and would bring to bear upon the trace evidence laboratory of the Cuyahoga County Medical Examiner's Office. The explosion at the Bingham would seem a petty inconvenience by comparison. The Spanish Inquisition would seem a petty inconvenience by comparison.

'By the way, where did you put it?' Theresa asked.

'Huh?'

'My box from the Bingham? You said you put it back in the garage but I couldn't find it. I assume you didn't climb to the top of that pyramid and place it there.'

'You assume correctly.'

'So, where is it?' He gazed at her for a moment, his mind clearly on some more pressing subject such as the expected lifetime of his current employment, then shook it off with a sigh.

'I didn't care to approach that critical mass in the garage and dumped it in the basement supply room. Come on, I'll show you where.' She snatched up her lab coat and used the elevator ride to propound her theory further. 'I know it's all circumstantial evidence, but *every* piece of it points to Lambert. We found olefin on Kadam's body from the Bingham explosion, and Lambert wears those disposable Tyvek jumpsuits in his workroom. He built an orphanage in Abkhazia, so he'd know about the Georgian splinter group when he needed a fall guy.'

'You're saying four people, each of whom were in pretty dire straits, had been living in Cleveland all this time with the knowledge to destroy a very rich man, and they never acted on that knowledge? How likely is that?'

'They couldn't implicate Bruce without indicting themselves. Ken and Lily were the weakest links, but no one would listen to them anyway. They already had enough trouble with the law without handing over another crime to charge them with. McClurg's death could be prosecuted as murder, with no statute of limitations. David needed to appear as the perfect parent. Marty would have lost his job as a police officer, the only real thing he had in life. All four needed to keep the past buried every bit as much as Lambert did.'

'Then why kill them?'

'I'm assuming that if loyalty didn't keep them silent, self-interest would. But after the explosion Lambert couldn't afford to assume. He needed to be one hundred per cent sure.'

'So he took the incredible risk of killing all his ex-friends just to be *sure*? Hardly seems worth it.'

Theresa grasped her boss's elbow, feeling the bony joint beneath a sheer coating of muscle. 'Next week Bruce Lambert will become, at a *minimum*, the richest man in the country, not to mention hailed as the world's

energy savior. Yes. It's worth it.' The elevator shuddered
to a halt. The basement of the Medical Examiner's Office was a warren of thick walls and storage rooms,
where no one ventured unless necessary and certainly
not on weekends. No one who worked at the M.E.'s office had a fear of ghosts, but everyone found the oppressive odors and even more oppressive silence unnerving.

Leo stopped outside one of the many nine-by-nine
storage rooms and Theresa yanked on the latch. The
storage rooms used to be walk-in refrigerators, and still
had the heavy doors and solid metal latches of an industrial cooler. Shelves of clear and brown glass bottles and
plastic jugs appeared as the fluorescent lighting came to
life. The aisle between them only allowed one person,
and Theresa moved down it, searching for a brown cardboard box among the chemicals. Typical of Leo to be too
lazy to get the garage key, go outside into the spring air,
fiddle with the ancient door lock merely in order to put
an item back where it belonged. Much simpler to drop
it in a place he had to go anyway. 'I don't see it.'

'At the back,' Leo said. 'So you're positive Bruce
Lambert was DaVinci?'

'Positive. And I'll prove it. The man came into my
home while I was sleeping. He killed three people so far
and did his best to kill both me and Frank. I'll never let
him go now.' She reached the end of the aisle, stopping
at the cold metal wall.

'No,' Leo said, 'I don't believe you will.' No box. She
turned, to see Leonardo DiCiccio holding a 1.5-liter bottle of hydrochloric acid.

Facts lined up with dizzying speed. Theresa had
assumed that Lambert had contacts in the police department—he could certainly afford them—but maybe his

contact had been much closer than that. Leo and Lambert were the same age, both attended CSU.

How had Lambert known David would be coming to the Eastman garden? How would he know Theresa was pursuing Lily's death and talking with David? How would he get into her house without leaving a trace? Simple. He hadn't. Leo had brought her the tote bag and the water bottle yesterday, along with a sad look. As if saying goodbye.

'Lambert wasn't DaVinci,' she said, her voice stupid with shock. 'You were.'

'I wish you could have left it alone, Theresa. I tried everything I could to deflect you.'

'I see that now,' she nodded. 'You argued the idea that the explosive could be nitrogen triiodide. You tried to keep me from visiting Lambert's factory and bowed yourself out of the alumni function, then told him to keep an eye on me. You told me to leave the explosion to the Feds. You told me to stay away from David Madison. You freaked when you saw the box from Payne Avenue. You poisoned me, then steered me toward blaming it on David. And since I didn't die you used it as a reason to take away all the samples from all the cases. You told Lambert where David would be, to kill him before he could blurt out Lambert's identity to me. Or yours.'

'Not mine,' Leo said. 'Bean has no idea I work here. He never knew my real name.' Leo, always so careful to keep his picture out of the paper and off the newscasts. And she had thought it had something to do with a poor body image. 'Lambert was Doc.'

'Yep.' He did not look away from her, the bottle precariously balanced in his gloved hand. They were the only two people on the premises—except for the deskmen, who were one thick floor up and at the other end of the building with the TV turned on. There were no cameras or other security in the basement. All that technology would be part of the new building, that promised land she wouldn't live to see.

'Then who was Joe McClurg?'

'A guy from my organic chemistry class. We were training him to take over cooking the stuff, phasing ourselves out.'

She needed time to think. 'No nickname?'

'We called him Red,' Leo admitted. 'But Ken Bilecki wouldn't know that. We were phasing him out too.'

'He'd become unreliable.'

'Yes.'

'You weren't concerned until I found the box from Payne Avenue, and brought back that lump of plastic from Lambert's workshop.'

He winced. 'I had no idea if it would match anything from Marty Davis' crime scene, but I couldn't be sure. All Lambert's stuff is most likely unique, and—you and that damn FTIR.'

'And Lambert was already worried; I'd been turning up too often. That's when you decided to drug me. If I *did* stumble on to anything, my abilities would be completely discredited.'

'Not much of a plan, but time seemed of the essence.'

'Are you going to kill me, Leo?'

'I don't have a choice, Theresa. We're scientists, after all, experts in facts, reality. It's you or me. That's the reality. I can bury the Payne Avenue stuff, say it got lost in the move. I can alter the tox reports, keep your cousin off the trail. I can control it all—except you.' She would have given anything not to believe him. But she had worked with the man for ten years, and thought she knew him. She had seen him fire people, hire people,

research attorneys before giving testimony, wield the
media like a sword and evict his own son from his home.
He had already killed, or helped to conceal the killing
of, three former friends. As much as he could drive her
to distraction, they had gotten along amiably enough
and he liked her. But he did not love her.

'I'm sorry, Theresa. I really am.'

'But—' She began to protest that she had already
told Frank, but before she could get the words out Leo
smashed the bottle on the concrete just inside the door.
Then he slammed that door shut.

Theresa knew exactly what would happen now. The
hydrochloric acid would turn to a toxic, corrosive gas
that her lungs would know better than to breathe in. Her
body would seize up until she choked and then suffo-
cated. It would seem like a tragic accident—she hadn't
propped the door and then accidentally broke a jar. Leo's
fingerprints would not be on the jar or the latch, and even
if they were he could explain it—he worked there. Unless one of the pathologists doing Sunday autopsies ran
short of an item, no one would find her body until next
week. She would have begun to decompose by then, not
too badly, just her veins marbling under the skin, cells
starting to ooze.

She also knew what to do. She clapped the bottom
of her T-shirt up over her lower face with her left hand,
and put her right one on a large bottle of sodium bicarbonate. She needed an extremely exothermic reaction.

The only way out of the room was to blow it up.
While she was still inside.

If she thought about this for even a split second she
wouldn't do it. She picked up the bottle and threw it,
knowing it would probably kill her.

Theresa didn't wait to watch the bottle arc through

the air, but dropped to the floor and huddled up against the cool metal wall, her face pressed to her knees, mouth open, arms over her head. This cure could well prove worse than the disease, even if the disease was death.

The sodium bicarbonate would neutralize the hydrochloric acid and produce hot carbon dioxide as a by-product. The air in the room would suddenly need to expand and without any place to go, no vents, no windows, would exert its full force on the weakest point in the metal box—the door, on its old and if possible rusty hinges.

Theoretically, anyway.

The same force she hoped would blow open a four-inch-thick metal and wood door would press her against the metal wall at her side. This would not be pretty.

Her life exploded into a ball of very loud, airless noise. A giant hand slapped her flat against the abruptly burning steel, pushing every molecule of air out of her lungs and giving her nothing to replace it except fire. Her body had abandoned her. She could not feel it, nor get too interested in what it might be doing.

Then, nothing.

THIRTY-EIGHT

SHE MUST BE DEAD, since all was nothingness. A white nothingness. Peaceful and floating and unending, except it was a little too close to her burned face for comfort and she pushed at it. It came back at her and she batted with both hands and the budding panic of the claustrophobe. Not quite as peaceful as she'd imagined.

Because the soft white nothingness was stiff white plastic with a black zipper running down its middle. She didn't like it, wanted out. Right. Now.

Luckily her body cottoned on to the situation long before the rest of her and ripped out with her hands, finding the zipper and pulling it apart. Cool air rushed in. Not that it did her much good—she still couldn't get a decent breath with lungs singed with hydrochloric acid and then hot carbon dioxide. And she could barely open her eyes against the blinding light. Maybe this really was heaven.

Though she was fairly sure that heaven would not have a ceiling paneled in acoustic tile. At least she hoped not.

She was in Lambert's laboratory, his very brightly lit, recently blown-up workroom. Once her pupils adjusted to the light she could see the high windows of the catwalk hallway, the desks, sections of automobile scattered here and there, the track for the crane that stretched from one end of the room to the other over her head, the freshly plastered section of fixed wall. The fishbowl room.

Then she caught the odor, just a whiff through her damaged sinuses.

'Don't move,' someone said. 'You'll blow yourself and everything around you into little tiny pieces. Including me.' She sat up slowly and shaded her eyes. Leo stood only five feet away, holding a cardboard box—her cardboard box. She herself had been surrounded by thirty blocks of whitish crystals, fanning out from her across the linoleum. She did not doubt what the crystals were.

Nitrogen triiodide. She didn't move.

Lambert sat at one of the desks, his fingers hovering over a keyboard. He stared at her. 'Shit. She's not supposed to be alive.'

'I forgot about the bicarb,' Leo admitted. He seemed to have aged about twenty years in the past hour as he straightened up from where he had been adjusting a small metal box—probably the detonator. 'Don't shuffle around in there either. If you step on the tiniest crumb, the pressure will set it off. And you know what happens then.'

'You're still here,' she said to Leo. 'Sounds almost worth it. Besides, blowing up the meth lab taught Bruce here how to stabilize nitrogen triiodide.'

'Only from decomposition,' Lambert said, not even looking up from his computer screen. 'Not percussion. Just ask Nairit Kadam.' The image of Kadam's incinerated body took her breath away for a moment.

The bricks appeared to be three by four by two inches, perhaps.

One cubic foot per block. Thirty cubic feet of NI—if it were TNT, there would be about a ton and a half.

Enough to take out the building. Enough to take out the building and the city block it stood on.

She looked around, up, willing someone to walk along the catwalk from the lobby and see them. 'What about your security? Isn't this all on camera?'

'Hello. Whose factory is this? That's right, it's mine. That means I get to turn the cameras on and off when I like. I also get to send everyone home until the recent blast is investigated and their security can be assured.' She stood, carefully, her feet still swathed in the folds of the body bag. She took her cell phone out of her pocket and opened it. Just as promised, no signal, which explained why neither man objected or even seemed to notice.

'So,' she asked. 'Is there a plan, here?'

Lambert said, 'Yes, but it's not one you're going to like.' All she had to do was get on to the other side of the spread of bricks. She hadn't been restrained or tied and neither of the two men had a gun or any other type of weapon. Except that she had never been much of an athlete—hell, except for a loping jog she wasn't *any* kind of athlete—and was pretty sure she couldn't pull off a standing long jump of five or six feet. A millimeter less and she could land on a brick or even a loose crystal, enough to ignite one tiny, infinitesimal reaction as the beginning of a long and loud chain of others. Also, in the past few days she'd been blown up twice and poisoned once and really wasn't feeling up to gymnastic feats.

'Where did you get all this?' she asked, looking at Lambert. 'I thought your supply went up with the Bingham.'

'Most of it,' he admitted, still concentrating on his computer screen. 'Damn idiot. We had enough material to power my engines for six months even if they sold like hot cakes, plus plenty of extra for side projects in those crappy little countries always looking for cheap weapons…gone in a split second.'

Theresa said to Leo, 'I guess I was wrong when I thought he had nothing to do with terrorism.' Leo winced as if in pain.

'It was just a sideline,' Lambert said. 'An extra benefit. Airline cargo screening looks for nitrogen compounds—but if the material already *is* a nitrogen compound, then what are they gonna do?' Theresa had no idea how to get herself out of the room, but with luck, Frank and a search warrant might show up before Lambert finished whatever he was doing.

'It was all good until Marty pulled you over. It meant nothing that Marty saw you with Kadam, until Kadam became the prime suspect in the explosion. The explosion *could not* be linked to you—no one would buy a fuel that could single-handedly destroy an entire building.'

'And I'd never convince our brain-dead citizens that the amounts used in the engine couldn't take out a small cardboard box.'

'So Marty had to die. And Lily.'

He gave what appeared to be a final tap to the board. 'Lily wasn't my fault.' Leo took up the narrative, perhaps defending his former partner, perhaps finding some weird solace in a complete confession. Perhaps distracting himself from the thirty or so cubic feet of explosive in the room with him. 'He couldn't be sure if Marty had told anyone, especially after the news outlets released Kadam's picture. Marty had to be discredited as well as killed. He planted his latest experiment at Marty's apartment, the supercharged meth. If the cops bothered to analyze it, the weird composition would keep them running in circles looking for Marty's drug dealer and would explain any wild tales Marty told about an old college acquaintance. The cops never found the meth, but Lily did, stole it, used it and died.'

'Two birds,' Theresa said.

'Exactly,' Lambert said. 'I'm always willing to accept my failures and move on, but this time, failure was not an option. After Monday's IPO I'll have more money than Buffett and Gates combined.'

'You honestly think this is still going to work?' Theresa said.

Lambert ignored her and said to Leo: 'Transferring to you now.'

'Divided among the three accounts?'

'Yep.' Theresa aimed her tiny cell phone camera at them and pressed the button to create a video. 'What, he's paying you off? Have you thought this through, Leo? He killed anyone who might be a threat to him, going back twenty years. Do you really think he's going to let you walk out of this room?' Both men glanced at her, and her phone, with a terrifying lack of concern.

'Yes, Theresa,' Leo said. 'We've thought it through. I very much have to stay alive, so that I can manage this crime scene. Your body will not be found here, not even as the macroscopic bits of flesh it will become once this goes up. Those bits will belong to some yet-to-be-named employee of Lambert Enterprises and I'll have the DNA tests to prove it. You will simply disappear.'

'But Don—'

'I couldn't ask him to do the analysis when he's so upset over your unexplained absence. Same goes for your cousin. He'll want to pry and he'll have plenty of suspicions, but without any proof his superiors will give him a leave of absence to deal with his grief. And if he did succeed, if the police department can put together some sort of case against Doc here, then guess what, his remains will be found in the ruins of some new terrorist attack. Probably City Hall. It's a convincing target.' She couldn't quite breathe with that image in her mind, either. Her phone ran out of space and she closed it. She couldn't send the video anyway, and the phone would wind up in the same shape as her body. In pieces.

'It's not as if I like any of this, Theresa. But I'll do what I have to. I always have.'

'What about your empire?' she asked Lambert. 'What about your IPO?'

'It will dip a little,' he said, quite seriously, 'what with two explosions in my lab in the same week. But I'll still end up with more money than God, and I can access my accounts from Bora Bora just as easily as I can here.'

'You'd leave your home? Spend the rest of your life in exile?' Lambert closed his laptop, unplugged it and moved it closer to the nitrogen triiodide. Whatever was on its hard drive, he wanted it disintegrated along with Theresa.

'Not saying I'm happy about it, but every failure is a new beginning. I'll miss my homies, but America? I've been ready to shake off the dirt of this puritan, everybody-is-special wasteland of idiots for a long time.' He turned to his former, and current, partner. 'Thanks, DaVinci. And if you're ever in the south Pacific—don't look me up.'

'Wouldn't dream of it,' Leo said. The two men nodded at each other, and the soon-to-be richest man in the world left the room. He did not so much as glance at Theresa.

Theresa's boss returned to the small metal box and touched it. She heard something click. Then he looked at her. The sheen of bravado he'd kept up with his old friend now faded from his face. He seemed deeply concerned, and almost sad.

Almost.

'Goodbye,' he said. Then he walked out as well, moving briskly, leaving her behind.

'Hell with that,' she said.

THIRTY-NINE

SHE HAD TO work quickly. All Lambert and Leo had to do was clear the building and get out to the street, which would take, what, four minutes at the most? No reason to set the detonator for any longer than that. She checked her Swatch. 9:15.

She could not jump over the bricks. The two men had obviously moved them somehow but she didn't know how and couldn't risk it. She could see wires running underneath them as well—possibly a booby trap.

The only way out was straight up.

The ceiling of the workroom stretched far above, but the suspended track for the crane had been built to help workers move large car panels on and off the working chassis. The beam passed only three or four feet above her head. She could not reach it but with luck she could lasso it.

Leo hadn't even bothered to empty her pockets, leaving her not only the useless cell phone but her set of keys. The mini Swiss Army knife was too short to be considered a weapon, but still sharp enough to function as a knife. She held up the body bag with her left hand and sliced down the middle of its back, anchoring the bottom with one foot so that the loose ends didn't flop on to any of the explosive bricks. There might be tiny crystals around her feet, but she didn't have time to be *that* careful.

Body bags were constructed to carry up to four hundred pounds without complaint, so slicing through its interconnected fibers made tough work even for a sharp knife. At least half a minute gone already.

Now she had two halves of a body bag, still connected at the foot area. She took one half, held it in one hand like a ranchero, and began to twirl. Being careful, of course, not to let even the lightweight plastic brush the tops of the stacked bricks lest it disturb the crystalline structure of its molecules, just enough to blow her to bits. Then she let go, thrusting the bulky plastic toward the ceiling.

It went up nicely, but came straight back down, prompting a frantic grabbing collection to keep any of it from landing on top of the crystals. She needed it to go up and over, but didn't have a lot of room for footwork.

She gathered it up, began to twirl again, trying not to think about how much time had already elapsed. Threw it.

The loose end sailed over the oily beam at least. But it was like trying to throw a ribbon—it didn't sail far enough, and the anchor side wasn't stiff enough to push it further. So she wiggled it, hoping to snake the free end down to her upstretched hand.

9:17.

She wiggled too hard, and the whole bag slid back down on top of her. Another frantic grab to keep it from striking the tiny molecules of the crystals. She prepared for another throw, acutely aware that if she could not do this, and immediately, she would be vaporized, leaving her child motherless and her own mother grieving.

She threw, all the desperation in her body traveling through her arms and into the lifeless plastic.

It went over the beam but not far enough. Reason failed her and she began to jump for it. Leo and Lambert had put the crystals in place somehow, surely they could stand a little vibration. On her third try her fingers brushed the dangling end and on the fourth, she grasped it.

The next step required some thought. She had to pull on both ends equally or one end would slide over. She could twist them together—but then they'd simply untwist as she climbed. Wasn't the rope-climbing thing in gym class what all boys feared? Though she'd never seen a rope in her high school gymnasium…if she could slice a third strip, she could braid it.

9:18.

She opened her knife again and made horizontal cuts in the white plastic, first on one side and then further up on the other. Another two stretching as far as she could reach, then she carefully stowed the knife in her front pocket where it could not fall out. The small but heavy object would certainly set off the nitrogen triiodide. Then, grasping her makeshift ropes with one in each hand, she slid one foot into her first makeshift rung.

Finding the second was considerably more difficult, but once she did she could distribute her weight equally, stabilizing the structure just enough for her to slide her hands up to a higher point, grasp, and move her feet to their next toeholds. She did all this with the sinking sensation that she would never get away from the crystals in time. Any split second now the entire room was going to erupt in a fireball of her own personal hell. Would she even know it when it happened? Or would she already be dead?

Remarkably, the last toehold brought her in reach of the crane's beam. She strained upward to reach around the track but this left her feet, which were at uneven levels, to balance the two sides of her snowy rope, and it shifted rapidly. A quick grasp with both hands arrested it, leaving her swaying above the explosive crystals.

She reached again, caution using up seconds she did not have. She should be dead already. Surely by now Leo and Lambert were in their cars and exiting the parking lot? Her boss would not have left extra time on the detonator. Leo did not take chances.

Her fingers met over the greasy beam and intertwined. She then swung both legs up and around it and somehow managed to climb on top, a surprisingly painful effort. The beam was not solid, more like two flat sides that bit into her palms with a chain track running inside the hollow center. On top of that neither foot would slide easily out of her makeshift rungs so arms, legs and torn body bag wound up wrapped around the beam in a mess. At least it kept the bag from falling on to the crystals.

As soon as she was on top of the beam instead of dangling below it she began to slide, using hands and knees like a child straddling a log. Her tangled feet weren't much help and the thin sides of the beam felt like they were slicing her palms. Water could set off NI3. Could blood?

She couldn't help but catch sight of her watch face out of the corner of one eye. 9:19.

When she cleared the crystal pile by two precious feet, she threw herself flat on the track and slid both feet off one side of it. The last thing she wanted was to end dangling from the beam in the shreds of a body bag, or have it catch at least one foot so that she landed on her head. The rest of her body followed without hesitation and it felt a lot further than nine or ten feet. At last she landed back on the linoleum, knees bending to absorb the shock.

One foot had managed to free itself but she had to waste another precious moment yanking the other loose from the white bundle, not wanting to drag it alongside the crystal bricks. Then she could finally approach the small metal box.

Unlike detonators on television, this one had no handy digital read-out showing how many seconds of life she had left. In fact, it had nothing at all, just a smooth, plain, unadorned metal face with a thin wire protruding from either side. This wire, she could now see, circled and entered the ring of white crystal bricks. Flat grommets occurred every six inches along the wire.

She had no idea what it was or how it worked. All she knew was she had to get rid of it if she wanted to take another breath.

Theresa whirled around to the desks about her. This room was full of tools—there had to be one here somewhere. She ran to one, then the next, looking among the printouts, Post-it notes and leftover lunch scraps. She opened a drawer or two. To have gotten this far just to go up in a ball of flame—maybe she should run, just run, but she'd never make it. *Don't* think about Rachael.

She found possible salvation on the desk with the fluorescent Post-Its and the four-foot-long pipe cutter. A pair of wire cutters sat next to the blotter.

She returned to the detonator and opened the cutters over the thin wire protruding from its side, fully aware that her action might set it off instead of disabling it. But she didn't have time to ponder…everything she knew about Leo and Lambert told her that they were careful not to over-think things. Speed was more important than durability here. They wouldn't have had time to install fail-safes, only to make the explosion occur as quickly as they could clear the area.

She squeezed the handles.

Click.

She encircled the wire from the other side. *Click.*

Still alive, she didn't waste time breathing a sigh of relief but picked up the metal box and carried it away. She didn't know what it would do and didn't intend to take the chance. Halfway to the nearest desk, it clicked and shuddered in her hands.

9:20.

She breathed, staring transfixed at the little device. Had she really come that close? Or had it been clicking and shuddering all this time? Would it really have worked at all?

Yes.

She had cheated death with about one second to spare, and the knowledge made her knees buckle. So she pushed it away and resolved not to think about it. Not now. Not *ever.*

Instead she set the box down next to Stitch and picked up the pipe cutter, which felt like her thirty-pound barbell. She moved to the door, took up a position to the right of its opening.

And waited.

Exactly three minutes later, Leo stepped inside. She swung the metal object as hard as she could.

Cell phone use might have been impossible, but the landlines on each desk worked just fine. She called her cousin and told him that Lambert was in the wind, but she had Leo.

'Your boss? What the hell is he doing there?'

'Long story.'

'You sound grim. Is he alive?'

'I don't know,' she told him. 'And right at the moment, I don't much care.'

FORTY

THERESA PLACED THE Cavs sweatshirt worn by an unlucky convenience-store clerk face downward on a sheet of treated photographic paper, so that the bullet hole just beneath the team's logo sat in the center of the paper's rectangle. Then she placed a piece of gauze, soaked in a different set of chemicals, on the fuzzy inside surface of the shirt and applied a steam iron to it. The chemicals in the gauze and the paper reacted with the gunpowder left on the victim's shirt to form a new compound, one that would turn bright orange against the white paper.

Everything was chemistry.

Chemicals had nearly killed her in the basement of the M.E.'s office, and then they had saved her. Chemicals still coated one side of her face and both her hands as the mild burns there healed. Chemicals had kept David Madison alive during his time in the ICU.

What were humans, really, but electrons and protons and neutrons, whirling in constant motion, more empty space than anything else? Atoms stuck together because each had a gap in its orbit of electrons, a gap it could fill by sharing the electrons of another. Each completing the other to become something new, something bigger, something stronger.

And sometimes it wasn't even that definite a bond, not a covalent bond, only an ionic one. Just mutual attraction.

She and David Madison could have continued in their

own orbits, but mutual attraction had brought them together. It should have made them both stronger, giving her a life outside her job and worrying about her daughter, helping him to feel like a man again, able to stare the world down when it brought up his ex-wife.

Instead he had lied to her about knowing Lily and Ken, and pretended not to recognize the Payne Street address. He might have saved Ken's life if he had spoken up after Lily died. He had to know then it was Lambert, that no one else would have the ability or the resources, but he said nothing lest he implicate himself. He truly hadn't known that Leo was her boss, or made any connection between Lambert and the Bingham explosion. But still, Marty, Lily and Ken, once his *friends*, all dead. And he kept his silence.

Then he invented the media frenzy regarding his wife in order to get his kids out of town and fled to *Theresa's* house, with Lambert out to erase his past and the people in it. David didn't want to endanger his children— admirable—but qualms about her or her child or her family? Not so much.

The bond had begun to weaken, her own electrons drawing back to their own orbits.

Theresa had showed up at the alumni tour of Lambert's factory and then during the Bingham excavation, asking about nitrogen triiodide, and suddenly Lambert had a problem just as pressing as his old college gang. He called his old friend and business partner.

She still couldn't wrap her head around Leo's betrayal. Rumors were already circulating that she had somehow framed Leo for her near-murder, perhaps because she herself had fallen under Lambert's sway. Or because she really wanted to be supervisor. Or because she and Leo had had an affair years ago and a new spat gave her motive for revenge. This did not occur because Leo had so many friends at the Medical Examiner's Office; quite the contrary, he had none. But government employees thrive on gossip and nothing beats a good conspiracy theory. So while her fellow employees amused themselves, Theresa felt like crawling into a hole and staying there forever.

Frank appeared in the doorway and stopped, held back by the acetic acid fumes. 'The prosecutor's working on the Lambert indictments,' he said by way of greeting. 'For all the good it will do him. He's going for culpable negligence in the McClurg death and seven counts of first degree in the Bingham explosion, plus Marty Davis and Terry Beltran. He's not even going to try for Lily and Ken, too hard to prove. Beltran is a weak one. We think Lambert got in disguised as an air-conditioning guy, but again, proof. But he has to go for it, otherwise Lambert could say Beltran was behind everything since he had the gun that killed Marty.'

'How is that possible?'

'I think Lambert planted the gun along with the bomb. As soon as Beltran opened that drawer and stumbled on them both, he'd be blown up and also implicated at the same time. Lambert didn't know it would happen while I was coming up the steps, of course, that was just gravy. Beltran kept his contraband cell phone in that drawer and I think that's what he was going for after he saw me and Angela. Hard to prove, though. Everything about this case is going to be hard to prove, even if we get a chance.' After Cleveland's resident genius had left Theresa hovering over thirty cubic feet of explosive, he had not headed across the parking lot as she had calculated but went to the roof, where his helicopter and pilot waited. This had bought her the extra minute while the engine warmed. She wondered what he had thought, hovering above the city skyline, when East Sixth did *not* turn into a giant fireball. Unlike Leo, he resisted the urge to come back and try again. He had disappeared into a cloak of connections and bribery and no one in the world had yet admitted to catching even a glimpse of Lambert, his helicopter or his pilot. Theresa said, 'He's got to turn up somewhere. The IPO might have been a disappointment but Lambert's still filthy rich, a genius and a sociopath. A man like that can't hide for long. His ever-ballooning ego will float him to the surface.'

'Let's just hope it's in a country that extradites.' She set the iron aside, removed the gauze and pulled the sweatshirt from the photographic paper. A cloud of orange mist and dots filled its center. The clerk had been shot at nearly point-blank range for whatever had been in the cash register. When it came to motive, size didn't matter.

'Has Leo said anything?'

'Not a word. Admits nothing, denies nothing. Hard to believe that your boss knew Lambert all these years and never let on.'

'Everyone had a reason to keep their college days hidden. And Leo never wanted fame like Lambert did. He just wanted complete rule in his one little corner of the world. This lab is his life. Was.'

'It's yours, too.'

'No, I have a mother and a daughter and you, I have friends, I go on vacation. Leo had nothing. There are jobs where running a meth lab in your college years would *not* get you fired, could be brushed off as youthful indiscretions long outgrown. Directing a crime lab is not one of those jobs.'

'Don't tell me you actually understand him.'

'Not a chance.'

'Good. So after the Bingham explosion, Lambert must have asked Leo to look out for their mutual interests. Leo couldn't do much at first with Homeland Security getting their noses in everything, but then you stumbled on the college meth lab explosion and his former classmates, Lily and Ken Bilecki.'

'I got them killed,' Theresa said, 'and all because I had a crush on David Madison.'

'No. They were killed because Lambert's Porsche had a bad brake light. But hey, look at it this way.' She watched him, waited.

'The supervisor slot just opened up.'

* * * * *

NOTES AND ACKNOWLEDGMENTS

I REQUIRE HIS help for just about every book I write, but I definitely could not have written this one without the assistance of my former CSU chemistry teacher, Dr Andrew Wolfe. It's a wonder that our emails have not come to the attention of appropriate government agencies. At least, not that I know of.

That said, anyone who tried to actually concoct methamphetamine from the descriptions in this book is doomed to disappointment. I got all the original information via my great good friend Google—and then left a few things out.

I'd also like to thank my equally brilliant cousin's son Tommy, who tried to explain to me how electric cars work. My husband Russ is always available for a quick question or two or three.

And of course my terrific agent Vicky Bijur, as well as everyone at Severn House. They are true professionals.

BIBLIOGRAPHY

Reding, Nick. *Methland: The Death and Life of an American Small Town.* NY: Bloomsbury, 2009

Lafave, Owen and Bill Simon. *Gorgeous Disaster: The Tragic Story of Debra Lafave.* LA: Phoenix Books, 2006